NEW
FEARS

ALSO AVAILABLE FROM TITAN BOOKS

NEW HORROR STORIES
by masters of the genre

NEW FEARS

Edited by **Mark Morris**

TITAN BOOKS

NEW FEARS
Print edition ISBN: 9781785655524
Electronic edition ISBN: 9781785655586

Published by Titan Books
A division of Titan Publishing Group Ltd
144 Southwark St, London SE1 0UP

First Titan Books edition: September 2017
2 4 6 8 10 9 7 5 3 1

A CIP catalogue record for this title is available from the British Library.

Printed and bound in the United States.

CONTENTS

INTRODUCTION

I believe that the first adult horror novel I read was James Herbert's *The Fog* back in 1976, when I was twelve or thirteen years old. But I'd been reading horror fiction for several years before then. Like many writers of my generation, I cut my genre teeth not on novels, but short stories—dozens of short stories, hundreds, maybe even *thousands*. From an early age I'd been a voracious reader—I still am—and in between the Enid Blytons, and Anthony Buckeridge's Jennings series, and *Doctor Who* novelisations, and children's classics like *101 Dalmatians*, *Charlotte's Web*, *Charlie and the Chocolate Factory* and *Treasure Island*, I read anthologies—mostly ghost and horror stories, some of which I owned, but many of which I borrowed from my local library.

Anthologies I remember reading and loving in my pre-teen years include *Nightfrights*, edited by Peter Haining, *Ghosts, Spooks and Spectres*, edited by Charles Molin, *Alfred Hitchcock's Ghostly Gallery* and a Target book edited by Freya Littledale called *Ghosts and Spirits of Many Lands*.

There were anthology series too—fifteen volumes of *The Armada Ghost Book*, six volumes of *The Armada Monster Book*, and four volumes of *Armada Sci-Fi*.

And then, of course, there were the annual Pan and Fontana Books of Horror and Ghost Stories.

My first encounter with one of these august editions

was in 1972 when I was nine. The book in question was *The 7th Fontana Book of Great Horror Stories* edited by Mary Danby, and I was immediately captivated by the yellow-green photographic cover, depicting a rat slinking between glass containers on a laboratory bench. The book was owned by my cousin, and as soon as she showed it to me I knew I had to read it. To be honest, I can't remember what I made of the stories at the time (though, perusing the contents, I see contributions from such genre luminaries as Gerald Kersh, Robert Bloch, Sir Arthur Conan Doyle, Marjorie Bowen and M.R. James), but I *do* vividly recall, a few years later, exactly how I felt after reading my first *Pan Book of Horror Stories*.

It was New Year's Eve 1975, and I was staying at a friend's house. I was sleeping in a camp bed on the ground floor at the front of the house, in some kind of box room or study. As I recall, there was quite a bit of clutter in the room—boxes, clothes hanging up, stacked items of furniture. At bedtime I settled down to read the book I'd brought with me: *The Eleventh Pan Book of Horror Stories.*

I'm not sure how much of the book I read that night, but I do know it was well into the early hours of 1st January 1976 when I finally turned out the lamp beside my bed and tried to settle down to sleep.

I say *tried*, because as soon as I closed my eyes I started to imagine I could hear rustling sounds in the darkness; started to believe that some *thing* had emerged from hiding and was creeping towards my bed.

Worse, opening my eyes to allay my fears only served to exacerbate them. Because in the gloom, with the only light a brownish glow on the closed curtains from the streetlight outside, I saw shapes that seemed to feed my imaginings. There was a tall figure standing by the wardrobe, a hunched mass beneath the windowsill. Snapping on the bedside lamp in rising panic, the tall figure would quickly disguise itself as a hanging item of clothing, the hunched mass a pile of boxes. But then I'd turn the light off, and after a few seconds the rustling would start again…

In my fevered state, the long hours to dawn became a waking nightmare, and I eventually fell into an exhausted sleep only when the sky outside began to lighten and the shadows began to dissipate. Yet, oddly enough, although the experience left me drained, I now look back on it with a sense of nostalgia, even fondness. It showed me how powerful good horror fiction could be, and it certainly didn't put me off seeking out more of it. On the contrary, over the next few years I devoured as many of the Pan and Fontana anthologies as I could get my hands on. They fuelled my imagination, and instilled in me a long-held belief that short fiction, perhaps even more so than novels, is the lifeblood of the genre.

There's nothing better than a well-crafted ghost or horror story. Short stories, if told well, can retain a real sense of dread throughout their twenty- or thirty-page length, and pack a real punch. All too often horror novels—perhaps because their authors feel a need to reward readers for the time they've invested in their work—end on a note of hope or redemption: the evil vanquished, the status quo restored. In short stories, however, there are no such restrictions, which is why short horror fiction tends to be darker and less reassuring, not to mention generally more ambiguous and experimental, than lengthier, more conventional works.

As a child I loved the fearful anticipation of reading an anthology and not knowing what was coming up next. Would the next story be scary, funny, baffling? Would it be supernatural or non-supernatural? Would it contain witchcraft, a haunting, cannibals, demonic possession? Or would it be something even stranger, darker, altogether more difficult to define?

The recent trend in the genre has been for *themed*

anthologies; collections of stories *about* a particular subject. We've had books of werewolf stories and zombie stories; books featuring stories sharing common characters, or all set within a particular location. Undeniably many of these anthologies have been excellent, their contributors showing a great deal of invention and flair in the way they've subverted the restrictions imposed on them, and interpreted the various themes in their own way. Yet whenever I read a themed anthology, I always secretly find myself craving the kinds of anthologies I read in my youth, anthologies in which *no* restrictions were placed on the authors, and their imaginations were given free rein.

This, then, is where *New Fears* comes in. In this first volume of what will hopefully become an annual showcase of the best and most varied short fiction that the horror genre has to offer, you'll find a wide variety of stories and approaches, which will hopefully demonstrate how very wide—indeed, how almost limitless—the parameters of the genre can be. Within these pages you'll find stories that explore ancient myths in new and innovative ways; stories of human evil; stories of unnamed and ambiguous terrors; stories where the numinous and the inexplicable intrude upon what we perceive to be reality in unexpected ways. There is humour here, and hope, and grief, and sadness, and regret, and impenetrable darkness. There are stories that will surprise you, and unsettle you, and shock you. But most of all there are stories that will grab you and draw you in and compel you to keep turning the pages.

There is *so* much that this amazing genre of ours has to offer.

New Fears 1 is only the start of the journey.

MARK MORRIS
February 2017

THE BOGGLE HOLE
by Alison Littlewood

Tim's grandad's house wasn't like a house should be. There were white lacy things on the chair arms, and the wallpaper had knobbly bits in it, and the television was too small and bulged out at the back. The carpet had a texture to it too, pale green ridges Tim could feel through his socks, and the worst thing, the thing he really didn't like, was the silence that hung over it. It was like it lived there, that silence, like a creature that had moved in and swelled to occupy the space. Tim didn't know how to banish it. He could only make it retreat, one leg at a time, into some corner or other; but he always knew the effect was temporary, that once he'd finished his game it would stealthily creep back, a bulbous, insidious thing that watched him always, waiting for its chance to pounce.

Tim's house didn't have a Silence in it. Now it didn't have Tim in it either, or his mum; she'd gone on holidays of her own, off to a golden beach with a man Tim scarcely knew. It wasn't even summer. It was late autumn, all the fallen leaves already lying soggy in the gutters. He scowled when he thought of her, miles and miles away and having fun.

"Penny for 'em, lad," his grandad said, and Tim realised he'd come into the room behind him, padding on silent slippered feet. Grandad's slippers were made of brown checked fabric and had holes in the toes. They were so ugly Tim wondered how he had ever come to buy them, but then old people were like that; they didn't seem to care what anything looked like. He scowled again.

"She'll be back soon enough, lad," Grandad said, and he glanced at the window, where the rain had begun to fall in a steady splutter. Tim couldn't hear it but he could see it spitting against the glass.

"I know you'd rather be in that there Bahaymas."

Bahamas, thought Tim, but he couldn't be bothered to correct him.

"'Appen I'll tek you to a beach," his grandad said. "You'll see, it's not ser bad. There's nowt on them furren beaches, son. Just wait—ours has got *treasures*."

Tim looked up.

"There's fossils, an—"

Tim sighed.

"Aye, well. You'd rather them Bahaymas. Fair do's, son." Grandad sighed and pulled open a drawer in the sideboard. He took out his pipe, hiding the curve of it in his hand. "I'll just pop for a puff, lad. She dun't like it in t'ouse, you know."

Tim frowned as he watched Grandad shuffle towards the door in his slippers. He knew he wouldn't bother changing into shoes to go outside. He always went in his slippers and he always talked about Grandma when he did it, and Tim didn't know why; his gran had died years ago, before Tim could even form the memories to remember her by, and yet Grandad still tiptoed around her. *She wouldn't like this. She wouldn't like that.* He would whisper, as if she was there and listening and disapproving. Tim had a picture of a stolid woman with her arms folded across her chest; it didn't tally with the photograph of a slender, dark-haired girl with laughter in her smile, which sat in an ornate frame on the mantelpiece.

He looked out of the window to see Grandad settling

into his usual seat on the rain-damp bench at the end of the garden, puffing on his pipe. The thumb of his left hand kept turning and turning the wedding ring on his finger, over and over, while he stared into the smoke.

Boggle Hole didn't look like much of a beach. It lay at the bottom of a narrow gully, a small cove of exposed rock with a stream running through it. The cliffs stretched away; they were the colour of pale sand. The beach was not the colour of sand. Mostly it was black, streaked with the bright-green slime of seaweed.

"What d'you think?" asked Grandad.

Tim tried not to scowl. *Boggle Hole,* he thought. *South of Robin Hood's Bay. Near Ravenscar.* Such a thrill he had felt at the sound of the words, and now the reality was grey and bare and boring. He remembered when Grandad first told him about it. *Boggle Oyle,* he'd said. *We'll go to Boggle Oyle,* and Tim had thought *Oil,* and wondered why they should want to go to an oily beach; the image in his head had been something he'd seen on television, blackened seabirds being dunked in washing-up bowls by solemn volunteers. Now he looked out at the dark beach under a dark sky and wondered how far off the mark he had been.

"Aye, well. There's a beach in summer. You can make sandcastles. It gets scoured off, though. Winter's on its way." Grandad sniffed the air, as if he could smell it coming.

Tim sniffed too, and got only cold briny sharpness. He wondered if that's what winter smelled like. He wondered too what kind of beach was only there for some of the time; that did have a whiff of the magical about it, as though it might appear when he turned his back.

"There were smugglers used this beach," Grandad said. When Tim looked up at him he winked, his face creasing in a hundred places. "Smugglers and maybe wreckers, too. And then there's the boggle."

"The boggle?" Tim had thought it was just a name, a strange one, like lots of other names around here. He hadn't known it was a thing.

Grandad's eyes brightened. "Come on, lad," he said. "I'll show you."

The cave was a dark focal point, which the cliff swept towards as if pointing the way. As Tim skipped ahead he found there was some sand on the beach after all; clumps of it clung to his trainers like mud, sticking strands of weed to the white leather. It occurred to him there was noise here too, not like in the house: gulls sounding like scrapping cats; the gritting of his feet; the distant growl of a car on the clifftop. Beneath it all the sea was shushing, as if telling everything else to shut up and listen.

Inside the cave, though, it was quiet. He could still hear the sea but it was as if the cave had its own Silence inside it, a presence that was trying to keep the noise out. Then Grandad huffed and puffed his way inside, and the thought was gone.

"This is it, lad."

Tim turned. "What?" He'd forgotten about the boggle, but he remembered when he saw the wink, the fissures in the old man's face.

"The boggle hole. This is it." Grandad waved his hand around the pocked grey walls. "This is where it lives."

"What's a boggle?"

Grandad put his fingers to his lips. "All right, I'll tell thee. But quiet, like. They don't like being talked about." He glanced around as he whispered, "A boggle is a sort of goblin. Some call 'em brownies, or hobs. This one 'ere's a boggle. Along t' coast there's another bay called Hob Hole. That one—well, some used to take their kids there when they got t' whooping cough. They'd ask the hob to cure 'em, and sometimes it did. It's true, lad." Grandad winked again.

Tim hadn't heard of the whooping cough, didn't know what it was. He shook his head.

"They say this 'ere boggle started out in Robin Hood's Bay. But they play tricks, see, and this one played a trick so nasty they banished him. So now he lives here."

Tim cast his eyes around the cave. It wasn't a big cave. There didn't seem to be anywhere a boggle could hide. He looked quizzically at his grandad.

"Oh, you can't see him. Not unless he wants to be seen." There was laughter in Grandad's voice; Tim was no longer sure if it was a real story or something he'd just made up. "Unless..." Grandad raised one shaggy white eyebrow. "They say, if you look in something shiny, you can see t' boggle's face. Here." He slowly worked the wedding ring from his finger and passed it to Tim. "Careful, now. Try that." He opened his eyes wide as if in fear.

The ring was old and heavy in Tim's hand. When he looked closely he could see there were layers of fine scratches in it, but between the blemishes, it still shone. He peered at the surface, then quickly looked at the old man, to see if he was being mocked.

Then, in the surface of the ring, he saw a dark outline against a bright oval. It looked a little like a face. He leaned closer and the shape grew bigger; it was nothing but his own reflection. He frowned.

"Aye, well. Maybe he din't want to come out today. Let's go and look for fossils. We might find some by t' beck."

The sea was loud again in Tim's ears as he walked by Grandad's side, talking now of boggles, now of smugglers and now of dinosaurs. The coast was Jurassic, Grandad said, and that made Tim think of T-rexes; he wondered if one could be buried, now, in the cliff. He looked at the beach with different eyes. When he knew the stories, the place was better. *Boggle Oyle*. He remembered what Grandad had said about his beach: *ours has got treasures.* He slipped his hand into Grandad's dry fingers, and when Grandad smiled at him, Tim grinned back.

The "treasure" was a small grey handful of stone, curled into a tight circle that was roughened at one side where the spiral had broken. It didn't look like treasure, but Grandad said it was a "hammonite", so Tim supposed it must be. He examined it while Grandad took out his pipe and lit it, sitting on a large smooth rock at the head of the cove.

After a while Tim stopped looking at the fossil and started watching the sea, and after that he watched Grandad.

"Why don't you smoke in the house?" he asked, and then caught himself. *Now that Grandma isn't there any more,* he had been about to add, but it struck him that it would be cruel, not a nice thing to bring up. When he looked at Grandad, though, he saw the old man knew what Tim had been about to say.

"She never did like it, son," he said, taking the pipe from his lips and staring down at the damp black stem. "She didn't like the smell, see. Said it lingered." His eyes went out of focus. "And she were right, as usual. Bad habit. So I always went outside."

"But—"

"Aye, I know." Grandad's voice was gentle. "I know she's gone, lad. I could smoke in t' house if I wanted. But—I sorter think her memory might not like it either, know what I mean? And I don't want to do something her memory wouldn't like. Case I chase it away."

He fell silent, staring into space, and Tim thought he should say something else, but he couldn't think what. And so he fell silent too, as if it were something catching, like whooping cough maybe. As if it had followed them from the house and onto the beach.

"Come on," said Grandad, tapping out the burnt contents of his pipe. "We'd best get on. Light's going already, and the tide comes all t' way up this beach. You can get stuck. Best put that fossil back, now."

"Put it back?"

"Aye, lad." Grandad's face broke into its steady slow smile. "You mustn't take anything from this 'ere beach. Din't I tell you that? It'll upset t' boggle, see. Take summat of his and he might just take summat from you. And how'd you like that?" He winked. "'S no lie, lad. Every word of it's God's honest truth."

They went back to the beach the next day. Tim walked up and down the seafront, peering into rock pools. Some had brownish-pink squashy things clinging to the rock, bulging and flexing as clear water washed over them. The rocks were made rougher still by barnacles, some with smaller barnacles clinging to their sides. Tim tried to grip one and pull it from the rock, but it wouldn't budge. He stomped instead on a thick mat of bladderwrack, trying to pop the blisters in its dark green fronds.

He looked back up the beach. By the beck—Stoupe Beck, Grandad had called it—two men were standing by the base of the cliff. One of them bent and slipped something into his pocket. Tim grinned. The man had found a fossil—maybe even the same one Tim had found yesterday—and that made him think of the boggle; the revenge it might take for stealing from its beach.

He turned towards Grandad. The old man wasn't smoking

his pipe; he was watching Tim. He grinned and waved and Tim ran towards him, laughing. He put out his hands to catch him when Tim drew close.

"Let's have a look for the boggle, Grandad." Tim pointed towards his left hand.

After a moment, the old man understood. He fumbled the ring from his finger and passed it to Tim. "Careful, now."

Tim wasn't sure if he meant about the ring or in case he saw the boggle reflected in its surface. He peered into the gold, turning it in his fingers. He could see clouds, and the hazy shape that was him. Nothing else. He frowned. *God's honest truth*, the old man had said.

Grandad tapped the side of his nose before holding out his hand for the ring. "Only when he wants to be seen, son," he said. "Now, how's about I teach you to find something shiny for yourself?"

They walked up and down the beach, but it didn't work. Grandad stopped and bent with a "pfft" and scraped through the stones with his fingers. There was nothing.

"You have to walk with the sun behind you, see," he said. He pointed at their shadows, dim and hazy. Tim turned and tried to make out the sun; there was only a place where the clouds were a little brighter.

"It's best at sunrise or sunset. You walk with it behind you and it shines 'em up, see, like they're polished. Sometimes there's agate, or carnelian. You can't see 'em for looking, normally. They're dull, like pebbles. But when the sun's low and shining on 'em—they glow. You can see t' gemstones then. They shine right back at you." He winked. "Maybe it's the boggle. They're his treasure too, see. P'raps he won't let 'em go, not today."

Tim lit up. "Tomorrow, then?" He looked once more over his shoulder at the faint trembling light.

Grandad sighed, then smiled. "Aye, lad. Tomorrer."

The next day, Tim fidgeted through games and sandwiches and television programmes. Sometimes Grandad caught him looking at the window, watching anxiously for rain, and each time he did they would share a smile; sometimes, they laughed. It wasn't until later, when they were about to set off, that Tim realised he hadn't thought about the Silence at all. It had retreated, hiding at the back of the airing cupboard or under a bed, somewhere quiet and small and still, until it could come out again. *Maybe tomorrer*, Tim thought, and grinned to himself as they got into the car.

The sun was bright and low, shining straight into Tim's eyes, dazzling him. It was going to work. He knew it even as they pulled into the little car park above the beach and saw the fossil hunters packing up to leave. Their car was grey and looked older even than Grandad's, and when Grandad saw it, he gave a low whistle. "Look at that," he said in a low voice. "'Appen t' boggle's nicked their hubcaps."

Tim grinned even wider. *Take summat of his*, he thought, *and he might just take summat from you.*

At first, Grandad watched while Tim carefully set the sun at his back and walked along the seafront, crunch, crunch over the pebbles. He said he was keeping an eye on the tide just in case, but Tim knew he was really having a puff on his pipe.

When he'd walked a distance away he turned and walked back and then he tried again. This time, the sun seemed— not brighter, but redder. *Readier*, he thought, and he turned towards the boggle's cave and stuck out his tongue.

His shadow was sharper where it lay against the pebbles, each stone sharply delineated with a black crescent. Every fissure and crease in the sand had its own crisp shadow. *Now*, Tim thought. He stretched out one foot in a long stride and let it fall again. *Crunch.* Then again. *Crunch.* The sun was at his back. His shadow was long before him. It looked like some kind of giant: *for scaring boggles away*, he thought. *So he can't hide his treasures.* And something shone amid the grey and the murk and the stone. It glowed like living sunset fallen to the beach, a footprint marking the way to the boggle's hoard.

Tim pounced on it. When he straightened and looked at what was in his hand, though, he frowned. It was nothing but a dull pebble about half the size of his thumb, reddish perhaps, but with a surface that was greyed like old skin. It wasn't even a nice pebble, and he drew his hand back ready to throw it into the sea when he had a thought.

He turned and the sun glared into his eyes. He held the stone between thumb and finger, and the light shone through it. It was like something alive, the bright orange-red of carnelian. He turned to his grandad with a look of triumph, but the old man was busy tamping out his pipe on a rock. Then he stood and raised a hand, half waving, half beckoning.

Tim looked down at his feet as clear frothing water rushed over them, stirring the tiny stones as if in offering: *take one of them instead.* He closed his hand over the gemstone and slipped it into his pocket. Then he started to make his way back up the beach.

It was in the car that Grandad made the sound. It was a little choking cough, way back in his throat. Then he started breathing really loud and patting at his coat, wriggling in his seat to check his trouser pockets.

"What's up, Grandad?" asked Tim.

Grandad didn't answer; he only looked back at the boy with wide open eyes. They were watery at the edges.

"Grandad?"

"It's me ring," he answered at last, and he held out his left hand, the fingers spread. "Me ring, see. *Her* ring." He panted and patted some more. "I must 'ave dropped it." He stopped, gripping the steering wheel as if holding on. "I must 'ave." He looked down at his hand, at his broad fingers. Tim remembered the way he'd worked the ring off his finger, twisting and pulling until it came loose.

"You looked in it, din't you, lad?" He turned to Tim, his eyes lighting up. "You did."

Tim shook his head. "That was yesterday," he whispered. "Yesterday, Grandad, remember?"

But Grandad hardly seemed to hear as he turned away from Tim, staring out of the window. "It's too late," he said, breathless. "Tide's coming in. It's too late to go and look."

That evening, the Silence was back. It had grown while they were away, stretching itself into corners and around walls and seeping through doorways that should have kept it out. The television was on, but there wasn't any sound. Grandad stared at it without seeming to see. His eyes hadn't dried. He kept nodding to himself, as if listening to something Tim couldn't hear. He kept turning towards the photograph of a grandmother Tim didn't remember, a woman he didn't know. He'd glance at it and then away, quickly, as if he couldn't bear to look any longer.

Tim hunched himself into the chair, trying to make himself smaller. Silence expanded to fill the gap he left behind.

His hand went to his pocket and he found the thing he'd put there. The stone was small and smooth and cold. Tim ran his fingers over it, but it didn't seem to get any warmer. He turned and turned it in his pocket, and he tried not to think, and he closed his eyes.

The next day Grandad didn't talk about the beach. He didn't seem to want to talk about anything. He made breakfast, his hands shaking, and then he switched on the television and sat there without looking at it.

Tim went to his side. "We'll find it today, Grandad, won't we?"

Grandad shifted, but he didn't reply.

"We'll go back to the beach, won't we?"

The old man shot him a quick look and put out a hand and ruffled Tim's hair. It pulled, but Tim didn't protest. He was thinking of the stone in his pocket. *Me*, he was thinking. *You should have taken something from me*. It wasn't right. It wasn't fair.

"Please, Grandad," he said, and this time his voice got through.

Grandad turned. "I s'pose. Aye, all right then." Tim had to lean closer to hear him. "Come on, lad."

A short time later they got out of the car and walked together down the narrow lane, towards the sea. The sky was packed with low gathered clouds and the sea gave back the grey in a dull shine. The waves were slow and effortless, giving way to the beach in tired little wafts.

Grandad stood where he'd sat the day before, looking at the ground. He gestured to Tim. "Go and play now, lad."

Tim nodded and turned away. He knew where he was going; it was all right. Better that he should go alone. He made his way up the beach. When he looked back, Grandad wasn't watching. He was staring down at the ground, at the millions of pebbles, and he wasn't moving.

Tim started to run. He only stopped when he reached the mouth of the boggle hole, listening to the silence coming from inside; and then he stepped forward and went in, and the cave swallowed him.

His hand was in his pocket. He clutched the stone.

He opened his mouth to speak but his voice was hoarse. He cleared his throat. "I brought this for you." He took the carnelian from his pocket and held it out. "I want you to give the ring back."

He looked into the corners of the cave. It was no good, it wasn't here. Instead he felt the Silence massing behind him, coming from the sea. He turned and found he could hear it after all, mocking him: *Hush. Hush.*

He stepped out into the light and stared. Had the sea taken the ring? It came right up to the cliffs, Grandad had said. Right into the cave. It would have crept over the beach in the dark, greedily sucking and reaching for any bright thing it could find. His gaze went to the roughened rocks between here and the shore, just as the sun cleared the clouds for an instant; it shone back from a watery surface and was gone.

Tim started to walk towards it, picking his way. It was a rock pool, a wide one, its bottom lined with dregs of sand and fringed with black fronds like hair in bathwater. The sides were sharp overhangs; no telling what could be hiding beneath. Crabs, maybe. Fish. Fish with teeth. Tim narrowed his eyes as the light caught the surface of the water once more. *Shiny*, he thought, and shuddered.

And then he saw what lay beneath the water. He gasped and rushed towards it, falling to his knees onto the rock. It hurt, but he didn't think about that.

There, lying on the pale sand under the clear water, was a thick gold ring. Tim looked up; his grandad was a small figure standing on the beach, staring into the waves. Maybe it was better that way. Tim could imagine the surprise on his face when he ran to him and held it out. He let out a spurt of air, almost a giggle, and thought he heard an answering sound somewhere behind him.

He tried to turn; there was nothing there. It was an echo, that was all, coming from the cave or the cliff; the sound of water trickling through stone.

When he looked back into the pool, the ring remained.

He pushed up one sleeve, gripped a spike of rock and leaned over, pushing his hand into the icy cold. He opened his fingers, grasping for the ring—and they closed on nothing. There was only sand, fine grains of it, the sand he'd wanted to find when he first came here; now he didn't want it. He let it slip through his fingers with a little cry. He withdrew his hand. When the drips and circles on the water subsided the form took shape again, a golden ring sitting on the surface of the sand. No, not on the surface; *above* the surface.

Tim frowned and reached for it again, leaning further this time. He poked at the ring with one finger, meaning to spear it through its heart, but there was nothing there.

He sat back again, letting the water grow still. There; a ring, but nothing he could grasp. And then he understood.

"It's here," he muttered. "Here. Have it." He took the carnelian from his pocket and held it over the water a moment, seeing it dull and lifeless in his hand. He let it drop.

The carnelian fell into the water with a plop, and it vanished.

Tim frowned. He leaned in again. There was no carnelian; he couldn't see it anywhere. He poked at the sand again to see if the stone had been covered in its fall, but there was nothing.

Then he saw a bright glow coming from the other side of the pool; an orange-red glow, something small at the bottom of the water. He shifted his knees, shuffling his way over the rocks. There was something there. He could see it when the sun shone behind him. He glanced at where he'd been. Blinked. He couldn't understand how it had passed from there to here. Perhaps this water was flowing after all, going back to the sea, and had carried the stone with it. Or maybe it was a reflection, something about the nature of the pool and the sun and his eyes. He shook his head; it didn't matter. What mattered was, he could see the carnelian below him. It was deeper here. He'd have to lean all the way out, his face nearly touching the water.

He gripped the rocks tightly with one hand and eased himself out over the pool. He plunged in his other arm almost to the shoulder, grasping below him, raking the surface of the sand. There was something cold and hard and smooth under his fingers. He grabbed it and pulled himself back, cold, dripping. When he saw what was in his hand he nearly dropped it. It was an old scratched ring. It was his grandad's ring.

Tim looked up at the cave mouth and slowly grinned. He gestured with the ring: *thank you.*

And something caught his eye in the pool as the sun passed overhead: a brief bright shine, and the suggestion of a face, ugly and distorted and fringed with shaggy hair, laughing on the surface of the water. It was there for a moment and then gone. *A reflection,* he thought, *that's all it was.* But he still wasn't sure as he pushed himself up and started to make his way back over the beach to his grandad, who was motionless, staring at the waves as they broke, over and over, against the shore.

There was something in Grandad's eyes. At first they had lit up. It had been just as Tim had imagined, him holding out the ring and the fissures appearing, deep lines of joy written into the old man's skin. He hadn't been able to speak. He had only taken the ring and pushed it, trembling, back onto his finger. Then he had opened and closed his hand before wrapping his thin arms around Tim, and they'd looked at each other and they'd laughed.

It was later that the look appeared. A small frown, and a single line between his eyes. It deepened when he looked at Tim. "Where'd you say you found it?" he asked.

Tim pointed up towards the cave. "The boggle had it, Grandad," he said, and the line grew deeper still.

They walked along the beach some more, but it wasn't

long before they both turned, as if by some unspoken agreement, towards the car.

"We din't go thee-er," Grandad muttered as he fumbled the keys from his pocket.

"What, Grandad?"

Pardon, his mother would have said, but his mother wasn't here.

"We din't go up near t' cave yest'day," said the old man. He didn't meet Tim's eyes. He just looked at the keys in his hand. No: at the wedding ring that nestled beneath them. "We din't go near it."

"No," Tim said.

"Did you see owt?"

Tim swallowed. "What?"

"When you looked in t' ring."

Tim looked at him, and this time the old man looked back. The thing in his eyes was still there.

Me, Tim thought. *You should have taken something from me.* Slowly, he shook his head. "I didn't take it, Grandad. It was the boggle."

"Aye. Aye, you said." Grandad heaved a sigh. "Well, it's back. That's t' main thing. Come on then, Tim. Let's get going, eh."

Tim, he'd called him, and for the first time it struck him as odd. Grandad never called him Tim. He called him lad, or son; never by his name. It was strange he'd never noticed that before. Now he didn't know what he was supposed to think about it. But there was nothing to be done but get into the car and start heading towards home as the rain, viciously, began to spit.

The Silence was there. This time it wasn't hiding and it wasn't creeping. It was a fat, sullen thing, sitting in the middle of the room so that Tim could almost see it. He stared at the window, watching the rain streak the glass, time passing outside. Soon his mother would be home. She would come to fetch him, laughing and tanned from her holiday.

Grandad was doing a crossword in the newspaper, his reading glasses perched on the end of his nose and his wedding ring shining on his finger. They hadn't spoken about it since they came back from the beach. They hadn't been back there, either. They had been here, in this house, with the Silence sitting between them.

Tim drew a deep breath. "Grandad, about the boggle."

Grandad buried his nose deeper into the paper.

"If the boggle took summat from you, and you took—"

"That's enough o' that now." Grandad let the newspaper drop with a loud rustle. "Enough o' that." After a moment his look softened and he gave a small smile.

"But, Grandad—"

"It's nowt but a story, Tim," the old man said. After a moment, he raised the newspaper again, holding it close to his eyes.

Nowt but a story.

Tim thought of the thing he'd seen in the surface of the water, its bright cruel grin; a whisper of laughter heard over his shoulder. He closed his eyes tightly. Grandad was surely right: things like that couldn't be. It was nothing but a story, and Tim had been lucky to find the ring, and that was all.

'S no lie, lad. Every word of it's God's honest truth.

He remembered the way they had laughed together. The way they had winked. It had been different then, when there was the story between them. Something that was for them, and them alone.

He thought of the fossil hunters, trolling their way along the base of the cliff. Them returning to their car and finding their hubcaps gone, being tormented perhaps by whispers and nips and things missing from their pockets; things they'd never get back.

He was forgiven; he knew that. But he knew the old man would never forget, no more than he could forget his dead wife's face when he stared into his pipe smoke. It was there, an intangible writhing thing.

Me, he'd thought. *You should have taken something from me.*

But as Tim watched the old man intent on the newspaper, that line still there between his eyes, he knew that was exactly what the boggle had done.

SHEPHERDS' BUSINESS
by Stephen Gallagher

Picture me on an island supply boat, one of the old Clyde Puffers, seeking to deliver me to my new post. This was 1947, just a couple of years after the war, and I was a young doctor relatively new to general practice. Picture also a choppy sea, a deck that rose and fell with every wave, and a cross-current fighting hard to turn us away from the isle. Back on the mainland I'd been advised that a hearty breakfast would be the best preventative for seasickness and now, having loaded up with one, I was doing my best to hang onto it.

I almost succeeded. Perversely, it was the sudden calm of the harbour that did for me. I ran to the side and I fear that I cast rather more than my bread upon the waters. Those on the quay were treated to a rare sight; their new doctor, clinging to the ship's rail, with seagulls swooping in the wake of the steamer for an unexpected water-borne treat.

The island's resident constable was waiting for me at the end of the gangplank. A man of around my father's age, in uniform, chiselled in flint and unsullied by good cheer. He said, "Munro Spence? Doctor Munro Spence?"

"That's me," I said.

"Will you take a look at Doctor Laughton before we move him? He didn't have too good a journey down."

There was a man to take care of my baggage, so I followed the constable to the harbour master's house at the end of the quay. It was a stone building, square and solid. Dr Laughton was in the harbour master's sitting room behind the office. He was in a chair by the fire with his feet on a stool and a rug over his knees and was attended by one of his own nurses, a stocky red-haired girl of twenty or younger.

I began, "Doctor Laughton. I'm…"

"My replacement, I know," he said. "Let's get this over with."

I checked his pulse, felt his glands, listened to his chest, noted the signs of cyanosis. It was hardly necessary; Dr Laughton had already diagnosed himself, and had requested this transfer. He was an old-school Edinburgh-trained medical man, and I could be sure that his condition must be sufficiently serious that "soldiering on" was no longer an option. He might choose to ignore his own aches and troubles up to a point, but as the island's only doctor he couldn't leave the community at risk.

When I enquired about chest pain he didn't answer directly, but his expression told me all.

"I wish you'd agreed to the aeroplane," I said.

"For my sake or yours?" he said. "You think I'm bad. You should see your colour." And then, relenting a little, "The airstrip's for emergencies. What good's that to me?"

I asked the nurse, "Will you be travelling with him?"

"I will," she said. "I've an aunt I can stay with. I'll return on the morning boat."

Two of the men from the Puffer were waiting to carry the doctor to the quay. We moved back so that they could lift him between them, chair and all. As they were getting into position Laughton said to me, "Try not to kill anyone in your first week, or they'll have me back here the day after."

I was his locum, his temporary replacement. That was

the story. But we both knew that he wouldn't be returning. His sight of the island from the sea would almost certainly be his last.

Once they'd manoeuvred him through the doorway, the two sailors bore him with ease toward the boat. Some local people had turned out to wish him well on his journey.

As I followed with the nurse beside me, I said, "Pardon me, but what do I call you?"

"I'm Nurse Kirkwood," she said. "Rosie."

"I'm Munro," I said. "Is that an island accent, Rosie?"

"You have a sharp ear, Doctor Spence," she said.

She supervised the installation of Dr Laughton in the deck cabin, and didn't hesitate to give the men orders where another of her age and sex might only make suggestions or requests. A born matron, if ever I saw one. The old salts followed her instruction without a murmur.

When they'd done the job to her satisfaction, Laughton said to me, "The latest patient files are on my desk. Your desk, now."

Nurse Kirkwood said to him, "You'll be back before they've missed you, Doctor," but he ignored that.

He said, "These are good people. Look after them."

The crew were already casting off, and they all but pulled the board from under my feet as I stepped ashore. I took a moment to gather myself, and gave a pleasant nod in response to the curious looks of those well-wishers who'd stayed to see the boat leave. The day's cargo had been unloaded and stacked on the quay and my bags were nowhere to be seen. I went in search of them and found Moodie, driver and handyman to the island hospital, waiting beside a field ambulance that had been decommissioned from the military. He was chatting to another man, who bade good day and moved off as I arrived.

"Will it be much of a drive?" I said as we climbed aboard.

"Ay," Moodie said.

"Ten minutes? An hour? Half an hour?"

"Ay," he agreed, making this one of the longest conversations we were ever to have.

The drive took little more than twenty minutes. This was due to the size of the island and a good concrete road, yet another legacy of the army's wartime presence. We saw no other vehicle, slowed for nothing other than the occasional indifferent sheep. Wool and weaving, along with some lobster fishing, sustained the peacetime economy here. In wartime it had been different, with the local populace outnumbered by spotters, gunners, and the Royal Engineers. Later came a camp for Italian prisoners of war, whose disused medical block the Highlands and Islands Medical Service took over when the island's cottage hospital burned down. Before we reached it we passed the airstrip, still usable, but with its gatehouse and control tower abandoned.

The former prisoners' hospital was a concrete building with a wooden barracks attached. The Italians had laid paths and a garden, but these were now growing wild. Again I left Moodie to deal with my bags, and went looking to introduce myself to the senior sister.

Senior Sister Garson looked me over once and didn't seem too impressed. But she called me by my title and gave me a briefing on everyone's duties while leading me around on a tour. It was then that I learned my driver's name. I met all the staff apart from Mrs Moodie, who served as cook, housekeeper, and island midwife.

"There's just the one six-bed ward," Sister Garson told me. "We use that for the men and the officers' quarters for the women. Two to a room."

"How many patients at the moment?"

"As of this morning, just one. Old John Petrie. He's come in to die."

Harsh though it seemed, she delivered the information in a matter-of-fact manner.

"I'll see him now," I said.

Old John Petrie was eighty-five or eighty-seven. The records were unclear. Occupation: shepherd. Next of kin: none—a rarity on the island. He'd led a tough outdoor life, but toughness won't keep a body going forever. He was now grown so thin and frail that he was in danger of being swallowed up by his bedding. According to Dr Laughton's notes he'd presented with no specific ailment. One of my teachers might have diagnosed a case of TMB: Too Many Birthdays. He'd been found in his croft house, alone, half-starved, unable to rise. There was life in John Petrie's eyes as I introduced myself, but little sign of it anywhere else.

We moved on. Mrs Moodie would bring me my evening meals, I was told. Unless she was attending at a birth, in which case I'd be looked after by Rosie Kirkwood's mother who'd cycle up from town.

My experience in obstetrics had mainly involved being a student and staying out of the midwife's way. Senior Sister Garson said, "They're mostly home births with the midwife attending, unless there are complications and then she'll call you in. But that's quite rare. You might want to speak to Mrs Tulloch before she goes home. Her baby was stillborn on Sunday."

"Where do I find her?" I said.

The answer was, in the suite of rooms at the other end of the building. Her door in the women's wing was closed, with her husband waiting in the corridor.

"She's dressing," he explained.

Sister Garson said, "Thomas, this is Doctor Spence. He's taking over from Doctor Laughton."

33

She left us together. Thomas Tulloch was a young man, somewhere around my own age but much hardier. He wore a shabby suit of all-weather tweed that looked as if it had outlasted several owners. His beard was dark, his eyes blue. Women like that kind of thing, I know, but my first thought was of a wall-eyed collie. What can I say? I like dogs.

I asked him, "How's your wife bearing up?"

"It's hard for me to tell," he said. "She hasn't spoken much." And then, as soon as Sister Garson was out of earshot, he lowered his voice and said, "What was it?"

"I beg your pardon?"

"The child. Was it a boy or a girl?"

"I've no idea."

"No one will say. Daisy didn't get to see it. It was just, your baby's dead, get over it, you'll have another."

"Her first?"

He nodded.

I wondered who might have offered such cold comfort. Everyone, I expect. It was the approach at the time. Infant mortality was no longer the commonplace event it once had been, but old attitudes lingered.

I said, "And how do you feel?"

Tulloch shrugged. "It's nature," he conceded. "But you'll get a ewe that won't leave a dead lamb. Is John Petrie dying now?"

"I can't say. Why?"

"I'm looking after his flock and his dog. His dog won't stay put."

At that point the door opened and Mrs Tulloch—Daisy—stood before us. True to her name, a crushed flower. She was pale, fair, and small of stature, barely up to her husband's shoulder. She'd have heard our voices, though not, I would hope, our conversation.

I said, "Mrs Tulloch, I'm Doctor Spence. Are you sure you're well enough to leave us?"

She said, "Yes, thank you, Doctor." She spoke in little above a whisper. Though a grown and married woman, from a distance you might have taken her for a girl of sixteen.

I looked to Tulloch and said, "How will you get her home?"

"We were told the ambulance?" he said. And then, "Or we could walk down for the mail bus."

"Let me get Mister Moodie," I said.

Moodie seemed to be unaware of any arrangement, and reluctant to comply with it. Though it went against the grain to be firm with a man twice my age, I could see trouble in our future if I wasn't. I said, "I'm not discharging a woman in her condition to a hike on the heath. To your ambulance, Mister Moodie."

Garaged alongside the field ambulance I saw a clapped-out Riley Roadster at least a dozen years old. Laughton's own vehicle, available for my use.

As the Tullochs climbed aboard the ambulance I said to Daisy, "I'll call by and check on you in a day or two." And then, to her husband, "I'll see if I can get an answer to your question."

My predecessor's files awaited me in the office. Those covering his patients from the last six months had been left out on the desk, and were but the tip of the iceberg; in time I'd need to become familiar with the histories of everyone on the island, some fifteen hundred souls. It was a big responsibility for one medic, but civilian doctors were in short supply. Though the fighting was over and the forces demobbed, medical officers were among the last to be released.

I dived in. The last winter had been particularly severe, with a number of pneumonia deaths and broken limbs from ice falls. I read of frostbitten fishermen and a three-year-old boy deaf after measles. Two cases had been sent to the mainland for surgery and one emergency appendectomy had been performed, successfully and right here in the hospital's theatre, by Laughton himself.

Clearly I had a lot to live up to.

Since October there had been close to a dozen births on the island. A fertile community, and dependent upon it. Most of the children were thriving, one family had moved away. A Mrs Flett had popped out her seventh, with no complications. But then there was Daisy Tulloch.

I looked at her case notes. They were only days old, and incomplete. Laughton had written them up in a shaky hand and I found myself wondering whether, in some way, his condition might have been a factor in the outcome. Not by any direct failing of his own, but Daisy had been thirty-six hours in labour before he was called in. Had the midwife delayed calling him for longer than she should? By the time of his intervention it was a matter of no detectable heartbeat and a forceps delivery.

I'd lost track of the time, so when Mrs Moodie appeared with a tray I was taken by surprise.

"Don't get up, Doctor," she said. "I brought your tea."

I turned the notes face down on the desk and pushed my chair back. Enough, I reckoned, for one day.

I said, "The stillbirth, the Tullochs. Was it a boy or a girl?"

"Doctor Laughton dealt with it," Mrs Moodie said. "I wasn't there to see. It hardly matters now, does it?"

"Stillbirths have to be registered," I said.

"If you say so, Doctor."

"It's the law, Mrs Moodie. What happened to the remains?"

"They're in the shelter for the undertaker. It's the coldest place we have. He'll collect them when there's next a funeral."

I finished my meal and, leaving the tray for Mrs Moodie to clear, went out to the shelter. It wasn't just a matter of the Tullochs' curiosity. With no note of gender, I couldn't complete the necessary registration. Back then, the bodies of the stillborn were often buried with any unrelated female adult. I had to act before the undertaker came to call.

The shelter was an air-raid bunker located between the hospital and the airfield, now used for storage. And when I say storage, I mean everything from our soap and toilet roll supply to the recently deceased. It was a series of chambers mostly buried under a low, grassy mound. The only visible features above ground were a roof vent and a brick-lined ramp leading down to a door at one end. The door had a mighty lock, for which there was no key.

Inside, I had to navigate my way through rooms filled with crates and boxes to find the designated mortuary with the slab. Except that it wasn't a slab; it was a billiard table, cast in the ubiquitous concrete (by those Italians, no doubt) and repurposed by my predecessor. The cotton-wrapped package that lay on it was unlabelled, and absurdly small. I unpicked the wrapping with difficulty and made the necessary check. A girl. The cord was still attached and there were all the signs of a rough forceps delivery. Forceps in a live birth are only meant to guide and protect the child's head. The marks of force supported my suspicion that Laughton had been called at a point too late for the infant, and where he could only focus on preserving the mother's life.

Night had all but fallen when I emerged. As I washed my hands before going to make a last check on our dying shepherd, I reflected on the custom of slipping a stillbirth into a coffin to share a stranger's funeral. On the one hand, it could seem like a heartless practice; on the other, there was something touching about the idea of a nameless child being placed in the anonymous care of another soul. Whenever I try to imagine eternity, it's always long and lonely. Such company might be a comfort for both.

John Petrie lay with his face toward the darkened window.

In the time since my first visit he'd been washed and fed, and the bed remade around him.

I said, "Mister Petrie, do you remember me? Doctor Spence."

There was a slight change in the rhythm of his breathing that I took for a yes.

I said, "Are you comfortable?"

Nothing moved but his eyes. Looking at me, then back to the window.

"What about pain? Have you any pain? I can help with it if you have."

Nothing. So then I said, "Let me close these blinds for you," but as I moved, he made a sound.

"Don't close them?" I said. "Are you sure?"

I followed his gaze.

I could see the shelter mound from here. Only the vague shape of the hill was visible at this hour, one layer of deepening darkness over another. Against the sky, in the last of the fading light, I could make out the outline of an animal. It was a dog, and it seemed to be watching the building.

I did as John Petrie wished, left the blinds open, and him to the night.

My accommodation was in the wooden barracks where the prisoners had lived and slept. I had an oil lamp for light and a ratty curtain at the window. My bags had been lined up at the end of a creaky bunk. The one concession to luxury was a rag rug on the floor.

I could unpack in the morning. I undressed, dropped onto the bed, and had the best sleep of my life.

With the morning came my first taste of practice routine. An early ward round, such as it was, and then a drive down into town for weekday surgery. This took place in a room attached to the library and ran on a system of first come, first served, for as long as it took to deal with the queue. All went without much of a hitch. No doubt some people stayed away out of wariness of a new doctor. Others had discovered minor ailments with which to justify their curiosity. Before surgery was over, Rosie Kirkwood joined me fresh from the boat. Dr Laughton had not enjoyed the voyage, she told me, and we left it at that.

After the last patient (chilblains) had left, Nurse Kirkwood said, "I see you have use of Doctor Laughton's car. Can I beg a lift back to the hospital?"

"You can," I said. "And along the way, can you show me where the Tullochs live? I'd like to drop by."

"I can show you the way," she said. "But it's not the kind of place you can just 'drop by'."

I will not claim that I'd mastered the Riley. When I described it as clapped-out, I did not exaggerate. The engine sounded like a keg of bolts rolling down a hill and the springs gave us a ride like a condemned fairground. Rosie seemed used to it.

Passing through town with the harbour behind us, I said, "Which one's the undertaker?"

"We just passed it."

"The furniture place?"

"Donald Budge. My father's cousin. Also the coroner and cabinet maker to the island."

Two minutes later, we were out of town. It was bleak, rolling lowland moor in every direction, stretching out to a big, big sky.

Raising my voice to be heard over the whistling crack in the windshield, I said, "You've lived here all your life?"

"I have," she said. "I saw everything change with the war. We thought it would go back to being the same again after. But that doesn't happen, does it?"

"Never in the way you expect," I said.

"Doctor Laughton won't be coming back, will he?"

"There's always hope."

"That's what we say to patients."

I took my eyes off the road for a moment to look at her.

She said, "You can speak plainly to me, Doctor. I don't do my nursing for a hobby. And I don't always plan to be doing it here." And then, with barely a change in tone, "There's a junction with a telephone box coming up."

I quickly returned my attention to the way ahead. "Do I turn?"

"Not there. The next track just after."

It was a rough track, and the word bone-shaking wouldn't begin to describe it. Now I understood why the Riley was falling apart, if this was the pattern for every home visit. The track ran for most of a mile and finally became completely impassable, with still a couple of hundred yards to go to reach the Tullochs' home.

Their house was a one-storey crofter's cottage with a sod roof and a barn attached. The cottage walls were limewashed, those of the barn were of bare stone. I took my medical bag from the car and we walked the rest of the way.

When we reached the door Nurse Kirkwood knocked and called out, "Daisy? It's the doctor to see you."

There was movement within. As we waited, I looked around. Painters romanticise these places. All I saw was evidence of a hard living. I also saw a dog tethered some yards from the house, looking soulful. It resembled the one I'd seen the night before, although, to be honest, the same could be said of every dog on the island.

After making us wait as long as she dared for a quick tidy of the room and herself, Daisy Tulloch opened the door and invited us in. She was wearing a floral print dress, and her hair had been hastily pinned.

She offered tea; Nurse Kirkwood insisted on making it as we talked. Although Daisy rose to the occasion with the necessary courtesy, I could see it was a struggle. The experience of the last week had clearly hit her hard.

"I don't want to cause any fuss, Doctor," was all she would say. "I'm tired, that's all."

People respect a doctor, but they'll talk to a nurse. When I heard sheep and more than one dog barking outside, I went out and left the two women conferring. Tulloch was herding a couple of dozen ewes into a muddy pen by the cottage; a mixed herd, if the markings were anything to go by. Today he wore a cloth cap and blue work trousers with braces. I realised that the tweeds I'd taken for his working clothes were actually his Sunday best.

I waited until the sheep were all penned, and then went over.

I told him, "It would have been a girl. But…" And I left it there, because what more could I add? But then a thought occurred and I said, "You may want to keep the information to yourself. Why make things worse?"

"That's what Doctor Laughton said. Chin up, move on, have yourself another. But she won't see it like that."

I watched him go to the barn and return with a bucket of ochre in one hand and a stick in the other. The stick had a crusty rag wrapped around its end, for dipping and marking the fleeces.

I said, "Are those John Petrie's sheep?"

"They are," he said. "But someone's got to dip 'em and clip 'em. Will he ever come back?"

"There's always hope," I said. "What about his dog?"

He glanced at the tethered animal, watching us from over near the house. "Biddy?" he said. "That dog's no use to me. Next time she runs off, she's gone. I'm not fetching her home again."

"A dog?" Nurse Kirkwood said. She braced herself against the dash as we bumped our way back onto the road. "Senior Sister Garson will love you."

"I'll keep her in the barracks," I said. "Senior Sister Garson doesn't even need to know."

She turned around to look at Biddy, seated in the open luggage hatch. The collie had her face tilted up into the wind and her eyes closed in an attitude of uncomplicated bliss.

"Good luck with that," she said.

That night, when the coast was clear, I sneaked Biddy into the ward.

"John," I said, "you've got a visitor."

I began to find my way around. I started to make home visits and I took the time to meet the island's luminaries, from the priest to the postman to the secretary of the grazing committee. Most of the time Biddy rode around with me in the back of the Riley. One night I went down into town and took the dog into the pub with me, as an icebreaker. People were beginning to recognise me now. It would be a while before I'd feel accepted, but I felt I'd made a start.

Senior Sister Garwood told me that Donald Budge, the undertaker, had now removed the infant body for an appropriate burial. She also said that he'd complained to her about the state in which he'd found it. I told her to send him to me, and I'd explain the medical realities of the situation to a man who ought to know better. Budge didn't follow it up.

The next day in town Thomas Tulloch came to morning surgery, alone. "Mister Tulloch," I said. "How can I help you?"

"It's not for me," he said. "It's Daisy, but she won't come.

Can you give her a tonic? Anything that'll perk her up. Nothing I do seems to help."

"Give her time. It's only been a few days."

"It's getting worse. Now she won't leave the cottage. I tried to persuade her to visit her sister but she just turns to the wall."

So I wrote him a prescription for some Parrish's, a harmless red concoction of sweetened iron phosphate that would, at best, sharpen the appetite, and at worst do nothing at all. It was all I could offer. Depression, in those days, was a condition to be overcome by "pulling oneself together". Not to do so was to be perverse and most likely attention-seeking, especially if you were a woman. Though barely educated, even by the island's standards, Tulloch was an unusually considerate spouse for his time.

Visits from the dog seemed to do the trick for John Petrie. I may have thought I was deceiving the senior sister, but I realise now that she was most likely turning a blind eye. Afterwards his breathing was always easier, his sleep more peaceful. And I even got my first words out of him when he beckoned me close and said into my ear:

"*Ye'll do.*"

After this mark of approval, I looked up to find the constable waiting for me, hat in his hands as if he were unsure of the protocol. Was a dying man's bedside supposed to be like a church? He was taking no chances.

He said, "I'm sorry to come and find you at your work, Doctor. But I hope you can settle a concern."

"I can try."

"There's a rumour going round about the dead Tulloch baby. Some kind of abuse?"

"I don't understand."

"Some people are even saying it had been skinned."

"Skinned?" I echoed.

"I've seen what goes on in post-mortems and such," the

constable persisted. "But I never heard of such a thing being called for."

"Nor have I," I said. "It's just Chinese whispers, David. I saw the body before Donald Budge took it away. It was in poor condition after a long and difficult labour. But the only abuse it suffered was natural."

"I'm only going by what people are saying."

"Well for God's sake don't let them say such a thing around the mother."

"I do hear she's taken it hard," the constable conceded. "Same thing happened to my sister, but she just got on. I've never even heard her speak of it."

He looked to me for permission, and then went around the bed to address John Petrie. He bent down with his hands on his knees, and spoke as if to a child or an imbecile.

"A'right, John?" he said. "Back on your feet soon, eh?"

Skinned? Who ever heard of such a thing? The chain of gossip must have started with Donald Budge and grown ever more grotesque in the telling. According to the records Budge had four children of his own. The entire family was active in amateur dramatics and the church choir. You'd expect a man in his position to know better.

I was writing up patient notes at the end of the next day's town surgery when there was some commotion outside. Nurse Kirkwood went to find out the cause and came back moments later with a breathless nine-year-old boy at her side.

"This is Robert Flett," she said. "He ran all the way here to say his mother's been in an accident."

"What kind of an accident?"

The boy looked startled and dumbstruck at my direct question, but Rosie Kirkwood spoke for him. "He says she fell."

I looked at her. "You know the way?"

"Of course."

We all piled into the Riley to drive out to the west of the island. Nurse Kirkwood sat beside me and I lifted Robert into the bag hatch with the dog, where both seemed happy enough.

At the highest point on the moor Nurse Kirkwood reckoned she spotted a walking figure on a distant path, far from the road.

She said, "Is that Thomas Tulloch? What could he be doing out here?" But I couldn't spare the attention to look.

Adam Flett was one of three brothers who, together, were the island's most prosperous crofter family. In addition to their livestock and rented lands they made some regular money from government contract work. With a tenancy protected by law, Adam had built a two-storey home with a slate roof and laid a decent road to it. I was able to drive almost to the door. Sheep scattered as I braked, and the boy jumped out to join with other children in gathering them back with sticks.

It was only a few weeks since Jean Flett had borne the youngest of her seven children. The birth had been trouble-free but the news of a fall concerned me. Her eldest, a girl of around twelve years old, let us into the house. I looked back and saw Adam Flett on the far side of the yard, watching us.

Jean Flett was lying on a well-worn old sofa and struggled to rise as we came through the door. I could see that she hadn't been expecting us. Despite the size of their family, she was only in her thirties.

I said, "Mrs Flett?" and Nurse Kirkwood stepped past me to steady our patient and ease her back onto the couch.

"This is Doctor Spence," Nurse Kirkwood explained.

"I told Marion," Jean Flett protested. "I told her not to send for you."

"Well, now that I'm here," I said, "let's make sure my journey isn't wasted. Can you tell me what happened?"

She wouldn't look at me, and gave a dismissive wave. "I fell, that's all."

"Where's the pain?"

"I'm just winded."

I took her pulse and then got her to point out where it hurt. She winced when I checked her abdomen, and again when I felt around her neck.

I said, "Did you have these marks before the fall?"

"It was a shock. I don't remember."

Tenderness around the abdomen, a raised heart rate, left side pain, and what appeared to be days-old bruises. I exchanged a glance with Nurse Kirkwood. A fair guess would be that the new mother had been held against the wall and punched.

I said, "We need to move you to the hospital for a couple of days."

"No!" she said. "I'm just sore. I'll be fine."

"You've bruised your spleen, Mrs Flett. I don't think it's ruptured but I need to be sure. Otherwise you could need emergency surgery."

"Oh, no."

"I want you where we can keep an eye on you. Nurse Kirkwood? Can you help her to pack a bag?"

I went outside. Adam Flett had moved closer to the house but was still hovering. I said to him, "She's quite badly hurt. That must have been some fall."

"She says it's nothing." He wanted to believe it, but he'd seen her pain and I think it scared him.

I said, "With an internal injury she could die. I'm serious, Mister Flett. I'll get the ambulance down to collect her." I'd thought that Nurse Kirkwood was still inside the house, so when she spoke from just behind me I was taken by surprise.

She said, "Where's the baby, Mister Flett?"

"Sleeping," he said.

"Where?" she said. "I want to see."

"It's no business of yours or anyone else's."

Her anger was growing, and so was Flett's defiance. "What have you done to it?" she persisted. "The whole island knows it isn't yours. Did you get rid of it? Is that what the argument was about? Is that why you struck your wife?" I was aware of three or four of his children now standing at a distance, watching us.

"The Flett brothers have a reputation, Doctor," she said, lowering her voice so the children wouldn't hear. "It wouldn't be the first time another man's child had been taken out to the barn and drowned in a bucket."

He tried to lunge at her then, and I had to step in.

"Stop that!" I said, and he shook me off and backed away. He started pacing like an aggrieved wrestler whose opponent stands behind the referee. Meanwhile his challenger was showing no fear.

"Well?" Rosie Kirkwood said.

"You've got it wrong," he said. "You don't know anything."

"I won't leave until you prove the child's safe."

And I said, "Wait," because I'd had a sudden moment of insight and reckoned I knew what must have happened.

I said to Rosie, "He's sold the baby. To Thomas Tulloch, in exchange for John Petrie's sheep. I recognise those marks. I watched Tulloch make them." I looked at Flett. "Am I right?"

Flett said nothing right away. And then he said, "They're Petrie's?"

"I suppose Thomas drove them over," I said. "Nurse Kirkwood spotted him heading back on the moor. Is the baby with him?"

Flett only shrugged.

"I don't care whether the rumours are true," I said. "You

can't take a child from its mother. I'll have to report this."

"Do what you like," Flett said. "It was her idea." And he walked away.

I couldn't put Jean Flett in the Riley, but nor did I want to leave her unattended as I brought in the ambulance. "I'll stay," Nurse Kirkwood said. "I'll come to no harm here."

On the army highway I stopped at the moorland crossroads, calling ahead from the telephone box to get the ambulance on its way. It passed me heading in the opposite direction before I reached the hospital.

There I made arrangements to receive Mrs Flett. My concern was with her injury, not her private life. Lord knows how a crofter's wife with six children found the time, the opportunity, or the energy for a passion, however brief. I'll leave it to your H.E. Bateses and D.H. Lawrences to explore that one, with their greater gifts than mine. Her general health seemed, like so many of her island breed, to be robust. But a bruised spleen needs rest in order to heal, and any greater damage could take a day or two to show.

Biddy followed at my heels as I picked up a chair and went to sit with John Petrie. He'd rallied a little with the dog's visits, though the prognosis was unchanged. I opened the window eighteen inches or so. Biddy could be out of there like a shot if we should hear the senior sister coming.

"I know I can be straight with you, John," I said. "How do you feel about your legacy giving a future to an unwanted child?"

They were his sheep that had been traded, after all. And Jean Flett had confirmed her wish to see her child raised where it wouldn't be resented. As for Daisy's feelings, I tried to explain them with Tulloch's own analogy of a ewe unwilling to leave its dead lamb, which I was sure he'd understand. John Petrie listened and then beckoned me closer.

What he whispered then had me running to the car.

I'd no way of saying whether Thomas Tulloch might have reached his cottage yet. My sense of local geography wasn't that good. I didn't even know for sure that he was carrying the Flett baby.

I pushed the Riley as fast as it would go, and when I left the road for the bumpy lane I hardly slowed. How I didn't break the car in two or lose a wheel, I do not know. I was tossed and bucketed around but I stayed on the track until the car could progress no farther, and then I abandoned it and set myself to fly as best I could the rest of the way.

I saw Tulloch from the crest of a rise, at the same time as the cottage came into view. I might yet reach him before he made it home. He was carrying a bundle close to his chest. I shouted, but either he didn't hear me or he ignored my call.

I had to stop him before he got to Daisy.

It was shepherds' business. In the few words he could manage John Petrie had told me how when a newborn lamb is rejected by its mother it can be given to a ewe whose own lamb has died at birth. But first the shepherd must skin the dead lamb and pull its pelt over the living one. Then the new mother might accept it as her own. If the sheep understood, the horror would be overwhelming. But animals aren't people.

I didn't believe what I was thinking. But what if?

I saw the crofter open his door and go inside with his bundle. I was only a few strides behind him. But those scant moments were enough.

When last I'd seen Daisy Tulloch, she'd the air of a woman in whom nothing could hope to rouse the spirit, perhaps ever again.

But the screaming started from within the house, just as I was reaching the threshold.

NO GOOD DEED
by Angela Slatter

I sobel hesitates outside the grand door to the chamber she'd thought to share with Adolphus. It's a work of art, with carven figures of Adam and Lilith standing in front of a tree, a cat at the base, a piece of fruit in transit between First Man and First Woman so one cannot tell if she offers to he, or otherwise.

Her recent exertions have drained what little strength she had, and the food she'd found in the main kitchen (all the servants asleep, the odour of stale mead rising from them like swamp gas) sits heavily in a stomach shrunk so very small by a denial not hers. The polished wooden floorboards of the gallery are cold beneath her thin feet—so thin! Never so slender in all her life. *A little starvation will do wonders*, she thinks. As she moved through the house, she'd caught sight of herself in more than one filigreed mirror and seen all the changes etched upon her: silver traceries in the dishevelled dark hair, face terribly narrow—who'd have known those fine cheekbones had lain beneath all that fat?—mouth still a cupid's bow pout and nose pert, but the eyes are sunken deep and, she'd almost swear to it, their colour changed from light green to deepest black as if night resides in them. The dress balloons around her new form, so much wasted fabric one might make a ship's sail from the excess.

How long before the plumpness returns? Before her

cheeks have apples, the lines in her face are smoothed out? She can smell again, now, but all she can discern is the scent of her own body, unwashed for so long. *A bath*, she thinks longingly, then draws her attention back to where it needs to be: the door.

Or, rather, what lies behind it.

She reaches out, looks at the twiggish fingers, the black half-moons of dirt beneath the nails, how weirdly white her hand appears on the doorknob shaped like a wolf's head, so bulbous she can barely grasp it properly. She takes a deep, deep breath, and turns the handle.

Isobel woke with a weight on her eyes, cold and dead.

Her mouth, too, was similarly burdened: lips pressed down and thin metallic tendrils crept between them. Her forehead was banded by something chill and hard, a line running the length of her nose, her cheeks and chin encased, as if she wore a helmet she had no memory of donning before bed. She had no memory either of going to sleep. Her throat and arms were mercifully free, but chest, abdomen and hands were encumbered. Not a cage, then.

Remain calm, she told herself, *slow your breathing*. She'd been taught at St Dymphna's to assess situations carefully; easier said than done when you couldn't open your eyes.

Rings, she thought. *Rings on my fingers and bells on my toes*. She tried to wiggle her feet, found them unwilling to respond, still quite numb; pins and needles were beginning, however, so some sign of hope. Wrists encircled, entrapped by… bracelets and bangles. She twitched her digits; only one finger bore a reasonable burden, a thin metal ribbon. Her husband's family, no matter their wealth, always insisted on a wedding band as plain as day. For love, they believed, must be unadorned.

My husband, she thought, and wondered where he was. Adolphus Wollstonecraft.

Surely he'd not have deserted her? Not so soon at any rate. Then she recalled they'd only just been married. That this morning she was preparing for her marriage, surrounded by Adolphus's girl cousins, so numerous that she'd had to pause before addressing each one so as not to get a name wrong and thereby cause offence (excepting Cousins Enyd and Delwyn, of course, they'd become so close!). All of them dressed as bridesmaids for she had neither sisters, nor cousins, nor aunts, nor friends who might stand her this service; all of them a whirl of pastel colours and soft fabrics, the light from the candelabrums picking out the rich necklaces and earrings, brooches and hair ornaments, finer than any queen might own. Yet none as lovely as those Isobel brought with her, inheritances from mother and grandmothers, aunts and great-aunts, the items that came to Isobel because she was the last of her line, the single point where all things might end or begin again depending on the whims of her womb.

She ran her tongue over her teeth, prodded at the wires and was able to dislodge them with a dull, wet clink against the bone of her teeth. But there was something else: her canines were larger, augmented, and polished, a series of cool smoothnesses and sharp edges. She caught the tip of her tongue on one of those edges and tasted a burst of iron tang, imagined the blood as a red blossoming.

She opened her mouth wider, felt the weight on her lips half-fall into the cavity; she turned her head, spat, and the mouthpiece fell away; the wires, reluctantly giving up their grip on her dentition, hit the softness she was lying on with a slithering *plink*. Whatever had been attached to her canines remained, however, so firmly affixed she was wary of interfering with them after that first cut. They would wait.

The weights over her eyes and face had also loosened

with the movement of her head. She shook harder and with a tinkle and a chink they were gone, landing wherever the other things had. Whatever she reclined upon was soft but compacted by the weight of her body. How long had she been there?

Where was she?

Isobel opened her lids, though the lashes felt glued with sleep, with the sandman's dust. She blinked vigorously, but there was only blackness even when she widened her eyes. She closed them again, breathed slowly to calm herself, then shallowly when she realised the air was stale with a hint of old decay.

I am asleep, she thought. *I am asleep and dreaming in my marital bed.* But she still could not summon the details of her wedding eve, of either feast or fornication, and surely she should? Surely good or bad, she would remember that? The touches, the sighs, the delight? The pain, the weight, the imposition? Surely she'd recall at least one of the things the other girls at St Dymphna's had whispered of at night in their dormer attic when they should have been resting?

"I am asleep," she said out loud. "I am asleep and in my bridal bed."

"Oh no, you're not," came a voice from the darkness, brittle and raw, with a hint of amusement. Not Adolphus, no. A woman. A woman who'd not spoken in a very long time by the sound of it.

Isobel startled, jerked; things that weighed on her chest slipped and slid off with a jingle. She sat up, but her head connected with a rough low rock shelf; the skin parted at her hairline and she felt a slow welling of blood on her forehead. It was a while before she could speak.

"Who are you? Where am I?" The Misses Meyrick had always instructed their pupils to ask questions whenever they could: *You never know what skerrick of information might help you survive.*

"I am you," answered the woman, and Isobel wondered if she'd gone mad, prayed to wake from the dream. "Well, you *before* you, I suppose. And you are me, after me."

"Don't speak in riddles! Tell me how to wake! I bid you, spirit, release me from this delusion!"

"Oh, you think yourself ridden by the mare of night?" The pitch lightened with surprise, then fragmented into giggles, each as sharp as a pin. There was an echo, too, wherever they were. Then the tone steadied, though mirth remained in evidence. "Oh, no. Oh no, poor Isobel. You are sadly awake. Alert at long last."

"Who are you? Why am I here? Where is my husband? I was at my wedding banquet…" she trailed off, not truly able to remember if there was any trace of the feast in her mind. She thought she remembered someone—Adolphus's mother?—tugging the veil down over her face, readying her for the procession through the castle. Or was it Cousin Enyd? Or Cousin Delwyn? Or? Or? Or?

Someone had lifted the veil, certainly, for it was bunched behind her head, pillowing her neck. Surely later, after *Volo* had been said, the echoes of the vows running along the walls and floor and vaulted ceiling of the small chapel, barely big enough to hold that fine family. So small a chapel, in fact, that only relatives had been bid to attend at the Wollstonecrafts' isolated estate.

And the Misses Meyrick. She could not forget *them*.

Isobel's erstwhile school marms, not invited, had come anyway to watch, to witness the choice she'd made, all their good training, her mother's good money, gone to waste. They did not speak to her, neither Orla nor Fidelma, not a word of congratulation or censure. Naught but disappointed looks as she and Adolphus walked down the aisle as man and wife.

There!

A memory, solid and stable. Pacing beside her handsome

new husband, and the Misses Meyrick so far from their school for poison girls and looking at her as if she'd left their house to burn; left them to shame. So, not a happy memory but a memory nonetheless. A real one. A true one. Something to hold on to.

And another memory: the Misses Meyrick once again at the wedding feast, waiting by the doors while the happy couple were greeted and congratulated by their guests. Isobel thinking, *I must speak to them for they loved me in their own fashion!* So she'd picked her way through the crowd until she stood before her old instructors in their gowns magnificent, their eyes bright, Orla's left blue, her right yellow; in Fidelma the colours were reversed. Long moments passed before Fidelma spoke.

"Your mother," she said, "would be ashamed."

Orla stepped behind her and Isobel felt terror like she never had before; but the woman merely said, "Pish!" and showed her a hairpin with a long silver shaft and a jewelled head shaped like a daisy; the outer petals were of diamonds, and the floret, divided distinctly into two halves, of yellow topazes. Then she slid it into Isobel's finely constructed hairstyle, beneath the long veil so no one might see the ornament and note how exquisite it was. "This," said Orla, "is the last thing we can do for you."

Before she could reply, the Misses Meyrick seemed to fade from the room, although she knew she saw them move, saw them walk away with elegant contempt, yet somehow it seemed that it was not a mere exit they committed, but a departure.

Then the other voice repeated, "Wedding feast?" and Isobel was brought back to the Stygian confines of… wherever she was.

"Wedding feast, I remember my own. All those fine families, all those relations of blood, all of Adolphus's cousins and aunts and uncles. I had no one, myself, being an orphan of very rich parentage, but he said to me, 'Kitten'—Kitty, actually, for he called me by that endearment—'Kitty, my sweet, they all adore you! It's like you're one of our very own, a true Wollstonecraft. Cousins Enyd and Delwyn say the same.' And those very cousins sat beside me at the wedding feast, making sure I drank from my goblet the wine my husband poured for me and they considerately topped up." The woman in the darkness cackled. "Does this sound familiar?"

"Where am I?" asked Isobel in a very small voice. She did not say that it all sounded very familiar indeed. She carefully raised her hands until the fingertips touched the rough stone of the low ceiling. She inched them along, felt the scrape of rock, found a place where roof joined wall; but there was only the hint of a line, a thin parsimonious suggestion on her skin, not a chink, not a gap where air or light might creep in.

How many feet between where she lay and the ceiling? Two? Three? Ceiling? *Lid?* That last thought made her shudder and she shook it away.

"You're where you've been these past twelve months, sleeping like the dead." The voice dropped low, secretive. "But I knew you yet lived. I could hear the slow, slow beat of your heart, the slug-slug of your blood, the base breath that made your chest only just rise and fall."

"Twelve months? Don't be a fool. I'd have died!"

"And you were meant to! But when you're so very nearly dead, everything becomes *unhurried*; blood, breath, appetite. You'll be ravenous soon, now that I've mentioned it."

As if in response Isobel's stomach growled and cramped. She put a hand to it, discovered a kind of armour there, a lumpen embossed corset that might well turn aside a knife blade. At its sides she located small latches, which opened easily; presumably no one expected the deceased to undress themselves.

"The poison they used," mused her companion, "is a strange mix: too little and it will render you ill, too much it will send you into a sleep indiscernible from true death, but if the amount is *juuust* right, then and only then you'll die. And it was new when used on me, so I died. It was old when used on you and Adolphus panicked and used too much, so you but slept."

"You're lying. You're mad."

"Oh, ho! Mad am I? That's possible, I suppose; I've been here a long while with only my thoughts, waiting for you to wake, and before that no one but myself to talk to. Who wouldn't go a little mad?" A sigh shifted the blackness; Isobel was almost certain she could see it. "Shall I show you? Where we are? Then we can discuss my mendacity or otherwise. Well?"

"Yes," said Isobel faintly.

For a second there was nothing, no sound, no movement, and then: a light. A tiny pinprick of luminous green, a point that pulsed and grew, strengthened and increased its ambit. The glow lit upon the things that had fallen from Isobel when she sat so precipitously; it caught at their lovely edges, lodged in facets, made it appear as if a hundred small fires had kindled on the musty purple silk.

She was distracted by a king's ransom in jewellery, but not of a common sort. Rich and rare, the cut and settings were of ancient design, almost foreign it was so antique, and Isobel could not think of where she'd seen its like before. None of it was hers, not one piece of the Lawrence family jewels to be seen, not a *single* thing she recognised. She put a hand to the back of her head, beneath the veil which had become odd in its texture, and found the one gem no one knew she had − no one but the Meyricks − the hairpin, its cool, hard daisy arrangement reassuring.

Then she gazed around the space, found it to be a box, six feet by six feet by two and half, a flattened mattress beneath her. Such a small room! A bed-closet perhaps, but no sign of a door, of any egress. And that mattress... not like any she'd ever seen, without either ticking or calico, neither down nor rushes to make it plump, but there was the smell of old lavender... no, more like... the lining for a death bed.

She sought her companion. Saw...

Saw...

Saw nothing but a skeleton in a jaundiced wedding dress, blue-and-gold boots with silver buttons up the side, a manically grinning skull from which red hair and a lopsided veil hung. The body was adorned with strange bijoux akin to those Isobel herself had worn.

And the body was glowing; glowing with the same green luminescence that had shown Isobel her location.

Isobel remembered at last that she'd seen such exquisite corpses before, in places where the wealthy venerated their dead and turned them into glittering saints. Old families and High Church. The Wollstonecrafts carried both in their bloodline.

And Isobel, comprehending at last where she was, began to scream.

The room, the Master's Chamber, is redolent of stale alcohol, spent seed and strong tobacco or perhaps incense. Some kind of drug? Isobel notices a kind of pipe in one corner, perhaps three feet high, made of blown glass in colours that have the same sheen as oil on water. There are silken tassels and a mouthpiece and tubing. She'd heard of such things at St Dymphna's: Hepsibah Ballantyne had averred it a fine way to poison someone. Mistress Ballantyne had always said that to best murder another, you should discover their habits and run parallel to them, insert your lethal blow into the usual flow of their life, so that way the difference you made would most like not be noticed.

Isobel looks to the bed, which is located beneath a bank of diamond-paned glass. In said bed, so enormous that it might fit six, she sees three figures. The covers are thrown back, as are the window shutters, for the eve is balmy, moonlit; one of her nannies always said that sleeping in moonlight let madness in. How many Wollstonecrafts have slept thus?

Summer, she thinks, *as it was when I married*. A summer bride, lying winter-cold for so very long. *No mourning for Adolphus*, she notes, *and no sleeping alone*.

Her husband lies between the recumbent figures of Cousins Enyd and Delwyn, their dark Wollstonecraft locks spread tousled across crisp white pillowcases, their naked forms on crumpled sheets. Two girls Isobel had thought friends, or like to become so. Their slumber is that of the well used. There can be no mistaking it; the dead bride did not lie. She did not need to when she'd said, *The Wollstonecrafts breed only amongst themselves and they are* prolific, *hiding those whose parents are too closely related in attics and cellars, those who show too much the double, triple, quadruple blossoming of blood*.

Isobel thinks, memories flooding now, of all those Wollstonecrafts at the wedding feast, watching her so avidly. She wonders how she ever thought their eyes gleamed with love and happiness, their lips curved in welcome, not avarice. Perhaps she could not see their greed because her own was so intense as she gulped from the bridal cup held by Adolphus, offered so generously to her first—against tradition!—a sign of his devotion, his love for his young wife. She has, even now, no recollection of falling asleep at the table, of drifting into what her new family thought was death. There is only the memory of the cup, the dark liquid within, her husband's tender smile.

Nor does she even now recollect crossing the wide room, yet somehow she is standing beside the great bed, staring down at Cousin Enyd whose tiny waist she's always admired; on Enyd's left wrist is a diamond bracelet that had belonged to Isobel's mother. Isobel's hand goes to the back of her own head, fidgets beneath the friable veil and finds the hairpin that was the final gift of Orla and Fidelma Meyrick. The gems and metal are cool against her fingers and the pin comes out with no complaint. Isobel looks at it carefully, remembers the instructions from one of the weaponry classes, then gives a nod of satisfaction. These three have been drinking, smoking, heavily; all of them snore. They'll not wake easily.

She leans over Cousin Enyd, lowers the hairpin point-first to the cockleshell of the ear facing her, then depresses the left side of the daisy's centre. A single tiny drop of paralytic poison, so powerful she fears to get it on her own skin, oozes from the tip of the pin and drips into the shadowy coil of Enyd's ear. Isobel waits for a count of five, then swiftly plunges the shaft into the narrow canal; her fingers push the right side of the daisy design and the length of the pin splits into four very fine, very sharp, very tough lengths which tear into the brain. Cousin Enyd hardly moves, giving just the tiniest of shudders as she voids her bladder and bowels, but the stink of it barely registers above the other rich scents in the room.

Isobel creeps softly around the other side of the bed and repeats the process on Cousin Delwyn, whose rich thick curls she'd often envied; around this one's swan-like neck is the emerald and pearl locket that had belonged to Isobel's grandmother. Delwyn dies no more noisily than did Enyd, though she is fleshier, larger, there is less poison and the paralysis is not so entire; she twitches, kicks too close to Adolphus and Isobel must swiftly grab at the limb, hold it in place until the tremors still. Isobel feels a twinge of pride; the time at St Dymphna's was neither wasted nor its lessons lost. Orla Meyrick herself couldn't have executed these deaths any more tidily.

Adolphus still has not stirred.

Isobel slips her stolen jewellery into the hidden pocket

of her dress, then steps away, takes up position between the bed and the door. Her breathing remains steady—it did not change even as she slaughtered those false cousins—and what she feels moving through her is a cold thing, a passionless fury, a determination to one end. She takes a breath and begins to sing.

"Are you quite finished?" came the voice when Isobel at last ran out of breath and fear. "Pride of St Dymphna's you are."

"How do you know—"

"I've had twelve months to wander around in your sleeping mind—no point looking like that. I'm bored and have been for a very long time. A saint couldn't have stopped herself. I can't do anything else, can't move from here. I've only got a little energy and I'm saving that for something rather more special than comforting you or a mere haunting."

"How did I get here? How did *you* get here?" wept Isobel, stung by the corpse's callousness.

"Our husband, you little fool! Adolphus Trajan Wollstonecraft. We're not the first brides he's disposed of for the sake of their fortunes, but *you* were the first one who was supposed to kill him. And failed to do so quite spectacularly. Imagine all the trouble you could have saved. No doubt, there'll be more betrotheds after us when his goodly period of mourning is done, and all your wealth run through!"

"How many?" asked Isobel, shocked out of her sobs.

"Four. Buried on the other side of the altar. I'm sure they've got fresh new maidens picked out to take up residence beside us in the fullness of time."

"But you can talk, make this light…"

"And small, bitter consolation that it is. As I said, I can't haunt anyone. Hepsibah Ballantyne knows her business too well for that."

Isobel startled at the name, thinking about the poisons mistress who came to St Dymphna's and taught the girls to brew dark potions. There were whispers that the woman was a coffin-maker, too, and indeed that was where her renown lay; the facility with poison was a happy coincidence and a secret for St Dymphna's headmistresses and students. A lucrative habit born of her more-than-passing interest in death.

"My, what interesting things you keep hidden in your heart and head. I only knew her name from conversations I'd heard Adolphus and his mother have as they crossed the floor above my tomb—they've a fondness for plotting in the chapel; perhaps it makes them feel justified and holy." The corpse sounded sad.

"Poison," said Isobel.

"And there are these jewels, of course. Not content with paying a premium for death-beds to keep us beneath, they laid these cursed gems over us."

Isobel prodded at the attachments to her canines, and the dead bride said, "Those are to stop us from becoming vampires or some other such blood ghosts. They made us saints against our will, the ecstatic dead to cover their crimes, to keep us from haunting them, from ever getting vengeance."

"But I'm not dead," said Isobel softly.

"No, indeed you are not!" Gleeful now. "None of the chains the living have placed upon you have taken, sweet Isobel, and you are fit for my purpose!"

Isobel listened, watched the still form; there was only the sickly pulsing green light to tell her she wasn't truly alone, that the voice wasn't simply in her head. But what if it *was*? What if the light was a hallucination too? Perhaps this was her punishment.

Punishment for what?

For leaving St Dymphna's the moment her mother died?

For denying her duty?

For falling in love with the man she was meant to murder? For being so foolish as to trust?

"Why did you do it? Trust him? You were better off than any of us. You were trained. You had a goal, a duty."

"Get out of my head! I'm conscious now and I don't appreciate you using it as your playground!" Isobel shouted so loudly that her ears hurt in the confined space.

"I'm sorry," said the dead bride. "There's little call for etiquette down here, so I forget."

"For him. He was older by a little, funny, sweet and smart. He didn't care that I was fat. He was… kind. I met him before I was sent to St Dymphna's. I knew almost from the cradle what I was meant to do, that the very point of my life was to destroy another's—to avenge an ancient and dusty death, that of an ancestress of mine murdered at the hands of his forefathers." Isobel paused. "But I met him and I loved him from the first even though I knew I shouldn't. I thought… I thought I might draw it out, put off taking his life until after my mother died, until there was no one left to care. Then he and I could be happy, the past forgotten, dead and buried.

"Then my mother did die, sooner rather than later, before I'd even finished my schooling. I left St Dymphna's the very day after the news arrived. I went to him, went to his home, we planned our life together."

"They're not as fabulously prosperous as they appear, you know. There's much tat and shine for show, but the vaults are empty, more often than not with but a few pieces of gold, candlesticks and crested salvers. The family silver has been pawned and redeemed time and again—the silversmiths of Caulder know the Wollstonecrafts of old."

"But—"

"Rich brides are this family's business. We're lambs to them, meat on the table, money in the bank, brides in caskets. Did you not wonder that there were no friends invited to your nuptials? None there but Wollstonecrafts? That they live so far from anything despite their supposed wealth? It's hard to keep secrets in cities where everyone's watching to see what move you make, where the well-to-do keep better track of their daughters." A long sigh. "You signed over everything, didn't you? All the riches your mother gathered, the businesses she built, all the prosperity and majesty that clever merchant queen reaped from her investments over the years, and you signed it away for a piece of cock." A giggle, rueful. "Don't feel too great a fool; I did the same, and brides before me and thee who were otherwise reckoned clever. I… I was ugly, yet he convinced me he loved me, that he cared not a jot for beauty."

"But Adolphus *loved* me. He didn't know what I gave up for him, that I put his life first." But she thought of the tiny moments, the signs she'd ignored: all the occasions when plans for what came after the wedding were put off, discussions avoided. *Don't you worry about that, my dear, we've plenty of time for that later.* Yet how quickly he'd begged she sign documents that transferred her ownerships to him in case of a dreadful tragedy, which would of course never happen.

"You think not? The poison he used came from Ballantyne, who knew you at the school, who outfitted this very coffin-tomb, this death-bed just as she did the others—she's not so skilled with stone as wood, but she did a good enough job to trap me. You let him live, Isobel, but no good deed ever goes unpunished." The skeleton gave a rueful chuckle. "And I doubt you're the first poison girl to flee that venerable institution, to choose love over duty."

"I was, you know. The Misses told me with great relish and umbrage," confessed Isobel.

"Ah. My tale is your tale, or at least so close that the differing details barely matter. But at last something can be done." The voice rose like a victory hymn.

"You're dead," said Isobel, toneless, lifeless. "You're dead and I'm trapped. Even if he's betrayed me"—*if?*—"nothing can be done."

"Do you have the engagement ring he gave you? An enormous sapphire, if memory serves correct, blue as a hot afternoon sky?"

Isobel examined her fingers, looked to where the item in question should be, but there were only the ornate rings joined to each other by golden chains, the things meant to hold her in place. She pulled them off, added them to the glittering pile beside her.

"No. Just the wedding band," mused the dead bride. "The same for all of us. No point in wasting an engagement ring when you can reuse it, like a dog collar. They don't want to trouble themselves with a costly replacement, and they can't use *these*"—Isobel knew she meant the cursed things— "Gods forbid anything should happen to the *lamb* before the wedding, before the Wollstonecrafts get the fortune for which they've worked so hard!"

Isobel looked at the other's skeletal hands, wrapped around a posy of dead yet somehow intact roses. A strong breeze would interrupt their carefully held structure. On one finger she could make out the dull gleam of a ring identical to hers.

"I'll die here," she said. "I'll starve as a trusting fool deserves to. I'll suffocate." Suddenly the air felt thinner, staler, her lungs more demanding. "But I'll go mad first."

"And what a delightful change that will be," sniggered the dead bride. "You'll not likely starve any time soon, although you're looking thin, yet not so thin as I. There's plenty of air, you silly bint. As for madness, sometimes taking refuge in it is the only way to maintain a modicum of sanity."

Isobel realised then that her own dress—with all the ribbons and frills and bows meant to make her beautiful, but which just made her look even more enormous—was terribly, terribly large on her. That none of the weight she'd carried around all her life, that drove her mother and nannies to despair, remained. Reading her thoughts again, the dead one said, "Bet you never expected you'd be grateful for that fat! What do you think kept you alive all these months?"

"I don't want to live," wailed Isobel, knowing it was stupid as soon as the words were out.

"Ye gods, the stock at St Dymphna's is poor. A man betrayed you and you want to die?"

"No. I… I betrayed my mother, my teachers, by trusting him, by choosing him." Isobel thought of the Misses Meyrick and their steely countenances.

"And you think dying is the choice they'd want you to make? You, upon whom so much effort was expended to make you more *active*?" The dead bride tut-tutted. "It would be easier, certainly, to expire, but St Dymphna's girls, as I understand it, aren't made for easy paths. You weren't descended from milksops or weeping maidens; the women before you carried sword and shield, they fought in the open, their blood was red and rich and violent! It's in your veins, Isobel, so pull yourself together!"

"But I can't get out—"

"Of course you can; there's a way, a way for the living."

Isobel sat up as straight as she could and stared at the unmoving form. "How?"

"Ah, now that's information for which you must bargain, Isobel girl."

"Tell me now or I swear I'll scatter your bones, I'll grind them to dust even if it makes my fingers bleed!"

"That's the spirit! Now calm down. In return for my very useful knowledge, you will make me a promise, a promise by which you'll set more store than any ever before or so help me—"

Isobel did not pause. "I will promise you anything, just get me out of this tomb!"

The song is one the dead bride advised, tried to teach until Isobel comprehended that she already knew it from her old life, a tune sung by this nanny or that governess. Her husband does not stir, so she sings louder still for there's no one to wake but Adolphus. She wonders how he's spent his days since her death, then decides she can probably guess. Sings more loudly, more sweetly, until her patience runs out and she fair shouts, "Adolphus!"

He sits up, stunned, blinking in that strange mix of darkness and moonlight and receding sleep that render him blind for long moments. He does not notice the still bodies of his cousins on either side of him, does not spare them a glance. He sees only Isobel.

She imagines she must look close to the spectre he tried so hard to make her. She smiles and follows the script. "Adolphus, my love, fear not. You're simply dreaming."

She can see him struggling to recognise her and she remembers how changed she is from the lumbering lumpy girl he said he loved above all others. That all those places he caressed and fondled and fingered are so much easier to find now.

"It's Isobel, my love. See you dream me how I truly was, how I truly wished to be. Still you know my heart!"

"But you're dead, my Isobel." Fear silvers his tone.

"Oh yes! So very dead and you do but dream me, but there is something I must tell you, something that threatens your very house and future. My love has drawn me back. Will you follow and see?"

"But of course! That you should still care for me beyond death! It warms my heart," he says and creeps to the end of the bed so as not to disturb his cousins' rest. He reaches for her and Isobel holds up a warning hand.

"The living cannot touch the dead, my love! Lest you be drawn down to lie beside me." Adolphus nods. Isobel smiles. "Then come and allow me to render you this last service."

The moment she turns her back she knows it for a mistake, but she was brimming with confidence that her deception had worked, that she'd *won*. She can almost feel Orla and Fidelma's disapproving stares just as she can feel the steel of her husband's fingers closing around her left wrist.

"Little fool, little bitch! Do you think I've not created enough ghosts to know one? That I cannot tell the smell of warm blood from cold? 'My love has drawn me back.' Gods, what a lackwit you must think me, as much of a one as yourself."

Isobel struggles, but her strength is so depleted from her long slumber that she cannot make any headway.

"Fear not, sweet Isobel, I'll put you back where you belong."

Isobel kicks him in the groin, watches with not inconsiderable delight as he doubles over, then she remembers to flee. She flings the door closed behind her, starts towards the grand staircase. She is halfway down when she hears the crash of wood against wall that says her husband is in pursuit. Her strength is fading, her speed bleeding to nothing. At the bottom of the stairs she must cross the marble floor, pass through the darkened arched doorway, and down the few worn steps into the chapel, and thence to the altar.

What if he catches her first?

What if he takes it in his head to strangle her then and there? For there's no one who might look for her, no one to suspect she lives; there are no appearances to be maintained. Even if some family member of his might wander by, they've no cause to save her. From behind comes a growl, a roar of such surpassing anger and viciousness that she finds her feet have wings. An extra burst of speed gets her to the entrance hall, almost skidding on marble tiles as she goes. When she passes through the doorway she does not touch the steps, but rather flies several yards into the chapel, landing at the third row of pews, the impact jarring every bone in her body, so much so that she's sure she must rattle. She stumbles her way towards the altar with its shimmer of precious plate, and splashes of colour on the bright white cloth covering where moonlight pierces the stained-glass window.

Adolphus is enraged; he'll not see the open tombs, the floor slid back by dint of the secret switches the dead bride told her about, a handy bit of knowledge plucked from one of the passing ghosts of the Wollstonecrafts' castle, a stonemason who'd built the secret passages and the tombs at the request of a great-great-great Wollstonecraft grandfather whose terror was to be buried alive. But such escapes are no use to the dead, and the grandparent was indeed thoroughly deceased when put into the tomb—although his bones and those of other departed were shifted and shuffled when the present generation began their business of burying brides. The stonemason himself, another trusting fool, had been put to death as soon as the work was completed.

This plan, fumes Isobel, *was not best thought-out* and she resents the dead bride for not having formulated a better strategy in all her time lying in the crypt. Then again, perhaps she never was very practical in life. Isobel, St Dymphna's dropout though she might be, is quite certain she'd have come up with something—*anything*—better.

Adolphus does not see the four figures slumped in the front pews, and Isobel runs past them, skidding to a halt before the altar. Her husband comes to a stop a foot from her, cursing and spitting and telling her precisely what he thought of her in life and death; if she had any lingering doubts about his role in her demise they are dispelled once and for all.

"I will put you back in the ground, sweet Isobel. Although these months beneath have done you good, who'd have thought under all that fat you were so terribly lovely?"

"Would it have stopped you from murdering me?" she asks out of sheer curiosity.

He shakes his head, his grin a wolf's. "No. But I might have taken a little more fun with you. I might do so now. I have, after all, a husband's rights."

"Will you exercise them on all of us?" Isobel says so quietly, so calmly that he is thrown off by her lack of fear, her lack of panic.

"Us?" He tilts his head. "Madness, I suppose, from the darkness."

"Madness no doubt, but one you will share, my love. Come, greet your maidens. They wait at your back like good wives."

Adolphus, seemingly unwilling to take his eyes from her, turns his head only a little, but it is enough for him to see what waits in the periphery. Four of his spouses, skeletons all, released from their beds and gilded cages by Isobel, stand with effort, bones a'clacking and a'creaking, hair falling from heads to shoulders, and thence into empty rib cages. Their frocks have entirely decayed, leaving only threads and rags caught here in a joint, there on a bone, as if they might show their husband their nakedness entire, in mimicry of the wedding night he denied them. There is, however, no sign of cartilage or tendons or muscles to show how they might be held together. Sheer will and malice, imagines Isobel, and not a little magic resulting from both.

She takes in the skulls with their hairline fractures, the stains decay has left, the wisps of hair that was once so glorious. At least one has a limp, another lacks an arm; a brigade of the halt and the lame, the obese and the damned ugly, all especially susceptible to any scrap of kindness, and unwary that their value to their husband was no greater than monetary. She wonders if the dead bride—her companion and guide—was a witch in life, undiscovered, for her powers to remain so long after death. Or perhaps she was simply a girl with hopes and dreams that curdled dark and sour and kept the strongest part of her, the bravest part, the worst part, alive.

Adolphus has gone astonishingly pale, as if his blood has turned coward and fled. His lips move, producing only, "Whuh, whuh, whuh."

"'Whuh?' What are you trying to say, my love? What is this sorcery? None but what you created yourself by murder and deceit."

The brides shuffle forward, closing in on Adolphus who backs away, hands raised as if that will stop their awful progress with its accompanying symphony of clacking and rattling.

"What I want you to know, my love, is this: tonight your house will fall. I will put every Wollstonecraft here to the sword. Then I will make it my business to hunt down every bastard, bitch and by-blow who fell from your family tree and destroy them too. Your bloodline will be wiped from the face of the earth, and I swear before you and your wives that I shall make this my life's work."

The corpse brides reach towards their husband, thin fingers, bony arms, ravaged joints, and with a cry Adolphus steps backwards. He does not see the open maw behind him, so he falls, arms windmilling, then there is a silence as he drops, then the *whump!* and *crack!* as he lands, dust flying into the air.

Isobel and her sister-spouses peer over the edge.

Adolphus lies in the tomb Isobel so recently occupied, recumbent upon the form of the dead bride, her own cursed jewellery removed. Isobel is sure she can see some broken bones on the skeletal girl where the impact has been too much, but while Adolphus remains stunned the dead bride's arms begin to move. They curve up and over, around her husband, before he realises what's going on. The fingers of her right hand clench together into a spear and this she plunges into Adolphus's chest, the flesh of which parts as if it is no more than warm butter. There is the breaking of ribs prised apart and the wet sucking sound of red muscle meat being found and enclosed by a bony cage of palm and fingers.

"Your heart, my love," says the dead bride, "shall ever be mine."

And with that there is a great sigh as from many mouths. Adolphus ceases to move, his eyes glaze over. The girl in the tomb does not answer when Isobel calls, and she can no longer sense any presence other than her own. The chorus of brides falls to the flagstones, become dust even as Isobel watches. She is meticulous, though, ensuring they will have somewhere to rest, and brushes their final remains into the crypt. It falls on Adolphus and his final bride like confetti for the dead. Isobel, feeling bereft that she cannot say goodbye to her sisters, whispers farewell and hopes they will hear it somewhere, then locates the switch to close the lid of the tomb, and then the second one that puts the floor back in place. When she is done it looks as if nothing ever happened here.

Isobel rises. There are weapons to be had in the house, sabres and stilettos that hang on walls for display, but will be just as fine used for their true purpose. She will spill all the blood to be found, she will put them to the sword and then set fire to the hangings in the bedrooms, the parlours, the grand hall. She will burn the place utterly to the ground.

No full graduate of St Dymphna's could do better, she is certain. She'll not return to the Misses Meyrick, though she might write to them from time to time as she crosses another Wollstonecraft off her list. Isobel will not hunt Hepsibah Ballantyne, for she was merely doing her job, and the poison used on Isobel was not *intended* for her. Oh, she'll find the coffin-maker, employ her for her own ends—it's a fool who wastes a good poisons woman—but first of all she'll put a good scare into Hepsibah Ballantyne just for fun. She might even keep the gems on her canines long enough to give Ballantyne a glittering, terrifying smile.

Isobel takes one last look at the chapel, finds she cannot distinguish the joins where the floor might open up again if she were to press the right parts of the frieze carved into the altar. And she understands, then, the only thing that will truly haunt her as she goes upon her way: that she did not ask the dead bride, the one who came before her, for her name.

THE FAMILY CAR
by Brady Golden

Lindsay spots the car in her rear-view mirror. It's coated in a glaze of dirt. Spatters of a translucent crust have hardened on the windshield, and patches of rust spot the paint like lesions. There's no shortage of station wagons in the world, many of them white. Other than its filthy state, this one looks about the same as the rest. But it's theirs. She can't account for her certainty, but she is certain. It's her parents' car. She rode in it a thousand times, learned to drive behind the wheel. What she's seeing is impossible. Even as she feels her muscles tightening, she tells herself that. Impossible. Her family is gone, their car with them. To convince herself, to wrest control of her own body before panic overwhelms her, she adjusts her mirror to get a look at the license plate.

She hasn't seen the number in eight years, wasn't sure she even knew it anymore, but there it is.

It's dusk. The sunset's glare hits the roofs of the two lanes of cars stopped at the intersection, waiting for the light. She's second in line behind a silver minivan. For less than a second, she lets herself think the driver might be her dad, but it's not. Through the thick gunk on the windshield, she can't make out much—a dark lump and a pair of gloved hands hooked around the wheel—but she can tell it's not him. He wasn't a small man by any stretch, but this driver is huge. In order to fit into the car, he has to hunch into a question-mark shape. Who, then?

The light changes. When the minivan starts forward, she hesitates. A car further back in line—not the station wagon, not the mystery driver—lets out a blast of its horn. She drives.

Lindsay's last memory of the station wagon—of its square back shrinking towards the end of Euclid Street—is an invention. Her imagination conjured it up to provide a visual representation of her family's disappearance. She didn't watch them leave that day. She was still in bed, eyes slitted, counting the beats of her headache so she wouldn't think about how badly she needed to throw up.

She was sixteen when it happened. Since then, there's been a secret theory she's been unable to shake, no matter how absurd it is—the night before, she had managed to piss her parents off so fully, to disappoint them to such an absolute degree, that when they climbed into their car that morning, they decided, *fuck it, let's just leave this one behind and start fresh somewhere else.* Anyone who had seen the look on her dad's face when he'd come into her room would have to admit the idea wasn't as crazy as it sounded. They were supposed to be attending a birthday breakfast for Lindsay's grandmother— her dad's mom—but owing to her antics the night before, Lindsay was disinvited. Those antics had included a bottle of strawberry Boone's Farm, the pickup truck of a boy four years her senior, and a collision with a traffic light downtown. The last thing her dad said to her, once he'd let her know they were leaving without her, was, "You just do the dumbest things, over and over again."

They never made it to breakfast. As far as the police could tell, they never made it anywhere. Something happened to the King family in the two-mile stretch of residential streets between their home and their destination. Whatever it was, it happened to the family car as well. Neither they nor it were ever seen again. Until, that is, today.

As she drives, Lindsay's eyes keep drifting to her mirror. The station wagon is right behind her, close enough that if she checked her brakes, it would plow straight into her bumper. Does the driver know who she is? Does he want her to notice him? Christ, is he *following* her? They cruise down one long block after another, past shopping centers and gas stations. The streets are crowded with rush-hour traffic, but it feels like they're the only two cars out there. A knitting needle of pain sings in her chest, and she realizes she's been holding her breath.

Her purse rests on the passenger seat. She reaches inside and digs out her phone. Fingers shaking, she misdials twice before the call goes through. The 911 operator picks up. The voice is fuzzy and distant. Lindsay can't make out the initial greeting. She starts talking anyway.

"My name is Lindsay King. I'm driving east on Grand. There's a car following me. It's a white station wagon. We're just past—"

She looks up for a street sign, only to discover that she has rolled through a red light into an intersection. Her passenger-side window goes dark as another car fills it. The phone slips from her fingers. She jerks the steering wheel and stomps on the brake, but it's too late. There's a sharp squeal, cut off by a tremendous metallic bang. Glass explodes all around her. The impact flings her against her door, and the left side of her body lights up. Her car spins sideways, then stops. Outside, people are yelling, but their voices sound muffled. Something tickles her cheek. She touches it, and her hand comes away sporting a bright red smear. The blood keeps coming. It runs down her face and pools in the folds of her shirt.

Her grandmother meets her at the hospital. She sits with Lindsay while a doctor sews her forehead shut, then drives her back to her place. Lindsay's grandfather died three years ago. After that, Denise sold the house where she'd raised her son, then, for three years, her granddaughter, and moved into a trailer park. Now she lives in a narrow box with shingled walls and planters thick with wildflowers mounted in every window.

The police officer who comes to see them isn't the same one who worked the case when Lindsay was a teenager. It was dumb of her to have expected it to be. The world changes in eight years.

Lindsay and Denise position themselves on the couch. While Lindsay talks, the police officer takes occasional notes in a pocket-sized spiral-bound notebook. He has the round button-eyes of a rag doll. Denise places her hand on top of Lindsay's. Her palms are dry and soft like dough. Lindsay narrates up to the moment after the accident when she stepped out of her car and discovered that the station wagon was gone. He leaves room for several beats of silence before he speaks.

"What made you sure it was your parents' car, not just one that looked like it?"

I just knew, she almost says. "I saw the license plate."

Nodding, he flips back a few pages in the notebook. "What's that number again?"

He has it written down right there. He's quizzing her like a game show host. She should know the answer, did know it only a couple of hours ago. It's gone now.

"I can't remember," she says.

His shiny doll eyes never seem to blink. He asks, "Are you taking any medications these days?"

"Lexapro. Ativan."

"That's for anxiety?"

"And depression," she says.

"Are you currently undergoing any sort of treatment?"

"I'm not in therapy, no. Not right now."

Denise squeezes her hand. In that gesture, she gives away something that she would never say out loud—she doesn't believe Lindsay either. Not really. This car accident is the latest in an eight-year series of manifestations of her granddaughter's inability to move on. Lindsay doesn't blame her for coming to this conclusion, any more than she blames the police officer. Her only anger is with herself for not figuring out the same thing sooner.

She wasn't the only one to lose people that day. Denise lost her only son, and she found a way to keep going. How deep a reservoir of strength must that have taken? She kept it together, took in Lindsay, cared for her husband while he died slowly for two years, is keeping it together right now. Meanwhile, even with the pills that are supposed to make her mind run smoothly, Lindsay's seeing ghosts and driving into oncoming traffic.

After the police officer leaves, Denise makes tea. They sit on opposite ends of the couch. Steam ribbons upwards from their cups. For a while, neither of them speaks. The trailer's electrical systems hum faintly.

Lindsay says, "I need to leave."

"I can give you a lift," Denise says. "But you're welcome to stay the night if you want. You're always welcome."

"Thanks. No. I mean, I need to leave *here*. Town. I need to get better. I don't think I can do it here."

It's hard not to look away as she says it. Lindsay is the last of Denise's family, and she's abandoning her. Once she goes, her grandmother will be alone. It feels like a betrayal, so Denise's response comes as a surprise. A grin breaks out on her face. Her eyes well up with tears that couldn't be mistaken for anything but joyful. It takes Lindsay a moment to realize that Denise has been waiting years for her to say these exact words.

When the phone call comes, she's in her kitchen, watching a street-cleaning truck's lights blink a slow rhythm in the alley beneath her window. Brown snow stands in piles in the gutter. It's barely nine o'clock, but Paul's workday starts before dawn, and he's already sacked out in the next room, so Lindsay is sequestered in here. It's where she spends most of her nights.

It's been three years since she moved here, to a city halfway across the country. She hasn't been back. She still talks to her grandmother twice a week. Those phone calls are everything she needs and all she can handle. In six weeks, she and Paul are flying to Hawaii to get married. Lindsay's looking forward to a lot of things about her wedding, but near the top of the list is getting to see Denise again. Her grandmother will be the one to walk her down the aisle.

Her phone is on the kitchen table beside a glass of water and a book she hasn't gotten around to opening yet. The name and number flashing on the screen are her grandmother's. It doesn't register that tonight is not one of their regular nights to talk until after she's accepted the call.

"Hi, Grandma."

"Lindsay King?" It's a man's voice, gentle and with a drawl. Something cold tiptoes up Lindsay's spine. She straightens in her seat.

"Yes?"

"Is this Lindsay?"

"What's happened?"

He clears his throat. "My name is Gus Winkler. I'm a neighbor of your grandmother's. A good friend too."

"Please, what's going on?"

"I really hate to be the one to tell you this," he says. "Denise had a stroke this morning."

"Is she—" *Alive? Okay?* She can't finish the sentence.

"She hasn't woken up yet. The doctors aren't sure she will. They're suggesting, if you want to say goodbye, you might want to do it soon."

She and Paul work at an industrial engineering firm. She's in the front office, while he does HVAC installation at large-scale commercial properties. The city's in the midst of a construction boom. Downtown is a forest of cranes and skyscraper skeletons. Paul's slammed, and she tells him she doesn't need him to come with her, but he does anyway. She knew he would. By the next afternoon, they're on a plane flying west.

At first, she finds it odd that Denise has never told her about her good friend Gus, until she thinks that maybe she has. Her grandmother makes frequent mentions of a neighbor with whom she's always making plans—outings to movies, museums, and restaurants, and regular visits to each other's homes—but she's never used a name, nor, Lindsay now realizes, a pronoun. Lindsay has always assumed the friend was a woman, which was doubtless her grandmother's intent.

Paul rents a car at the airport, and they drive straight to the hospital. It's night when they arrive. The ICU waiting room is on the third floor. There are several people scattered around, slumped on couches and chairs. Gus Winkler recognizes her right away. He's an old man with dark skin and arms like broomsticks. His Hawaiian shirt looks to have been slept in. When he introduces himself, there's a moment when she can see in his eyes that he's considering hugging her. To her relief, he decides against it. They don't even shake hands. Paul stands just behind her and off to the side. In new situations, he likes her to take the lead, keeping just close enough that she can sense the weight and size of him.

Gus leads them past a nurses' station to her grandmother's room.

"Do you want me to wait out here?" Paul asks.

"Absolutely not."

Denise looks small in her bed. Her hands lie atop her sheets. Her face has lost its shape, like someone vacuumed all the meat out from under her skin.

"You should say something," Paul says. "So she knows you're here."

"I'm here." It's all she can think of, and it feels stupid. She takes hold of her grandmother's hand. It's hard and cold.

They stay with Denise until a nurse informs them that visiting hours are over. When they return to the waiting room, Lindsay's not surprised to find Gus fast asleep in one of the seats. Lindsay and Paul find a couch for themselves. Paul reclines into a corner and invites her to rest her head on his chest. When she's settled in, he uses his jacket as a blanket to cover them both. The contours of his muscles press into her cheek. For a while, she sleeps.

When she wakes up, the room is silent. Paul is out cold. His mouth hangs open. A spit bubble poised on his bottom lip quivers with each exhalation of breath. She slides out from under his jacket. At the disturbance, he shifts and snorts, but his eyes remain closed. The clock on her cell phone tells her they're still a couple hours from sunrise. The sensible thing would be to try to steal a little more sleep, but there's an acidic anxiousness in her stomach. She wants air.

An elevator carries her down to the main lobby. It's not quite deserted. She crosses it, passes through an automatic sliding door, and steps out onto the sidewalk.

The air is warm and smells of car exhaust. Until she moved away, she hadn't known that the whole world didn't smell like this. It's not an odor she's missed. Across the street, the parking garage stands against the sky, dark and severe. It's the tallest structure in sight, taller even than the hospital whose employees and patients it services.

Was moving away a mistake after all? There will be no getting those three years back now. She considers what it will mean to be the last of her family, then thinks about the fact that very soon, she and Paul will be starting a *new* family. First there will just be the two of them, but that won't last long. Paul wants kids. He's been clear about that. She does too, she thinks. Her family has contracted. Next it will expand. It feels cyclical, natural. Sad, but also okay.

The sound of a car engine coming to life pulls her out of her head. It sounds tinny and hollow, like the last dregs of water boiling in a kettle. She glances around, searching for its source. When she finds it, her breath catches in her throat.

Her parents' station wagon is parked at the curb thirty feet away. Somehow, it's even filthier than the last time she saw it. The crust of mud on its side is thick and chunky. Pale clouds of exhaust rise up around it. Past the windshield, the inside of the car is dark. She can't see the driver, but she can sense eyes fixed upon her, taking her in. Within the shadows, she sees something—a sudden flash of yellow light the size of a tennis ball. A moment later it winks out, leaving her uncertain as to what it could have been. A cigarette lighter, maybe? Involuntarily, she takes a step towards the car for a closer look.

The headlights click on, capturing her in their glare. Fear erupts within her. She imagines the Volkswagen surging forward, grinding over her like roadkill. For a moment, she cannot convince her legs to move. The engine's rattle gets louder as the car shifts into gear. Lindsay manages a step backward, then another, through the automatic doors into the dreary safety of the lobby. As the doors slide shut, she watches the Volkswagen speed past and disappear.

She rides the elevator back up to the ICU with sweat beading down the sides of her face. The doors open on a different scene than the one she left. Nurses and doctors whisper in clusters while others rush in and out of the room. Lindsay sees a man in a security guard uniform jog down an adjoining hall. Paul and Gus are awake now, standing together. They spot her as she emerges from the elevator and approach.

"Where'd you go?" Paul says.

Before she can begin to figure out what to tell him, Gus steps forward and declares, "She woke up."

At first the words don't register. When they do, she starts forward, ready to run to her grandmother's room, but Paul stops her with a hand on her arm.

"We don't know where she is," he says.

"What?"

"The nurses' station got a disconnect alert from her monitoring equipment. When they went into her room to check on her, she wasn't there."

"When was this?" Her voice comes out pinched and strained.

"Five minutes ago? Ten?"

"The doctors think she must be disoriented, confused," Gus says. "Doesn't know where she is. She wandered off."

Paul nods. "They're telling us there's nothing to worry about. She can't have gotten far. There are nurses' stations, watchmen, security cameras. She's still in the hospital, and there's no way she's getting out. She'll turn up. They'll find her."

An hour passes; then another. The squawks and hisses of security guards' walkie-talkies become the waiting room's new soundtrack. She and Paul sit together while Gus walks laps around the room, stopping to question anyone wearing any kind of uniform who's willing to listen. Lindsay can see in the slump of his shoulders as the understanding slowly sets in that something is deeply, deeply wrong here. Whatever words of encouragement Paul keeps whispering to her don't sink in. She's hearing the tin-kettle sound of the Volkswagen's engine, picturing the yellow flicker through the dark windshield.

At dawn, the police show up. Officer Button-Eyes is with them. Lindsay doesn't think he recognizes her, until he pulls her aside for a private conversation.

"I want you to know, there's absolutely no reason to think this has anything to do with what happened to your family."

She nods. He's wrong, of course. They're the Kings, the family that disappears. The family that gets taken. It's amazing to her that she could ever have considered tying Paul to this family, let alone having children. What would she be sentencing them to? How long would it be before someone came for them? She makes her way back to Paul's side, takes his hand, and threads her fingers between his. She's already decided—when he gets on a plane to fly back home, she won't be going with him.

The gun is wrapped inside a knitted red blanket. Lindsay's on a laundry kick, gathering everything she can find to which Denise's scent still clings for a massive haul to the laundromat. When she digs the blanket out of a drawer beneath the bed, it uncoils and the gun slips out. It hits the floor with a quiet thump. She picks it up. The grip is matte black with grooves for her fingers. Her face reflects back at her in the barrel. She's never touched a gun before. Until now, she would have assumed the same about her grandmother. It feels as though she's stumbled upon something private and embarrassing. The gun might as well be a vibrator. She returns it to the drawer.

It takes her a few days to work up the nerve to ask Gus what he knows about it.

He says, "For the past couple of months, Denise was getting… I hate to use the word *paranoid*. Suspicious. She thought someone was following her. Said she was hearing noises outside at night."

"Did you ever hear anything?" Gus's trailer sits just across a narrow lane from Denise's.

"Can't say that I did."

After that, she moves the gun up to the top of the nightstand.

It's her fourth month living in her grandmother's trailer. Paul spent a long time refusing to believe she wasn't going to change her mind and come back to him, and a while after that too furious to interact with her at all. Eventually he sent her things, but by then she'd grown so used to her grandmother's stuff that she never got around to unpacking much beyond her clothes. The trailer doesn't offer much in the way of storage, so the boxes have become furniture in their own right. They're stacked in columns in corners and piled against the walls.

Gus approves of her moving into Denise's place so much that he's never asked her about the fiancé she never mentions. "Someone's got to keep those plants of hers alive until she gets back," he said. Lindsay failed to keep them alive—she doesn't have the talent for it—and her grandmother hasn't come back. It is just like before. For the first couple of weeks, Officer Button-Eyes contacted her daily. Then he delegated those phone calls. Then the police stopped calling altogether.

Finding work has been a struggle, probably because she left her last job with no warning and broke the heart of one of their favorite employees in the process. That's assuming anyone's bothering to check her references, which they might not be. Lately, she's managed to pick up a bit of temp work, but it doesn't help much. Her savings weren't great to begin with. Four months later, they're gone, and she's sinking quickly into debt. Her sleep schedule has twisted itself into something unrecognizable. Her days are broken up by naps, and her nights are interminable stretches of alternating nervousness and boredom.

She spends her free time driving the flat, wide streets with her head on a swivel, on the lookout for a filthy white station wagon. The town is a broad grid. Residential neighborhoods give way to shopping centers and then back again with metronomic regularity. She does her best to stay ten miles per hour below the speed limit. There's never any worry of creating traffic. Everyone here moves slowly. The cars creep along. Pedestrians are somnambulistic. Kids on scooters move as though through transparent gel. The world's motor has been set at half-speed so that Lindsay won't miss anything, won't miss the fact that there isn't anything to miss.

One afternoon she wakes up on her grandmother's couch with her stomach stinging from hunger. A perusal of her refrigerator and cupboards comes up with nothing. She glances out her window and sees Gus on a wooden folding chair in front of his trailer. He spots her and offers a wave, which she returns. When she doesn't step away from the glass, he waves again, this time with a beckoning motion. She changes into a fresh T-shirt and goes out to him. His feet are propped on a white cooler. He holds a Bud Light bottle in his lap.

"Beer?"

"I probably shouldn't," she says.

"Too early?"

"I haven't eaten anything yet today," she says. Then, "You know what? I'd love one."

He lifts his feet off the cooler. "Help yourself."

She does, twisting off the cap and flicking it into an empty terracotta pot nearby. It clinks against thirty others just like it. The first sip hits her empty stomach exactly as hard as expected. Once she's recovered from her wince, she says, "You and my grandma spent a lot of time together."

"Sure did."

"I guess I've been kind of a shitty neighbor. I should be visiting you more."

"No you shouldn't," he says. Seeing the look on her face, he quickly adds, "Not that I'm not glad for the company. And I think it's a good thing you're doing, keeping the home fires burning. But I don't think for a second you're a surrogate Denise. People don't get replaced. You probably know that better than anyone."

He invites her to stay for dinner. They cook hamburgers on a grill. She eats two. When the sun sets and the air turns cold, they go inside, where she drinks several more beers. By the time she emerges, she feels sleepy and nourished in a way she didn't realize she'd been missing. Gus has nodded off in an armchair. She tries and fails to find a blanket to put over him. A rectangle of light spilling from his doorway forms a path from his trailer to hers. When she closes the door, the path vanishes.

She's just crossed the lane when a car rolls up behind her. She feels the heat of its engine on her back. With a heavy clunk, it drops into park. A barbed-wire ball of dread comes together in her stomach. Even before she turns, she knows which car it is.

For several seconds, nothing happens. It's as though the driver wants Lindsay to have a chance to take this all in. She tries to. Her sister's car seat sticks up into the frame of the back window. It's patterned with multi-colored elephants with big dumb smiles marching trunk-to-tail in horizontal lines. The passenger door opens, and she's looking across the seat at the driver.

Inside, it's dark like a tool shed. She can make out a floppy cap pulled low, a thick, ratty coat with the collar popped up, a pair of gloved hands on the steering wheel. The car stinks of mildew. The driver shifts to look at her. Lindsay's mouth goes dry.

The head is impossibly long and narrow, bulbous at the

top and coming to a phallic point at the chin, like an autumn gourd. Coarse dark hairs cover it. They quiver, exploring and tasting the air. The face has no mouth to speak of, just four inky orbs arranged in a vertical line down its center. Lindsay finds herself thinking of them as eyes, though they give no indication of sight, thought, or feeling.

Part of her knows that this is the time to start screaming, but something is happening with the orbs, and she can't look away. The color is growing lighter, turning first to amber, then yellow. The fading darkness leaves behind a shape in each orb's center, a black squiggle suspended in urine-colored murk. Four people, one in each orb. They are posed identically—arms out, heads bowed, legs dangling. From the top down, her father, mother, sister, and grandmother, suspended in liquid, not quite heavy enough to sink. No one has aged, not even the baby, plump and limp.

Lindsay says, "Are they dead?"

By way of an answer, the driver nods at the empty passenger seat. An invitation. *Only one way to find out.* It would be so easy.

She takes a step backward. From inside the car, there is a rustle, then a sudden burst of movement. It happens almost too fast to see. The driver launches itself toward her. Like a newspaper in a gale-force wind, it sails over the passenger seat and lands on its feet before her. Free of the car, it's able to rise to its full height. The driver is all joints and strange angles. Unfolding, it towers over her and gazes down.

Lindsay could succumb now. The inside of her head is a waterfall of noise and fear. She could collapse under its force, literally collapse into a pile and let the driver scoop her up and toss her into the backseat. It could take her to her family in that yellow-lit place, to answers. Depending on how much of her mind remains by then, she might even understand some of them.

Instead, she runs inside. The driver chases. It moves with a whispering sound. She slams the front door shut behind her, then hears it bang open again a moment later. A kitchen stool she tips over on her way past gets flung against the wall with enough force to rock the whole trailer. No lights are on. The trailer is cramped and difficult to navigate. Her shins catch the corners of furniture, her shoulders the frames of doorways. Stumbling, she keeps going, not looking back. She doesn't turn around until she reaches the bedroom, until she holds her grandmother's gun in both hands. The driver rises up before her. She doesn't have to aim.

Three shots, three flashes. The driver flops back, bounces off the wall, and hits the ground. It lies still, a heap of clothes and jutting angles. For a while, Lindsay stands there, panting, gun outstretched. Then she sets it down on the nightstand. Three shots. It took little more than a second to end everything. It was so easy, so meaningless. Her hand stings from the gun's recoil. She wants to cry. Instead, she goes to a window and peeks around the edge of the flimsy curtain.

Drawn by the noise, her neighbors are peering through their own windows or stepping cautiously out their doors. Some already have cell phones pressed to their ears. Next, the police will come. Then what? What will they make of any of this? How will they explain it?

As if it is hearing itself in her thoughts, the driver stirs. Lindsay stifles a gasp. The heap of clothes and jutting angles shifts and begins to rise, slowly, like a blow-up doll being inflated one breath at a time. Pressing herself against the wall, Lindsay inches past it to the bedroom door. She backs out of the room. Without taking her eyes off the driver, she retraces her route through the trailer. She reaches the front door just as it achieves its full height. It turns its head to regard her. Curls of smoke roll out of the bullet holes in its coat. It moves toward her. She runs outside.

The station wagon is still idling in the middle of the lane. The passenger-side door hangs open. She climbs inside and yanks it closed. The upholstery is patchy with mould. The engine's vibrations carry up through the seat. The driver emerges from the trailer. In an instant, it's beside the door. In another, it's reaching for the handle. She hits the lock down just in time. It rattles the handle, then lets go and brings its face close to the window. A ripple passes through the hairs on its face. It slams a gloved hand against the glass and leaves it there. Extra knuckles notch its over-long fingers.

Lindsay scoots backward over the parking brake into the driver's seat until she's pressed up against the door. A familiar keychain hangs from the ignition, swaying gently.

Up ahead, something catches her attention. A faint glow. She squints at it through the layer of grime on the windshield. Before her, maybe ten yards away, lights hover in the air. What she's seeing doesn't make sense. There's nothing there for lights to reflect upon, just empty space. It has to be an illusion, some kind of interplay of the filthy glass and a neighbor's porch lamp, only she knows it's not. She knows, because the lights are the same jaundiced shade she saw in the driver's eyes, and because the lights don't quite look like they're floating in the air—more like they're shining through it. The effect makes her think of tissue paper flattened over the end of a flashlight. The beam filters through, revealing the paper's thinness and frailty, its readiness to come apart at the slightest pressure.

On one side of her, the driver continues to paw at the door. On the other, Gus is emerging from his trailer. The sleepy look on his face turns to one of horror as he takes in the scene. He shouts Lindsay's name. Whatever he says next, she misses. It's been eight years since she sat behind the wheel of this car. Her father used to take her to empty parking lots to practice driving. He would set up orange traffic cones and drill her for hours on three-point turns and parallel parking. If she did well, her reward was getting to drive home. Eight years, but the muscle memory is still there, and she's already gone.

FOUR ABSTRACTS
by Nina Allan

A Life on Canvas: the art of Rebecca Hathaway, Burton Museum and Art Gallery, Bideford, August 2016

Rebecca Hathaway died in February 2015 from complications following a diagnosis of early-onset Alzheimer's four years earlier. She was forty-nine years old. Hathaway worked in a variety of media including ceramics and textiles, though paint was a recurring constant throughout her career. She herself described her work in oils as a kind of journal-keeping. The ten abstracts that comprise this exhibition have been drawn from all periods of her working life, beginning with a canvas painted for her graduation show at Reading College in 1984 and culminating in two previously unexhibited oils taken from her studio in Hartland, part of the series she was working on at the time of her death. The paintings on display grant a unique insight into the mindset of an artist whose troubled personal life was frequently reflected in her work.

You ask me how I knew her and what she was like. That's a long story.

1. *Junk*, 1984, 3'x4', oil on canvas. Hathaway's graduation show consisted of eight identically sized canvases, each depicting a massed multitude of common household objects, painted in a hyper-realistic style to fill the canvas entirely, leaving no blank spaces. The canvas on display here, No. 6 in the original series, features a number of objects taken from what Hathaway always referred to as the junk drawer of the dressing table in her bedsit on Leamington Road: lipsticks, nail scissors, orphan earrings and a pencil eraser. The objects are painted slightly larger than life size, and with their colours artificially heightened in a manner suggestive of 1960s pop art, although Hathaway always denied this influence. She described her graduation show as a series of "distilled observations", a visual diary of the year in which she painted them.

Not long after I first met her, Beck told me a strange story. This was in 1980, when we were both studying History of Art at the University of Reading. We were swapping childhood memories, which is most of what you do when you're first getting to know someone, and I'd just told Beck about the time I put a ladder up to the bathroom window to spy on my brother Robby as he lay in the tub. I was fourteen when I did that, Robby just twelve.

"Don't you think it's weird?" I said. "One minute you're running around naked together in the back garden, the next you're supposed to act like strangers. I think it's weird, anyway."

Robby's reaction when he found out what I'd done had been both tearful and furious. When I told him he'd become a prisoner of the social construct he told me to fuck off.

"It's instinct," Beck said. "The instinct that says you have to stop sharing baths at some point or you're going to end up shagging your own brother."

I made a gagging sound, and we both collapsed in shouts of laughter, bending ourselves double with our foreheads touching the carpet. I was secretly thinking it was Beck's brother Ben I fancied, not Robby; Ben with the reed-slender wrists and sweeping eyelashes. Ben was three years older than Beck and me, and he had a fiancée already, a girl called Ros who was at Oxford reading PPE.

"You think that's weird," Beck continued. "When I was ten, my mother sat me down and told me the women in our family are all part-spider."

"You what?" I sneaked a glance at her, trying to work out if she was being serious or taking the piss. Her eyes were closed, head tipped back to rest against the side of the bed. Beck had the same long, fair eyelashes as her brother, but whereas Ben's eyes were dark brown, Beck's were hazel, so pale in certain lights they looked almost colourless. Topaz, Beck said, the same as her mother's.

"I know you think I'm joking but it really happened," she added. "Mum said I'd start my periods like everyone else, only mine would last longer and be more painful because the lining of my womb had silk in it and it was difficult for the human body to break it down. She said I'd soon get used to it. When I asked her what else would happen she said probably nothing, because the spider genes had become very diluted over the centuries and I'd most likely go my whole life without even noticing I had them."

She paused, and while it seemed that she was giving me the chance to butt in, to ask a question, to get angry even, I couldn't think what to say. It was obviously a wind-up—I mean, how couldn't it be?—and yet even as I waited for Beck to fall on her face laughing, to knee me in the side saying she really had me that time, it was the best one ever, she refused to do any of those things, just kept leaning quietly against the bed, saying nothing and waiting until I actually began to feel a bit creeped out.

"It can't be true, though," I said in the end. "Why would your mum tell you something like that?"

Beck made a "huh" sound, midway between a laugh and a snort of contempt. "You don't know my mum," she said. "It was probably just her way of explaining puberty to me."

The room was almost dark—aside from the narrow fluorescent tube above the hand basin we had switched all the lights off—but when I turned to look at her I caught sight of a tear glistening on the curve of her cheek. I watched as it slid down her face and plopped into her lap.

"Last year my periods stopped completely," she said. "The doctors don't know what's wrong with me. They think it's just stress—exams and starting college and all that. I think it's because I'm a freak."

"You're not a freak."

I leaned sideways and hugged her. She pressed her face against my shoulder and cried. I could feel the wetness soaking through my T-shirt. I wasn't sure what she was crying about—her mum being weird, or her stopped periods, or something else, hidden between the lines of those other things, but it didn't seem to matter. What mattered was that she could cry and I was there to hold her. I felt a thrill of secret excitement, not so different from what I'd felt perched at the top of that ladder, staring at Robby's new, alien body through the misted-up glass.

After a bit, Beck lay on the floor with her head in my lap and we carried on where we'd left off, talking about who we'd hated most at school and what we hoped we'd do when we left university. We talked until two in the morning. We were inseparable, even then, just three weeks into term. I was scared—scared that something would come along to fuck us up. Even getting off with Ben would fuck us up, I reasoned, because that would mean I'd have to think about Ben all the time and what a drag that would be, once the novelty had worn off.

I actually felt relieved that Ben had a girlfriend, that Ben and I was never going to happen.

I knew all along that Beck's mother was the photographer Jennie Hathaway. Jennie was the reason I made friends with Beck in the first place, if I'm honest—I had the crazy idea that I could write my final year dissertation on her—although in fact I didn't meet her until Ben's wedding the following summer. Jennie seemed nervous to me, as if she were permanently on the lookout for an escape route, as if the wedding, the guests, the whole day was too much to cope with. Small, almost spookily thin, hair even straighter and paler than Beck's. Constantly glancing about herself, searching for images.

There was something about her that made me feel uncomfortable, maybe because she was so different from my own mother, who worked in a bank and who still went to Yates's wine bar with her girlfriends on the last Friday of every month. Came home hammered too, usually. I got on better with Beck's dad, Adam. He seemed much more easy-going, more like Ben.

It wasn't until I began work on my postgraduate thesis that I discovered that Jennie Hathaway had produced a little-known series of photographs of the naturalist Terezia Salk, who died of a rare wasting disorder she contracted during an extended period of field studies in the Amazon basin. Some reports said the disease was the result of a spider bite, although it was more likely that Salk's immune system had been compromised through repeated bouts of fever, and the disease was able to gain a foothold as a result.

I was unable to source the whereabouts of the original negatives. Salk's family bought the lot, apparently. They were determined to suppress the photos, which they saw as a gross invasion of Salk's privacy.

Jennie Hathaway photographed some pretty weird shit— one newspaper reviewer referred to her as the British Diane Arbus—but I came away with the feeling Salk's death affected her more than she'd bargained for, that she took it personally.

Which could help explain why she fed Beck all that spider nonsense. Terezia Salk's unborn child died in the womb, I do know that. Salk's doctors had to perform a caesarean because Salk was too weak by then to undergo labour.

Jennie photographed the baby too, apparently. There's no way that wouldn't get to you, especially if you had young children. It could be that she was suffering from some strange form of survivor guilt.

2. *Sticklebacks*, 1988, 3'x2', oil on canvas. This canvas, which formed part of Hathaway's first major London show, is painted in a similar style to the works in her graduation exhibition, although the colour palette is more subdued and there are indications of the looser, more painterly style that came to characterise her work over the following decade. On closer inspection we see that the closely packed shoal of "sticklebacks" that throng the canvas are actually Yale keys, more than two hundred of them, collected by Hathaway specifically for the purpose of painting them. Questioned in an interview about the meaning of *Sticklebacks*, Hathaway spoke of the significance of keys as symbols of secrecy and confinement.

In the autumn of our second year at university, Beck

dropped out of her History of Art course and transferred to Reading College. She wanted to be an artist, she insisted, not a professor. We had a massive row about that and for a while afterwards she stopped speaking to me completely. She told me years later the reason she cut ties was because she was terrified of losing me, which didn't make much sense even then and was agony at the time.

She was living in a grotty bedsit off London Road and spending most of her time with a postgraduate named April Lessore, who made collages from strips of pre-war fabric and old bus tickets. I refused to call April an artist, although textiles are really big now and so I suppose you could say she was ahead of her time. Whatever she was, I loathed the sight of her. I even began to loathe the month of the year she'd been named after.

I think Beck and April were probably lovers, though I never asked. By the time Beck and I were properly back on speaking terms, April was history.

A week after Beck's funeral, Ben called and asked me if I would help him clear out her place. I didn't know who was speaking at first. I mean, I recognised his voice but I couldn't place it. Ben and I had never spoken on the phone before that, not even once.

He had been a part of my life for thirty years—longer—yet if you took all the time we'd spent physically in each other's presence, it would probably have added up to less than a weekend.

"Don't feel you have to say yes, Isobel," Ben said. "But if you think you could face it I would be grateful. I haven't been down there, you see, not since last winter. It became too difficult."

I felt a rush of self-righteous gratitude: so it hadn't been just me.

"What does she want to bury herself out there for?" That's what Ben's wife Ros said, when Beck announced she was leaving London to rent a cottage on the North Devon coast. Not a bad question, although in fact the answer seemed more obvious to me than I let on at the time. In my experience, people tend to do one of two things after a bad breakup: either shag themselves into oblivion or head off to the back of beyond and pretend to be finding themselves.

As I stepped on to the platform at Exeter St David's I couldn't help thinking about the last time I'd made this journey—four years ago, or so I told myself, although in fact it was closer to seven. When I looked for Hartland on the map it didn't seem that isolated—in a country the size of England, nowhere is ever far from anywhere else, or so you'd think, which made it all the more unbelievable that the trip took five hours: the high-speed train to Exeter then a local line to Barnstaple then a bus ride along the coast road and into Hartland. That final stretch of the journey seemed to take forever. Barnstaple is a weird place—half historic port, half industrial estate—and from there the landscape only gets stranger. Stretches of desolate roadway through a flat, tussocky hinterland I never knew existed. Farmhouses and wind turbines, the odd ruined barn.

The village itself, when you finally get there, is one of those places you might have visited on holiday as a child: a bus stop and a convenience store, a cafe with a striped awning, a church and a tiny gift shop for the tourists. The cafe has a cappuccino machine now, which is sad and a relief at the same time.

Stepping off the bus, I felt my separation from London as I might feel a piece of grubby sticking plaster being torn from a mostly healed graze and tossed away.

Beck's cottage was at the far end of a dingy side street. The inside looked like a deliberate reconstruction of a typical 1960s interior, complete with vinyl wallpaper and a bulbous three-piece suite in Carnaby Street orange. There was a wood-burning stove though, and a monstrous iron Rayburn that provided the hot water. "The owners said I could redecorate," Beck told me excitedly, except she never did, just plonked her stuff down and forgot about it. The Fulham flat was just the same.

The best thing about the cottage was its position—backing on to open fields, with the sea just visible between the trees. The back garden was a mess: a grubby concrete yard, a tangle of brambles and cow parsley beyond that. The attached barn Beck was using as a studio was just about watertight, the chill taken off by an enormous mud-coloured storage heater that looked as if it dated back to VE Day. Removing it would have been a major work of demolition, which was clearly why no one had attempted it. The barn's rafters curved high above our heads, like the exposed ribcage of a capsized Viking longboat.

I shivered. I hadn't yet told Beck about Eddie moving out. Coming so soon after her and Marco I was afraid it might look ridiculous, a copycat breakup. I was still at the stage where I was missing him, more than I thought I would, even though I knew it wasn't Eddie I missed so much as the familiarity of our routine, up to and including our constant sniping at one another. After ten years together, Eddie and I had the fine art of bitching pretty much nailed.

I didn't feel like discussing it, I guess. I hoped we wouldn't have to talk about Marco either. Beck had spent most of the past eighteen months convinced it was only a matter of time before he came back, which was a delusion on her part, obviously. Marco had served his time and he wasn't about to get back on the merry-go-round.

The whole place smelled of damp, cottage and barn both. I was worried about Beck's health, even then.

That was the year Beck began working on the diadem paintings. I saw some of what she'd been doing—underwashes mainly, burnt sienna, overlaid with gritty layers of flesh tones and Naples yellow. They reminded me of the fields behind her home.

People tend to assume Beck and Marco split up because of Beck's breakdown, or that her breakdown was actually caused by Marco leaving. Neither thing was true. Marco left because of Beck's affair with Lila Nunez, or that's the excuse he used, anyway. But the real reason for Beck's breakdown was her mother's suicide.

"The same thing is going to happen to me," she said when she called me. I didn't have a clue what she was talking about. She was sobbing hard. I told her to slow down. That's what you say to someone when they're not making sense, isn't it, slow down, regardless of the speed they're actually talking at?

Most of what Beck was trying to say was drowned out in tears. "Mum's dead," she said at last. "No one's allowed to see her body. She jumped off the roof of a multi-storey car park."

My blood ran cold. Another idiotic cliché but in this case that really was how it felt, as if cold liquid had been injected directly into my veins.

Jennie Hathaway had killed herself.

"Did she—?" I said, after the requisite fifteen minutes of being horrified and outraged and sympathetic all at once. Did she leave a note? was what I meant to ask, and Beck must have understood this because she answered my question as if I'd spoken all the words aloud and not just the first two.

"She didn't need to, did she? Dad knew. We all knew.

She was changing. She must have known she didn't have much time."

We talked for almost an hour.

"I'm not going to do what she did," Beck said just before we hung up. She'd stopped crying by then but her voice was still rough with catarrh, bunged up with old tears. "No one can make me do that. It's not my fault I'm—"

She never finished her sentence.

A freak, I thought. Like Beck had done with me, I knew exactly what she was trying to say. There was no need for her to spell it out.

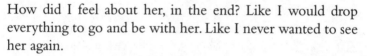

How did I feel about her, in the end? Like I would drop everything to go and be with her. Like I never wanted to see her again.

The doctor who gave evidence at Jennie Hathaway's inquest confirmed that she had been suffering from a chronic degenerative muscular condition for several years. The prognosis had been uncertain, he added, because the exact nature of her condition had not been agreed on.

"A rare form of muscular dystrophy," the doctor suggested, "with additional complications."

When asked what these complications were, he hesitated, then stated that Jennie Hathaway had been suffering from what he referred to as calcification of the epidermis, and that she had also undergone a full hysterectomy after an exploratory operation had revealed large numbers of fibrous growths attached to the lining of her womb.

"Silk," Beck said. "Only no one was going to admit that, were they? According to their bloody textbooks there's no such disease."

"Beck," I said. "You can't be sure of that." Get real, was what I wanted to say. This spider shit is all in your head.

People make television programmes about the nature of genius and speak in hushed tones of the pain of alienation and outsider status. What doesn't get talked about is how time-consuming these people can be, the hours you waste talking them through their latest crisis, only to have them chuck your advice down the toilet an hour later. And still you're supposed to be there to pick up the pieces.

And if you put your foot down and refuse to do that? You're seen as a callous bitch, drowning in bitterness and jealousy, most likely. It never occurs to anyone that you're just tired. You listen for hours and weeks and years, you hug them and hold their hand and never once do you tell them to shut up or get a grip or stop being so bloody selfish, because that would mean you didn't get it, that you weren't sensitive enough to understand how thin-skinned these geniuses are, how vulnerable, how barely able to cope with being in the world.

How about those of us who just have to soldier on? Who's going to come running when we feel like going off the rails?

Not your genius friend, that's for sure.

The only reason Beck and I were able to stay so close was because I went long periods without having anything to do with her.

3. *Jorōgumo,* 1995, 4'x3', oil on canvas. Sometimes known as "the binding bride", the jorōgumo in Japanese mythology is a woman who can turn herself into a spider or vice versa. She is often represented carrying an infant, later revealed to be an egg sac bursting with spider eggs. Strongly influenced by the late work of the Portuguese artist Vieira da Silva, a painter Hathaway greatly admired, *Jorōgumo* is crosshatched with narrow bands of white, pink

and mauve, the layers of paint building in places to a thick encrustation. At close quarters, the effect is suggestive of densely woven fabric. When the canvas is viewed from a distance, however, the greyish outline of a female figure becomes visible, the strands of her long, purplish hair intermingled with the crosshatched background and finally indistinguishable from it. *Jorōgumo* is Hathaway's best known painting, and earned her the silver medal in the 1996 Siemens Painting Prize for European artists under fifty. The award included a travel bursary, which Hathaway used to extend her residency in Berlin. It was during this time that she met the painter who was to become her husband, Marco Teich.

I liked Marco. As an artist, he was brilliant and surprising. As a human being he was resilient, engaged, and interested in other people, which isn't the norm when it comes to artists, believe me.

I would never have seen him getting together with Beck, not in a million years. Even then, she was so brittle, so self-absorbed. People have the idea she was a party animal but she wasn't; the only thing she liked about parties was that they gave her an excuse to sit in the corner and drink vodka and not talk to anyone. Marco did the talking. He was a wonderful host when he was in the mood, which was most of the time when he wasn't actually working.

He knew Anselm Kiefer back in the day, though he never traded on that fact; he didn't need to.

I remember him saying to me that Beck was squandering her talent.

"She drinks far too much." As if Beck could solve her issues by consuming less alcohol. Marco liked a drink too, but never before 6pm, when he finished work for the day. You could argue that Marco's strict work ethic was part of the problem, making him believe that Beck's afternoons in the pub were the root of her troubles when they really weren't, they were just a mask she put on.

The pub was where she felt safest, in the end. Most of the fights that break out in pubs are of the common or garden, bloody-nose variety, no demons allowed.

It's important to say that Beck really did believe she was a jorōgumo, a spider-woman. I believe she was an undiagnosed schizophrenic, like her mother. The difference was, Jennie had Adam. Adam Hathaway protected Jennie not just from the world but from herself, which is why she was able to survive for so long without coming unstuck. Marco couldn't do that for Beck, firstly because he was selfish, like all artists, and secondly because he refused to admit there was anything wrong with her.

For Marco it was all about discipline, or rather Beck's lack of it—if Beck would only organise her life properly then she would get better. He may even have had a point—half a point, anyway. God knows Beck had a singular talent for living in chaos.

In West Africa and the Caribbean, the spider is the avatar of Anansi, the trickster god, the storyteller, the finder of pathways. In Hopi and Navajo mythology, the Sussistanako or Spider Grandmother taught her people how to hide in plain sight. Throughout the world the spider goddesses—and with the exception of Anansi they are female deities: black widows, secret sharers, whisperers in darkness, keepers of the flame—teach patience and cunning as the cardinal virtues. Among the Inuit people, string games—passed literally from hand to hand, generation to generation—bring schoolgirls on the playground closer to their spider heritage.

Arachne, weaver of silk, of tapestries so rich and so

articulate the gods of Olympus grew jealous of her talent.

After Beck won her prize for *Jorōgumo* I decided I would write an essay—maybe even a monograph—on the famous Doré etchings on the theme of Arachne, considering them alongside a series of pen-and-ink studies by the Japanese-American artist Helen Ogawa. At first glance, the two sets of images are remarkably similar, depicting the horrific metamorphosis of a woman as her body is bent, wrenched and coerced into an alien form. Study them more closely and you will begin to see that whereas Doré's images are concerned with the agony of loss, Ogawa's reveal the ecstasy of transgression and rebirth.

The jorōgumo is more powerful in her spider form, and she knows it. Her transformation is hard-won, and in spite of its evident discomforts, passionately desired.

By the time the bus pulled in opposite the pub it was almost dark. The bus ride had been chilly but the air outside was bitter, sharp as razors. I could smell fish and chips. My stomach growled—I hadn't eaten a thing since Exeter—and I seriously considered ducking into the pub, ordering something hot and greasy from the bar menu, forgetting Beck and Ben and the whole sorry mess. For an hour or so, at least.

I asked myself why I'd agreed to this—staying in Beck's house, especially. It had been a mistake.

I couldn't pretend Ben wasn't waiting though, waiting for me to arrive so we could both get some supper, probably. I left the pub behind, carried on down the road and turned left into the narrow cul-de-sac where Beck's cottage was. I was relieved to see there were lights on, in the porch and in the downstairs front window. I rang the bell and waited, shivering inside my coat, a ratty old parka I hadn't worn since the last time I was there.

Would Beck still be alive if I'd done more for her? Being back in Hartland made the question seem more present somehow, and certainly more brutal, probably because it was harder to avoid.

Beck was doomed—everyone who knew her had known that. Doomed and sick. The doctors had confirmed her illness at least, a condition that could not be halted, or even accurately named.

The front door opened, releasing the familiar smells of damp, old newspapers and mild discomfort, the kind it is easier to come to terms with than to try and change.

"Isobel," Ben said. "You look exhausted." He had his coat on, and I realised he'd been about to leave the house—to go to the pub, most likely, if he had any sense. He hovered in the doorway, clearly undecided over whether he should invite me in or suggest we both go out.

"Shall we go and get something to eat?" I said, deciding for him. "I'm actually really hungry."

"If you're sure that's all right. I mean, you've only just arrived. I can easily go and fetch some fish and chips."

"The pub's just down the road. And I still have my coat on."

"Beers are on me, then." His voice caught in his throat suddenly, as if the mention of alcohol, even in such an innocent context, was still and always would be problematic. He slammed the front door hard, which was the only way of ensuring that it closed properly. It juddered in its frame, warped with damp.

I'd seen Ben at the funeral of course, but everything was different then. He had looked ghastly: too thin, traces of stubble on his cheeks, his black suit old-fashioned in cut and obviously hired for the occasion. Ros, by contrast, seemed to be thriving, her schoolmarmish, charcoal-coloured pinafore dress bizarrely and coincidentally in fashion for the first time ever. She was wearing one of those fake Russian earflap hats, which could have been classed as a faux pas had the weather not been so cold, cold enough for snow almost.

I'm being a bitch again, aren't I? Dear old Ros, she always did do everything by the book. Which is why she has a tenured fellowship at an Oxford college while I'm still a tottering freelancer and always will be, a glorified temp. If Ros is order and Beck was chaos, what the hell am I?

The pub smelled comfortably of beer and there was a good fire going. We ordered two plates of the homemade lasagne then grabbed our beers and went to sit in one of the alcoves. I found myself wondering if Beck had ever occupied the same seat. I realised I knew next to nothing of Beck's daily life, here in the village. What I knew about was her work— the contentment she had found here at first, her increasing isolation as the disease took hold. What she did when she wasn't working I had no idea. Had she made friends here, people she went to the pub with on a regular basis? I knew she had friends from London come and visit from time to time—Nuala Reinhard, April Lessore of all people, even Marco—but that was hardly enough to call a social life.

Had she been lonely? Probably. I decided it was better not to think about it.

The guy from behind the bar brought our lasagne. "You're the family of the young woman who died," he said. A statement, not a question. I always thought that thing about village gossip spreading like wildfire was a cliché but apparently not.

"Ben," Ben said at once. He offered the man his hand.

"I'm Rebecca's brother. And this is her best friend, Isobel."

Her best friend. I smiled a wan smile, the kind of gesture you see people make in films, when you know the person smiling is really thinking fuck off. I was still caught on the words "young woman", snagged on them like a plastic bag flapping about on barbed wire, because Beck had been getting on for fifty and worn down to the bone. I wondered how anyone might look at her and think young woman, then supposed that must be how we looked to people here, all of us Londoners, young in mind if not in body, pink as peeled prawns and as raw, shuffling along the high street like children on a school outing, whining about the cold and not understanding why we'd been brought here or what we were supposed to do with ourselves until we went home.

"Thank you for coming, Isobel," Ben said, once the more immediate issue of hunger had been resolved. "I mean really. I couldn't have managed this alone. I'm truly grateful." He paused. "Ros didn't know Beck, not properly. She thinks I should call house clearance, get rid of the lot. She's probably right—sensible, anyway. But I can't bring myself to do it. Does that sound silly?"

"Not even remotely. There's Beck's work, apart from anything. We need to catalogue it, find out what's there."

"Exactly." He let out a sigh. "I knew you'd understand. You and Beck—"

I didn't let him finish. I wasn't ready to talk about her. Not yet. "How is Ros, anyway?"

"Ros is great. She's pretty wrapped up in Chantal, actually. Which is probably why she doesn't have much left over for— well, this."

I forgot to mention that Ben has a child now. After four decades as a dyed-in-the-wool bluestocking, ghastly cardigans and all, Ros suddenly decided she was going to give birth. Ben was thrilled, naturally. You can tell he's the good-father type just by looking at him. You wouldn't imagine Ros would know what to do with a baby—submit a paper on one, perhaps—but as it turned out she was born to it, the complete earth mother. She had even gone part-time at work. The last I'd heard she'd set up an online hub where people could swap fairy tale variants or whatever.

She didn't want Chantal anywhere near Beck, that went without saying. Beck was a bad influence, a nightmare of an aunt complete with vodka bottles stashed under the sink and overflowing bin bags.

And Ben? Did I catch a hint of that familiar man-baby wail in his voice as he told me just how busy Ros was these days? Was he trying to let me know, in his roundabout, non-judgemental, Bennish way, that his wife didn't understand him now that her attention had been diverted towards their daughter?

Men are all the same when you get down to it. Even the nice ones.

"Would you like to see some photos?" he asked, a question you can't say no to, not if you still want to be considered a member of the human race. He began scrolling through his picture library: innumerable images of a moon-faced little girl with pursed lips and wide-open eyes, Ros looking obscenely comfortable in her new range of pinafores and so pleased with herself you'd think she'd produced the baby single-handed.

I was glad of the diversion, actually. Cooing over little Chantal, it was almost possible to forget the reason we were there. To pretend that everything was normal when we both knew that it wasn't and never would be again.

"Do you think I let her down?" Ben said, much later, when we were back at the house, a half-drunk bottle of Merlot between us on the kitchen table.

"No more than I did." Probably the most honest words I'd spoken since I got off the bus. We looked at each other then looked away again.

I felt as close to him then as I was ever going to feel, and it wasn't pleasant.

I slept in the spare room, the same as I had the last time, when Beck was alive. The room was drab but clean and seemed unchanged, even down to the unstable stack of cardboard boxes in the corner by the window, their flaps iced with dust, their logos—Brillo, Campbell's, Bird's—pointing towards a past buried somewhere in the last century.

I'd glanced into the top box when I was last here. It was full of school exercise books, the kind of stuff I could never imagine wanting to see again, let alone keep. I imagined the boxes following Beck around, from her parents' place near Peterborough to the bedsit in Lewisham, then the Fulham flat, then here. From the thickness of the dust it was clear the boxes hadn't been moved since being dumped here.

Possessions are like a safety blanket, a proof of identity—a proof of existence, even. Then suddenly when you die, they're just rubbish to be cleared.

"How much of this do you think we should keep?" Ben asked me, sometime during the morning of the following day. We'd been wandering from room to room, picking things up and putting them down, undecided, undecided, undecided.

The big things—the furniture, the odd bits of garden equipment, Beck's clothes, even—these things were easy because they were worthless. They could be loaded into a van and taken away. After a couple of hours of dithering I called a house clearance company and booked them to do just that.

"They're coming Friday," I told Ben. "Between ten and twelve." I hoped I'd be gone by then, although I supposed that would depend on how quickly we sorted through the other stuff: the schoolbooks and diaries, the pads of A4 graph paper covered in coffee rings, wine stains and shopping lists and—occasionally—the ghosts of ideas that were undoubtedly worked out more thoroughly in Beck's sketchbooks.

Then of course there were the sketchbooks themselves, enough to fill a sizeable wardrobe and many of them in dubious condition.

If it had been Lee Krasner or Joan Mitchell the place would have been swarming with art experts and their legal executives already, sealing everything into strongboxes and trying to prevent anyone from sneaking out the odd sketch while no one was looking. But Beck had died while she was still in the process of becoming someone. She had a course mapped out, a small but significant following of those in the know. But the real movers and shakers—those with the money—barely knew Rebecca Hathaway existed, much less that she was dead.

There was no team of experts, no archive. If we—or rather, if Ben—decided he was going to keep this stuff, he would have to find somewhere to store it until the higher echelons of the art world decided that Beck was someone worth making a fuss about. At which point the scavenger-curators would descend, and make Ben feel like an arsehole for accepting money for what they would happily have shovelled into landfill just six months before. Because he would accept the money they offered; he'd be an idiot not to.

Beck would have thought so, anyway. She would have wanted him to have it.

The cottage wasn't in too bad a state. I'd suffered waking nightmares about what I might find—blocked toilets and soiled sheets, the kitchen sink overflowing with dirty dishes—but in fact there was just dust and drabness, an exited cocoon. A house where someone had lived but lived no longer.

There had been whispers in the last years of her life that Beck might end up in an old people's home, stinking of urine and brain like cheese. None of these grim predictions had come true. She had merely deteriorated, or so it seemed, to the point where she had no further use for life. Where she had, to all intents and purposes, moved beyond it.

"She's not eating much," her carer Gaby had told me over the phone two weeks before Beck died. "I don't think she realises I'm here, most of the time. But she seems comfortable enough."

Gaby was solidly built, broad-shouldered and slab-cheeked, thick-legged from the hundreds of miles of cycling she did every week, a professional carer who worked for a local charitable organisation called Pro-Nurse, the epitome of competence and practical caring without a sentimental bone in her body.

Under normal circumstances, Beck would have admired her, whilst feeling daunted by her own utter lack of an entry point into Gaby's world. She would have tiptoed round her. Which, I suppose, is what she did do in any case.

I used to call and speak to Gaby every ten days or so, both of us managing to avoid the embarrassing subject of my physical absence, a failure of nerve on my part, professional tact on hers. Beck stopped speaking to me—or to anyone— about a fortnight after Gaby arrived. The first time this happened I heard Gaby calling Beck to the phone, then a long silence, then Gaby again.

"I don't think she feels like talking just now, do you, my pet?" she said. "I wouldn't worry, she's fine otherwise. Try again tomorrow?"

In a way it was business as usual. I remembered the long, dismal months following Beck's first, pre-Marco breakdown, when I'd call and have to listen to the ring tone going on and on, until finally the technology gave up on me and sent a piercing, remorseless weeeeee sound deep into my ear. I always knew Beck was there at the other end, though, sprawled on her bed and not giving a shit about anyone, least of all me.

I liked to think that just hearing the phone ring might make a difference, knowing that I was trying to get through to her, that someone cared. But she never referred to the unanswered calls afterwards—when she was better, I mean—so how would I know?

Gaby told me that Beck weighed less than six stone when she died.

"She was transparent. No point forcing her, though, not when she was so peaceful. She knew her time was up, that's all. Best to let her go."

Transparent. The word sounded strange, coming from Gaby, fanciful almost. I wondered if she'd said the same to Ben.

Ben had arranged to have Beck's body shipped back to Oxford for cremation. At some point during the late afternoon of that first day, when we'd been sifting and sorting for what seemed like aeons, I asked him how she had looked.

Ben glanced up at me briefly then went back to what he'd been doing. "Like a child," he said. "Or a very old lady. Curled on her side. Completely—absent. Her hair was so thin."

I was looking down at something I'd found, an A3 sketchbook, filled with detailed anatomical drawings of the common garden spider, *Araneus diadematus* as she was labelled in drawing after drawing, as Beck had pointed her out to me in the back garden of the cottage the summer I visited. The drawings were skilful and technically accomplished, the kind of thing you might expect to find in one of those beautiful scientific textbooks from the nineteenth century: part myth, part forensic examination, rendered lovingly by hand then transferred to an etching plate and inked into reproduction for the reading masses.

Beck loved those old textbooks. She told me she'd first learned to draw by copying the illustrations in her father's copy of W. S. Bristowe's *The World of Spiders*.

The drawings in the sketchbook took the art of copying to another level, working outwards from closely observed line studies towards cloudy ecstatic conflagrations of shading and light.

I was looking at the preliminary studies for her diadem series.

"What have you got there?" Ben said.

I passed him the pad, trying to make the gesture seem offhand, as if the sketchbook meant nothing, as if it were just one more stick of flotsam in an endless sea of it, trying to hide the fact that I did not want to relinquish it, not even for a moment. The drawings were too precious, too much Beck.

I was thinking what a crime it would be to dump this stuff, whatever it was worth, or not worth. What mattered was the quality of the work, and although I had frequently doubted Beck's sanity I had never once questioned her talent.

I think that was the moment—going through those sketchbooks with Ben—that I first admitted to myself that I meant to write about Beck, I mean seriously, that my personal grief was already being transcended by the bigger picture.

"Look," I said to him. "We can box these things up and store them at mine, if you like. There's all that space over the garage. It's not being used."

"Are you sure?" His voice leaped upwards, like a cricket from grass. "That would be such a huge weight off my mind, you have no idea. Ros—well, she's not too keen on having Beck's stuff at our place. She says we don't have the space and she's right really but…"

"It's fine. Honestly."

At around six-thirty we knocked off and went back to the pub. We sat at the same table, even ordered the same food, though in other ways that second evening together was very different. It was as if sorting through Beck's things had unlocked something in both of us, finally allowing us to talk properly to each other—to swap memories, to share confidences—in a way that had not seemed possible before. As the evening wore on and our intimacy deepened, I could not help thinking about the closeness Ben and I might have shared—as friends, as comrades—had Beck been balanced and well, the kind of person who spent time with her family like everyone else.

We arrived back at the cottage just after closing time. I knew we were going to have sex, had known it for the whole of the walk back, mainly because by then we'd stopped talking almost entirely, yet our connection with each other remained intense. Without wholly intending to, we had become fixated on one another, temporarily at least. Shit happens.

We went straight upstairs.

"Not in there," was all I said, meaning not in Beck's room. Horny as I was, the idea was horrifying. We used my room instead, the guest room. The curtains were still open but that didn't matter because we didn't put the light on. I watched Ben undressing in the glow from the streetlamp, thinking how this should feel like unfinished business, only it didn't. I hadn't thought of Ben in that way for years—decades. The idea that I'd been harbouring fantasies all that time was so wide of the mark it was almost laughable.

We were simply two people who happened to want the same thing at the same time and were determined to make best use of that opportunity. I hadn't had sex since a short-lived and ill-advised affair with a postgraduate student eighteen months before, and from the way Ben grappled and drove I guessed he hadn't had much to do with Ros in that department—or she with him, more likely—for some time, either.

There were no complications afterwards. Not only did we both know the score, we were both old enough and sensible enough not to need to discuss it. We talked about Beck instead, I mean really talked about her. Mad things she'd done as a kid. How loopy she'd been at university. How Ben had never really got on with Marco and how devastated I felt by my own inability to deal with her illness and all it entailed.

The more we talked, the more I couldn't help noticing how we both seemed to be skirting around the subject of Jennie.

If I don't ask him now I never will, I thought, then told Ben the story Beck had told me soon after we met, about how all the women in their family were part-spider.

"What was it with Beck and spiders?" I said. "Would your mother really have said something like that? To a ten-year-old?"

Ben sighed. "You never knew Mum that well, did you?"

"I met her at your wedding. And at that party for Beck's twenty-first."

"God." He flopped backwards onto the pillows. "That seems like another world now, like an old TV series. Do you know what I mean?"

"Of course. It feels like that to me, too."

When does the past become properly the past, inaccessible to us except through the most urgent application of memory? The schedule varies, I suppose, depending on how completely that past has changed us.

"I think I was Mum's favourite, you know? I've always felt bad about that. Mum was hard on Beck in all sorts of ways. Because they were so alike, probably, although neither of them would ever have admitted it."

"While you're more like your dad, you mean?"

He nodded. "We're not that close either though, not any more. Probably because we both feel guilty."

"What about?"

"For being basically okay. Mum was—well, I can't really remember a time when she wasn't ill. And Beck was always shut off somewhere in her own world. I used to tell myself that was just the way she was, that she was happy that way. Away with the fairies, Dad used to say. I think now she was probably lonely. And scared. Of ending up like Mum. Or worse."

He turned to me abruptly, the planes of his face made strange by the orange lamplight through the window. "That spider story is exactly the kind of weirdness Mum would come up with. Mum was always terrified of getting ill—physically ill, I mean, of things going wrong with her body. She saw that as the ultimate humiliation, the ultimate loss of control. When she was bad she sometimes used to imagine that her hands were rotting away, or that her hair was falling out. It was awful. Especially at the end, when she began to waste away for real, just like she always said she would."

"Beck once said she thought the spider story was probably just Jennie's way of telling her about puberty."

Ben laughed. "She could have been right, you know. That's Mum all over."

Could *Jorōgumo* simply have been Beck's way of trying to resolve the conflicts and tensions between herself and her mother? The spider-mother, the black widow?

As a theory it seemed plausible enough. I lay there in the darkness, thinking about how Beck had weighed next to nothing when she died, and wondering if she had contracted the same disease that had killed her mother, after all. Gaby had told me the weight loss was normal, that people with the strain of Alzheimer's Beck had eventually stopped eating almost entirely.

"It's the body's way of letting go," she had said.

Like my theory about the jorōgumo, it sounded plausible enough.

But what if Jennie's fears for her daughter were grounded in fact? A hereditary disease, passed down through the female line.

When spiders die, their bodies shrivel away to nothing, too, I thought. Whenever you find a dead spider it looks like a little ball of unravelled string.

Desiccated.

Curled on her side like a child, or a very old lady.

Ben's breathing evened out and then deepened, snores catching at his throat like the dreams of cats. I began a desultory chain of thought in which I wondered if shagging him had been a good idea after all. Sod it, I thought, too late now. I fell asleep myself soon after.

The last time I spoke to Beck on the phone, she was already spiralling downhill into what would become the final phase of her illness, although even at that stage it was still difficult to tell what was sickness and what was just Beck.

She started talking to me in what sounded like the beginning of a sentence, as if returning to a conversation we'd just broken off from, even though it had been at least a week since we'd last spoken.

"You remember Mita, Issie—Mita Bomberg? You will ask her about it, won't you? I sent her the drawings."

I had a feeling Mita Bomberg was a niece or cousin or something of Marco's, although why Beck was so keen for me to contact her I had no idea. I said yes anyway, of course I would, Beck shouldn't worry.

"It's happening," Beck said then, very quietly. Her voice seemed to have shrunk—it was like listening to a child speaking, the child-Beck I had never known but who had always been there, underneath, all along. "I'm not afraid though, not any more, because it means I'll be free."

What do you say in response to something like that? I found I couldn't speak. I thought it was death she was talking about, which she was in a way, but not entirely, not really.

When someone falls ill, and there is no hope of recovery, a gulf opens up. They are on one side, you are on the other, and there is no closing it. You don't want to close it. You would never admit this, and you don't have to, but all you can think, feel, intuit as you switch off the light at night is that you are alive, that you still have a chance to do all those things you meant to do and you mean to take it. The other person—the person you once loved as an equal—is already gone, or as good as. In a real and secret way, you have washed your hands of them.

If you walk along Hartland's Fore Street and into Springfield you'll come to a gate, and then to a path that will take you all the way down to the cliff edge if you follow it far enough. Long before you reach the sea you'll find yourself in a narrow valley, bursting with flowers and foliage and so secluded you will find it hard to believe you're standing less than fifteen minutes' walk from the village centre.

When I first went there with Beck, it was summer, a day of scorching yellow heat and that blissful species of lassitude you remember from childhood. The valley thrummed with insects, anaesthetised with the scents of clover and wild garlic. We stood together in the waist-high grass, enchanted, and I caught a glimpse of what it was that had drawn Beck to such an isolated outpost in the first place. The idea of a nature cure—a concept I would not normally have dwelled upon for long enough even to despise it—began seeping into my brain like pot smoke.

"And you say the rents are really cheap here?" I heard myself saying. A cottage, I thought. Whitewashed walls and window box geraniums. Basic provisions from the crummy yet nonetheless charming village store. Radio 4 left on all day long and no need to lock the door when you went to the post office.

Wasn't it at least worth considering? It was only once I was back in London that I began admonishing myself for letting my desire to "show Eddie" threaten to overrule my logic. Radical gestures are all very well, but had I forgotten how absurdly long the journey time was, how slow the broadband speed. Now, sneaking out of Beck's cottage in the chill of a March morning, it was easy to feel smugly self-satisfied, that I had finally dismissed the idea of marooning myself in Hartland as the madness it was.

It was just after six, not quite light. Ben was still sleeping—one of my main reasons for leaving the house was to give him the chance to wake up and get out of my room before I returned. Not that I regretted what had happened—I was past that by then—but I had no intention of repeating the incident and I wanted things back to what passed for normal as soon as possible. There was no one about, I mean no one, and as I made my way along the darkened street I felt spooked by my solitude and on a high at the same time. I couldn't remember ever feeling so alone. Not lonely, but by myself.

The entrance to the path was pitch black, tunnel black, and as I stepped into its coagulated nothingness I remember thinking this is the moment in the horror film when you'd be thinking don't go down there, don't be such a *dick*, and then willing the character to do it anyway, because of course you wanted to know what was lurking in the woods and there would be no film otherwise.

Real life is usually more prosaic. I smelled damp earth, wet leaves, and as light crept into the sky the massed tree trunks and the peculiar, dipping shape of the valley they stood in began to take on the bleached, curiously flattened aspect of an over-exposed photograph. It was chilly out, but I barely registered it. I was too busy thinking about Beck, wondering if she had ever come down the path in the dark, if she had ever seen the wood willing itself into existence in the strange dawn light.

Do you ever believe you are dying, even as it happens?

I reached the valley floor, a whitish tube of light now snaking out behind me. The bushes directly ahead of me seemed to glow, exuding a soft, greyish luminescence, the same as the light in the sky only more intense. Then I saw that the glow was actually spiders' webs, an intricately woven blanket of them, glinting with dewdrops, like threads of tinsel.

The sight was wonderful, miraculous, but at the same time deeply unsettling. I felt a shudder pass through me, and the urge to run, that queasy, stomach-in-free-fall sensation you get when you think you're alone, then realise someone's been watching you all along.

I turned my head, looking back up the path. There was no one there. The bushes stirred and nodded in the breeze.

Beck's dead, I thought. That moment when you finally realise the truth of it, that someone you loved and who was part of you is gone forever. That they are out of this world. No further questions, nothing.

I thought of Doré's Arachne in her bent-backed agony. Was it better to live on as a monster, or vanish to nothing? The doctors had intimated that Beck would turn into a monster before she died: a creature that pissed and shat and vomited with no awareness of itself, a creature that would no longer remember it had a name. None of that had happened, though. On my way back up to the cottage I remembered how Beck had reacted to her diagnosis.

"That's rubbish," she said. "They're wrong." I imagined her shaking her head, then going back to rubbing paint into a canvas with her bare fingertips. She refused even to discuss it after that.

Ben was in the kitchen, making breakfast.

"I smell bacon," I said. "Yum."

I'd been gone two hours. Ben raised an eyebrow, then smiled. We were OK, it seemed, and if Ben felt any curiosity about where I had been he kept it well hidden. "Who's Mita Bomberg?" I asked, once he'd dished up.

"Marco's sister's sister-in-law," he said, just like that. "Why?"

"Just wondered. Beck mentioned her on the phone once."

"She's an academic. A historian." He paused. "I think she and Beck had a bit of a thing once."

"'Ask Mita', she said. Ask Mita what?"

"No idea."

Ask her if she had a thing with Beck the same way Beck had a thing with April Lessore, who turned up at the funeral, by the way, as if the day hadn't been difficult enough already. I didn't recall seeing Mita there, though I probably wouldn't have recognised her even if she were. Ask her if she'd been the cause of Beck's breakdown? Ask her if she gave any credence whatsoever to the notion that my best friend had turned into a spider?

"I went for a walk," I said. "Down the woods' path."

"You must have been freezing."

"I can't remember the last time I was outside at that time in the morning. Really outside, I mean, not just dashing for a train or something."

He looked up from his plate. "Beck and I used to sneak out all the time when we were kids. It drove Mum mad—she was worried about us being too tired to concentrate at school—

but that didn't stop us. We'd see the milk float driving around but that was all. We felt like we owned the world."

Once we'd established that the bulk of Beck's archive—and it's amazing what the use of a judiciously chosen word can do to bring a previously chaotic situation under control—would be stored at my place, the job of clearing the house became much easier. I told Ben that if he dealt with the domestic stuff—Beck's clothes, furniture and other personal effects—I would sort out the rest. Any completed artworks could be shipped direct to Beck's gallery for evaluation and cataloguing. The notebooks, sketchbooks and diaries would go to mine. I telephoned a removals company in Bideford to order packing crates and arrange transportation.

I asked Ben if he wanted to cough up for a professional house-clean once we'd finished. He seemed reluctant at first, then agreed. Beck's lease ran for another five months, but Ben had already decided not to sublet.

"At least that way you should get Beck's deposit back," I said. "Plus we'll be able to leave here as soon as the packing's finished. We can leave the keys with the estate agent."

Ben wanted shot of the place and who could blame him. As I moved carefully around Beck's studio, sorting papers into piles and stuffing rubbish into bin bags, I briefly entertained the idea of taking the place myself, just for the summer, just to see how I felt. I could catalogue Beck's archive properly, in situ, begin drawing up an outline for the monograph, maybe.

I pushed the thought away like the obstruction it was.

Gaby turned up mid-morning. I felt uncomfortable seeing her in the flesh. She seemed extraneous to requirements somehow, a character from a novel, her role in my life played out. I watched as she chained her bike to a lamp post and came up the path, looking with dismay on her ruddy cheeks and windblown hair and thinking how much we resent the people who happen to encounter us when we are vulnerable.

"I won't stop," she said. "I can see you're busy. But I wanted to pass on my condolences. And to give you this." She held something out—an envelope, a package? I grabbed it without thinking, just for something to hold. "She said you were to have it, that I should give it to you myself. I've not opened it," she said. "About three days before, this was."

A brown A4 envelope, fat with papers. "Will you stay for a cup of tea?" I asked. I didn't see how I couldn't.

She shook her head. "I'd best get on. But thank you."

"Thank *you*," I said. "For everything you've done, I mean."

We stared at each other. I felt spoiled and incapable and offensively inadequate. This woman had held my friend's hand as she lay dying.

We would not see one another again, Gaby and I, and I was glad.

Once she was gone I made a pot of tea for myself and returned to the studio. Ben was out, fetching provisions from Bideford. Bald March light streamed in through the skylight and spread in a thin film across the concrete floor. I put my mug down on the bench and opened the envelope, working my finger beneath the flap in an attempt not to tear it and then wondering why I was being so circumspect. It was just an envelope.

Inside were some letters, sent from Germany and addressed in a handwriting I didn't recognise but guessed—correctly— must be Mita Bomberg's. A cellophane folder, containing four drawings. A diary from the year 1980, our first year at college. A sheet of paper folded in half, my name written on the flap in shaky capitals.

The letter wasn't dated, but from the state of Beck's writing I estimated that it had been written sometime in the past three months.

Isobel—
It is almost time but I don't mind now, I want this. I
am no longer in your world and I thought that would be
terrifying but it's not, it's easy.
I do remember you.

She had signed the note with a spidery "X": a kiss, or an acknowledgement that her name was no longer important? In the diary I read:

Went for coffee with Isobel Hampton. She's reading Art History, like me, but unlike most of the others she actually seems interested in art. She has some wonderful books. She has a birthmark on her face, shaped like a baby's hand, like a map-mark for sanity. I long to draw her but don't dare ask. She swears a lot. She makes me feel less of a freak.

The second week of October, that was, and less than a week before our night-time conversation about Robby and Jennie and Beck's unlikely heritage. Spider-silk in the womb, for goodness' sake. I felt my throat fill up with tears. How different things might have been, had I supported Beck's decision to drop out of uni.

The row we had. It was still painful to think of, even now she was dead.

I told her she was a loser, that she'd never make it as an artist, that she was sabotaging her future.

How would I choose to explain in the official account? Come clean, admit that I was jealous of her talent? Sounds good, doesn't it? Dramatic *and* plausible.

I don't think it's the truth though, or not the whole truth. I think I was scared she would meet someone else, someone she would love more than me. And she did, didn't she? She met April.

But maybe April was my fault, all along.

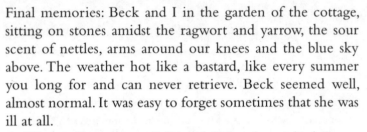

That time she called me from Berlin, when she went to find Marco. She was drunk and I was angry. I told her to pull herself together, that Marco was a dick anyway, that she was well rid of him. Then I put down the phone.

Final memories: Beck and I in the garden of the cottage, sitting on stones amidst the ragwort and yarrow, the sour scent of nettles, arms around our knees and the blue sky above. The weather hot like a bastard, like every summer you long for and can never retrieve. Beck seemed well, almost normal. It was easy to forget sometimes that she was ill at all.

"Sit as still as you can," she said. "There's one, look."

She raised one finger, very slowly, to indicate the fat brown garden spider that had just that moment emerged from under a leaf. It was spinning itself a support rope, letting itself gently down from the gabled upright of a colossal stand of what I thought was cow parsley, only Beck said it was garden chervil, not cow parsley, that cow parsley was mostly over by the end of June.

"You never used to know stuff like that," I said.

"How do you know I didn't?" she said absently. "Look at her go."

The spider ratcheted back and forth, staking out its mainframe. I found the spectacle fascinating and vaguely repulsive.

I gazed up into the sky, shading my eyes against the glare.

What the fuck am I doing here? I thought. Beck and her bloody spiders. I could be back in town having a beer with someone normal.

4. *Saint Joan of Arc,* 2012, 2'x2', oil on canvas. Following
the breakdown of her marriage in 2009, Hathaway
moved from her long-term residence in Fulham to
the isolated village of Hartland, on the North Devon
coast. Responding to her new surroundings, Hathaway
became increasingly preoccupied with the natural world,
choosing as her subject matter the colony of orb-weaving
spiders that flourished in the overgrown back garden of
her rented cottage. Hathaway's observations ran to many
hundreds of pencil studies and pen-and-ink drawings, as
well as the fifteen major canvases known as the diadem
series and first shown in a posthumous exhibition at the
Artemis Gallery in Chelsea earlier this year. Spiders have
very poor eyesight, and experience the world primarily
through touch and through sound vibrations. *Saint Joan of
Arc* is an attempt to convey the textures and sounds of the
natural world as they might be experienced by a spider.
Pictorial elements such as grass stems, tree bark, drystone
walls, spores and seeds have been deconstructed, redacted
to an abstract, highly textured surface from out of which
individual features appear to alternately dissolve and
coalesce as we focus our attention upon them.

Mita's letters were chaotic and rambling, not what you'd
have expected from a scholar of her standing—but then,
we're all different when we're off-duty. There were pages of
reminiscences of their time in Berlin—a period I knew little
about, given that Beck and I had not been in contact at the
time. Mita kept mentioning a studio Beck had rented while
she was living there. It had become vacant again, apparently,
and there was an intimation—for the space of two or three
letters, anyway—that Beck might move back out there. The
move never transpired though, and without Beck's own

letters to refer to it was impossible to work out why.

If I was serious about writing Beck's biography I would have to get in touch with Mita at some point, find out whether she still had the letters and if she would grant me access to them. Not a task I relished, I have to say, especially as the parts of the correspondence I did have suggested that Mita might be as difficult to deal with as Beck. It wasn't just the letters that made me think that, though they were odd enough. What really made my heart sink were the photocopied newspaper clippings that often accompanied them. One related to a medical negligence case in Annecy in south-east France, in which a woman's family were prosecuting her doctors for failing to diagnose what was later recorded as a rare form of endometriosis. The woman's reproductive organs and stomach lining had been colonised by fibrous growths of such unusual tenacity that numerous operations failed to eradicate them. The woman later died from complications following a radical hysterectomy.

Another news clipping was from an American paper, and recounted the story of a college lecturer who contracted a mysterious condition that caused the skin of her arms, legs and lower abdomen to sprout dense masses of ultra-fine, silky hairs. A third piece related to a woman who had lived in Cumbria in the 1660s. Allergic to light and with very little spoken language, the "spider woman of Whitehaven" spent the majority of her life sequestered in a tiny back room, wrapped in numerous shawls to disguise the coarse black hair that, it was rumoured, covered the whole of her body. She made her living from casting fortunes, a gift that ensured her reputation and standing among the townspeople until the bubonic plague swept through the region, at which point the tide of opinion turned against her and she began to suffer persecution for being a witch.

The woman left Whitehaven in 1670. According to some

reports she left town of her own accord, although there was one notable account that stated she had been pursued and captured by a band of local vigilantes and stoned to death.

How ghastly, I thought. I could not think what had possessed Mita, filling Beck's head with stuff like that. She was suggestible enough as it was. At the bottom of the third clipping, the one about the so-called spider woman of Whitehaven, Mita had underlined and circled the woman's surname, which was Chilcot. I puzzled over this for a long time, before remembering that Chilcot had been Jennie Hathaway's maiden name.

I had to laugh. There are people—people like Mita Bomberg, apparently—who will take a simple coincidence and dress it up as a grand conspiracy in the space of a heartbeat, but I have never been one of them.

Ben left Hartland on the Friday afternoon. The house clearance people called round in the morning to give us a price for taking Beck's furniture and then I helped Ben pack some crates with books and knick-knacks that he wanted to drop off at a charity shop on his way home.

I'd told him I planned to stay on for a bit. I'd reckoned on a fortnight at least and maybe more, but soon changed my mind. With Ben gone, the atmosphere of the cottage seemed to darken, becoming claustrophobic and faintly threatening. It was the memories, I reasoned, the sense of loss, all the usual platitudes.

Yes and no. I'm sure a part of what I felt was simple regret, that I had not made more effort, more time for her when she was alive. But as one day passed and then the next I found myself dwelling increasingly on the strangeness of it all: Beck's loneliness, there in that place, the terrible and pitiless nature of her final illness, the confusion that must have overcome her at the end.

The cottage, now that I was alone there, seemed drenched in these things, wrapped in bindings of fear and hopelessness so thick and dark I frequently found myself having to escape outside to avoid being spooked.

I've come to believe that being haunted is actually just belated understanding.

In the end I admitted defeat. I told myself the work of cataloguing Beck's archive would advance more quickly in London anyway, what with all my accustomed resources close to hand. I made arrangements to have the house cleaned, as Ben and I had planned, then spent a hectic two days packing up Beck's papers and wrapping the canvases in bubble wrap, ready for collection.

As for what I did immediately before leaving, what can I say? I believe the usual expression for such actions is moment of madness. I guess I'm not as rational as I thought I was.

There had been plenty of spiders before—when I was there with Beck, I mean. This time it took me ages to track down even one. I put it down to the weather, though I had no idea if that was right or not. Did spiders dislike the cold? I didn't know. The creature I finally found was one of the plump-bodied, brown ones with the striped legs that Beck had called St John spiders.

"Because of the cross on her back. See? She should be St Joan really."

Come along, Joanie, I thought, as I coaxed the thing into a matchbox. Time for a change of address. It entered reluctantly, scuttled around in confusion for a couple of seconds then hunched itself in a corner, its legs gathered around its body, a fence of upturned "V"s. The thing was miffed, clearly. I didn't blame it, to be honest.

I put the matchbox in my bag and tried to forget about it, though for the whole of the journey home I kept imagining tiny footfalls on the back of my neck. Once, when I went to the buffet car, I thought about leaving the matchbox on the counter in a fake act of absent-mindedness, then realised I would be just as freaked out by losing it as having it with me.

The moment I arrived home I released her in what I hoped would be a safe place: down the side of the garage, beneath the overhang. She dashed straight up the wall, legs unfolding and flashing like a nest of daggers, then disappeared into a crevice behind the guttering.

I felt better after that. Stupid, I know.

[This essay first appeared in the anthology *The Life and Magical Afterlife of Rebecca Hathaway, Artist*, which was published to coincide with the second anniversary of Hathaway's death following a fall at her home. In the interview that accompanied the essay, its author Isobel Hampton described the piece as an "imaginative memorial", and stressed that the events it chronicles should not be equated with lived reality, nor should the persons described be confused with the artist's surviving friends and relatives, or even with the artist herself. Isobel Hampton is an art historian and critic. She is currently at work on a full-length biographical study of Rebecca Hathaway, who was her close friend for more than three decades.]

SHELTERED IN PLACE
by Brian Keene

It didn't take the cops long to respond. When they arrived on the scene, smoke from both the guns and the bomb still hung thick in the air, curling up to the ventilation panels in the ceiling. The bomb hadn't been an explosive. It was just a smoke bomb, spewing confusion in an oily white cloud. Shots still echoed throughout the baggage claim area. People were crying and screaming. The smoke was overpowering. It burned my nose and throat, and made my eyes water, but I could barely hear the sounds over the ringing in my ears. You ever see that movie, *Saving Private Ryan*? Remember at the beginning, when the soldiers are trying to take Omaha Beach, and Tom Hanks is sitting there amidst the chaos, detached from it all, watching the carnage unfold, and his ears are ringing and everything is muted? That's exactly what I felt like.

The cops charged through the terminal, guns drawn, shouting at everybody to get down. I'd heard once on TV that there was a reason they did this during an active shooter incident. The theory was that a gunman would remain standing, while innocent civilians would immediately comply with the order. That seemed to be the case now. I certainly complied, dropping quickly to my knees, and then lying flat on the floor, almost on top of a dead businessman. I knew he was a businessman because of how he was dressed, and the expensive watch around his wrist—the face of which was now shattered—and the briefcase he still clutched in one hand. I knew he was dead because the back of his bald head was missing. I lay there on the floor, his blood still warm on the tiles beneath me, and stared into the wound. I was close enough to see his brains. To smell them. They looked like pinkish-white cottage cheese covered in bits of red jelly.

"Everybody get down! Down, down, down!"

The ringing in my ears faded. The screams and cries grew louder. I raised my head cautiously. Then, three new gunshots rang out. This time, it was one of the cops shooting. I turned my head to the right, and saw a man slam back into the wall. He slumped down, leaving a smear of blood, and then collapsed.

Someone whimpered behind me. "Was that the shooter? Did they get him?"

The police continued bellowing. From my vantage point, it was hard to tell if everyone in the baggage claim area had complied. I did my best to stay still and remain calm. I didn't want to be the next one to get shot. I lay there, staring into the back of the bald businessman's head, and suddenly I had to pee very badly. I wriggled, pressing my groin against the floor, trying to alleviate the pressure. The dead man's blood seeped through the fabric of my pants and shirt.

"Everyone just stay down," another officer ordered. "Shelter in place. No sudden movements. Don't stand up. If you are injured, just hang on. Help is on the way."

I wondered if the cops were local airport police or TSA or Homeland Security. Probably the former, judging by their uniforms. In hindsight, their response had been impressive. How long had it taken, between the time the first shot was fired and the moment they arrived? It had seemed like minutes, but in reality… maybe forty-five seconds? Maybe a minute, at most? How many more people would have been killed had they not gotten to the scene so quickly? Indeed, how many were dead? It was hard to say, given the smoke and the chaos.

The gunshots had faded now, and the screams had stopped. New sounds emerged. More crying, of course, but also prayers, and whispers, and one small child calling for "Mommy". I couldn't tell if the kid was a boy or a girl, and wasn't about to stand up and see. A lot of people were coughing; I guess because of the smoke. Someone else retched, followed by the unmistakable sound of vomiting. I heard English and Spanish, and what may have been Swiss French. Somebody muttered in a language I didn't recognize at all, other than it was Asian. I know that's not very politically correct, but again, I wasn't going to risk getting shot by a cop just to determine the nationality of a fellow airport commuter. Many people moaned in obvious pain. One person—it sounded like a woman—kept urging someone named John to "Breathe, just breathe."

I tilted my head carefully to the left and spotted another dead person. A young woman, dressed in pink yoga pants and a black hoodie. One foot was clad in a sandal. The other foot was bare. She'd been shot in the throat, and the ends of her long blonde hair, tied up in a ponytail, had turned strawberry-colored from the blood. Another man was sprawled next to her, unmoving, eyes staring sightlessly. One of his arms was thrown across her. I wondered if they knew each other. Then I wondered how he had died. He hadn't been shot. I didn't see any obvious wounds. Heart attack, maybe? Shock?

The baggage carousel still turned. The wheels and pulleys squeaked. Suitcases and duffel bags rotated past on the conveyor belt, stuck in a seemingly endless loop. I wondered why someone didn't turn it off.

"Did anyone see the shooter?"

The speaker was directly in front of me. I raised my

head just a bit, and saw a guy in a Hawaiian-print shirt. I remembered seeing him before, from across the baggage claim area. I wondered dimly how he'd ended up on this side of the carousel.

"I didn't see shit," somebody answered.

"I'll bet it was a fucking terrorist," Hawaiian shirt muttered. "Fucking Muzzies."

"I think it was that guy the police just shot," a woman volunteered.

"Nah," someone else piped up. "That guy wasn't a Muslim."

"Who says the shooter had to be Muslim?" The woman's tone had grown angry.

"Quiet down," a cop ordered. "Everyone just remain calm. Help is on the way."

I heard an electronic squawk and then a burst of static from one of the officers' radios. A dispatcher mumbled something, but she said it so quickly and her voice was distorted, and I couldn't tell what it was. A recorded announcement came over the airport loudspeakers, reminding us to keep our luggage with us at all times, and to not accept any strange packages from strangers, and to report any suspicious activity to airport security. Oddly enough, this caused some giggles from a few people in the crowd.

Cell phones began to ring and ding and beep. The first reports of the shooting were probably exploding across social media and the news outlets—going viral, they call it. Concerned loved ones were probably trying to contact friends and family. I imagined there were a lot of people parked outside of the airport, unable to get inside. Surely the authorities had put up a security cordon by now.

"Nobody move," a cop reminded us. His voice sounded shrill, like a guitar that's been strung too tight. "Just let them ring. We need to secure this area first."

"My husband has been shot," a woman yelled. "Won't you please help him?"

"Just hang in there, ma'am. We're doing all we can. We—"

"You're not doing shit," she shrieked. "He's over here dying!"

I heard people around me gasp. I raised my head and saw a young officer pointing his weapon. His arms trembled.

"Ma'am, get back down! Get down on the floor!"

"My husband—"

"*Get on the fucking floor, goddamn it!*"

Other people started telling her to get down. Others cursed the police. The woman began sobbing, but she must have complied, because the cop lowered his weapon again.

The businessman with the hole in his head started to vibrate. The floor rattled around him. It was his phone, set to mute. For one bizarre second, I had the urge to answer it. It buzzed for another twenty seconds or so and then went silent. The police radios squawked again. I still couldn't make out what was being said.

It occurred to me that my fear had subsided. The nervous ball of tension that had been sitting in my stomach like a bag of cement since this whole thing began was gone. Just dissipated. These mass shootings—they seem to happen all the time now. Once a month, sometimes more than that, you see the breaking news. Another mass shooting. Schools, train stations, college campuses, movie theaters, nightclubs… airports. I remember the first time I heard the term "shelter in place". It was after the Boston marathon bombing, when the cops basically imposed martial law and went door to door, searching for the bombers. The media said residents were being told to shelter in place.

I used to always wonder what the people in those situations were going through. What were they thinking? How did they feel? Now, I knew. I didn't feel anything.

I still had to pee, though.

The pool of blood I was lying in began to cool. It stuck to my palms and in between my fingers like maple syrup. Amazingly, the dead businessman was still leaking. Blood trickled steadily from that hole in his head, like a spigot that hadn't been turned off all the way. I guess I should have been repulsed by it, but I wasn't. It was sort of fascinating really.

Paramedics arrived on the scene. The cops huddled with them for a moment, and then turned to us. All of them still had their weapons drawn and at the ready.

"Okay, people, listen up. We're going to clear this room. One by one, you're going to be frisked, stand up, and then go through these doors over here. You will follow all orders and keep your hands over your head at all times."

I glanced at where he was pointing. The sun shone brightly through the glass. It looked like a nice day outside.

"Don't stand or move until we tell you to. If everyone complies, this will be over a lot quicker. We know you're scared. Some of you are injured. But we can't take any chances until we've confirmed that none of you are the shooter."

He didn't ask us if we understood, but several people murmured their consent and understanding. Several more moaned in pain, growing frantic at the sight of the paramedics—so close, and yet still so far.

The cops fanned out in pairs, going through the crowd. One by one, they frisked us where we lay. One of them did the deed while the other kept a gun pointed at us. When they were satisfied that we weren't the shooter, they had us stand. The people that couldn't stand were helped to their feet. Then they pointed us toward the door, where more law enforcement officers were waiting. Each of us had to leave the baggage claim area with our hands held high over our head, as ordered.

Soon enough, it was my turn. I lay still while the officer

patted me down. He was close enough to me that I could feel the heat wafting off him, and smell his cologne. His partner kept her weapon trained on me. That urge to pee grew almost unbearable. Then, they were done. They told me to stand, put my hands over my head, and walk out the doors to where the other officers were waiting. That's what I did.

They never noticed my pistol, shoved underneath the still bleeding corpse of the bald businessman.

Nor did they notice the burn the smoke bomb left on my finger when I set it off.

I made it home, and just finished typing this up. I don't know how long it will take, but I suppose they'll figure it out soon enough. They'll learn that I was the shooter. Maybe they'll find security camera footage of me, or maybe someone with a cell phone snapped a picture of me when I opened fire, before the smoke obscured everything. Or maybe they'll find my fingerprints on the handgun.

I'm sitting here, trying to decide what to do next.

Go out in the streets and pick up where I left off.

Or I can wait for them to come to me, while I sit here, sheltered in place.

THE FOLD IN THE HEART
by Chaz Brenchley

"I don't understand," she said, gazing discontentedly around the churchyard, "why we always want to hold on to everything, regardless. We don't even let our dead go, for God's sake."

I said nothing. I who had spent a long year trying to hold on to the living, and failing badly. I had an urn full of ashes in my wardrobe, and no idea, none, what to do with them; only that I couldn't let them go.

Rowan was—well, sometimes I called her my favourite niece, sometimes my god-daughter. Neither was actually true, but she was the first child of old friends and she mattered to me more than blood, far more than belief.

She said, "I want a woodland burial, a woven wicker coffin, no marker. Just stick a tree on top of me and forget which one it was."

"I could bury you at sea," I said cheerfully. "Sewn into a hammock, with cannonballs at your feet to hold you down."

"Hey. Can you actually do that?"

"Sure. I'd need a licence, and I was joking about the hammock; you have to have a coffin weighted with steel and concrete, but it's doable if you want it."

She thought about it as we clambered over the stile into the ninety-acre field; then she shook her head. "Nah. I never did like boats that much. Or fish. Sorry, I know I'm a disappointment."

"You are that. Trees it is, then. I can't promise to forget where we plant you, but I'll make sure your parents don't put in a rowan."

"That would be tacky," she agreed. "Something to grow old and bent and hoary, please. No good for building boats. I don't want you cutting me down for timber."

"Pity. You'd make excellent planking: long and straight and lissom."

I stuck my elbow out, as I used to do. Obligingly, she slipped her arm through mine as we plodged through heavy wet turf in pat-proof wellies. There was no beaten path between the stile and the sea cliff. This was cow pasture; we took a different route every time, veering around new pats and high-stepping over old ones. Even in wellingtons. Even so, there was a midpoint, a waymarker that was hard to avoid. From the stile to the sheepfold, from the fold to the sea; it was native, inherent, absolute. A given.

When she was little, the fold meant a break in our journey, a necessary pause while she clambered over drystone walls and played King of the Castle on top of it, hide-and-seek within it, while we made up stories about wizards snared in lonely towers and the brave princesses who came to rescue them. In later years she'd join local kids and visitors in rowdy games of tag or kiss chase, where the fold was always home, safe ground.

Now that she was grown, now that I was far beyond rescuing and she wouldn't dream of running from a kiss, she laid a hand on the upper coursework and said, "Someone's been working on this." Almost accusatory, as though it should properly have been left in the state of half-collapse that she remembered.

A sheepfold in a cow pasture has no obvious purpose, and other enemies than time; but even so. "People do," I said mildly. "Every now and then a lad gets interested, wants to know how to wall. There's always a farmer willing to teach him. This is where they learn. Cows are always rubbing their arses on it, knocking stones off. Sometimes they bring down a whole corner, over time. Well, you know; you've seen it at its worst. Then it's a job of work to put it back up again. But it does get done." There hadn't been sheep on this land for a hundred years or more, but the fold was here yet, blunt grey walls in a green field.

She grunted, a little sceptical, and leaned her own trim arse against a hip-high wall as if tempted to give it a nudge, see if she could knock off a coping stone.

Her eyes on the horizon, she said, "Tell me about Bruce."

"Tell you what about Bruce? You knew him all your life."

She said, "Yeah, but I was a kid and he was an old man, and—well, you know. Not at all grandfatherly. He really didn't want me in the yard, where I had to be watched all the time because of the tools, and—"

"And that took my eye off him and my mind off the work, and he didn't like either of those, no. And he didn't want you in the cottage either, because you were too loud and again, my eye off him. It wasn't you as such, just kids in general. Just anyone in general; he didn't much like me having friends around either."

"Right. I didn't really get that when I was little, but later I did. When I was a teen, I mean, and he still didn't want me there."

"And you still came, so bless you for that."

She came to his funeral too, by herself, which might almost have been her first truly adult act; and I might have seized the moment now to say so, except that she pre-empted me. "It was toxic, though, wasn't it? He was just controlling your life, and I don't see how you could let him do that."

Of course she didn't. She was twenty, and free in ways

that I had never been; his being dead didn't change a thing. I said, "Toxic maybe—but people say that about tomatoes and potatoes, just because they're the same family as nightshade. Poison is as poison does; whole civilisations have been built on potatoes. Bruce was never easy, but he took a feral kid at risk of growing into pond scum, and he made something decent out of me. By his lights, and my own." Which in fairness were entirely of his making, indistinguishable. He'd trained me in more than joinery and sailcraft.

"Oh, you're better than decent. You are. But even so. You shouldn't ever have let him dominate you that way."

"Sweetheart, I'm not even going to pretend I had a choice. That's how dominance works; you don't elect it, you don't get to vote it down. And I remain grateful. Best thing that ever happened to me."

"The only thing that ever happened to you, more like. You lived the life he chose, and you still do. His boatyard, his business. His cottage."

"Mine, now. He took over my life, sure—when it wasn't worth anything, except to him. He gave it value. He gave me everything; which is fair trade, it seems to me, for everything he took."

She sniffed. "I still think he groomed you."

"Of course he did. I was fifteen when he took me in. Nothing but clay, ready to be made into whatever he wanted. He was forty." I could shudder yet, just at the memory of the strength in his hands, in his will. "Twenty-five years, love, it's a lethal distance. I never stood a chance."

"That's the distance between you and Josh," she said, eyeing me a little sideways.

"It is—and between you and me, too. But you were never clay. We took care of that. By the time you were fifteen you were sharpened steel. As for Josh, well. I didn't know him at fifteen. He came to me fully formed." All of twenty, like herself, which was why she'd swallow the lie, because she believed it wholeheartedly of herself.

She nodded and stood up, ready to go on. Holding her hand out, not ready to go on without me.

"Not yet," I said, smiling. Leaning on the wall of the fold. "Dusk is coming. Things are about to get noisy."

She blinked, looking up a little wildly into the empty sky. "Oh—are they still here?"

"Not all of them; but Easter's early this year, and they haven't all gone. Still enough left to make a noise."

"Oh, lovely…"

She perched again beside me and we watched the sky, the sea, the boats, and the horizon until they came.

From October through April, the starlings gather in great roosts along the cliffs and inland, on church roofs and pub window ledges, on every tree that offers. In daylight they scatter, to forage in smaller flocks all across the parish and further yet. As the sun sets they all converge, to wheel and dance and display in extravagant, astonishing flights that write patterns in the air. *Murmuration* was the word that Bruce had taught me. *The noisy sky*, Rowan had called it once when she was little. That worked for us: noise in three dimensions, figured by forces far beyond the random. White noise loosed into the world, given shape and substance and a name.

We watched it happen, we saw the sky fold itself in sheets and curves and angles, in blasts of sound and shadow that gave momentary solidity to the wind, as though they outlined all its fluid edges.

There's a native human urge to see patterns in what's random, to give significance to what is incidental. We have a word for it, even. We see shapes in clouds and call it pareidolia, as though we understand it. As though there were anything to understand.

If I saw faces, one face, making itself again and again and

again—well, nobody could blame me. Besides, I didn't need to say what I was seeing, so long as I didn't ask her.

At last the light began to fail and the birds spread themselves more thinly, diving this way and that, tearing themselves out of all coherence. We stirred, gathered each other silently and trudged on arm in arm again, and here came the cliff edge.

"Careful now," I said, pulling free and guiding her behind me. "The council's done nothing to make this path any safer, and the cliff face is still crumbling."

"Of course it is. It's not going to stop, just because a parish council finds it inconvenient. Or expensive. I'll step where you step." She put both hands on my shoulders, to be sure. When she was small we'd go down just like this, except the other way around: I'd set her in front and steer her slender frame, keep fast hold and think how fragile she was, and how robust. She could outlive any boat that left my yard, and I knew exactly how well those were put together.

Down and down, winding back and forth until we came to where the path splays out onto the beach. It is, in honesty, not much of a beach. More rock pool than sand, and more simple rock than either one; at high tide there's a bare margin between sea and cliff, at spring tides none at all. Tourists head to the other side of the bay, to the wide sprawling spaces and the cafés and the tat. Ramblers following the coast find their way down sometimes, if they're serious, but mostly not.

Which suited me, because at the end of the beach, in that marginal questionable territory where the river runs into the sea, just on the point, there was my yard. Formal access came from the other direction, along the riverbank. Approach from this side and all you saw was a wall of timber and corrugated iron, reaching from cliff to water. In fact, there was a gate, but you might not spot it at first: like the whole stretch of wall, it was compounded of wood and iron, painted with pitch to protect against the actions of storm and sea. Black on black, salt-stained and discreet.

There was no more an established path down here than there was in the ninety-acre; what the cows achieved above, surf and tide worked to match below. Pools and puddles shifted, new weed was laid down while old was washed away. Even I stepped somewhat differently from sand to rock to sand again, every time I crossed the strand. Rowan hopped and cursed and giggled, slipped and shrieked and drew her foot up *sans* boot, leaving it stuck in a crevice. Batted me away when I went to the rescue, then grabbed for me again; couldn't decide whether to cling to my side or hold my hand more distantly or spurn me altogether.

"Piggyback?" I offered neutrally.

"Uh, yes. Please…"

First I rescued her waterlogged boot while she balanced stork-like on one leg, then I bent my back so that she could climb aboard. With her legs jutting forward at waist-height, I used her feet as a battering ram to knock the gate ajar, and carried her through like a queen.

We built our boats from wood, with handheld tools. Nevertheless, noise was no stranger to the boatyard, echoing off the cliff and out across the water. Nevertheless, the racket that evening was exceptional. One boy, one mallet and a heavy copper sheet; he'd laid an old folded tarpaulin between sheet and concrete, and even so. Sixteen square feet of copper will sing when it's beaten.

So also will a boy sing, when he's thumping something in rhythm. At least until he looks up, to see that he's no longer alone.

The Japanese are a quiet folk, by and large, with a yen for quiet art, low-cal, static. A solitary flower in a *wabi-sabi* vase, three characters in slow ink with a swift brush, a garden of raked gravel. A single square of paper folded whole—uncut, untorn—into a formal stylised figure: a crane, a unicorn, a frog. A boat.

There was nothing Japanese about Josh, and nothing quiet. Rather it was a restless energy that had led him to origami, simply to give him something to do with his hands. All through our first interview—in the pub, which doubled as my office—his swift neat fingers had transformed sheets of coloured paper into a little line of figures: Darth Vader and R2-D2, two copulating unicorns, a cat in a box. Classic technique married to pop culture in a crisp and reckless style as inappropriate as it was charming. Mix that with tools, materials, and the space to scale up; the result had proved robust. Noisy. Origami unleashed.

The Boat of Going Nowhere was a yacht flying a jib and a mainsail, folded from four-by-four copper rather than paper. It had cost me one sheet already as proof-of-concept, a practice piece to learn how to fold and crease metal sharply; now he was working on the thing itself. Technically in his spare time, outside working hours—but my young apprentice shared not only my yard and my home, but also my casual approach to timekeeping. Sometimes we'd be up half the night, working under arc lights until the task was done; some days we'd start at noon or quit at three or never reach the yard at all. Just now I couldn't have turned his mind away from *The Boat of Going Nowhere* if I'd tried.

Rowan was unsure how to feel about Josh, the idea of him or the boy himself. In other circumstances I could have been amused by her wary detachment, her inability to figure out which of us was the more vulnerable, who was exploiting whom. She saw me replicating what Bruce had done—for me, with me, to me—and so forging one more link in a chain I might have broken. She could disapprove of that quite thoroughly. At the same time she could thoroughly distrust the motives of a young man latching onto an older one in his grief, at his time of least resistance. She loved me, was protective of me, knew what was best for me far better— of course!—than I did; and that best did not include a boy less than half my age; her age.

Now she was here, face-to-face with the reality of him, in the cottage and in the yard. Angular beauty and heedless charm, the relentless driving energy and the sudden slamming walls; she might have been his next conquest, or he hers, if it wasn't that he occupied that unexpected, unnegotiated space, the bed that Bruce built.

She was quite bewildered about what to feel. And I hated to see her in such a muddle, so confused where she ought to have felt most comfortable; and I could think of no resolution except to do as Bruce had done, live with the boy for the rest of my life and see if that was some kind of reassurance to her.

Just now, I set her down on an upturned cable drum and handed her lost boot back to her with a courtly bow. Knowing, as she knew, that Josh was watching, mallet poised, work suspended.

"Hey, Cinders," he called. "Aren't you supposed to leave the slipper and run away?"

"Yeah, well. I can't get anything right. He's not even my Prince Charming." Slight emphasis on the *my*; bless her, she was really trying. She might disapprove of both of us, but she'd do her best not to let it show. At least to him.

Freshly shod, she walked over to view his progress and admire the crispness of his creases. "But will it float, when it's finished? We learned how to fold boats at school one time, but they were different, more like barges. Those floated. And you could load them up with cargo, beads and stuff. Until you overloaded them, and they sank."

"I guess this would float," he said. "You can make boats out of concrete, so copper ought to work. I think she'd turn turtle, though, first thing. The sails make her top-lofty, see, and there's not enough keel to counter that. Unless you load the hull with ballast, but then I guess she'd sink anyway."

"Just as well it won't be going to sea, then. Or going anywhere."

"Aye that."

He left his model lying on its tarp, rose and stretched—slowly, fastidiously, like a roused cat reaching back into itself—and smiled across the yard at me. All physicality, all purpose: wickedly deliberate. Rubbing her nose in it, but that was incidental. If he knew how she was feeling, he didn't let it trouble him. Or stop him.

Oh dear God, but he reminded me of me, so much. Sometimes too much. A young man aware of his own power and reckless with it, heedless with it, willing to give it away. Willing to give it all away, in exchange for—what? A life, a companion, a craft, a home. Everything I had from Bruce, I was handing on wholesale, the complete package. Unless that whole package existed separate from ourselves, and we merely inhabited the roles for a while, each in turn. It could feel that way sometimes, that we were groomed by some force outside ourselves, shaped to fit and held in place by a nameless inevitability. I had been him; he would be me. We would both of us be Bruce in the end, ashes in an urn. Lessons learned; lessons passed on. Someone else's duty.

Something stirred in the sky. At first I thought it was one more late flight of starlings, turning in unison towards a cliff-side roost, their wings catching some fugitive final glimpse of light from the sunken sun. The other two hadn't noticed, intent as they were on building some kind of awkward *detente* on sand sodden with resentment and distrust. I had the words in my throat before I recognised what I was seeing; the words were out before I could swallow them down. "Hey, look, look up—"

They turned, lifting their heads just at the moment when I would have called them back, when I would have said, *No, don't look, don't see that…*

In the dark of the sky was his face again, impossibly, irresistibly. No matter if it was only scudding cloud lit from beneath, each of us saw the same thing. Pareidolia. And each of us knew whose face that was. Two of us had known the man himself; Josh knew him only from photographs, but that was enough to put a bewildered certainty into his voice.

"That was, that was…" It was a sentence that couldn't end, certainty notwithstanding; so he ducked it. "Was that awesome, or what? The way that looked like Bruce?"

Josh was at my elbow, though I hadn't seen him come; and Rowan was just as sudden on my other side, taking my arm and clinging tight with no hint of adult irony. "It did," she said. "Didn't it?"

It did; and no, it was not awesome. At least, not in the way Josh meant it. A portrait like a sidelong glance, painted with twilight and cloud and suggestion—but not randomly, and not in our heads. If Josh was sure, who'd never met the man; if Rowan was sure, who'd known him and disliked him, how much more sure was I, who had known him and loved him and lived with him for thirty years? All three of us stared up and saw clouds shredded by the wind, saw the first pale stars in the looming gloom, saw no hint of any face at all, and even so.

"Come on, kids. You know he never took his eye off me. Why should death make any difference?"

Humour struck a jarringly false note, but what could I do? Give one last lingering, anxious glance upward, then grip each of them by the shoulder and turn them bodily. Sometimes the inexplicable is too great for challenge, for question, for curiosity. You have to just stand under the reality of what's numinous, and then walk away.

It's hard to turn your back on the sky, but we could at least set the sea behind us. And a bare dozen paces ahead lay the workshop, with a light already burning and the side door set ajar.

Far more than the cottage, this was home and shelter to me, since I had been that feral teenage boy. I used to sleep down here more often than not, curled in a nest of blankets, my dreams scented with wood shavings and diesel. I would wake to brew coffee on the paraffin stove and sharpen yesterday's tools on the oilstone and call greetings across the water to friends on the day-boats as they chugged out in pursuit of shoaling mackerel or pilchard. All with one eye on the cliff path, waiting for the day's first sight of Bruce, a distant potent figure heading down.

There was electricity in the building now; a new floor beneath a new roof and proper plumbing; a real bed for Josh or me or both of us together, those nights we never made it home. Even so, it was still essentially the same place, imbued with the same long history. Even the paraffin smell still lingered. Perhaps that was only in my mind, like fugitive glimpses of that same distant figure with that same familiar stride. I could almost find a comfort in those moments, believing that he still kept watch over me. Especially when I turned my head and looked more closely and of course he wasn't there. He was still dead, and I was still dealing with it. What better comfort could he give me than these occasional reminders that I really could get by without him?

No comfort now. Here I was moving beyond mourning and with my own apprentice, this sudden shift, a turning away that could seem quite like abandonment; and here was Rowan too, ever a thorn, a trouble, a wall between us where nothing should ever have come; and now his face was in the sky, and no comfort meant. Something else, something more, some expression of fury or claim of possession and death apparently not a factor.

But here we were, all three of us under my roof—mine now, mine!—and cut off from the sky's glare, his glare. The workshop had no view out to the slipway and the sea; that wall was all door. The window looked out to the river and the road.

Just as I steered them both inside, Josh glanced back and yiked, ducking free of my grip and slithering outside again. I half-turned to follow and felt myself seized by indecision, there in the doorway with her on one side and him the other. Chase or stay, him or her? It wasn't possible—and then thank God it wasn't necessary, because Josh was no sooner gone than he was coming back.

With *The Boat of Going Nowhere* snatched up from the concrete apron, tucked securely under his arm.

"In case it means a storm, that sky," he said, laughing, shrugging. "I'm not leaving her out there for some stupid flood tide to take away."

People think that way. We all do. It's what makes me a blue water sailor, why I want a hundred miles between myself and any land when weather's on the way: because danger lies in that liminal space where the ocean meets the shore. It comes from the deep and hits the land and God help you if you lie between the hammer and the anvil. It's why we stand and look outward, why we have lighthouses and foghorns, barriers and sea walls and defences.

Sometimes we should look the other way. Inland, where everything is fixed, reliable, coherent; where structures have weight and certainty, where the variable moon harbours no influence, where wind and rain together must work hard to achieve a little local damage. Where it's all too easy to forget how everything from peak to valley bottom is designed to channel trouble to the sea.

Water finds its own level, they say. That would be here, where the rushing river meets the rising tide.

Perhaps there was a natural dam high up on the moor somewhere: a fallen tree, accumulated blockage, with no one to notice. Perhaps there was a freak of weather, rain beyond measure just where a lake could build and build. Or perhaps water is somehow an expression of malevolence, or of will, or of endurance. Perhaps Bruce could just make water happen. All at once, in flood.

It started as a rumour, a distant rumbling, something ripping deep in the fabric of the world. The kids looked to me for reassurance, enlightenment, anything. I had nothing to offer except a mirror for their blank questioning stares. I shook my head at them, and turned to the window.

It was dark out there, but not dark enough. I could see what was coming all too well. The village upstream gave me a horizon of light, a beacon that drew us nightly to pub, to cottage, to dinner, to bed. This night I saw half those lights go out, almost all at once. Those that survived on higher ground served only to frame that darkness. Everything happens at the margins; at that lit edge there was a churning chaos, a moving roiling wall in silhouette, sound made solid, that growing growling roar...

"Get out," I said. "Out now. Not that way," as Rowan turned hesitantly towards the door we'd come in by. That way lay my truck, the gateway, the road and the village and the world; but half the village was gone, heading our way in shattered pieces. It was breaking the road to ruin as it came.

"The river's in flood," I said, as mild a way as I could find to say, *It's over, that world you knew; death is coming, and it's meant for us.* "We'll go along the beach and up the cliff. Keep together and we'll stay safe." Quick as I was to herd them out, I was almost too slow. Floods should lose their power as their reach broadens, as a narrow valley riverbed opens to the sea—but this one met a wind and tide that should never have come together, that neither clock nor calendar was ready for. We were a week past springs and three hours before the full, but even so: here was the tide, too high and too soon, racing up the slipway as I heaved open the workshop door. And the wind that battered me, that tried to force me all the way back inside, was a storm wind out of season and unforecast, implausible, as close to impossible as weather ever had been.

The wind held up that rushing wall of river; the tide thrust underneath and lifted it higher yet, the water and the rubble that it swept along, half the village in its seize. I stood on the slipway and saw it hurtling towards my gate, my truck, my workshop—towards *us*, head-high and lethal with rocks and beams and filth and sheer force.

Sheer force of will, but I didn't want to think about that.

I snatched for Rowan's hand and Josh's too, where they stood mesmerised and struggling to stand in the blast. I tugged each, and they each came with me grimly, step by step. It was a hard slog just to reach the side-gate, even with the impetus of what was following, that brute blunt fear to drive us on.

The gate still stood open. The wind was slamming it back against its hinges, slam and slam again; something in me wanted to stop and pull it shut, give it a chance of surviving the night.

But nothing here would survive the flood when it hit, and I had no free hand in any case. My true interest lay in their survival, the two youngsters who clung and hauled alongside me as we made a difficult panicked passage over the rocks of the beach with tidewater swirling about our feet, and behind us the dreadful sounds of destruction as the flood took my gateway, my truck, and my workshop in strict order.

A sudden wave took us from behind, soaking us waist-high and floating Rowan off her feet for a moment. After that she clung closer. I ploughed on doggedly, letting Josh foray forwards while I trod more or less in his footsteps, making myself the anchor of our trio. That wave must have been the flood's last gasp. But we still had wind and tide to face, not out of the water yet.

And something more.

"Single file," I yelled above the wind's howl as we reached the foot of the cliff path, "hand in hand, slow and careful. Keep tight against the rock. Josh, you first." I was in the middle, keeping a grip on them both. The path might give way before us or behind us, or underneath all three; but if we went, we would all three go together.

Mostly I kept my eyes on my own feet, for what little good that did, and my back flat against the cliff to give the wind least possible purchase. Rowan copied me with care; but Josh was leading, looking ahead, inclined to step out to see better. Each time, the movement of his feet snagged the corner of my eye, pulling my head up in anxiety, having me tug at his hand to draw him back into the rock wall's mockery of safety.

Maybe he was getting confident, thinking the worst was behind us; maybe he could see the end of the path, the top of the cliff. At the last he didn't let me do that; this time he tugged back teasingly, tried to draw me forward into his body's better shelter.

I was distracted, not ready, taken aback. Just for a moment I went with him, took a step too far, lost my place as the body-bridge between him and Rowan.

I broke my grip on her hand. She was too far behind; she couldn't stretch that far. I felt her fingers slip between mine and away.

I flailed blindly to recapture them, before my head could whip around to see; and I felt a strong hand close with mine again.

Strong and wet and bitter chill, compounded of salt and wind and water, and so very very much not Rowan's hand.

Familiar none the less. Not Rowan, and not supposed to be here. Anywhere.

We always want to hold on to everything. We don't even let our dead go.

Sometimes, the dead don't let us.

Now I looked.

I couldn't see Rowan at all, through the dark and the wind and the figure that stood between us. Broad-chested, raw-boned, standing four-square on the path; known, integral, unmistakable. Dead. Holding my hand.

I took a second; I needed that one second just to stand there, to be back, to be sheltered and watched over and held.

Then I plunged: straight through whatever there was of him contained within that shaping, the sea spray and the wind and all, a great stillness made of movement as we all are, as all things are.

I hurled myself recklessly and blindly through, to reach Rowan.

Doing that, I had to let go of Josh.

Every story is about betrayal, in the end. We lucky ones, we're allowed to choose who we betray.

If the briefest breathless moment can truly be forever, then I honestly never thought I'd find her. I thought she'd be gone: over the edge, or the path collapsed beneath her, or just not there, not anywhere.

But I hurtled into her very physical self, and for a moment we clung, almost going over; and then we scrambled to some awkward mutual desperate balance, and if that was some kind of Sophie's choice, apparently I'd made it.

Made it and couldn't conceivably regret it, when she was right there wrapped around me, damp and chill and trembling; and even so already it rived me, that I had let Josh slip. I gazed yearningly back over her head, thinking that Bruce must have taken what I had abandoned, sure that I would never see the boy again—and suddenly there he was, plunging out of a darkness deeper than the night, just as I had.

Again we teetered, and again we didn't fall. Now I had them both within the circle of my arms, and Bruce had lost his advantage. Whatever choice I'd made, there were others free and able to make choices too.

"All together or not at all," I said, and this time I set Rowan before me, with my hands on her shoulders as they used to be, as they always should be. Josh took his cue from me, without being told or asked: he set young strong fingers on my shoulders, stood close enough behind me that I could feel his breath on my neck, even in that wind; was young enough to brush a kiss against my nape, even in that danger.

I nudged Rowan forward, and that's how we climbed the last of the path: caterpillar-style, stepping all together and gripping tight. I suppose I was still making the same choice, Rowan the one I gave my strength to, trusting Josh to hold to me; but now it didn't feel like betrayal. Recognition, rather. Something new between us, a shift of state, that I lay within his compass as much as he in mine.

Up and up, step by step; and here we were at the top and the wind was almost helpful now, blowing inland, pushing us to greater safety, away from the cliff edge. It was hard even now to believe that I had lost neither one on the path below, when I'd thought to lose them both. And now I could fling an arm around each and march them forward, laughing almost in the teeth of the night. Bruce had had his chance, I thought, and missed his mark, and—

Of course that's when he came again, in that moment of stupid confidence, when we thought the worst behind us. He'd always had a knack for catching me off-guard, keeping me off-balance, so that I'd forever be falling into him, needing him to catch me once again.

Again he was a storm shadow, woven from dark and wind and water. He shaped himself out of nowhere, and stood before us, undeniable as death—and then he walked away, across the ninety-acre, as though he were a guide in the night.

Towards the sheepfold, where of course we were headed anyway: somewhere to pause, to catch our breath, to huddle in an angle of the walls and let the wind batter itself against stone while we wrapped our heads around what we had just survived.

He led us and we followed, because what else could we do, where else go? There was no path to better safety, no path at all. If we had him in sight, at least we knew where he stood.

Besides, the wind hustled us neatly at his heels. I leaned back against it, tried to drag my feet, to act as a brake for all three of us. Even so, I could barely keep us from catching him up. We dogged him, and he led us exactly where we had all meant to be. Every step felt inevitable, preordained, irresistible.

The sheepfold had a gateway, though no gate. He brought us there and paused, and turned—I want to say to face us, although the weather mask he wore offered no suggestion of a face.

We came to a halt, all three of us together. Even the wind seemed to pause for that breathless confrontation, until he moved again. Reshaped himself. Made a frame around the gateway, like an open invitation: *come on in.*

Like a lychgate, a threat as much as a promise.

Not wide enough for three of us abreast, however close we huddled. He wanted to force me into choice again, and this time there would be no reprieve. Whoever I left outside, he would take. And he had tested me once already, and he knew—we all knew—which way that decision fell.

Maybe he wanted a new apprentice.

Not this time.

I could feel Josh stiffening at my side, seeing what I saw, leaping to the same conclusions. Waiting to feel me pull away.

Not this time.

This time, I made a different choice.

I stepped away from both of them at once, one brisk pace back. I took a wrist of each, before they could protest it, and locked their two hands together; then I gripped them by the neck, one in each hand, and propelled them forwards.

The young cling by instinct. If either of them knew what I was doing, if they understood, they had no time to overcome that instinct and unlatch. I pushed them by main force through the opening in the fold's wall, through the gate mouth Bruce had made.

He didn't touch them; I don't believe he could. The fold was home, safe ground, always had been. Even the wind couldn't reach them, I thought, in there.

I was alone out here, my choice made, and I didn't even try to follow them in.

Instead—well. Hand in hand and two by two, that's the way we chose to go.

I reached out my hand to touch the nebulous near column of that strange shimmering gateway, and felt my hand seized again by the same strong frigid fingers as before. There he was again in almost-human form, his own size, his own shape.

If he had all the powers of wind and water, he chose not to use them. Perhaps bonding himself into an almost-body, as near as he could come, gave him only that body's strength.

The memory of mortality with all its limits implied.

At any rate, I could pit my own body's strength against his and not make a mockery of myself. I could tug him, indeed, against the wind's shove, back towards the cliff edge and the path. It may be that he was willing to be tugged. Denied what he'd expected, the cruel choice, one child or the other, he might be bewildered now; he might be intrigued. If he was capable of either, or capable of anything but malice. I couldn't tell: was he a ghost; was he himself remade with all his old attributes and antagonisms; was he only a memory or a lingering aspect somehow cut off from death and left behind?

It didn't matter. Nothing mattered except this moment, this determination: to take him away from the kids, away from the world if I could.

Young or otherwise, the human instinct is to cling. *We always want to hold on. We don't even let our dead go.*

I was gambling, I suppose, that I could hold on to him now, and take him with me one last time. That he wouldn't have the strength or else the will to leave me.

I was almost running now. And hauling him along, and if he thought anything at all—if he was capable of thinking— he must have thought I was headed for the path and trusting him to keep me safe in a foolish, hectic descent.

Not I. I ran him clean off the edge of the cliff.

That was all I had. My way to save the kids, if it could work; to keep him bound to me and end myself. I had no time for regrets, for second thoughts, for fond farewells. Just straight to the edge and over.

Hurling both of us into that wind, almost rising before we could start to fall; hoping he would, what, disintegrate perhaps? Lose coherence and fray away into the air that he was made from? I'd had no time for analysis either, or I might have thought myself foolish, hopeless, illogical. Lost.

I thought I was lost anyway. Dead myself and not reckoning to come back, malevolently or otherwise.

I leapt, almost flew, almost fell—and didn't, quite.

He had always had the saving of me in his hands. Always been the saving of me, always made that choice.

Now, one more time—who knows why?—he did that again.

I had thought myself so grown-up in my pride, in my strength, mature and responsible and knowing. Now suddenly I was a child again, while a grown-up swung me by one arm.

That grip I had, I'd thought I had; turned out to be his grip after all, his on me, as ever. He swung me high and hurled me, back to the land again.

I hit the ground hard, and couldn't breathe for a while. I couldn't see for a while after that, because of the wind and the night. The wind died, though, in time. Then I could stand, and see that there was nothing to see, walk to the fold, and find Josh and Rowan still huddling there.

Did he linger, did he depart, did he dissipate? I had no way of knowing; only that he was not there.

Nor was the yard there, when I went down, when I could. Nor the bulk of the workshop. The roof and doors were gone; some walls survived, but none worth keeping. There was nothing in me, no will to build again. It had been his, and barely mine before he took it back; and the village was in ruin, and my life there.

Besides, I had insurance. His insurance, transferred to my name just before he died; he always had been careful with everything that was his, including me. That money bought me a yacht; none so fine as those we used to build, but good enough. Blue water worthy.

The cottage I gifted to Rowan, if she should decide to want it. If not, to Josh; if not him, then to the distress fund for the village, all my friends and neighbours.

From the cottage, I took nothing but Bruce's ashes; from the wreckage of the yard, nothing but the wreck of Josh's copper origami, *The Boat of Going Nowhere*. Crushed and mangled as it was, no kind of seaworthy, I would take it out, far and far, and pour the ashes into its deepest crevice, give them to the ocean, watch it drink them down.

And then—well, not come back. Not yet, not now. Let the winds have me for a while; winds and blue water.

DEPARTURES
by A.K. Benedict

She has no idea where she is but, judging from the lager farts rising from the fabric under her forehead, she'd say she was face down on a pub banquette. Someone must've called her out last night for a quick one and the quick one turned, as they do, into a lengthy ten. Maybe she lucked out at a lock-in. Maybe she was held, if only for a moment.

She sits up slowly and opens her eyes. The world lurches. Yup—she's in the corner of a pub, an empty bottle of gin on the table in front of her. Her head, though, doesn't feel like a piñata under attack. And there's no burst of guilt, shame or screaming nerve endings. If she's lucky, her eyeliner is still in place and not smeared across her, or someone else's, face.

Something's wrong, though. She knows that as surely as her name. Something is off-kilter, like the illusion of a straw kinked in a cocktail glass. She doesn't know what. She can't even be sure if she's been in here before. The generic pubness—Christmas tree slouched in the corner; decorations that look like they've seen better days but probably haven't; punters muttering; barmen buffing; smoke filling the room, confirming both a lock-in and a landlord with a lax relationship with the law—means it could be any number of bars in Dublin.

Two men turn from the bar. The nearest, a scowl of a man

in a barrel of a body, looks her up and down, then sneers. She sinks back into the seat. The other man is tall and gaunt with a very long neck. He moves slowly towards her, like an ambulant nebuchadnezzar of champagne.

"You're a weak man, Henrik. Can't you mind your own fucking business for once?" the sneering man says.

"Leave it, Carny," Henrik says. He has difficulty walking, as if he's moving one frame at a time. "You're awake, then," he says when he reaches her. He sits down. "Don't mind Carny. He's always been at war with the world." He grins, making his face look like a crumpled hankie. "You'll be feeling pretty rough, I should think."

"Could be worse. You were here last night, then?" she asks.

"I'm always here."

"You're the landlord? Tell me if I've broken anything, will you? You know, tables, chairs, laws, hearts? I've no idea how I got here."

"No one does." He crosses his legs infuriatingly slowly, like a skeletal Sharon Stone in slo-mo.

The coffee machine fumes behind the bar. "I need coffee," she says. At some point, memories are going to surface and she needs to be in a fit state to apologise/call the police/run.

"It won't do you any good, I'm afraid," he says. "You know that, deep down." His hand moves haltingly across the table to hers.

She tries to yank her hand away but it's stuck in place. This is one weird hangover. "Do I know you?" she asks. She attempts to cross her fingers, hoping that they hadn't crossed a line last night. Her forefinger twitches but otherwise won't budge. And she has never been this cold. This is more than too many shots of Jägermeister.

"No, but I hope we'll be friends. I'm Henrik. I'm the welcoming committee."

"Isn't there usually more than one person in a committee?"

"Our numbers have dwindled lately. Maybe you'd like to come on board?"

"I'm not much of a joiner."

He looks at her, head on one side. "You really don't remember what happened, love?"

"Could you just tell me what I've done, who I've offended and what the fuck I drank last night and then I can go home or have my stomach pumped?" She's no one's love.

"Do you know where your home is?" he asks.

"I wasn't that drunk, thanks. Soon as I know where I am, then I can make my way back. I can't be that far out."

"You're at the airport. The pub in Departures."

Okay, maybe she can be that far out. "Then I'll get a cab."

"I'll call them from the bar. What's your address?" he asks.

"It's…" But the words don't come.

"Which side of the river?"

She should know this. She knows she knows this but she can't even picture her front room.

"And who shall I say the taxi's for, miss?"

Again, she opens her mouth to tell him but the word that represents her has gone. She can't find her first name, or her second. She doesn't even know if she has a middle name or what her job is, or if she has one. It's like searching for something in her handbag that she's sure is there but there are only old mints, ticket stubs to a film she doesn't remember and Tippex. And now someone's tipping the Tippex over everything she knows. Even facts and trivia are whiting out. She doesn't even know which Monkee's mum invented Tippex. Or was it Post-its? At least she knows that she doesn't have a partner. That one she knows deep inside her, where the yearning lurks.

"Not so easy, is it?" Henrik says.

"Someone must have given me something," she says, panic rising. She can't remember her own fucking name; what else is she blotting out? "I need to go to the, what's it called? Building with off-white corridors, smells of disinfectant?"

"The hospital."

"That's it. Tell the taxi to take me to hospital."

"I think it's a bit late for that, sweetheart."

She tries to stand but nothing happens. "Was it you? Did you do this?" She's shouting but her voice sounds far away.

"Ssh," Henrik says. "Take things slowly. No one here did anything to you. Take a good look around. You'll get it soon enough."

"Can you just fuck off?"

He doesn't just fuck off. "Notice anything odd about the smoke?"

There *is* a lot of smoke in the room, even for after a lock-in. So she still knows her pub etiquette. Trust that to be the last thing to go. Also, the smoke isn't hanging in ribbons; it courses round the room as if it has a destination in mind. The room doesn't smell of smoke: it smells of bleach, coffee, greasy chips and beer. And if no one's smoking, the doors are open and the fire isn't lit, then there shouldn't be smoke at all.

"You're almost there," he says. He looks sad. His tone is tissue soft. "Look closer."

She gazes into a streak of smoke as it passes the table and feels as if her heart has been placed in the ice bucket. There are faces in the smoke. Noses, mouths, eyes that do not see and limbs that move quick as a flick-book. See-through and swift, there are people, almost people, moving en masse like mist.

Or ghosts.

She tries to get up but her legs won't move. "What are they?" she says.

"Don't worry, they can't harm you."

"That's not what I asked."

"What do you think they are?"

"Don't give me this Socratic shit, you know what I think they are."

"Tell your little friend to shut up," Carny shouts over without even looking at them. "Or I'll shut her up."

"Nice place you've got here," she says. "Arseholes at the bar and ghosts taking up valuable drinking space." She watches two spectral faces turn her way as if they can hear, then they're gone. "What do they want, anyway?"

"A drink before their flight, a drink after their flight, a break from working on security, a few minutes not to talk, a burger and chips before their sister arrives… they're all here for different reasons, just like us."

"Us?"

"They're the ones with busy lives. We're here to watch them."

The air around her feels thickened, as if it has skin. She reaches for her glass, able to move now but it takes a huge effort, as if pushing back something she can't see. She needs just one drink to steady her nerves. Her fingertips reach the glass, and pass straight through.

"What's going on?" she asks.

"You'll remember soon enough," Henrik says. His eyes are the soft amber of a cloudy pint.

"Remember what?"

"How you died."

"What're you talking about now? I haven't died, they're the ones who are—" She breaks off. One of the spirit people, a man, leans over to grab the glass. His arm brushes through hers, making her feel colder than ever before. He looks straight at her, blinks and shudders, then whisks back into smoke. And then she knows. It's the way he looks at her: she is the ghost.

Three days have passed, three days in which she's pushed Henrik away; tried to leave but couldn't move from her booth; wrestled with death and being yet dead, denying it, crying over it; tried to remember something, anything. You'd think she'd recall, wouldn't you, how she died, at the very least? But no: she just sat here, staring into the table as if it'd open into a brown pool where she could tickle out memories as if they were trout. But nothing surfaced. All the while the giggling river of the living flowed past, eddying, flitting, alive. At least she thinks it's been three days, it's hard to tell, minutes go so quickly: hours pass across the face of the clock over the bar like micro-expressions. Clocks should have days and years on them. They should hold onto time more tightly.

She should've held onto life more tightly. This wallowing has got to stop. She's all for spending your life in a pub, but what's the point if you can't drink?

"Henrik," she calls out.

Henrik looks up from trying to soothe an exchange between Carny and another customer.

"It won't make a difference, you know," Carny says, his mouth contorting, as Henrik walks over to her. "You can help as many people as you like but you still failed her. You're weak. You're water to her whiskey, you always were. You'll give in, down the line."

Henrik closes his eyes as he sits down next to her.

"What was all that about?" she asks.

"There's something he wants to know and I won't tell him. Never mind that. You're looking a little brighter," he says. "I was worried about you. We all were."

"Apart from Carny."

"Carny only cares about himself."

"What is this place?" she asks. Her voice comes out stronger. "Hell? Limbo? Valhalla?"

"You didn't say heaven," Henrik says.

"We may be in a pub but this isn't heaven. I'd be feeling more guilty if this were heaven."

"It's none of those, as far as we know, although limbo is nearest. We've no real idea, though. There's no authority figure to tell us what's happening, only guidance passed on by, and to, the passed on."

"'The passed on'. So life looked at me and said, 'I'll pass on her having her thirty-third birthday.'"

Henrik clapped his hands together. The sound was empty. "That's a good start, you know how old you are."

"Maybe it's all coming back."

"Give it time. Anyway, sometimes it's the other way round. People pass on life for their own reasons."

"I'd never pass on life," she says.

"Good for you," Henrik says. "As far as what this place is, we think it's a literal last chance saloon."

"What's the last chance?"

"The chance to do it again, to relive a section of our life and make decisions that will lead to us not dying, not so soon anyway."

She feels hope flow. "What do I need to do?"

"That's the tricky bit," Henrik says. "You're going to have to remember who you are."

"And then what?"

"The people you see moving around you are, in a way, ghosts—they're in the past. Each one is in their own timeline running up to their death. At some point in your past, you came here. Your job is to wait and then find yourself among the millions."

"Then what?"

"Then grab hold of you, fold your future spirit into your past body and persuade it not to die."

"Piece of piss, then," she says, clinging to sarcasm like splintered driftwood at sea. "Seeing as I've no idea what I look like, what my name is or how to move in this weird space/time fuck-up."

"We'd better get you moving, then," Henrik says.

An hour, a day or a year later, she has managed to cross halfway across the pub. Somehow, knowing that she is on a different plane to the febrile world of the living helps her move through it. A year, a day or an hour later, she's standing in the Departures hall. Streams of the living weave in and out like DNA strands. They twist round her, flinching as one if they accidentally touch her.

Spectres gather. Lots of them. They stand by departures boards, check-in desks and cafés. Heads slowly turning, scrying for past selves in the smoke. Henrik says that the dead are found in places where large numbers pass through—museums, concert halls, terminals. She'd never liked airports, found them too crowded and frantic, but maybe she knew, deep down, that the dead were waiting, that it was far busier than the living imagined.

She wanders slowly through security and into the perfumes hall; the mist of sprayed fragrances feels heavy on her spectral body, as if walking into doorway beads. What had she been thinking about? A man. She'd been talking to a man. In a pub. Memories of him are disappearing like flights from the departures board. Henrik. That's it.

People pass, leering at each other as if in masks, mouths stretched wide. So many of them, as overwhelming as the intersecting smells of alcohol and aldehydes. And she has to recognise herself among them. It's impossible. She'll never get out of here. She sinks to the floor and curls up as the feet of the fleshed flow past.

"Didn't I say, 'Don't go too far on your first trip'?" Henrik says when she comes round. She's back in the pub.

"You did, but then I didn't remember." All she wants is to lie down on her banquette and sleep.

"That's why you shouldn't go too far. The pub keeps our memories, don't ask me how. It's like they're pickled in alcohol. Staying conscious helps, if you can."

She concentrates on the poster by the bar. It's a traditional Irish prayer that appears on tea towels, magnets and beer mats. You've probably seen it on a mug at your auntie's house—it starts with the words, "May the road rise up to meet you," and ends with the blessing, "May God hold you in the hollow of his hand." In this poster, though, the last three words have been eroded, either by time or sun or adjacent packets of pork scratchings.

Henrik follows her line of sight. "It's why we call this place the Hollow." He crosses himself then says, "May God hold us in the Hollow."

"I thought the aim was to leave," she says.

"We've been given the opportunity to redo parts of our pasts, I don't know if everyone is as lucky. As far as we know, some people go straight to the next stage, if there is one. Or go nowhere at all. Being held in the Hollow is an opportunity, a blessing."

"Tell him that," she says, watching Carny stalk the smoke in the room. The living move away from him as if he were bellows. She feels their panic. It changes the taste in the air, adds iron, like a mouth filling with blood. The ghosts stay away too.

"What's his problem?" she asks.

"He was killed," Henrik says. "Don't ask me the whys and wherefores, and definitely don't ask him, but that's what drives him—finding his murderer and killing him."

"But he's a ghost. I saw him struggle to smash a pint glass.

He wouldn't be able to kill anyone."

"Well, that's the other side of the blessing," Henrik says.

"Isn't the other side of a blessing a curse?" she asks.

"You could say that, although the curse is on both us and the living: if, for example, you think you've found your past self and embrace her but get the wrong person, then you've marked that human for death."

"Shit."

"Yes, they may die straight away, in weeks or years, but before their time. And *you'd* fade away instead of living again. We only get one choice. One chance."

"This is what I'm here for? Who made up this game?"

Henrik shrugs. "Don't know. But those are the rules."

In the smoke, a family passes, pulling suitcases, then two women, hand in hand, kissing: happy people off on blink-quick holidays.

"Fuck you," Carny shouts into the smoke, nostrils flared, hands in fists. She knows how he feels.

After that, she only goes into the airport on short sorties before circling back to the Hollow. Atoms of memory reattach themselves. She knows now that she lived in Dún Laoghaire and that Shirley Bassey recorded three James Bond theme songs.

And she's remembered her name. *Sian.*

That evening, or another, she sits with Henrik in the Hollow, staring into the people stream.

"What do I look like?" she asks.

"Well," he says, squinting at her. "You've got dark brown eyes, like stout. Got as much in them as stout as well."

Sian laughs.

"Your hair is brown with blonde bits in, like my wife used to have. And cheekbones that could crack open a can of Batchelors."

"You don't talk about your wife much."

"No. Well," Henrik says, looking away. "I don't like to. She's my angel's share."

Moaning comes from the booth next door, as if someone were writhing in pain.

"That's my cue," Henrik says. He gets up, then turns to Sian. "Do you want to help?"

She shrugs. It's something to do.

A newly made ghost is on the neighbouring banquette, arms looped about her knees, rocking. She whimpers. She's young, in her mid-twenties.

"It's all right, everything's all right," Henrik says.

Sian stops herself saying that it really isn't.

The young woman looks up at Henrik; then, on turning to Sian, her eyes widen, her pupils slowly eclipse the blue. It's as if she knows Sian. Has known her. She shakes and Sian wishes she had the ability to hug her. Her eyes close.

"We're here when you need us, just say," Henrik says softly, and leads Sian away.

The next day, the young woman is more alert, looking around the pub. When she sees Sian, she almost smiles. Sian moves over from the bar and sits down next to her while Henrik begins his slow, kind unveiling of the Hollow, the airport and the search that goes on inside. The words drift past Sian as she takes in everything about the woman: tight jeans, Flaming Lips T-shirt two sizes too big; her hair, shaved at the sides and a rumpled quiff. She is lucky enough to remember her name: Marta.

"Have you got any words of wisdom, Sian?"

"What?" Sian says.

"Any sage advice for Marta, here? You've been through this recently."

"I don't think I'm the one to ask. I've only just worked out what my name is."

Marta looks down at her lap as if disappointed.

"I can tell you one thing," Sian says quickly. "The living look scary but they're frightened of us, for some reason. We're not out to hurt them." She looks across at Carny. "Not all of us, anyway."

"But we can hurt them. Get it wrong and we condemn them to an early death. They know that by instinct. The living haunt the dead and the dead the living; that's the way it's always been," Henrik says.

"Well, that's a cheery thought to wake up dead to," Marta says. Her voice is quiet. Her sarcasm is as refreshing as the first pint at the end of the day.

"I'll leave you to it," Henrik says, then walks slowly over to the corner where Carny has the ghost of a guitar player backed against the wall. Carny holds out a warning hand to Henrik; Henrik backs away.

"Who's that man?" Marta says. She's staring at Carny, her hands making claws and trying to grab the edge of the seat.

"That's Carny. Not a happy man. There are plenty of good people in here, though. It's got that waiting room spirit thing going on. If we were alive we'd be passing around sweets. All we've got to share are stories and I haven't got many of those."

"Why not?" she says. As she looks at me, a current of past and future runs between us.

"I don't know how I lived or how I died. Henrik says memory loss can happen in death, during trauma. So I think we can say I didn't die well."

"Who does?" Marta asks.

"Joan Crawford. Apparently her housekeeper prayed for her and Joan shouted: 'Damn it! Don't you dare ask God to help me!' Don't ask me how I know that. I didn't know I did."

"The last words Bogie said to Bacall were, 'Goodbye, kid, hurry back.'"

"Wouldn't it be great to know someone as well as they did, to have them know you?"

"It would," Marta says.

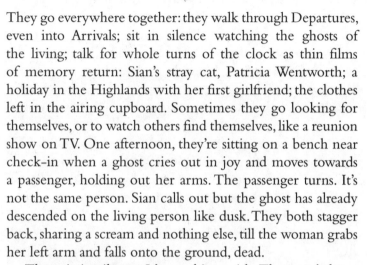

They go everywhere together: they walk through Departures, even into Arrivals; sit in silence watching the ghosts of the living; talk for whole turns of the clock as thin films of memory return: Sian's stray cat, Patricia Wentworth; a holiday in the Highlands with her first girlfriend; the clothes left in the airing cupboard. Sometimes they go looking for themselves, or to watch others find themselves, like a reunion show on TV. One afternoon, they're sitting on a bench near check-in when a ghost cries out in joy and moves towards a passenger, holding out her arms. The passenger turns. It's not the same person. Sian calls out but the ghost has already descended on the living person like dusk. They both stagger back, sharing a scream and nothing else, till the woman grabs her left arm and falls onto the ground, dead.

They sit in silence. It's too big a risk. They can't leave each other for that. Anyway, having found each other, the importance of finding themselves is receding. Marta turns to her and moves forward. Their lips do not touch, as they never can, but they miss each other in the same space and that's almost nearly good enough for now.

There's a lot of almost kissing after that. They're nearly kissing in Sian's booth when Carny kicks off.

"He's here. The cunt's here," Carny says, pointing into the smoke. His face is a red knot.

"Who's he talking about?" Marta whispers.

"The man who killed him, I think," Sian says, standing up.

Carny strides around, herding the billow of smoke. The adrenaline tang in the room soars. Sian moves towards him.

"Let it go, Carny," Henrik says gently. "You tell me to

mind your own business, how about you do the same?"

"He murdered me. He placed his hands round my neck and strangled me into this place. This *is* my fucking business," Carny says, staring at the large man he's isolated from the flitting living. The man runs towards the door but Carny is there. Wherever the man goes, Carny is there. Carny reaches for his throat.

"Maybe you're part of it. Have you thought about that?" Sian says. She doesn't know how she's doing it but she's moving quicker.

"Fuck off back to your girlfriend," Carny says, turning on her.

"Maybe you're here so that you can go back and make it right. Just by going back and altering one thing, the timeline will have shifted. You have one chance and you're wasting it on him." Out of the corner of her eye, she sees the man move away, fear stretching his face into a scream.

"He *killed* me. Would you let someone get away with that?"

"If I had the chance to live again, yes," Sian says. "I'd replay it, change the ending."

"I *will* replay it," Carny snarls. "I'll replay that cunt killer's death, over and over as I die."

"I'm afraid you won't," Henrik says, over Sian's shoulder.

Carny looks around. His intended victim has gone. "You cost me my chance," he says to Sian, his face twisting. "And you'll pay."

"A ghost can't kill another ghost, can it?" Sian asks.

Henrik says nothing.

They, along with Marta, are walking round the airport in the early hours. Shops and check-ins are shut and the only noises are from the living snoring on beds made from suitcases. They'll jump up soon and run to fidget in line as the place comes alive, but for now, there is calm across the airport.

"I mean, I don't have to worry about him unless I find my living self?"

"Not necessarily. I think the best thing to do is to find your living self as quickly as possible," he says. "And then stay away from this airport."

"So there *is* a way," Marta says. "But how, if we can't even touch?"

"Few of the dead know about it. I don't even know if it's real. Don't think I'm going to tell you, either, or anyone else, even though they beg me," Henrik says. "I'm not having that as well on my conscience." His voice is all pain and edges.

They walk on, not talking, past a family slumped over a bench. Their sped-up snoring sounds like pigs talking.

"Is there a way, though," Marta says, her little finger an ache of an inch from mine, "that we *can* touch?"

We both look at him. He sighs. "Over time, just as you adjust to moving in a different dimension and affecting the living, you become stronger in this one. It's not touching as you remember, but it's as good." He screws his face up and closes his eyes, as if pushing back a memory.

"You said that you didn't want 'that as well' on your conscience," Sian says. "Is that something to do with your wife? Your angel's share?"

"What's the angel's share?" Marta asks.

"It's the small percentage of alcohol that evaporates from the casks," Henrik says.

"And you call your wife that because...?" Sian says.

"Because she got away. Because I wasn't brave enough to follow. Now, please," Henrik says. His eyes ghost with tears. "I've tried to help you. Leave me be. Stay away from Carny; get away from here. Anger is the only thing fuelling him and you've removed his method of revenge. He'll be looking for another one. And I don't know if I can hold him off." He walks off, as quickly as Sian's seen him walk.

"I shouldn't have pushed him," she says.

"We both did," Marta replies.

Whenever they're there, Carny taunts them. He stands close. Watching. His jaw works backwards and forwards as if chewing gum. "Enjoy yourselves while you can," he says. "I'll always be here."

Henrik sidles over. He can't look them in the eyes. He seems paler, even less substantial. "He knows," he said. "He knows the method. He's building up the strength but you must find your bodies."

They avoid the Hollow after that, only going back to refresh memories. The more they know about themselves, the more likely they can find their living bodies as they roam slowly round the concourse, Carny following. They hear him whistling even when they can't see him; can smell the cologne of beer, stale smoke and semen that follows him even in death.

Moving through the crowds, they search the faces of thousands of women, Marta looking for Sian and Sian Marta, as they know each other's faces better than their own. And then, one day, Marta turns to Sian with a face of fighting micro-expressions.

"What is it?" Sian asks.

"You're over there," Marta says, pointing to Accessorize where a woman is buying a white woolly scarf.

"That's me?" Sian says. She can't connect with that woman but the memory of the scarf loops round her. It was warm and slightly scratchy, like fingernails at her neck.

"Go. Quickly," Marta says, pushing her away. "And don't come back."

Sian walks up to the woman with brown hair and stout eyes. The woman opens her mouth and there is a moment of recognition and sadness before Sian opens her arms and walks into her own.

It takes time to find room inside Sian. Her ghost tries to snake into her thoughts but they're taken up with her job of writing questions for TV quizzes and factoids for crackers, and her evenings are taken up with booze and near lovers. It's hard to hold onto the Hollow and what happened there. The ghost in the living can feel the memories leave. She tries to get herself to write the words "Marta" and "Henrik" and "Carny" but they only appear in dreams. Soon, there isn't much room between future and past Sian, only a thin space where a memory might be.

Sian carries certain things around with her, though. She has a fondness out of nowhere for a certain Irish blessing, a fear of being followed and an aversion to flying. It's trains, buses and boats or she's not going anywhere. Her friends don't know why this change has taken place and neither does she, only that she's going nowhere near Departures and there's a hollow in her heart.

A day, a week, a year later, Sian's sister, Yvonne, is flying back from New York for Christmas. "Pick me up, would you?" Yvonne said when she called. "It'll cost a fortune in a taxi."

"Are you joking? With the dollar as it is? And it's not as if you're not making money."

"You sound like Dad."

"Ouch."

So she is picking her sister up at the airport. She couldn't find a good enough reason why she shouldn't, and it wasn't as if she was going to Departures.

Sian sits, scarf on to counteract the draught of the automatic doors, hands around a huge coffee. She went for the gingerbread latte. It's Christmas, after all. She looks up, and a man is staring at her. He isn't tall but he's got broad shoulders. A chill that has nothing to do with the draught flows down her spine as if she's being unzipped. She pulls the scarf tighter around her.

He moves slowly closer. The cup slips between her fingers, sending hot coffee everywhere as she realises—she can see through him. Other people move around him without seeing or acknowledging him but he is coming for her. She knows that. She doesn't know how she knows, but she does.

She scrambles up, kicking the chair away and stumbles out of the café, looking back to see where he was, but he's closer. And there's something familiar about him. About his sneer.

She runs up to the information desk, out of breath. "Help me, please, I'm being followed. I think I'm in danger."

"Slow down there, madam," the smooth-skinned, groomed woman behind the desk says. "Who is it that is chasing you?"

Sian points to the man walking slowly towards her.

The woman, whose name badge says Rhiannon, smiles at her, eyes as cold as the River Liffey. "There's no one there, madam." Her pencilled eyebrows flick reverse Vs.

Sian turns away. The man is there, inches from her. She can smell him—a blend of whiskey, tobacco and decay. "I told Henrik he was weak and I told you you'd pay," he says. His hands reach for her.

"No," says another voice.

A young woman is standing behind him. Her hands are on his neck, her sinews straining, her eyes closed. She squeezes, pulling him back, away from Sian.

"How are you doing this?" he spits out, each word a struggle.

"Henrik," the girl says. "Said he had to do something to make up for it all."

Sian's heart contracts and expands as if breathing. "I know you," she says.

"You do," says Marta. "And I know you."

The man, Carny, collapses to the floor, holding his throat. He is pulsing, like a faulty light bulb.

"We don't have much time," Marta's pulsing too.

Sian walks towards her.

"No, we can't," Marta says, backing away, but Sian is quicker. Their fingers touch and their lips kiss and for one moment she is held.

"Hurry back," Marta says.

Sian opens her eyes. Marta and Carny have gone and she is in the middle of a stream of people, alive and dead, and she is totally alone.

As soon as she gets home, Sian writes it down. All of it. Not on a computer, but on paper she can hold to her and read when the memories fade, and when the ink fades she writes it out again. She writes facts for crackers and quizzes for idiots but knows she knows little. Sometimes she sits in the Hollow, watching the terminally slow Styx of the dead, waiting for what is stalking her. She doesn't know how long she's got. Maybe Marta will be there in some way. Maybe she's here already. May she hold her in the Hollow. May she hold her in the hollow of her hand.

THE SALTER COLLECTION
by Brian Lillie

"When you enter a grove peopled with ancient trees, higher than the ordinary, and shutting out the sky with their thickly intertwined branches, do not the stately shadows of the wood, the stillness of the place, and the awful gloom of this doomed cavern then strike you with the presence of a deity?"

—Seneca

Alice led Mr. Caul and his ever-present cart through the various stacks and vaults and twisting hallways of the Special Collections wing in silence. They passed a few bleary-eyed grad students and Terry from the third floor, busy pulling yellowed survey maps from a huge drawer in the McIntyre Collection. Terry rolled her eyes comically when she saw whom Alice was escorting.

Everyone who worked at the library had at least one Mr. Caul story. The little weirdo always wore a black three-piece suit and black tennis shoes, eyes scrunched up beneath a fault-lined brow as if perpetually tasting something rancid. He was infamous for never looking at anyone when he deigned to speak, and for having the social graces of an insect. For all of Caul's annoying traits, though, he was also well known for being able to fix just about anything, which is why Alice had called him.

When they reached the Salter Collection, Alice swiped her card, punched in the key code, and ushered Caul into the dark hallway beyond. A moment after he and his cart disappeared in musty blackness, the automatic lights kicked in with a crotchety splutter, revealing the face of a red-cheeked huntsman surrounded by pine trees, gazing intensely from his frame across from the entrance. Alice had been working at the library for close to three years, and yet the painting always startled her, no matter how many times she had accessed the collection.

Hello, Mr. Salter.

Alice pointed to the left, down the circular marble hallway crowded with inset bookcases and shelves stacked with a surfeit of neatly labeled boxes. Near the door was an open crate with the latest batch of papers that had come over from the Salter estate the week before, which Alice was slowly making her way through. "The listening room is—"

"I know which one it is."

Alice glanced at her watch as she held the listening room door open. She couldn't believe it wasn't even eight-thirty. She was going to need a triple cappuccino from the atrium café after this.

Caul gasped. You would think he had just walked into a real crime scene, with blood splashed onto the walls, but it looked exactly like Alice had found it twenty minutes earlier: an empty room with white plaster walls, two oak tables, four oak chairs, and a basket of outdated headphones on a shelf. The only thing out of the ordinary was a small brown tube lying on the floor, obviously cracked down its middle.

It was this last detail that had elicited Caul's response. He practically threw himself to the floor to get a closer look. "That's how I found it," said Alice. "I figured I shouldn't handle it, so—"

"Quiet!" snapped Caul. He got up on his knees and

pulled his cart closer, removing a pair of gloves and a small cardboard box from the jumble of its lower shelves.

"I'm going to need you to watch your tone," said Alice, not able to contain herself.

Caul snorted. "Perhaps if you spent less time watching your 'tone' and more time safeguarding the items under your care, we wouldn't need to have these unpleasant interactions." He pulled on his gloves and carefully prodded one of the cracked areas on the cylinder with what looked like a crochet hook.

"I had nothing to do with this and do not appreciate the insinuation. I only ever open the cylinder collection for Professor Hastings and his students and they haven't been up here in weeks."

Caul stopped what he was doing and made actual eye contact with Alice from his spot on the floor, which was unnerving. "You are implying, then, that one of the antique cylinder recordings let *itself* out of its locked cabinet, somehow rolled into this room and then shattered itself on the floor?"

"No, that's not what I'm saying."

Caul took a deep breath. "In any case, I would ask that you refrain from speaking for a few moments while I attempt to triage the damage here."

Alice sighed, willing herself not to say any of the dozen things she wanted to at that moment. "I'll be in the hall," she said finally, turning on one heel and leaving before the bastard could respond.

She wasn't just frustrated by the pompous gnome— it nagged at her that none of this should have happened, *period*. In order to even just look at one of the wax cylinders, somebody would have to present written permission from the musicology department and leave their driver's license at her desk. Alice would then have to take that person back here personally, utilizing two different key cards and the combination to the correct cage. And to top it all off,

Professor Hastings (who basically *was* the musicology department) always sent one of his grad students along to supervise anyone accessing the audio collection. There was just no feasible scenario for how someone could have gotten in without her knowing about it.

Not that it mattered, at all.

Sometimes, especially on mornings when she wasn't caffeinated enough, being an archivist felt to Alice like living out a long prison sentence, with her crimes long forgotten and no release date in sight.

The automatic light in the audio media storage room flickered even more than the ones in the circular hallway, and for a moment Alice worried it would burn out—the perfect capper to a wonderful morning. Before she could stamp her foot in further frustration, the old fixture finally groaned to partial life, revealing the walk-in cages lining one side of the room and hints of their shadowy contents.

Different formats of audio recordings from Eaton Salter's private collection took up the bulk of the cages—acetates from the first commercially available flat-disk dictation machine in one; two cages full of gramophone records and several original model gramophones in another; but the true jewel of the collection was housed in the cage farthest from the door—the wax cylinders.

Alice entered the combination and pulled the gate open, feeling the metallic shriek of the hinges in her teeth. She tugged the string light and looked for anything out of the ordinary. On her left were three shelves housing the cylinder players and recorders—an original Bell Labs Graphophone from the late 1880s, and three Edison models from around the turn of the century.

The rest of the cramped space was taken up by several

antique cabinets, some stacked two high. Alice opened the first cabinet and scanned its contents, squinting to read the small handwritten labels in the anaemic light. The three shelves within held a total of three dozen cardboard tubes on spindles, each containing a brown wax cylinder recording (some in better shape than others judging by the water stains and warping of a few of the cardboard jackets). This first cabinet was filled mostly with popular musical recordings of Salter's day, including many from "George J. Gaskin and his Manhansett Quartette".

All of the cylinders in the cabinet were accounted for. The same went for cabinets two through six—nothing out of place, no empty jackets or spindles. She opened the last cabinet, seven, and was immediately confronted by an empty spindle in the back of the second shelf, standing out like a missing tooth. Alice nodded to herself. *We have our winner.*

Alice traced her finger along the location map on the inside of the cabinet door until she found the culprit—the space for the missing cylinder was labelled *White Hill Inventory, October 11, 1899* in Salter's own blocky handwriting. She could not recall offhand what was recorded on that cylinder, even though she must have heard it during digitization. In some ways, it was a relief that the broken cylinder was one of these personal recordings. Any surviving wax was, of course, worth curating, but having heard several of the lumber magnate's blustery monologues Alice didn't think the world would miss one.

Mr. Caul was still in the listening room when Alice returned. He had moved his operation to one of the tables, where he was busy with a pair of tweezers and a lighted magnifier. "So, is it salvageable?" she asked, knowing full well that it was mostly impossible to repair a cylinder.

Caul turned in his seat, eyes wide. "This is a remarkable find."

"What do you mean?"

"Look here—the cracked outside layer is hiding another recording underneath."

"What?" Alice rushed over to the table. Caul had removed a good third of the damaged wax, laying each piece on a blue cotton pad at his elbow. Sure enough, revealed beneath this shell was another recording altogether, muddy gray and looking almost freshly cut.

"Amazing," said Alice, forgetting her annoyance in the face of something truly interesting happening at the library. "They must have shaved this other cylinder down practically to its core to be able to fit it inside like that."

"It is rather impressive work," said Caul.

Alice surprised herself. "I say we listen to this thing before I call Professor Hastings."

Equally surprising, Caul nodded. "Agreed."

Alice unpacked the Archéophone and wasted no time in calibrating it for the mystery cylinder. It fit one of the machine's common spindles and didn't require much tinkering as far as balancing the rotation. She set it to record to a WAV file, blew a stray bit of hair from her face and turned to Caul. "I think it's ready," she said.

Mr. Caul raised his eyebrows.

Alice flipped on the power switch, keeping her hand on the machine's speed adjustment knob as the cylinder began turning on the Archéophone's spindle. After several seconds of scratchy white noise, the recording began.

Caul's eyes went wide with disbelief.

Before she could stop herself, Alice reached over and switched off the machine. The now silent room still echoed with what they had just heard.

"What the hell *was* that?" said Alice. Had that been Salter's voice? What language had he been speaking? And what were those… *other* sounds?

Caul looked like he had just been slapped across the face. Without a word, he began gathering up his equipment and putting it back into his haphazard cart.

"That wasn't real, right?" said Alice. "It couldn't be. Could it?" She could swear she smelled smoke, but the Archéophone wasn't overheating and the cylinder sat innocently on the spindle, undamaged.

"I have no idea what we just listened to, but I suggest we let someone else deal with it."

"Were those dogs? Didn't it sound like dogs were attacking somebody?"

"Enough, woman!" said Mr. Caul, raising one finger into the air. "Please show me out of here, *now*."

Alice busied herself after lunch by helping Connie put together a complicated pull for the classics department. Alice didn't mention the situation with the wax cylinder, and Connie was too flustered to worry about anything other than finding several issues of *Hesperia* that seemed to have gone missing from their prescribed shelf. At about three-thirty Connie ventured back into the stacks for one last look and Alice immediately picked up her desk phone. Rafael answered after several rings.

"Security, Fuentes."

"Have you found anything?" blurted Alice.

"Well hello to you, too, missy."

"Sorry."

Rafael laughed. "No problems. So, I checked the key card log for Special Collections and nothing registered after ten last night, until your card around seven-thirty this morning. Even if somebody used a skeleton key, it would've still registered as a hit on the log."

"What about the camera footage?"

"Like I said, nobody opened the Special Collections door last night after ten. I don't see what the recording would show us."

"Please," said Alice. "As a favor to me, would you consider looking at our lobby footage from last night? I'm trying to find an explanation for something odd."

Rafael sighed. "Okay, for Alice the Librarian I will do this thing."

"Thank you," said Alice. "Let me know if you see anything out of the ordinary, okay?"

"Will do," said Rafael. "By the way, I prefer chocolate-chip cookies."

"Done," said Alice. She hoped he wouldn't mind Chips Ahoy!, since she hadn't baked anything since high school, and wasn't about to start again now.

Whoever designed Market Street back in the 1920s had done a brilliant job of harnessing the gusts off of Carlyle Lake, creating a ceaseless wind tunnel between the tall buildings there, and making the trudge from the bus stop to Alice's apartment as godawful cold as possible. She was not what anyone would ever describe as a "winter person", but tonight the icy lashing actually felt good, helping to break the drowsy spell of the bus.

As per routine, the lobby of Alice's building was deserted and she had no mail. Her apartment still reeked of wet dog, nearly a full week after Lester had gone back home to Mags and Lisa. The smell hit her the moment she opened the door. Though it had been a pain in the ass walking that grouchy old mutt twice every day in the snow and slush, the place did feel emptier than usual now. She had even gotten used to him snoring on the rug next to her bed.

At that image, her mind suddenly flashed to the secret recording—the canine gnashing, the screaming, the look of utter horror on Mr. Caul's pinched face. The alien words.

Alice shook her head as if she could dislodge the memory physically. *Worry about this tomorrow*, she told herself, hurriedly unbuttoning and unwrapping all her myriad wintertime layers and slipping into the old moccasins she kept by the door. Five minutes later, she was on the couch with a beer and a Tupperware full of last night's fried rice, her mom's old quilt across her lap.

In her more optimistic youth she had imagined that by now, well into her thirties, she would be living in a warmer state, in a sunny house with huge gardens, and writing full time. Zero out of three. On winter nights like this one, the weight of that became almost surreal. She sighed and took a swig of beer, which she could barely taste.

Eventually, to take her mind off the wax cylinder and her sour mood, Alice put on some music and picked up the book she'd been hammering away at for the past couple weeks, Herman Melville's *Pierre; or, The Ambiguities*. The only ambiguity was why she was making herself finish the ponderous thing, since no one else on earth cared if she was a Melville completist or not.

No wonder she lived alone.

Alice woke around two a.m., disoriented. For a moment she thought she was back at the library, that she had somehow fallen asleep at her desk. She panicked. Had she been looking for something in the Salter Collection?

The familiar smell of the quilt snapped Alice back to reality. She flashed for a moment on her tiny, severe, disappointed mother, and flung the blanket away as if it had bitten her. She couldn't find her moccasins so she switched off the living room lamp and hurried barefoot across the icy floor to her bedroom, where she slipped under the equally icy covers. Her mind refused to calm and let her go back to sleep. She spent the rest of the night listening to the wind rattle the old windows, while trying not to think about the recording or why she hadn't yet called her boss, Greta Green, or Professor Hastings about it.

Alice arrived late the following morning, having missed her regular bus. No amount of Tylenol nor a scalding shower had managed to touch the throbbing in her head. After hanging up her coat, she slumped into her desk chair wanting nothing more than to lay her head down and go back to sleep. She noticed the message light on the phone was blinking.

It was Rafael. "Hey, Alice the Librarian," the message began. "When you get this, bop on down to first floor security and find me."

Rafael was leaning across the front security desk, flirting with a work-study student at least half his age. "Ah, there you are," he said when he saw Alice. He excused himself and hustled Alice into a closet-sized room across the hall. It consisted of an ancient table with two chairs, a bank of old monitors showing blurry black-and-white shots from around the library, and a keyboard with a big toggle switch. "Welcome to the nerve center."

"Impressive," said Alice.

After they squeezed themselves into the seats, Rafael spent a few minutes trying to cue up one of the monitors. Alice half watched the camera feeds on the other five screens. Things looked slow all over the library, which was pretty common on Friday mornings, exacerbated by the day's weather prediction for heavy snow by noon.

"Almost there," said Rafael, using the toggle to fast-forward through footage from the Special Collections lobby. The only thing onscreen that appeared to be moving was the time stamp in the corner and some wobbly scan lines, otherwise nothing much was happening. "I barely caught this the first time as I was fast-forwarding," he said. He slowed the playback to regular speed, where the time stamp read 12:38:45, and tapped Alice lightly on the shoulder. "Now, missy, watch the door."

The door in question was the one between Alice and Connie's desks, the entrance to the Special Collections wing. The camera angle was above and to the right, so only about two thirds of the entryway was visible. "What am I looking for?" asked Alice, leaning toward the monitor.

"Wait for it…"

There was no movement for another several seconds, but just as the time stamp turned over to 12:40:00, a tall figure walked purposefully out of Special Collections, causing Alice to flinch. The man on the video made a beeline across the lobby, off screen, and was gone. Grand total, maybe two seconds of footage.

"Who was that?" said Alice.

"I was hoping you'd tell me." Rafael paused the video and toggled it back until the figure was caught midstride in the center of the screen. "Look familiar?"

"Can you, you know, enhance the picture or zoom in or something?"

Rafael laughed. "Silly librarian. These monitors are practically steam-powered."

Alice stared at the fuzzy image on the screen, and had no idea who the man could be. "Oh, wait," she said, before she could stop herself. "Mystery solved. I know who that is. It's Steve something-or-other, a grad student from Professor Olvidar's Civil War Studies class. I forgot I gave him permission to stay after close if he needed to. Which explains the whole key card thing."

Rafael squinted at Alice. "You have a terrible memory," he said.

"I'm sorry I dragged you into this. I feel like an idiot." Actually, she felt like a big fat liar, and couldn't fathom what she was up to.

Alice was alone at her desk all morning, the only living thing on the fifth floor. No students, no TAs or faculty, nothing but the thumping of the library's ancient pipes, the wheezing of its heat ducts. She hated being situated in the echoey lobby to begin with, but today it felt even more like working in a huge cave.

Connie called around nine-thirty to say that she wasn't going to be able to make it in. Her vanpool had been canceled as the weather reports had turned more ominous, and she couldn't afford to be stranded.

Alice logged in to the digital archive and searched "Salter, Eaton" for something to do. After putting together the finding aids for the last few major donations to the collection, she already knew a lot about him: Salter had come over from England around 1860, had died in the famous Minton lumber mill fire in 1911, and in between had become one of the richest men in the Midwest. He and his partner, Cornelius Wilks, had made a fortune clear-cutting the state's ample virgin-white pine forests and selling the lumber to builders and shipwrights on the east coast. Their company,

S&W Lumber, had built several logging towns throughout the state, most of which had been abandoned by the 1930s. Salter had erected his famous log mansion, Castra Saltus, on the banks of the Barrow River near Carlyle Lake. The little settlement that sprang up around the mansion eventually became the town of White Hill, home of the university.

Salter was an avid hunter and outdoorsman. Many of the online photos, Alice noted, were the same as those that hung on the walls back in the collection. They featured Salter at various ages: paddling in canoes, climbing huge trees, standing proudly on a bluff with his rifle at the ready. She had seen all of the images several times before, had handled hard copies of most of them. But this time, one particular photo caught her eye, one that she could not recall seeing. It featured Salter and Wilks, middle-aged and both in double-breasted coats and silk top hats, standing unsmiling in a forest clearing before a pair of huge metal wheels. To one side of the photograph, Salter's side, a pair of large dogs sat imperiously. On the other side stood a group of grimy-looking men in suspenders, staring at the dogs, as if expecting them to attack at any moment. The caption read "July 29, 1903. Arlington County, Camp 12. One cannot discern with true conviction whether the assembled lumbermen are spooked by the proximity of their employers, or by Sköll and Hati."

After lunch, which she ate alone at her desk, Alice grabbed her key cards and a third cup of coffee, and entered Special Collections. It was rare to be in there alone amongst the archived flotsam and jetsam of the past, all neatly codified and put away. It was so quiet that the air seemed cottony, swollen. Maybe she was coming down with something.

Without consciously planning it, Alice found herself outside the Salter Collection. She held her mug of coffee close to her face, breathing in the steam as she swiped her card and punched in the code. She opened the door and was about to step through when the lights came on fully, illuminating the portrait of Salter at the entrance.

She stared into his painted eyes.

Strange words echoed in her head.

Her life felt so…

"My dear, how are you on this blustery afternoon?"

Startled, Alice let out a shriek and spun around, almost dropping her coffee. She came face-to-face with Professor Hastings, who took a step back, eyes wide. "I'm sorry if I frightened you," he said sheepishly. "I thought you had heard me approaching."

Alice caught her breath. "No, no, it's okay. I get a little high strung sometimes." She looked down and realized she was holding a black document case. When had she picked *that* up?

Hastings was as dapper as ever in a bow tie, his bone-white hair coiffed. "I assumed everyone would have stayed home today, what with this glorious weather we're having," he said.

"I'm beginning to think I should have."

Hastings smiled and nodded toward the open door. "Were you about to visit old Eaton's treasure trove?"

Alice's mind went blank. What *had* she been doing back here? She waved the document case. "Actually, I was just grabbing some papers and locking up," she said, pulling the door shut. "What are you up to back here, if you don't mind me asking?"

The professor sighed. "I have been working on an article on Alexander Scriabin of all people and realized I needed Nemtin's arrangement of his *Prefatory Action*, a copy of which I happen to know resides in the Casey Collection." He held up a slim, buckram-bound volume. "So, I thought I'd hightail it over here and abscond with the little bugger before the polar vortex shuts the whole city down."

Alice escorted Professor Hastings to the lobby, only half listening to him babble about Scriabin's *Mysterium* and how performing the unfinished piece was supposed to have ushered in a new golden era for the world. She couldn't shake the feeling that she'd left something behind.

Hastings gave a little wave as the elevator doors slid closed, and it wasn't until that moment Alice realized she had failed, yet again, to report the situation with the cylinder. She hadn't mentioned it to Hastings, nor had she called Greta. Alice hoped Mr. Caul had been similarly tight-lipped, but had no idea why.

The document case held several old newspaper clippings in Mylar sleeves and a book called *Timber Tramps & Widow Makers: A Short History of Logging in the Midwest*. Alice spread the articles out across her desk. A cursory read showed that most were accounts of S&W's unstoppable growth during its heyday, successful business dealings and the like, all ranging from the late 1800s to 1905. The final clipping was Cornelius Wilks's obituary from the *Minton Messenger*, dated April 17, 1905. "Inflammation of the lungs" had been the cause of death.

Alice picked up the book and riffled through it. There were a few chapters devoted to S&W and its competitors in the state, with several photos interspersed. A sidebar article grabbed her attention:

WHERE OH WHERE HAS OUR LITTLE MILLIONAIRE GONE?

One enduring mystery from the annals of our lumbering past is this: where did Eaton Salter disappear to between July and November of 1909?

The story goes that he embarked on a solo camping

trip (of which he was quite fond) just after Independence Day '09, boarding the Suttree Special in Iron City, and getting off 200 miles north, somewhere near what is now Walleye Lake State Forest. The plan was for the gray-haired but still hearty lumber baron to camp and fish for a few weeks before meeting up with Cornelius Wilks's sons, Edmond and Grant (who had inherited their late father's share of S&W), for the annual summer business meeting in Minton.

When Salter failed to return by mid-August the company sent a small army of searchers north, via train, to find him. Some say that it was all for show and that the so-called "rescuers" spent most of their time drinking and playing cards, waiting for winter to arrive so they could call off the search and so the Wilks brothers could announce Salter's death. In fact, a death certificate was drawn up in early November of that year. S&W was within days of filing it with the state, and had brought back most of the men they'd sent up, when Salter stumbled into the train depot in Calhoun, a good sixty miles from where he'd walked into the forest more than four months earlier. The story goes that he didn't have a scratch on him.

Information gets murky after his return, but we do know that this was the beginning of Salter's late-period "eccentricities". After returning home from his extended hike up north, Salter divested himself of his share of S&W and became what could only be described nowadays as an early "tree hugger". All of this would come to a head just two years later, in Minton, when he set fire to his own lumber mill, killing himself, his beloved dogs, and Edmond Wilks in the process.

At the bottom of the page were two photos. One of them was the famous shot of a gray-haired Salter standing on a bluff with his rifle, his eyes bright and full of confidence. The other was a photo of Edmond Wilks, and when Alice saw it, she almost screamed.

Around three p.m. Alice delivered her one and only order for the day, a pull for a pair of linguistics students in the second floor carrels. Just as she was walking back to the elevators, an announcement came over the tinny PA that, because of the blizzard, they were closing the library for the day. Alice took the service elevator back up to the fifth floor, her head swimming with visions of Edmond Wilks somehow sneaking into Special Collections a hundred years after his death. As the chipped doors slid open to deposit her in the fifth-floor lobby, she was shocked to see Mr. Caul, *sans* cart, standing nervously by her desk. He looked up as she left the elevator.

"Did you forget something?" asked Alice.

Caul rocked on his heels for a moment and stared down at the floor. "No. I…"

"Well, I'm outta here. Didn't you hear the announcement?" said Alice, brushing past him to grab her coat from its hook behind the desk. "If you're here to yell at me some more, you can save yourself the trouble."

"No, nothing like that," said Caul. "I just wondered if you were perhaps thinking along the same lines as myself." He rocked again, hands shoved nervously in his pants pockets.

Oh god I hope not, thought Alice. "What do you mean, exactly?"

Caul stared right at her. She noticed how pale he looked, how bruised the flesh was around his eyes. "How many of those hidden recordings are there, do you suppose?" he said.

Alice didn't reply but set her coat down on the desk. That was exactly what she'd been wondering, though she hadn't realized it until that moment. "As you said earlier, that's a matter for Professor Hastings or Greta," she said.

"Is it? Then why haven't you told them yet?"

"I've been busy. Why haven't you?"

Caul removed his right hand from his pocket. He was holding a gray-handled utility knife. "Suppose more of the cylinders were to be found mysteriously cracked in their cabinets. We would have no choice but to investigate, yes?"

Alice thought about that for a moment. Finally, surprising herself yet again, she nodded and unlocked the desk's top drawer. "I suppose we'd better make sure none of the others are cracked," she said, grabbing the key cards.

By the time the wavering light in the storage room kicked fully on, Alice was already entering the combination on the wax cylinder cage. She pulled the complaining door open and they stood for a moment in the entrance, shadowed cabinets looming before them.

"Which one?" asked Caul.

Alice pulled the string light and pointed to the back of the locker. "Number seven." The pair approached the cabinet. Breaking the shared silence, Alice opened the cabinet door and took a step back so that Caul could peruse its contents. "Which one should we start with?" he asked.

Alice glanced at the map on the inside of the door, trying to deduce a likely suspect. "That one," she said, pointing to a cylinder on the middle shelf: *County Platte Dispute Notes, November 21, 1899*.

It was hard for Alice to reconcile the nit-picking Mr. Caul with the person who stood before her now. This new version reached into the cabinet, grabbed the cardboard tube in question and removed the cylinder within, all without hesitation. Before either of them could change their minds, he sliced right into the dull brown material with his utility knife. Alice held her breath as he pulled off a large chunk and let it drop to the floor.

"*Merde*," he said and coughed. Poking out through the hole in the brown layer like a rat was another gray recording, looking as freshly cut as the first. Caul locked eyes with Alice. She nodded. He handed her a twin utility knife.

They limited themselves to the second shelf of cabinet seven, deciding they might still be able to plead insanity if they were caught. By the time they removed the outer layers of brown wax, all eleven remaining cylinders were revealed to contain secret gray recordings beneath.

Caul was wheezing heavily by the time they finished, and bent over to catch his breath for a moment.

"Are you okay?" said Alice. "Do you have an inhaler or something?"

"Not asthma," said Caul. "If I were... allergic to dust... this building would have killed me long ago."

"Well, let's get you out of this room, anyway. Maybe you're having a mould reaction."

Alice placed the flayed recordings into an empty cardboard box. As they turned to leave the locker, there was a flash from above as both lights died, dropping the room into instant full dark. "Dammit!" said Alice. "I don't even have a flashlight in here."

Caul responded by switching on a pocket flashlight and smiling. "Let there be—"

A horrible wet thudding interrupted him, coming from behind cabinet seven as if something big were trying to move it out of the way. Both Alice and Caul cried out and rushed out of the locker and through the door. The circular hallway beyond was just as dark as the storage room. Caul's little halo of light barely penetrated the gloom, but they didn't hesitate.

"What was that?" wheezed Caul, as they ran for the front door of the Salter Collection.

"No idea," said Alice.

When they reached the door, Alice took the light from Caul and handed him the box of cylinders. She tried to calm herself long enough to swipe the key card and enter the code. Though her right hand was thoroughly shaking, it had performed this particular act so many times that it went into autopilot. There was no response, even though the keypad was unaffected by the blackout. Usually, if she made a mistake on the code, the little red light to the side of the pad would blink. This time, however, nothing.

"What's… the matter?" said Caul.

"Not sure." Alice attempted the swipe and code a second time. Still nothing. In the middle of her third attempt, the keypad went dark. *This can't be happening*, thought Alice. Security was on its own protected circuit. Even if the whole building were to lose power, the backup generators should instantaneously bring the alarms back online.

"Let *me* try," said Caul.

Alice fought down a spike of annoyance and handed over the card, shining the flashlight on the keypad. "What's your code?" asked Caul.

"Um…"

"Quickly!" he shouted.

"1234."

Caul frowned, looking extra caustic in the heavy shadows of the flashlight. "Are you *insane*?!"

"Either try the goddamn card or get out of my way so I can, you pedantic little prick!"

Without a word, Caul turned to make another attempt. Nothing happened. He handed her the card, eyes wet. "It's no use," he said.

"Look," said Alice. "I'm really sorry."

Caul wiped at his eyes with one sleeve. "I realize I am a… thoroughly unlikeable person… but that's no excuse to—"

Another wet thud. Alice pointed the flashlight into the darkness from where they came, revealing nothing but bookcases and the scuffed marble floor receding into blackness.

"Come on." Alice grabbed Caul's sleeve and dragged him away.

Almost as soon as they had locked themselves in the listening room, the lights came back on. The pair stood, trembling, waiting for whatever it was out there to break down the door. Nothing happened for several minutes. Alice realized she was still clutching the box of wax cylinders to her chest, so she set it down on the table next to the Archéophone.

Caul, still wheezing, stared at the machine for a moment. He removed one of the cylinders from the box and raised an eyebrow at Alice. "I believe… we're supposed to… play them," he said.

Alice had a sudden and vivid recollection of the dream that had awakened her the night before. In it, she had been searching through the Salter Collection for something she couldn't remember, but desperately needed. The hallway had turned to mud beneath her. She'd slipped and fallen into the cold ooze, but before she could pull herself back to her feet there was a tumultuous roar as rushing water filled the hallway. She was swept away by the freezing rapids.

Eventually, Alice had clawed out of the river and up a bank into some trees. She pushed through the dense thicket, branches scratching at her face, until breaking out on the other side into an empty clearing in the middle of an endless moonlit wood. Dogs howled in the dark.

A voice from out of the night had whispered to her and slipped something into her pocket.

Alice took the cylinder from Mr. Caul. It pulsed in her hand like an egg sac and in that moment she remembered what Salter had said to her. *"It is returned."*

She smiled and placed the cylinder onto the spindle.

Sköll and Hati came at the end of the ninth cylinder. By that point, Mr. Caul had accepted his part in the ritual and did not even scream when they tore him apart. Blood sprayed everywhere, much more than one would expect from such a small man. Alice had to wipe the tenth cylinder on her blouse before playing it, and even then it skipped and had to be played twice.

The fire started on its own as soon as the twelfth and final cylinder began playing.

Alice followed the hounds' tracks through the snow. The mansion was lit up like Christmas. She could see its glow long before she climbed the final hill and looked down upon the massive wooden structure.

A backlit figure stood in the open front doorway.

Alice began laughing. She laughed harder than she had in years, possibly since she was a child in that tiny gray house, before disappointment had curdled her. It hit her how hilarious it was that all the emptiness and longing and lying to herself and worrying—it was all just a shadow cast across fertile ground, a cloud passing before the sun. She could feel her true roots stirring, readying themselves to burst up through the frozen earth of her being.

Alice shucked off her old life like wiping a spiderweb from her sleeve. Her heart was buoyant as she stepped down the snow-covered slope, toward the figure in the doorway.

She heard the elevator doors slide open just beyond the edge of the woods. Rafael's gasp was comically loud even from this far back, hidden by the trees. She knew Hastings was with him, though only because she sensed the older man's horror. Perhaps he had expected the new era, when it came, to be something a little less…

Wild.

She smiled to herself.

"Alice?" Rafael shouted. "Are you in there?"

"No," she said quietly. She followed the vibrations of their fear to the edge of the wood, where the pair stood on the polished floor with their mouths hanging open, unable to take in what was unfolding before them, what was stretching up to scrabble against the high-domed ceiling.

Sköll and Hati slunk out of the trees to join their master, stopping to sit on either side of her, coiled but obedient.

Hastings edged backward, away from the hounds, away from the trees, toward the still open elevator doors. Rafael took a step toward her and reached out his hand. "Come on, missy, let's get you out of here," he said.

She smiled, opened her mouth, and spoke the primordial forest back into existence.

SPEAKING STILL
by Ramsey Campbell

As soon as I opened the door of the Hole Full of Toad I saw Daniel. I'd meant to be first at the pub and have a drink waiting for him, but he was seated near the bar with his back to me and talking on his phone. I was crossing the discoloured carpet between the stout old tables, scarred by cigarettes and at least a decade old, when he noticed me. "Goodbye for now, my love," he murmured and stood up, pocketing his phone. "You look ready for a drink."

It was our regular greeting, but I could tell he hoped I hadn't overheard his other words. Embarrassment made me facetious. "What's tonight's tipple?"

"Mummy's Medicine," he said and pointed at his tankard. "Not as urinary as it might appear."

"It's what the doctor ordered, is it?"

"It's what this one prescribes."

Though we'd performed this routine in the past, it felt too deliberate now. "I'll be the second opinion," I said to bring it to an end.

When he brought me a yeasty pint I found it palatable enough. We always tried the guest ale and then usually reverted to our favourite. Daniel took a manful gulp and wiped foam from his stubbly upper lip. He'd grown less plump over the last few months, but his skin was lagging behind, so that his roundish face reminded me of a balloon left over from a party, wrinkled but maintaining an unalterable wide-eyed smile that might have contained a mute plea. He kept up the smile as he said, "Ask me the question, Bill."

"How have you been?"

"I'd prefer to forget most of that if you don't mind. I've seen colleagues lose patients, but that's nothing like the same." Daniel opened his eyes wider still, which looked like a bid to take more of a hold on the moment if not to drive back any moisture. "The job's helping now," he said, "but that wasn't the question I thought you'd have."

"I'd better let you tell me what it ought to be."

"Weren't you wondering who I was talking to when you came in?"

"Honestly, Daniel, that's none of my business. If you've found someone—"

"You think I'd be involved with someone else so soon. Or do you think I already was?"

"I'm sorry for presuming. I must have misheard."

"I don't think so. Perhaps you missed the obvious." As if taking pity on me Daniel said, "I was talking to Dorothy, Bill."

I thought this was quite a distance from the obvious, but stopped my mouth with a drink. "No need to be confused," Daniel said. "She's still there. Would you like to hear?"

"Please," I said, though it didn't feel much like an invitation.

He took out his phone and opened an album to show me a photograph. "That's the last I have of her. She wanted me to take it, so I did."

It had the skewed look of a hasty shot. His wife was sitting up in a hospital bed. She'd lost far more weight than Daniel and was virtually bald, but was matching if not besting the smile I imagined he'd given her. "I wasn't talking to her there tonight, though," Daniel said. "Bend your ear to this."

He brought up a list of calls received, and I leaned towards the phone as he retrieved one. "Don't bother visiting me this afternoon," Dorothy said. "They'll be having a look. I expect I'll be out of it this evening, so I may not be worth your journey then either."

I found I'd grown shy of meeting Daniel's eyes, especially when he said, "That's the last I ever heard from her. I went in, and I didn't leave her after that till the end."

"You did say."

"That isn't all I've kept. I'm only glad I haven't erased anything since last year."

The calls skimmed up the screen until he touched a listing with a moist forefinger. This time his wife was telling him which supermarket aisle she was in and which items he should find elsewhere in the store. "She sounds more like she used to, doesn't she?" Daniel said.

Her voice was far stronger and brisker than it had been in the call from the hospital. As I tried not to feel too saddened by his need to preserve every trace of her Daniel said, "But that isn't really her either."

It seemed unsafe to say more than "How is that, Daniel?"

"She built herself up around the self she never quite got rid of. Sometimes I think the children we all used to be are lying in wait inside us, maybe hoping we won't rouse them." As he returned the phone to his pocket he said, "Thank God she's free of her mother at last."

"I thought her mother died years ago."

"Not in Dorothy's mind," Daniel said and shut his eyes so hard that he might have been trying to crush a memory. "Tell me an exciting tale of accountancy, Bill."

This was another of our old jokes that I hadn't heard for weeks. I did my best to generate suspense from a call I'd made on a client's behalf to the tax collector, and then I was glad to hear news from the medical world. When the pub shut we went in opposite directions, having established that we'd meet next week. I glanced back to see that Daniel had stopped beneath a streetlamp and taken out his phone, but I couldn't tell whether he was speaking.

My wife Jane was in bed and on the way to sleep. "How was your friend?" she said most of.

"Missing Dorothy."

"Well, I should expect so. I hope you'll miss me too."

I rather wished her sleepiness hadn't let that slip out, though of course she only meant if she was first to go when the inevitable came, surely quite a few years hence. I'd managed to put all this out of my head by the time I joined her, and Daniel's situation had gone too. I can't say I thought about him much in the ensuing week, but when Monday came around I looked forward to catching up with him. Given his concern for all his patients, I was hoping a week's work might have helped him.

The pub was in sight when I saw him outside. Since he was talking on his phone, I wasn't sure whether to hang back, especially since I couldn't see his face. I compromised by making for the entrance, which he wasn't far from, and heard him say "You'll be all right, Dorothy. You've still got the right kind of strength."

As I tried to steal into the pub the door creaked. Daniel turned, belatedly hitching up his smile, and shoved the phone into his pocket. "Yes, I'm ready for a drink."

He dodged into the pub at once, so that I wondered if he meant to restrict the conversation we might have had. When I brought two pints of Hound's Howl to the table, however, he was ready to talk. "Some of the doctors who are coming up," he said, "you'd wonder if they need a doctor. There's a call to reclassify schizophrenia as a spectrum instead of a disease."

"That isn't your area, though."

"I know more than I'd like to about it." He downed a cloudy mouthful as though to douse his fierceness. "I'm just glad they weren't taking that approach," he said, "when they diagnosed Dorothy's mother."

"I didn't know she had that problem, Daniel."

"Dorothy never wanted it discussed, even with friends. Her mother brought her up never to talk about her. Even I didn't realise what was wrong till her mother couldn't hide it any more."

"How recently was that?"

"Too recently. For most of our marriage I didn't know about Dorothy's childhood."

So we hadn't strayed so far from his preoccupation after all. "What was it like?" I said.

"I'll tell you just one thing I won't forget. When Dorothy was little, before she was even at school…" This time his gulp of ale seemed intended to fortify him. "If she did anything her mother thought was bad, and there was no predicting what that might be next," he said, "she'd be locked in her room with no light, and she'd be told that something worse than she could possibly imagine would come for her if she dared to put the light on."

I felt bound to ask "Did she?"

"Not till years later, and do you know what the old, do you know what her mother did then? Took the bulb out of the socket and wouldn't let her have one in her room."

I was running out of questions I wanted to ask. "How did all that affect Dorothy, do you think?"

"She told me not at all by then. She said she challenged whatever she was meant to be scared of to show itself, and of course nothing did. She assured me that toughened her up and she was never afraid of anything her mother imagined again."

"More power to her."

"If it was true. I'm just afraid she kept it hidden deep down in herself."

"Daniel, please don't take this the wrong way, but at least you needn't worry any more."

I thought he'd opened his mouth to speak, but he gave himself a drink instead. His throat worked before he muttered "You didn't meet her mother."

"And if I had…"

"Call me fanciful, but whenever she came into a room you'd feel as if she'd turned it dark."

"I suppose you might when you knew what she'd done to your wife."

"I felt like that before I knew." Daniel reinforced this with a stare that looked trapped by the memory. "And I think having her committed brought everything back," he said, "even if Dorothy tried not to show it did."

"Surely she'd have been relieved that her mother was being taken care of."

"You'd hope so." With more conviction than I thought was warranted he said "She kept telling Dorothy that if we had her shut away she'd make sure Dorothy was with her."

"But she wasn't, so I should think—"

"It was all she talked about when she was dying. She said she'd wait for Dorothy in the dark, and she'd be made of worms."

"That's second childhood stuff, wouldn't you agree? I hope your wife thought so."

Daniel's tankard stopped short of his mouth. "Whose childhood, Bill?"

"You know I meant her mother's. I never knew Dorothy to be anything but strong."

As he took a drink I saw him ponder how to go on. "You caught what I was saying earlier."

"I didn't mean to eavesdrop."

"I might have myself." Even more like an apology he said "I wouldn't ask this of anyone except a good friend."

With no idea where this was leading I could only say "Then you can ask me."

"Do you think Dorothy could hear me?"

"When do you mean?"

I was bracing myself to be told that he had her last moments in mind, and was nowhere near ready to hear him say "Now."

"We can't know, can we?" In a bid to raise his spirits I said "In a way we're keeping her alive by talking about her."

"I wasn't thinking of you." Though his smile winced in case he'd sounded rude, he carried on. "I mean when I'm speaking to her on the phone," he said.

I took all the care I could over answering. "You'd like to think so."

"Yes, but I'm asking what you think."

"I won't say you're wrong, Daniel."

"All right, Bill, you're discharged. The ordeal's over." Humour deserted him as he said "I wonder what your wife would say. She's the computer expert, after all."

I'd begun to wonder how potent our drinks were. "How did we get on to computers?"

"They've been on my mind a good deal recently. I'm starting to believe they may have made a kind of afterlife."

"All the photos of Dorothy you'll have, you mean." When he didn't respond I said "Her voice."

"That's what I've kept, my wife in electronic form."

"And you still have all your memories of her."

"I don't want you to think I'm being maudlin." As I made to deny it he said "I just wonder how much of her that is."

"I'm afraid I'm not following."

"All of us are electronic where it counts, aren't we? What they used to call the soul, that's a mass of electronic impulses in the brain. Even if they didn't have a place to go before, perhaps they have one now."

Though I might have liked to take a drink rather than speak I said "We're still talking about computers."

"Yes, the Internet. That's where everything we know is turned into electronic form. Perhaps I haven't got it right, though," Daniel said, and I was hoping rationality had overtaken him until he added "Perhaps it gives us access to a place that was already there."

I no longer knew how to respond. I was lingering over a mouthful of ale when Daniel said "I realise you aren't going to accept it without proof."

"That would be a help."

He took out his phone at once. "There's another message," he said.

He left a moist print on an entry in the list before turning the phone towards me. His wife's voice sounded weaker or more distant than it previously had. "Are you there? You're not there, are you? Don't be—"

I assumed she'd cut herself off by mistake, since I'd heard a trace of nervousness. "Was she asking you not to be long?"

"I hope that's it, but that isn't the point. That's her most recent message, Bill."

"I thought you told me the one you played yesterday was."

"It was then," Daniel said and showed me the phone. "As you see, now this is top of the list."

"But it hasn't got a date."

"And don't you wonder how that could happen?" When I had no explanation, though I might have pointed out that the caller was unnamed as well, he said "Would you mind asking your wife?"

"I'll call you when I have, shall I?"

"No need for me to trouble you so much. Next time we meet will be fine."

I thought he was doing his best to put the issue out of his mind, despite forgetting to make his accountancy joke.

Instead he told me at considerable length how medicine and surgery would soon be able to prolong life, though I couldn't tell whether he regretted that the developments came too late for his wife or was glad that they hadn't been there for her mother. I felt as though his monologue was postponing what he was anxious to say, and then I grasped that I mightn't be the person he was desperate to address.

We'd hardly parted outside the pub when I heard him on his phone. Either he wanted me to hear or no longer cared whether I did. "Dorothy, I'm sorry I missed your call. I don't know when it was, because I didn't hear it ring. I'll keep an eye on the phone whenever I can, just in case. I know we'll be together again soon, and then we'll have all the time there is."

He sounded like someone I hardly knew—as unlike the self he presented to the world as he'd said his wife differed from hers. As I headed for home the call I'd heard made the autumn night feel as cold as black ice. Jane was asleep, having driven fifty miles to revive all the computers in a large office. When I caught up with her at breakfast I found I was anxious to learn "Do you know if there's a reason why a missed call wouldn't show a date?"

"You can't withhold those, only the number."

"I thought so, but Daniel has one with no date."

"He'd have had to delete the information himself, though I don't know how." Jane abandoned the delicate frown that had narrowed her keen eyes and said "How was he this week?"

"I'm not sure he's coping that well. He's kept all the messages his wife left on the phone, but he seems to be convincing himself he can still hear from her."

"Maybe that's how he's coping. I don't see the harm if it doesn't put his patients at risk."

I couldn't believe Daniel would let that happen. If he thought he was growing incompetent, surely he would take leave rather than risk botching an operation. Perhaps Jane was right, and his preoccupation was no worse than a comfort to him. However irrational it was, I came to accept it on his behalf as the week went on, until Samira stopped me as I returned from convincing a client to keep receipts for six years, not just one. "A Dr Hargreaves was asking for you, Bill," she said. "You aren't sick, are you?"

"No, he's a friend."

"It was only that it sounded urgent. He says don't call unless you have to, otherwise he'll see you tonight as usual."

Friday was by no means usual, and if Jane hadn't gone away overnight to deal with an office-wide computer crash I would have felt unreasonable for leaving her alone two nights in a week. I reached the pub earlier than normal, only to find Daniel already at a table. He'd been drinking fast or for a while, since his tankard was less than half full, and when he brought me a pint of Mohammed's Prohibition he treated himself to its twin. "There's another message," he said.

His smile looked determined not to yield but close to meaningless. When he brought out the phone I saw that the new message was undated and unidentified. "Jane doesn't know how there can't be a date," I said and risked adding "Don't you think that means it needn't be new?"

"It wasn't there before. I'd have listened if it was."

"I'm saying it could have been delayed. Maybe there's a glitch that left out the date as well."

His only response was to set the message off and turn the phone towards my ear, waving my hand away when I made to take the mobile. Even when I ducked towards it I could scarcely hear for the mass of unchecked conversations in the pub. The voice was feebler than before, barely recognisable as Dorothy's. "I don't like this. I don't know where I am." I could have thought it was as small as a child's. "It's dark and wet," Dorothy protested. "I think it's wriggling, or I am.

Can't you hear?"

A hiss of static followed, which sounded as if some kind of collapse had overwhelmed the call. Once he'd pocketed the phone Daniel gazed expectantly if not beseechingly at me, but I was loath to share my first thought—that Dorothy had inherited her mother's mental problem, which had overtaken her at her lowest ebb. I compromised by saying "Do you think that's how she felt when she was waiting for you at the hospital? She wasn't like that once you got there, was she?"

"She was barely conscious. She hardly seemed to know I was there."

"I'm sure you must have made the feelings go away, so she couldn't have had them at the end."

His smile had begun to look less studied. "You're suggesting she made this call from the hospital."

"I'm sure that has to be it. I've had calls that got lost in the ether for days. I'll ask Jane what's the longest delay she knows about if you like."

"I've already spoken to the hospital. They say she wasn't capable of phoning once they'd run the tests."

"That proves they're wrong about this call then, doesn't it? She'd already made the one asking you not to be late."

"I don't believe she did say that, or from the hospital." His smile was making itself plain now—amusement so wry it was more like regret. "I don't think she was cut off," he said. "She was saying someone wasn't there, if you remember. I think she was telling them not to be."

"Come on, Daniel," I said, perhaps too heartily. "Who could she have been talking to on your phone except you? And you're the last person she would have wanted to put off."

Either this persuaded him to some extent or he preferred not to answer. Soon he was expounding on the merits of euthanasia and assisted suicide. I suspect that he sensed I was glad to be spared more of his obsession, because when we left the pub he said "I should think you've had enough of me for a week."

"I'd be less of a friend if I had. Let's make it Monday as ever," I said and was relieved not to see him take out his phone as he vanished into the dark.

Jane's task was more complex than she'd anticipated, and she wasn't home on Saturday until I'd gone to bed. On Monday morning I was ashamed to realise I'd forgotten to quiz her on Daniel's behalf. "How long do you think a call to a mobile could be held up?" I said.

"Quite some time," Jane said and poured herself a coffee even blacker than the one she'd just had. "A client of mine had a call turn up months late."

"I knew it," I said and thought of phoning Daniel at once. "Daniel keeps getting calls from his wife that he thinks are new. You'd say they're delayed, wouldn't you? I'll tell him."

"I don't know if you should do that." Jane took a sip so black that sensing its harshness made me wince. "I've never heard of staggered delays, if that's what you're describing," she said. "I wouldn't think it's possible."

I decided against phoning Daniel. By the time I saw him that night I might have worked out what to say. I hadn't when I reached the office, and meetings with clients left me no chance. I was at my desk and working on an email in which words were shorter and less abundant than numbers when the receptionist rang me. "There's a gentleman to see you, Bill."

"Could you ask him what he'd like to drink? He isn't due for half an hour."

"He isn't your appointment. He says you're a friend." With a hint of doubt Jody said "Dr Hargreaves."

For a moment I was tempted to declare myself unavailable, and then I felt worse than remorseful. I hurried into the lobby to find Daniel crouched on a chair. He was consulting his phone or guarding it, and his stance looked close to foetal. When he glanced up I thought he was struggling to remember how to smile. "Can we talk somewhere private?" he said almost too low to be heard.

Six straight chairs faced six more across a bare table in the nearest conference room. Daniel slumped onto a chair while I shut the door, and as I sat opposite him he said "She's there again, Bill."

"Jane says calls can be delayed for months."

"I don't think they were calls in the first place." He laid his phone between us on the table and rested his distressed gaze on the dormant screen. "I'm sure this one isn't," he said.

"What else could it be?"

"I believe I've made some kind of connection." He planted his hands on either side of the phone, and moisture swelled under his fingers. "Maybe keeping her on the phone helped, and I'm sure trying to speak to her did," he said. "I think we're hearing her as she is now."

I might have preferred not to listen to the evidence, but I was determined to help if I could. "Let me hear then, Daniel."

The marks of his hands were still fading from the table when he brought up the latest entry on the list. This one was bereft of details too. Even though he'd switched the speaker on, the voice was almost inaudibly faint. "It's dark because I've got no eyes. That's why the dark is so big. Or it's eating its way in because it's made of worms. They're all I'm going to be..."

Daniel dabbed at the phone with a moist fingertip once the thin diminished voice fell silent. Though I was appalled by the way Dorothy's terrors had reduced her to the state of a fearful child, I tried my best to reassure him. "It has to be an old call, Daniel. It's sad, but it's only more of the thoughts you cured her of by being with her at the end."

"You haven't heard it all yet." He raised a finger, and a qualm plucked at my guts as I realised he had only paused the message. "Tell me what you hear," he said like some kind of plea.

"That's me. It's only me, or it's the dark. I can't really feel it, it's only dark. Like being asleep and dreaming. Just dark and my imagination." The voice might have been drifting into a reminiscent stupor, but then it grew louder. "Who is that?" it cried, and a rush of static unpleasantly suggestive of moisture seemed to end by forming an answer. "Me."

Daniel clasped the phone protectively, to no effect I could imagine. "You heard, didn't you? You heard the other voice."

"I heard Dorothy, Daniel." However sharp and shrill the final word had been, surely that signified no more than impatience. "She was saying what she said before," I insisted. "Don't let it upset you, but she meant she was by herself. And then you came and stayed with her till the end."

"I wish I could believe that." Although he was staring at me, he appeared to see a sight considerably less welcome than I hoped I was. "I'm afraid I didn't just bring her by calling," he said. "I think I attracted something else."

I could have argued but confined myself to saying "Do you mind if we discuss it tonight? I need to get ready for a meeting soon."

"I'll give tonight a miss if you don't mind. I have to be prepared as well."

I imagined him sitting alone at home with the phone in his hand while he waited for yet another tardy message. Should I have insisted he came out for a drink? All I said was "Next Monday, then."

"Monday," Daniel said as though the prospect was irrelevant if not unimaginably remote.

He scarcely seemed to hear me wish him well as I saw him out of the building. Interviews and official phone calls took up my afternoon, and a job kept Jane away overnight. Our empty house felt like an omen of a future in which one of us would be on our own, and I was more than glad when she called me at breakfast to say she was starting for home. "And here's something to tell Daniel if you think you should," she said. "I've found a case where somebody made several calls in an hour but the person they were calling kept receiving them for most of a week."

I thought this was worth passing on to Daniel, and as soon as I'd said goodbye to Jane I rang him. His phone was unresponsive, refusing even to accept messages. I blamed his interpretation of his wife's calls for making the utter silence feel like darkness so complete it could engulf all sound. I phoned the hospital where he worked, only to learn that he'd cancelled all his operations. They had no idea how long he would be on leave, and wished they knew.

My first meeting of the day was after lunch. As I drove to the suburb next to mine I tried to think what to say to Daniel. I was hoping to persuade him that he needed someone else's help. His broad house—one of a conjoined pair—was emptily pregnant with a bay window and shaded by a sycamore that had strewn the front lawn with seeds. Sunlight muffled by unbroken cloud made the front room look dusty if not abandoned. I was ringing the bell a third time when Daniel's neighbour emerged from her house, pointing a key at her car to wake it up. "He went out earlier," she said. "He'll be at work."

At once I knew where he might be. In five minutes I was at the graveyard where I'd attended Dorothy's funeral. Her plot was in the newest section, where the turf wouldn't have looked out of place in a garden centre and the headstones were so clean they could have advertised the stonemason's shop. Once I'd parked the car a wind followed me across the grass, and I heard the discreet whispering of cypresses. My footfalls weren't much louder. I was trying to be unobtrusive, having seen Daniel.

He was kneeling on Dorothy's grave with his back to me. He hadn't reacted when I shut the car door, admittedly as quietly as I could. While I was reluctant to disturb him, I wanted to know what state he was in. I strained my ears but heard only the reticently restless trees. At least I wouldn't interrupt Daniel at prayer or in attempted conversation, and as I approached he stirred as though he was about to greet me. No, a shadow was patting his shoulder, a faint ineffectual gesture on the part of a cypress. In fact, he was so immobile that I couldn't help clearing my throat to rouse him. This brought no visible response, and I'd grown nervous by the time I came close enough to see his face.

He wasn't merely kneeling. His chest rested against the headstone, and his chin was propped on the sharp edge. However uncomfortable that might have been, he showed no sign of pain. His fixed smile looked fiercely determined, and his eyes were stretched so wide that I could only wonder what he'd been striving to see. They saw nothing now, because nobody was using them. When I closed the lids I imagined shutting in the dark.

His phone had fallen from one dangling hand and lay beside the headstone. I retrieved it, finding it chilly with dew, and wiped it on my sleeve. For a moment I was pitifully relieved that I wouldn't be able to look for any messages, since the phone was activated by a passcode, and then I recalled seeing Daniel type his birthdate. Before I could panic I keyed in the digits and brought up the list of messages. All the latest ones were unnamed and dateless, and there were two more than I'd previously seen.

I opened the first one and held my breath. The pleading voice wasn't much louder than the cypresses, and I fancied that it sounded afraid to be heard or else acknowledged. "Leave me alone. You're just the dark and worms. You're just a dream and I want a different one." At first I thought the noise that followed was just a loose mass of static, and then it began to form words. "Mother's here now," it said. "She's what she promised she would be. There's nobody for you to tell and nobody to see. She'll be with you always like a mother should."

I struggled to believe the explanation I would have given Daniel—that it was yet another deferred call from Dorothy, which was why she was referring to her mother in the third person—but not only the usage made the voice seem inhuman. It no longer resembled static so much as the writhing of numerous worms, an image I tried to drive out of my head as I played the last message. I almost wish I'd left it unheard. An onslaught of slithering swelled out of the speaker in wordless triumph, and in its midst I seemed to hear a plea crushed almost beyond audibility but fighting to shape words. I couldn't bear much of this, and I was reaching to turn it off when another voice went some way towards blotting out the relentless clamour. "I'm here as well."

It was unmistakably Daniel's, though it sounded in need of regaining strength. In less than a second the message came to an end. I closed my fist around the phone and tried to tell myself that Daniel could have recorded his voice over the last part of an existing message. The idea he'd left in my mind days ago was stronger: that the phone, or the way he'd sought not just to preserve all its recordings of his wife but to contact her, had somehow caused the situation. Perhaps I was mistaken, but by the time I doubted my decision it was too late. I found the edit button for the messages and let out a protracted shaky breath as I hit ERASE ALL.

I used Daniel's phone to call the police. Weeks later the inquest confirmed that he'd poisoned himself. When the police finished questioning me I drove from the graveyard to work. Though I yearned to be home, I managed to deal with several clients. At last I was at our front door, and when

Jane opened it she gasped as if my embrace had driven out all her breath. "No need to hang on so tight. I'm not going anywhere," she said, and I wondered how I could even begin to explain.

THE EYES ARE WHITE AND QUIET
by Carole Johnstone

18.02.19 (Clinic: BAR55, 14.02.19)
Consultant: Dr Barriga
Ophthalmology—Direct Line: 020 5489 9000/ Fax: 020
5487 5291
Minard Surgery Group, Minard Road, SE6 5UX

Dear Dr Wilson,

Hannah Somerville (06.07.93)
Flat 01, 3 Broadfield Rd, SE6 5UP
NHS No.: 566 455 6123

Thank you for referring this young lady, whose optician
suspected optic disc cupping. Her visual acuity is 6/6 in
the right eye and 6/4 in the left. Both of the eyes are white
and quiet. Intraocular pressure readings are 18mm/Hg in
the right and 16mm/Hg in the left. She has open anterior
chamber angles in both. The CD ratios are about 0.5.
There is no significant visual field defect.

Her eyesight does not appear to be deteriorating. Her
chief complaint is that of intermittent visual disturbance,
but this was absent in clinic. There is no family history
of glaucoma. I have not started her on any medication.
Unless she has any further problems, she will be reviewed

in the eye clinic in twelve months following a repeat visual fields test and central corneal thickness assessment.

Yours sincerely,

Dr Rajesh Roshan DRCOphth, FRCS
Staff Specialist in Ophthalmology

19.08.19 (Clinic: BAR55, 15.08.19)
Consultant: Dr Barriga
Ophthalmology—Direct Line: 020 5489 9000/ Fax: 020 5487 5291
Minard Surgery Group, Minard Road, SE6 5UX

Dear Dr Wilson,

Hannah Somerville (06.07.93)
Flat 01, 3 Broadfield Rd, SE6 5UP
NHS No.: 566 455 6123

This patient was reviewed in the eye clinic today at her own request. Her visual acuity is 6/6 in the right eye and 6/5 in the left. The eyes are white and quiet. The CD ratio remains about 0.5 in both. There is no significant visual field defect and no evidence of glaucoma.

We have seen this young lady at least three times in the last six months, and can ascertain no physical cause for her complaints of intermittent visual disturbance and periods of "complete blindness". These are reported as having lasted up to two hours on occasion, and she believes that their frequency is increasing.

I am of the opinion that we can do no more for her. I have referred her for psychological evaluation and discharged her from the eye clinic, with the advice to see her optician on an annual basis.

Yours sincerely,

Dr Rajesh Roshan DRCOphth, FRCS
Staff Specialist in Ophthalmology

"I mean, all that fuckin' gabbin' and over-sharin' like, everyone thinkin' they're bein' all civilised again, and look how quickly that went the way of everythin' else when they thought one had got in tonight." He rocked back on his heels; the dirt crackled against his boots. The fire warmed her face and she leaned closer to it. She was always so bloody cold.

"Sharin's never a good idea anyways. That posh divvy, he's half mad on that Debbie one, the auld arse don't know half as much as he thinks he does, Jimmy is more fuckin' terrified of wild dogs than anythin' could actually kill us. That's all it is, ain't it? Listenin', findin' out what makes folk tick, what makes 'em shit themselves. Survival instinct—if you're smart like. Say nothin' and let everyone else do the talkin'."

He was from Liverpool and he was on his own. He had terrible teeth; often she could smell his breath before he even spoke. His name was Robbo. That was all she knew about him. That, and he did a whole lot of talking for someone so against it. He liked talking to her; she had no idea why.

"Why don't you leave then?" she asked. It had started to snow: cold, glancing touches against her fire-warmed cheeks. She could hear the growing mutters and cries of dismay on the other side of the parked vans. They always built at least four fires now, one in each corner like a mobile Roman infantry camp.

"Nowhere to go is there? And folk need folk, like. That's

just survival instinct too, ain't it? Some folks, they got that more than other folks. And, I mean, it's not like you know which kind you're gonna be till it happens, ay? Soft lads like Jimmy are scared of their own shadow, then you got the likes of Bob fuckin' Marley runnin' straight at everythin' like a proper weapon. Debbie and that other bird—the Scottish one…"

"Sarah."

"Right. *Sarah*. I mean, what have they done since we all hooked up, eh?"

"They're just scared."

"*I'm* fuckin' scared. Don't stop me helpin' out, goin' on patrol. I mean, explain that, ay? You look at the animal kingdom, right? It's not like Peter fuckin' Rabbit wakes up one night and thinks, fuck it, what's the point? I can't be arsed runnin' away from anythin' that wants to 'ave me for brekkie. Might as well give up and die like. Or just cry meself to sleep in me nice comfy VW."

She smiled. "It's not the same." He was rattled. He was always wired, always opinionated, but the events of the day and then the wild dog that had snuck past the fires had got to him. His sweat was fresh, but it smelled bad; it reminded her of the days when no one had understood what was going on. When everyone had been trying so desperately to get away from a thing that they hadn't yet realised was everywhere.

"I mean, fuck, look at you, 'ann. You don't just go out on reccies, you fuckin' lead a few. And you can't see your arse from your fuckin' elbow."

She didn't answer.

"Arr ey, you can't, come on like. I'm not bein' a fuckin' dick. It's a valid fuckin' point."

She liked the way his *fuck*s and *like*s and *dick*s always sounded like the hissing hot water siphons of the coffee shops that she used to hide in when her sight started getting really bad. It was comforting somehow. She liked the way that he admired her too. Even before she'd proved her worth to everyone else, he'd always been the first to volunteer to sit watch with her. Back when she'd just been the blind girl.

There had been many convoys in those first few months, but none had stopped for her—or if they had, they'd moved on swiftly again without her. This one had initially said yes, she suspected, only because of Robbo. And as convoys went, it only just qualified. One of the vans was his beat-up Ford, still smelling of methylated spirits and paint and hash. The other—the VW—had belonged to a brethren couple whose names she had already forgotten.

Robbo swore when they both heard sudden movement behind him.

"Grub's up, ladies."

"Nice one," Robbo said, pretending that he hadn't cursed, that he couldn't hear Marley's low chuckle. "Want some scran, 'annah?"

She put out her hands and relished the sudden warmth of the foil tray. "Thanks."

Marley was big, she could tell. Sometimes—often—she could sense something other than scorn or tightly wound caution in him, especially when they were alone. Once, he had followed her to the shallow pit that they always dug on the periphery of their camp, and as she'd squatted and peed, she'd felt him watching; she'd breathed in the sea smells of him. If it wasn't for Robbo, she knew that she'd have a lot more to fear from Marley than she already did.

After Marley left them alone again, Robbo attacked his stew with gusto. She suspected that he always ate with his mouth wide open; she found the sound of that oddly comforting too. She ate quietly, mechanically, tasting nothing at all.

"Why won't this snow fuckin' stop?" he eventually muttered. "Last thing we fuckin' need is another fuckin' whiteout."

"I'll be able to hear them," she said, and he heaved a great sigh, even though it was a lie. It never failed to amaze her how easily that lie had been believed from the very start, as though the immediate consequence of her blindness should be a nearly preternatural sharpening of all her other senses. They did believe it though—all of them—and it was just as well. It made her useful, maybe indispensable. She knew that even Robbo's surrendered Peter Rabbits remembered the night that the Whites had ambushed them while they'd all been sleeping. She knew that they remembered her warning scream, the dead White at her feet next to the opened VW door, the bloodied crowbar in her hands. When the brethren couple had staggered out of the van, they'd pulled their coats tight around their bellies, crying and sobbing that God had saved them.

"Oh, aye?" Robbo had said, after discovering the body of a Pakistani man, whose name Hannah had also forgotten, lying by the makeshift entrance to their camp. "What he do to piss Him off then, ay?" The Pakistani had died badly. Even though Robbo had never told her exactly how, she'd been able to smell it; she'd been able to *see* it through the horrified witness of everyone else.

They'd burned both bodies on the periphery of their camp, and then buried the smoking bonfire under heavy, wet clods of grass.

"They almost look like us," Robbo had whispered to her later. "When they're dead at least, like. When they're not runnin'."

After that, they stopped sleeping in the vans. After that, not one member of the convoy voiced an objection when she started taking point, same as everyone else. There was always someone ready to hold onto her elbow and take the weight of her pack. A few weeks after the dead White, the brethren couple didn't return from an easy supply run. No one volunteered to go looking for them.

"So, what kind of folk are you, Robbo?" It wasn't what she wanted to ask, not even close, but she needed to start somewhere. They never talked about anything that was worth something. They never talked about where they'd come from, because none of them believed they'd ever be going back. And they never talked about where they were going, because they weren't going anywhere. They were just moving. And progress was slow. It was safer to scout routes and camps on foot before bringing up the vans behind. The vans weren't for travel any more; they were for escape. She'd been on point today, and the two days before that, and Robbo had held her elbow for all of them. That was why tonight of all nights, she needed somewhere to start.

"I'm still here, ay? What's that tell you?"

She swallowed. For a brief moment, fear swallowed her up, doubt pinched fingers against her windpipe. "Tell me something from home. Tell me something about before, about *you* before."

He sighed. It still rattled a bit inside his chest, even though he'd run out of the last of his bifters weeks ago. "Aright, 'annah. Don't see the fuckin' point like, but aright."

She heard him change position, move a little closer. "Anythin's better than bein' on your own, ain't it? That's just how it is. It's why we're all still here, ain't it? I had this mate, right. We'd been mates since school—not bezzies like 'cause he was a bit nuts, and you know what kids are like; you're not about to hang out with the soft lad. Anyways, we stayed in touch 'cause we lived on the same estate, we both worked in the Asda, and went to the same pubs on the weekend. And this guy, 'ann, he was somethin' else, man. He was like them abandoned puppies they used to show on ad breaks. He was built like a brick shithouse like, but soft as shite on account of his ma beatin' him up every time she took a drink when he was a kid, and his da tryin' to shag him every time she wasn't lookin'. All he wanted, right, was someone, anyone. You could fuckin' smell it off him."

When Robbo coughed, she nearly told him that it was okay, that he could stop if he wanted to. But she didn't. She shook the snow free of her blanket before pulling it tighter around her shoulders. She blinked her eyes, brushed icy fingers between her eyelashes, offering Robbo at least the illusion that she could see him. "Did he find someone?"

Robbo's laugh sounded angry, but she knew it wasn't. "Yer, he did. She likely didn't know her luck till she didn't. Folk never know what to do with unconditional love, like, d'you know that, 'annah? They think it's all they want till they get it. It wrecks with your head 'cause it makes no sense at all. It's like them pop-up targets at the shows. After a while you just need 'em to stay down, you know?"

She nodded, even though she had no idea at all.

"By the time they'd been seein' each other six months, she'd shagged half the estate behind his back."

"Did he find out?"

That angry laugh again. "Yer he did."

"What happened?"

When he didn't answer, she stabbed at the fire with a stick, sending up sparks of heat between them. Her heart was still beating far too fast. "Robbo?"

"He walked in on them," he muttered, and then suddenly he was talking too fast and too hard again; she struggled to keep up. "He whacked her over the 'ead with an 'ammer, and then he took a carvin' knife to the fella. And then he fronts up to my house, covered in their blood, and asks if he can come in like, if he can borrow a fuckin' towel. And I say go'ed, lad, no worries, have a shower while you're at it. And I phone the bizzies the minute he does."

He was breathing too heavily. She could nearly feel the hot, choppy distress of it. "You did the right thing, Robbo.

He'd killed people. What else could you have done?"

"Are you for real with this shit or is it just an act? I didn't call the bizzies 'cause he'd killed people and it was the right fuckin' thing to do, 'annah. I called 'em 'cause I thought he was gonna kill me. And he came to my house 'cause he knew I'd do it, he knew I'd grass 'im up."

She opened her mouth to speak, maybe to say sorry, but he hadn't finished. She could hear his boots scraping against the ground, and she could still hear the agitated puff of his breath.

"And as they're cartin 'im off, still fuckin' wet from me fuckin' shower, he says to me, *it's okay, Robbo*, like he fuckin' means it, and I stay standin' there on the doorstep in me skivvies and slippers, worryin' about the fuckin' neighbours."

"I used to be a troll."

He coughed again. "What?"

She gestured at the snow. "Before all this. When I still had my sight and the world still had the Internet. I worked nightshift in a petrol station as a cashier, and dayshift in online chat rooms as a troll."

She could nearly hear him blinking. It made her suddenly want to laugh.

"You mean, like, you were one of them blerts gets people to off 'emselves for shits and giggles?"

"No," she said quickly, though not for exoneration. "I just did what you said before. I watched and I listened. I worked out people's weaknesses and used them."

"You're pretty fuckin' good at it, like," he said, with a low, sheepish chuckle, because he was a lot cleverer than everyone else thought he was.

For a while, he said nothing else. She couldn't hear even the sound of his breathing any more, only the cracks of the firewood, the muffled conversations on the other side of the camp, the closing, echoless shroud of settling snow. In her mind's eye, she could see the clustered pine trees that she'd been able to smell just before they made camp. She imagined them padded with new white shoulders, their cones sparkling with frost, dark trunks in shadow. She imagined the abandoned towns and villages and cities made new, smothered under all that breathless white and quiet. And she imagined all the camps, doubtless just like this one: small bastions of fiery resistance, like coastal dun beacons passing along messages of doom.

She started when Robbo made a sudden movement, cleared his throat.

"What the fuck d'you do it for?" He sounded angry, and she could understand that at least. Robbo hadn't only thought that her blindness meant she could hear and smell better, he'd thought that it meant she *was* better. Better than anyone else.

And she'd thought about the why a lot too. Most often, she'd posed as a man, a predator, whose misogyny had hidden behind feigned interest and casually cruel charm. "I don't know. I just did."

She heard a sound: the cracking of a snow-heavy branch maybe, or a starving wild dog trying to hunt. In an instant she was afraid again, uncertain again. She reached out her numb hands toward the fire. "Do you ever get tired, Robbo?"

"Sure." That self-conscious chuckle again. "Do I wish I'd just stayed in the house and drunk meself to death instead? Deffo sure."

Some snow crept between her blanket and skin, cricking her neck. "Do you think we're both better people now?"

"No. Do you?"

"No." She smiled, and it hurt her chapped lips. "Is there any more of that nasty rum?"

"There ain't much left, but you're welcome to it."

"We can share it." She heard the screw of the hip flask, and then the tinny slosh of its contents. When Robbo got up to walk around the fire, she could hear his boots sinking into the snow, and the creak-like sound of them shifting inside it before lifting free. The snow had got deep fast. When he squatted down next to her, she could instantly smell the rum, his breath, his sweat. Goosebumps prickled her skin. Perhaps her other senses were getting better after all.

"You okay, 'annah?"

"Yeah," she said, feeling the cool smoothness of the hip flask against her open palms, putting her numb fingers around its opening before guiding it to her lips. She coughed as soon as she swallowed, and then put it to her lips again before pausing.

"It's okay, you finish it," Robbo said.

When he started getting up, she reached out for him, tugging on his coat. And when he squatted back down, she released a breath that she hadn't realised she'd been holding. She didn't take another drink, but she swallowed anyway.

"I can see them, Robbo. The Whites. I've always been able to see them. Right from the start."

He lost his balance. She heard his legs going out from under him, boot heels scraping against buried dirt, his arse hitting the snow with a nearly funny *whump*.

"They're all I can see." She felt a need to explain that was pretty much redundant now—but the omission had been too heavy. All those weeks of people trusting her, holding her elbow, thinking she was benignly special, their good luck charm. She'd helped them, but not enough. Not in the ways that she could have. And now there was this.

"That's boss, 'annah." But his voice was careful, guarded. Maybe even a little disappointed in her. "And I can understand, like, why you never let on. You'd be the same as them folk who didn't go blind in that triffid thing, ay? Every cunt'd want a piece of you."

She tried to smile when he immediately cursed—when he realised what he'd said and tried to take it back. It made her like him more. It made the choppy beating of her heart choppier.

"You're right, Robbo. You're right, it's the same." But it wasn't. She hadn't kept quiet about being able to see those fast and silent white horrors, like nets of bloated muslin twisted by the wind, because she'd been afraid of being exploited. She'd done it because she'd wanted to feel wanted, needed to be needed. Just like all of those yellow days spent hunched over her laptop in the grimy, freezing kitchenette of her bedsit. She'd needed to feel powerful.

She took another swallow of rum and it went down better than the first. This time she didn't cough. When she shook the flask, it gave a tinny, almost empty slosh. "You finish it," she said, pushing it against his coat.

"Why d'you make us stop here tonight, 'annah?"

She could hear the quiet neutrality in his voice, the clever, fearful certainty. She pictured those fiery dun beacons again.

"Do you know what I think, Robbo?" she said, feeling self-consciously histrionic despite herself, despite the circumstances. "I think the world would be better off without us. I think the land and the sea and everything living in both would be better off without us. And I think that God— if there is one—would be better off without us too." She stopped, wiped tears as well as fat flakes of snow from under her eyes before turning back towards Robbo, the heat and sweat and fearful certainty of him. "But I need to know what you think, Robbo. I need you to tell me what *you* think."

He shifted, got back onto his haunches. When he spoke, she could hear the smile in his words as well as all that fear. "I think we'd be the ones better off without fuckin' God, 'annah." He immediately tutted, as if his answer had annoyed him, and then sighed a long, low sigh. "I reckon love's just another excuse for hate."

"Good," she said. Her own breath left her in a shuddery exhale that she imagined as a silvery plume of smoke. "Me too."

The world will be white and quiet, she thought. *Nothing but white and quiet.*

"Aren't you going to finish the rum?" she said instead, and her teeth were suddenly chattering too much; she bit her tongue.

"It's okay, 'annah," Robbo said, taking hold of both of her hands and pulling them into the warmth of his chest. She could feel his frantic heartbeat against her knuckles.

She thought of his mate being led out to the police car, still wet from his shower, looking back at Robbo in his skivvies and slippers. She squeezed her eyes closed. *The world will be white and quiet*, she thought, *the world will be white and quiet*, like a mantra that she'd once believed in but now no longer trusted at all.

"I'm sorry," she whispered.

She kept hold of Robbo's hands as she lifted up her head, as she opened her eyes. She gripped them harder as she let herself see all those bloated fists of white wind around them. All those casually cruel eyes, hungry dark mouths. The hundreds—maybe now even thousands—of them crouched inside the expectant silent hush. They weren't waiting for her; they weren't waiting for anything. They were simply taking their pleasure, stretching it as far as they could.

She remembered how it had felt to know that she had someone caught and trapped by her smiling lies; how the anticipation of destroying all she had built up had so often loomed larger than the final act itself. And how that need to purge—to pass along all her fear and furious loneliness, like a contagion of fire along headland and cliff—had never waned, never ever lost its power. She was sorry for it now—sorry for all of it—but she'd never lied to herself. She'd never pretended that if the Whites hadn't come she would ever have stopped.

The world will be white and quiet.

"It's okay, 'annah," Robbo said again, pressing the wet prickle of his face against her own as those eyes, those mouths, all that eager, twisted white rushed over the camp in a suffocating fog that would soon not be quiet at all. "It's okay."

And she believed him, she trusted him, she clung onto him. Even though he was blind.

THE EMBARRASSMENT OF DEAD GRANDMOTHERS
by Sarah Lotz

Oh God. I'm almost sure she's not breathing. It's hard to tell, though, with that racket on stage. The Phantom of the bloody Opera. Her choice, not mine. Well, at least if she *is* dead I can blame Andrew Lloyd Webber. *Don't be flippant, Steven, this could be serious.*

She really is being unusually quiet. Especially considering she's one of those noisy breathers—on a good day her chest sounds like a Volkswagen Beetle with a cracked carburettor. And if she's not wheezing and rattling, she's making liquid smacking sounds as she adjusts her ill-fitting dentures. These less than pleasant sound effects normally drive me up the wall, but right now I'd give my left arm for a snort, a cough, or even a fart. Any sign of life will do. Her eyes are closed; she could just be dozing.

Okay, worst-case scenario. She's dead. What then? What the hell am I supposed to do? Do I stop the whole performance? Just the thought of it makes my skin crawl. I hate making a scene. I've never once complained about poor service in a restaurant, nor fallen foul to road rage (not an easy feat in London with all of those bloody cyclists).

Jesus.

This outing has been a complete debacle from the start.

First there was the thing with the teeth. Why take them out in the ladies' in the first place? My God, the look on the usher's face as he handed her the dentures wrapped in a wad of toilet paper. She's not *that* doolally. I can only surmise that she was doing it as some kind of warped practical joke. She is—(was?)—continually telling me to "lighten up, petal". And then we had to bribe the usher to let us in after last bell. It's no wonder I forgot to switch off my iPhone. And when we'd finally squeezed and shifted our way to our seats, I had to endure ten painful minutes of crackling and rustling as she unwrapped the cellophane from her box of Quality Street. And who offers chocolates to strangers in a theatre? Mortifying. And now this.

I'd better be sure though. Really sure, before I do anything drastic. Imagine the embarrassment if she's just having a snooze.

Without taking my eyes off the stage, I sneak my hand over to hers and pat it gently, as if I'm just trying to reassure her. Nothing. I pat harder. No reaction. Steeling myself, I pinch the skin on the back of her hand. Its liver-spotted surface is pliant, like cheap ham. It's also somewhat chilly, but then she's always going on about her poor circulation. Better check for a pulse. The thump of "The Music of the Night" seeps through the soles of my feet, but I can't detect the faintest timpani of a beat in Gran's veins.

I drop her wrist as gently as I can and wipe my sweating palms. Has anyone noticed? The meaty guy wedged into the seat next to Gran is transfixed on the stage, his lap littered with multi-coloured chocolate wrappings. He's silently mouthing the words, getting every second one wrong.

Must concentrate. *Think*.

I can't interrupt everyone's evening with the announcement of my gran's recent demise. It's just not the done thing. Best to hang on until the interval, then slip out and get help. That's it. Pretend in the meantime that nothing out of the ordinary has happened. Just sit here. Watch the show. *Shut it off, block it out, brick up the bad thoughts, Steven.* Yes. Sit here and watch the show. Sit here and watch the show with my dead gran.

Finally, the interval lights go up. The large fellow next to Gran hefts himself out of his seat and makes a beeline for the concession stand. Time to spring into action. Easier said than done, though. I've been sitting completely still for the last half an hour or so, and now my leg's asleep. I thump it to rid it of the pins and needles, and I'm half up when there's a tap on my back. I somehow manage to strangle a scream.

"Steven?" a familiar voice says.

I turn.

"It *is* you. It's me, Liz, from Litigation. Second floor? I thought it was you!"

"Liz, hi!" Oh God. How bad can this evening get? I've been trying to find an excuse to talk to Liz for weeks. And now here she is, within touching distance. And what the hell am I going to say to her? *Excuse me, Liz, gorgeous Liz, while I just pop out and phone for a hearse?*

"I didn't know you were into musicals, Steven."

"I'm not. Not usually, I mean."

"Me neither. A client sent us a bunch of tickets. Who are you here with then?"

"Oh, just my grandmother," I say, trying and failing to sound nonchalant. My thighs are aching from doing an awkward half-squat motion—not quite standing, not quite sitting. "She loves an outing."

"Oh that's so sweet."

I manage a rictus grin.

"Sorry," she says. "Don't let me keep you. Were you going

to the bar? I could keep your gran company if you like. You know, while you're gone."

I sit back down so hard I almost break my coccyx. I'd better tell her. It's going to look really odd if I don't say something.

"You all right?" Liz asks. "You're looking a bit peaky."

"I'm fine. Really."

"Well? Aren't you going to introduce me?"

"Excuse me?"

"To your gran, silly!"

Acid floods my stomach. *Bugger, bugger, bugger.* What to do? There's a chance that I can spin this in my favour. *I need help, Liz, I think Gran's had a turn; I'm really worried.* Perhaps she'll stay with me while the paramedics arrive; hold my hand, dish out the sympathy. I could shed a tear, show her my vulnerable side—women love that. Maybe she'll come with me to the funeral; she'd look good in black. Perhaps, in the future, we'll look back at Gran's demise and laugh sadly about it. It'll be our story. "How did you two meet?" people will ask, and we'll glance lovingly at each other, and finish each other's sentences: "Well, it's a funny thing…" But then again, it could easily go the other way. If I come clean now, I'll be *that* guy. The guy who took his dead gran to a—let's face it—sub-par production of a rather stale musical. Paralegals can be cruel; conveyancers can be brutal. I've seen the group emails that waft through the office like sarin gas. Sure, people might be sympathetic on the surface, but at the very least, I'll be the *Weekend at Bernie's* guy for the rest of my career at the firm. Am I being paranoid? No. No, I don't think I am.

Brazen it out for now, Steven. I lean towards Gran, and gently pat her hand.

"Gran. This is Liz. Liz, this is my gran."

"Pleased to meet you," Liz says.

Unsurprisingly, Gran doesn't respond.

"Sorry," I say. "She's a bit deaf." (This is true.)

"Shame, it's probably a bit late for her, isn't it? She must be dead tired."

Oh, Liz.

"Listen," Liz says. "This may sound a little bit presumptuous, but a few of us are going out for drinks after, if you'd like to join?"

"That would be great!" I blurt, without thinking. "I mean, I'd love to, but I have to sort my gran out."

"Oh bring her along! It'll be fun!"

The lights dim and the orchestra hums. Liz squeezes my shoulder and sinks back into her seat.

Now I'll have no choice but to wait until the end of the performance. Mind you, maybe that's not a bad idea. Yes, wait until the theatre empties, then call in the cavalry.

But what about Liz? *Thanks, Gran. Thanks a bloody lot.* Of all the times to die, she has to choose tonight. My one chance with Liz ruined. What if I don't go and she thinks I'm not interested?

Think, Steven, think.

But it's impossible to hear myself think with the caterwauling going on onstage.

The bloke next to Gran shifts in his seat, bumping his elbow into her side. I'm powerless to do anything as Gran's head slips onto my shoulder. I freeze. I can't shift her back—if I push too hard she might topple in the opposite direction and land on the fat guy's lap. So now I'm trapped. Gran's hair, which has always been lustrous for her age, tickles my ear. How long before rigor sets in? It's been ages since I read a Scarpetta novel, and I can't remember. Using minuscule movements, I take out my phone and quietly ask Google. The woman on my left (Gran's age, smells faintly of beef bourguignon) tuts as my iPhone's glow radiates up from my lap. *Don't make a scene.* I stash the phone back in my pocket. I *think* it's four hours. Yes. I should be fine. But how long before decomposition starts? I breathe in deeply. All I can detect is hairspray and fabric softener.

Big mistake. There's a catch in my throat. A weight in my chest. I bite my tongue to hold a sob at bay. Gran wasn't always a hindrance. She wasn't always a tooth-sucking mouth-breather. A long-buried memory surfaces. My parents' voices getting lower and lower, dropping to that dangerous hiss. Their bedroom door closing, a pause and then… *Don't make a scene.* Next: Me packing my school bag with Monster Munch and a spare T-shirt. Slipping out the back door and walking the two miles to Gran's flat, the winter light dying fast. "Don't tell them!" I begged her when she opened up. She didn't shout at me for running away. She gave me a hug, watched *He-Man* with me, made me a hot chocolate and put me to bed in the spare room. It smelled of her.

A smattering of applause brings me back. Everyone around us is up on their feet, clapping and cheering—a standing ovation. I don't move. I don't dare. Let them think Gran and I are just churlish.

It's only in the confusion of people rooting under their seats for their belongings that I'm able to shift Gran upright in her seat. Her head lolls forward, but she doesn't look *that* dead. The tutting woman tries to edge past me, but I refuse to move, and she's forced to exit via the other end of the aisle.

I spy Liz at one of the exits. She waves to me, and I feel myself staring at Liz like an inept stalker, frozen with indecision.

"Are you coming, Steven?" she calls. And I'm certain there's something extra in her voice. Something inviting. "Like I said, feel free to bring your gran!"

Don't do it.

"She's getting a lift from someone else," I hear myself shouting back, voice booming over the crowd with far more power than the actor who'd played the Phantom. Well it's true, isn't it? I can phone for an undertaker from the bar if I have to. *Not funny, Steven.*

"Cool, we'll wait for you outside."

I look down at the body. *Last chance.*

"Bye, Gran." I give her a kiss on her cheek; it's warmer than her hand, so there's that—and get the hell out of there, knocking my shins on the seats in my haste to join the others.

I turn back to see one of the ushers tapping her on the shoulder. She flops forward in slow motion, her forehead smacking the seat in front of her with enough force to send her teeth skittering.

And then I run.

EUMENIDES (THE BENEVOLENT LADIES)
by Adam L.G. Nevill

On his first day at work the only thing that had enthralled Jason was Electra and her legs. For the next two months his admiration developed into a fixation, lasting from morning until home time in the logistics office, at the distribution centre of Agri-Tech.

Jason found Electra's egresses away from his desk mesmerising. Whenever his wayward scrutiny lowered to her legs, she seemed to perpetually be doing only that, forever moving away from him, while tantalising him in a way that was more torment than pleasure.

Electra was the only light within the darkness of his working life, the sole distraction he welcomed. And even though his position at the distribution centre seemed intent on erasing the last of his individuality, and his hopes for anything better in life, he secretly tingled in anticipation of each working day because *she* was always in those days: sweetly perfumed, tastefully painted, soft, virtually mute, a silky presence with thighs that susurrated between the desks and the grey metal shelving. A siren mounted upon tipped heels that created their own strange music when she teetered along the concrete-floored aisles, or sent a staccato beat across the vast tarmacked spaces, designed for cars and delivery vehicles, under that forever grey of sky engulfing Agri-Tech.

Jason's job and office, both confined within the enormous but sparsely staffed "logistics hub" for agricultural engine and machine parts, was a place that did not matter. Agri-Tech and the town that hosted it, Sullet-upon-Trent, was a part of the North Midlands that wasn't quite the Black Country or Staffordshire, a bit of both but not regarded as either. Sullet-upon-Trent, or "Sully", had no meaning geographically, culturally, or politically. It boasted no public life or attractions for visitors. The area was a kind of anti-matter and stuck at the intersection of new, fast roads that swept people past it.

Within a week of Jason's hasty departure from another dead space just beyond the M25 in what might have been Buckinghamshire—where he had landed after university five years previously when aiming for London's media world—he'd become even more disappointed with Sullet-upon-Trent. It now seemed to him that his life was destined to waste away among dual carriageways, metal fences, eerily quiet industrial estates, white vans, new houses built on railway embankments, and warehouse-style shopping malls containing pet suppliers and white goods stores the size of football stadiums.

He'd found that Sullet-upon-Trent and its ilk offered the antithesis of a life that one could engage with, embrace, or be invigorated by on any level. Such locations offered existences rather than opportunities to attain any kind of essence. As a consequence, they remained areas devoid of vitality. He'd also discovered that the places of work within them were usually created, and peopled, by concentrations of the unimaginative.

Sully filled Jason with a particular apathy and inertia common to such zones. They made him listless but occasionally eager to scream or laugh hysterically, or to inflict physical damage upon his surroundings. Increasingly, the longer he lived in Sully, he thought of himself as a caged ape, dressed in a cheap suit; one left in a narrow and littered cement enclosure, forever bereft of visitors; a forgotten and unexceptional primate that incessantly slapped its own face with a big leathery hand.

Jason only kept his mind alive by ordering books online and reading them patiently in his room, seeking self-knowledge as well as answers about how to better deal with his lot until he managed to escape. His reading was also an attempt to cup his hands around the small, bright flame that three years at university had ignited. If that tiny fire was doused he feared who he might become, perhaps a man that would also forget who he had once been.

Here too, as with his last job, his colleagues were mostly men, painfully ordinary, but somewhat cynical and prescribed to a limited discourse that mostly revolved around football, cars, IT, gaming, drunkenness, and handheld gadgetry. Even in its briefest form the office discourse made Jason's heart smoulder with a frustration born of morbid boredom.

Online dating sites had only returned the profiles of eight single females within his reach geographically, and the profiles had all looked fake. Romantic opportunities to relieve his demoralising loneliness were slender. The Sully women that didn't leave the area appeared to marry early and become mothers even earlier. Only Electra appeared different. Who was she and what was she doing here? No doubt she had not long left further education and probably had a boyfriend.

Whenever he *came across* her during the lunch intervals, as she sat on one of the solitary benches set around the warehouses on grass verges that were criss-crossed by roads without pavements, he picked his way clear of subjects that might encourage any mention of a man in her life. If she did ever confess to such, Jason knew that his reaction would be so emotional that his powers to disguise his colossal disappointment would fail. For as long as she never revealed a significant other—a Gaz, Baz, Nigel, Anton, Leon,

Jay or Ste—his wishful thinking about her might continue undiminished. Even an innocent stock-related query before her desk, made by one of his male colleagues, evoked spasms of jealousy so intense that they left Jason dizzy.

Perhaps she was religious and saving herself. This was possible because the only jewellery she wore was a crucifix of white gold. He fancied he might convert to anything just to be with her.

In Jason's company, during his lunchtime intrusions, she remained passive, half-smiling and monosyllabic. But he often harboured a suspicion that she shared some knowledge with his colleagues about him, and that his interaction with her was embarrassing to her. He sometimes suspected that, at best, Electra was merely humouring him.

On the occasions Jason sat beside her, his head would thump with blood while his mouth issued inanities and observations so lifeless and charmless that self-mutilation seemed the only fitting antidote. She would twist strands of her shoulder-length hair around a finger and then peer at it intently with her young green eyes, not nervous but not restful either. Her legs would always be crossed, her lined skirt slithering back from the leading knee while one foot bounced a high-heeled shoe upon its hidden toes.

Such was his obsession with the girl, that on the final day of his probation period he summoned the courage to ask her out. As Electra made tea for the entire office, Jason followed her into the kitchen, opened the refrigerator door for no reason, and said, "We should go out sometime?"

After he'd made the request a silence thickened within the staff kitchen as if the very air had become gelatine, while the space inside his ears roared as loudly as an underground tunnel filled with freight trains. As quickly as his disintegrating thoughts could manage, he tried to remember his pre-rehearsed get-out clause.

What had he been thinking? He was at least ten years her senior. He was a *pest*. The insidious word hissed through his mind like a serpent in dry grass. To finally be reduced to this at his age. It made him want to tear his shirt from his untrained, freckled torso, the action accompanied by the howl of a thwarted beast. He had finally lost his reason and was no longer an acceptable person.

"Okay. Where'd you wanna go?" Electra said, without looking at him. Her indifference was created anew in his eyes as boredom.

She was bored. Bored with it all, like him. Not enigmatic, mysterious, coquettish or coy, or any of the things that his imagination had invested into her. She was merely young and bored. He perceived this as the stark walls of the room shuddered back to their former dimensions.

So certain was he of failure and rejection, Jason had not thought as far ahead as to where they might go. "Where's good to go… to go round here?"

Electra frowned. "Nowhere much. Beside the zoo."

Jason rented a room in a large, sub-divided Victorian house in the town's oldest street, an area unhappily separated from where it had originally been founded after the county's lines were redrawn in the sixties. Initially, Jason had hoped to have his own place in Sullet-upon-Trent, but even so far away from London, his credit card debt consumed most of his income and he was forced to cohabit.

All of the residents of the house were male, older than Jason, and appeared even more weary and disappointed than he felt. If he could not break his current encirclement of poorly paid employment without prospect, in negligible places set beside motorways, he perceived his new neighbours to be a communal portent of what awaited him in the future.

Only one resident of the house ever engaged him in conversation, though Jason wished Gerald had remained as secretive, sullen and retiring as the other grey figures that existed before the muttering televisions of their rooms. But Gerald was one of those unfortunate individuals who hated being alone, while being in possession of few social graces and no emotional intelligence. Gerald was also an autodidact on council politics, which he interspersed with political history, both moribund and local. He always spoke through a knowing half-smile too, employing an ironic tone of voice that helped Jason understand why housemates often murdered each other.

But Gerald liked an audience and had selected Jason to fulfil that function when Jason, making an effort to be the gregarious new boy, had been moving his meagre belongings into the house. A geniality he now paid a heavy price for whenever he used the kitchen.

That part of the building had become a kind of trap laid by the spidery and withered Gerald. His door on the first floor would click open whenever anyone entered the kitchen to boil a kettle or prepare a meal. The insect-like figure would then descend silently and hover about the kitchen door, as if weaving an invisible web that his victims would fail to break through, should they decide, quite reasonably, that hunger and thirst were better alternatives to Gerald's company.

But the night before his "date" with Electra, Jason saw a rare opportunity to employ Gerald's local knowledge to some purpose. An opportunity he had never before discovered in their one-sided interactions. Jason took a ready meal down to the ground floor kitchen, and, with a magician's flourish, hit the OPEN DOOR button of the microwave. The appliance's bell pinged loudly, and within three seconds the door to Gerald's room had clicked open.

"Evening," Gerald said from the doorway, and followed

this with his customary embellishment, "How's life down pit?" To which *he* chortled through his beard, close to tearing-up with delight at his own jest.

Jason cut out any preliminaries to Gerald's ubiquitous encirclement. Tonight, he'd let him in. "I had no idea that Sullet had a zoo."

Gerald stopped smiling and frowned. "It doesn't. Not in all the years I've lived here. And I would know. You can trust me on that."

Jason had such faith in Gerald's local knowledge that this news filled Jason's head with a terrible confusion that lapsed to dread. Electra had made a fool of him then? If Gerald said there was no zoo in Sullet, then none existed. And wasn't a zoo a place where older men, like dads and uncles, traditionally took younger girls, like nieces and daughters, on innocent days out? Electra's offer to meet him outside the gates of the zoo the following morning, on Saturday, must have been a disingenuous, mocking rejection that he'd been too stupid to recognise.

When Jason arrived at work on Monday and he accused her of playing a cruel trick, she would say, *Did you really think? No, tell me you didn't? I was only joking. No, wait, don't tell me you actually went and looked for a zoo? In Sully?* He could almost hear her voice. His disgrace and humiliation would reach the forklift drivers by elevenses. The material he'd gifted his colleagues with, for endless pranks and jibes about all things zoological, was limitless. Why had he been so gullible? Sullet had no cinema, no theatre, museum, bowling alley. It was simply a place where people existed. Recreation was sought out of town. So how could it possibly boast a zoo?

"But that was a roll up right there. Typical really." Gerald's voice returned to Jason's shocked stupefaction before the microwave oven. "As usual the money wasn't there. Gibbet was running the council into the ground at the time. So instead they used the budget on roads that no one needed."

Jason's horror at Electra's deception turned into anger. "What the hell are you wittering on about? I asked about a zoo, not budgets and roads."

Gerald grinned as if Jason was positioned exactly where the older man wanted him to be. "What you need to understand. What you need to know is how it all came about—"

"No I don't. There is no zoo. I know what I need to."

"Oh, but there was one once. Pentree Zoological Gardens. In ruins now. You can still see it from the A2546. If you're going towards Bunridge, just before you get to where the Man in the Moon used to be…" And this continued for some time. Another of Gerald's interests was interminable road directions using landmarks that no longer existed.

"Stop." Jason even held his hands up as if pleading. "Please, stop. The zoo. There was a zoo, but it's no longer open?"

"That's what I said. When Gibbet—"

"Stop. Slow down. Please. This zoo. The zoo itself is still there? So what else is there?"

Gerald frowned.

"In terms of leisure activities? Funfair? Restaurant? Pub? Whatever? Why would anyone go there now?"

"Well they wouldn't, unless they belonged to the local historical society. I was once the secretary, from—"

"Gerald! Why would the local historical society go there?"

"Because of the architecture of course. It's one of the last remaining Victorian zoos built by Bellowby. A testament to inhumanity. If you were an animal shipped over from Africa or Asia, then the last place you'd want to end up inside was Pentree Zoological Gardens. You see, what you need to understand—"

"So it's a museum, of sorts, open to the public?"

"Not likely. There's never been enough money to pull it down, let alone preserve it."

"So it's derelict? This is a derelict Victorian zoo?"

"More or less. Why do you ask?"

"I'm going there tomorrow. To meet a friend."

Gerald's eyes burned with an opportunist's glee. "Well, all right, I've nothing on. I'll come too. There's no point going unless someone's with you who knows the story."

"No. No. Thanks, but no. It's a date."

"A date? With a girl? There?" Gerald's shock was shared in equal amounts between the idea that Jason would even know a woman, and the idea they would visit the abandoned zoo together.

"The story we don't need. Sorry, local history, that sort of thing. Wouldn't quite work."

Gerald deflated at the rebuff. "Maybe she knows all about it then."

"I doubt that." And then Jason wondered if he was meant to find the zoo locked up and in ruins on Saturday morning, as if that were to serve as an epitaph to his romantic aspirations. Or was she suggesting that he were an animal that should be locked up? The best place for him after pestering her at work and staring at her legs for months? My God, he thought, and seemed to shrink inside. Was it that noticeable, his leering?

"A bad business. Religious nutters finished off what a shortage of funds began."

His miserable reverie broken, Jason looked at Gerald. "What? What did you say?" A question he'd never thought he'd ever ask Gerald. "What bad business? What nutters are you talking about?"

Gerald appeared to expand with the spirit that had so recently deserted him. "The animals all died. Horribly. Poisoned, they suspected, from chemicals that drifted over from the works out at Bunall. Place had been in decline, of course, for years, so the poor beasts were in bad shape. No money you see. Way before the animal rights lot got organised the animals' welfare was in serious decline. But a group of swivel-eyed evangelists had actually been going into the enclosures and poisoning the animals at night. The Sisters of the White Cross they called themselves. They had a temple out Ruddery way, but it's a teeth-whitening place now…"

And for the first time as a resident in the house, Jason stood still, without fidgeting or looking at his watch or breaking away to make phone calls that he did not need to make, and he listened to Gerald.

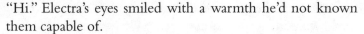

"Hi." Electra's eyes smiled with a warmth he'd not known them capable of.

Questions he wanted to ask her tripped over each other in his mind like clowns wearing long shoes. His thoughts were enshrouded by a fog of both confusion and desire that refused to lift. But there was no doubt that this was *a date*. The realisation made him shiver.

A young woman would not have worn boots with spike heels and tights so shimmery that they appeared wet, or a stretchy miniskirt and that much make-up, unless she intended to impress. She must have spent hours on her hair too.

"How do I get in?" He followed this with, "Why here?" when the girl he was now struggling to recognise as his colleague showed him a gap between a metal pole and the tented security wire attached to the upright. Electra didn't answer Jason's question, but smiled and dipped eyes, made entrancing by a pair of false eyelashes, when he said, "You look amazing, by the way."

One turnstile of the four attached to the ticket booths soon turned with a loud metallic knocking as they each passed through the original entrance. A long wooden frontage bore faded depictions of animals with humanlike faces. The mildly unpleasant notion of the turnstile's sound echoing far out to what lay beyond the gates, like a curious door bell, was dispelled when Jason was confronted with what stretched around him.

He found himself on a wide tarmac forecourt once designed to receive large crowds. Opposite the turnstiles was a boarded-up gift shop and a shuttered Go-Ape café. Facades of animal-themed sideshows stretched to a disused toddlers' fairground. In there, the gaudy plastic reds and yellows of the little fairground rides remained bright within the encroaching treeline. In the distance, a small train intended for children slumped on punctured tyres against a miniature platform that was embellished with gingerbread filigree ironwork. A toilet block with a flat roof had mostly been engulfed by moss and dead tree branches. Tall, busy weeds erupted through the footpaths. Food wrappers faded enough to appear bleached covered most of the ground.

But above the concessions, a steep hill, reminiscent of a small alpine mountain, rose into low grey cloud. Peering toward the mist-enshrouded summit, he glimpsed concrete enclosures, rusty metal poles and tatters of wire hanging from them, a decaying cable car ride, and signs of footpaths cutting through the wild deciduous foliage. The zoological gardens had been built into tiers around the hill, all connected by a winding path that began on their left.

The bizarre and exotic surroundings excited Jason as if he were a child. He wondered if he'd underestimated the girl at his side. Had she a sensitivity to the strange beauty of dereliction? An empathy, unfettered by intellectualism, to past grandeur? An interest, at the very least, in local history? He wanted to take her in his arms and kiss her pretty mouth hard and move his hands over her diminutive curves. She seemed to read his ardour and not be appalled by it. She smiled.

"This might be the only interesting thing about Sully." His remark also pleased her. Amidst such ruin her sudden laugh was melodic, magical. He'd never heard her laugh before.

"There's nothing like this anywhere else." She raised her

face to the hill as if in adoration. "Never makes me want to see it when it was open."

Jason wasn't sure he entirely grasped the sentiment but wanted to agree with her. Though there was something about Electra's enthusiasm that also made him suspect that she might be mad. Mad but beautiful, like the Sisters of the White Cross, according to Gerald. One of them had been a local beauty, who'd once been crowned Miss Great Britain. She'd taken the veil for the sect after succumbing to its obsession with the Garden of Eden before the fall of man.

"Why here? Why do you come here?"

Electra's face adopted the half-concealed smile he knew too well. He hoped it was merely playful. "Cus it makes me happy. Peaceful, like."

"You come here a lot?"

"Loads."

"On your own?"

"Mostly. Sometimes I meet friends."

The idea should have been reassuring, but such was his greed for the girl he preferred the idea of her being alone here, a place she would only share with him.

"They might be here later. We can meet up."

"Your friends are coming?" He hoped his disappointment wasn't obvious.

Electra set off up the path on their left, as much to cut off his interrogation, he sensed, as to show him more. Her face betrayed an eagerness to get higher more quickly than his new shoes would allow him to. Her posture also seemed looser, more limber, while her face remained angled upwards as if to catch the sun's rays. He was seeing a side to the girl he had never glimpsed at work and she was becoming harder to recognise as every minute passed. He tried to combat this estrangement by talking to her.

"You know what happened here, in the seventies, before

you were even born?" He found himself in danger of reciting parts of Gerald's monologue that had lasted for over an hour the previous evening; a discourse that had been rich with details about the cult who'd destroyed the zoo's complement of animals incrementally, embellished with council politics that had subsequently kept the place shut. More than the breathlessness caused by the ascent, a sudden horror at the insidious influence of Gerald in his companionless existence made him stop talking.

"Oh, you know about that?" There was a spine of sarcasm in Electra's tone. She stopped by a vast canopy constructed from steel poles and netting. Great rents and holes gaped in the overgrown enclosure's covering. Rotten logs and a deep lake of dead leaves consumed the floor. The middle of the area was a thicket of unmanaged tree growth. High on the rear cement wall were the unappealing mouths of two artificial caves. Electra grinned at the abandoned enclosure as if she had spotted a rare and shy animal inside.

Jason cleared the signage with one hand: a steel placard upon which a map of Africa was embossed. With a finger he traced the species of the former occupants: GELADA BABOONS. "How did they get in, I wonder. The women. The nutters who poisoned the animals."

Electra chose to remain mute. It irritated Jason. He filled the uncomfortable silence again. "One of the women was killed. But not by the lions or the tiger they had here, back then, like you'd think. An elephant got her. Can you imagine that?" According to Gerald, an ancient and blind pachyderm called Dolly had used its head to press one of the Sisters of the White Cross against the floor of its pen. She had been the beauty queen. She'd crept in to soak the straw with arsenic but had the life crushed out of her. The elephant had also placed its knees upon her legs and held its position, while pressing her with its vast skull, until she was dead.

Concluding her silent communication with the stained rocks and dead wood where primates had once scampered, Electra turned away from the railings and moved further up the hill. "They always get things wrong," she said, though Jason was confused as to who "they" signified. "People don't know what happened here," she added.

"Oh, they do. Nutters killed every animal except the reptiles. Apparently they bludgeoned the smaller ones they could corner. Doesn't surprise me at all that the... town"—he'd nearly said "council" and that would just not do on a date—"wants to keep the place quiet. Makes it all a bit eerie, don't you think, once you know the story? I think the surviving women were committed."

Jason was aware his comments were displeasing Electra; perhaps it was their morbidity, a tone that he could not shake from his thoughts now that he was inside the zoo.

"People don't know why it happened. They weren't there." She said this sharply, but with a sly look in her lovely eyes, as if she were privy to a need-to-know secret that she could not disclose. It made her seem simple and immature. "You shouldn't have opinions if you don't know the facts," she added. "Horrible things happen for good reasons. Don't you know that?"

"Yes, of course," he said too quickly, desperate to return her mood to what it had been.

He followed her in silence, was led past horribly small, overgrown cages for owls, kookaburras, macaques, scarlet macaws and amazon parrots. The ascent made Jason sweat and wheeze, which he tried to conceal by dropping just behind her line of sight. Electra clipped on, her small and lovely legs sheening in the thin metal light and effortlessly sending her ahead to the foot of a long cement staircase that led to another level.

A sign beside the worn metal handrail at the foot of the

stairs indicated that orangutans, gibbons, chimpanzees and lemurs once whiled away their captivity somewhere above. Dense branches of small trees arched over the steep passage, sealing out most of the natural light. Jason would have to bend over to get through.

"You coming or what?" Electra said.

He was almost too winded to speak. "Is there another way..." The heel of his left foot was now smitten with a hot and painful blister.

From the hilltop, from out of the fog-wreathed trees, came a sharp cry that he wanted to believe was human. And into his mind came suggestions of yellow teeth, of dust being kicked up in clouds by clawed black feet. He imagined thin, hairy limbs racing up tree branches in enraged pursuit of other furred shapes.

Electra giggled. And for a moment, before she slipped up into the dark tunnel that surrounded the staircase, her expression had seemed especially salacious. Wanton though cruel, and much older than it should have appeared on such a young face.

So quickly did he turn to where he guessed the noise had issued from, Jason fell against the railings at the mouth of the staircase. His sight groped about the dark, wet trees above. He peered into the distance, at the pointed cement roofs, vaguely alien in the way they poked through the mist and treetops nearer the summit. And where the mist hung about the peak he was also struck by the unappealing suggestion of a ruined temple returned to some steaming jungle on an Asian mountain range. The shriek, the fog, the wildness of the trees, all conspired in his mind to make him suspect that he had passed beyond the margins of Sullet-upon-Trent, a town not really belonging anywhere either.

Further up the stone staircase, Electra's tipped heels clicked through the shadows.

Jason followed. Her called her name twice and said, "Hang on!" She laughed, sweetly, from a greater distance than seemed feasible.

Within the smothering canopy of tree branches, Jason soon struggled to see where he was placing his feet. His breath was loud about his head, his heartbeat inside his skull. Stumbling forward, one hand flailed to where he hoped the railing might be. But amidst the scents of leaf mulch and wet earth, a trace of her perfume lingered. He chased the fragrance.

Daylight eventually formed a coin of white gold when he rounded a corner on the cement staircase. As he neared the top, Electra's lovely blonde head appeared and joyfully cried, "Keep up!" before vanishing. The comment made Jason feel twice his age.

He only stopped struggling upwards when startled by a second shriek, a cry at the side of the staircase, mere feet away from where he laboured. An animal scream followed by a boisterous scampering toward his position, which swiftly evolved into a determined progress of a presence that he could not see, passing over his head. It was aware of him below, though, of that he was certain, as much as he was certain of the speed and strength of whatever thrashed through the darkness above.

When Jason eventually made the top of the staircase he was near insensible with exhaustion and fear. But Electra was not waiting for him on the wide and greening concrete path.

He peered back into the narrow tunnel he had emerged crouching from, with the taste of blood and panic in his mouth. Down there, all was quiet again. But he was now certain that the Sisters of the White Cross had failed to destroy every animal that had been kept in captivity here, four decades earlier. Some kind of ape must have survived and bred descendants. Indigenous British wildlife included nothing that could have made such an infernal cry. Nor anything capable of such agility so high above the ground.

This must form part of the appeal to Electra and her trespassing friends; they knew that the zoological gardens were not quite as empty as the town thought. She'd wanted to surprise him with something special and secret that he could not see anywhere else. Her cryptic comments made more sense to Jason.

But where was she? He feared their date had degenerated into a childish game of hide and seek. He was too tired and shaken to ever get into the spirit of something like that now. Even if the taste of her mouth was waiting as a reward for his being a good sport, Jason wanted to go home.

Enclosures for animals lined each side of the only possible route onwards, fronted by raised viewing platforms. His repeated cries of "Electra!" were greeted with a misty silence that he mistook for anticipation in the verdure around him.

The only tolerable way out of here for him was forward and up to eventually get down again. The original design of the zoo was much clearer; visitors would move to the summit, circling the sides, while viewing the animal attractions on ascent. Other features must await on descent.

He was now flanked by the orangutan and chimpanzee houses. He worked this out from the badly painted depiction of an orange ape on a viewing platform. In the opposite pen, chains still suspended a complex arrangement of logs from which chimpanzees once capered. To his dismay, and a dread that he now tried to swallow like a lump in the throat, he noticed that some of the hanging logs were gently swaying as if from recent use. He expected to see a black face peer out from one of the lightless doorways that were burrowed into the cement wall of the chimps' old home. The detritus of tree stumps and dead tree branches littered the broad discoloured basin.

Behind him, in the orangutan area, there came a sound of

a heavy object flopping into water.

Wide-eyed and breathing like an asthmatic, Jason rushed to the railings closest to the sound, eschewing the viewing platform that looked structurally unsafe.

There was a moat twenty feet below. It must have once kept the apes inside their pen or provided recreation. It now brimmed with a thick soup of dirty rainwater, upon which bobbed a carpet of dead leaves, the mulch of ages, and woody flotsam. One portion of the surface had been disturbed. A circle of expanding ripples had stirred to lap greasily against the greening cement banks on either side of the moat. Whatever had just submerged did not resurface.

Beyond the moat stood a half-rotten tree house and two large and rusticated stone figures of apes. To Jason, they appeared like the crude effigies of imbecilic gods, forgotten and left behind in their polluted grotto.

A rich and bestial spore—sulphurous, fresh, nitrate rich, reaching brain-deep and in danger of turning his stomach—assailed Jason from each side of the path.

He moved away, quickly, and to a junction offering three new pathways: one down, one up, one straight ahead.

"Electra!" he roared in fear as much as anger, though his voice sounded feeble and broken amongst the damp trees. If he wasn't mistaken the air was now much warmer too, and odiferous with the scent of a wet forest floor.

A response seemed to come from high up. A horrible cry that whoop-whoop-whooped and then croaked into what could have been demented laughter. Another descendent of escaped apes he hoped. But what could they have found to eat in here?

Jason was closer to the summit now, about halfway up in fact, and had a better view of what waited up there, if he were to venture any higher. A series of domed cement roofs, like a miniature Sydney Opera House, poked between two large oaks. Perhaps this was one of the stylistic features that Gerald had attributed historical value to.

The head of a dirty penguin statue was also visible. The chipped stone beak was open beneath the blank and indifferent sky. The cement bird was forever poised to call out a lament of solitude and imprisonment, a shriek from the accursed place in which it had been abandoned.

Jason's imagination began to chatter like a frightened monkey in floodwater.

On the very summit, part of a red tiled roof was visible. Directly below that, where the tops of the trees parted, Electra walked into view. She was not alone. Electra was talking to at least three other people. Women, Jason thought, and all wearing dark clothing. But against a background of discoloured cement, the faces of her companions appeared especially pale.

They all turned and looked down at him. Electra waved enthusiastically. Her friends remained still and were content to stare.

At a trot, Jason rounded a walled paddock for giraffes, now filled with broken bricks and masonry. Where tapir, capybara, and Barbary sheep once paced back and forth, their fiefdoms had long been given over to choking bracken, blackberry vines and long grasses.

Hobbling past on blistered feet, he intuited an atmosphere pregnant with apprehension, or perhaps one even tense with animosity because he was intruding upon a territory in which he was unwelcome. Ridiculous to feel this way, or so he tried to persuade himself. A few feral descendants of the original apes had given him a turn. That was all. Once he reached Electra he'd make her explain the strange cries. But what could she offer as an explanation of what had slipped into that oily moat about the orangutan enclosure?

Steeling himself not to look beyond the iron bars he rushed

past, so as not to allow the rubbish-strewn and increasingly smelly dereliction to affect him, Jason finally arrived, out of breath and wet through with perspiration, at the place he had last seen Electra.

Once again, he found himself alone and overlooking a lagoon of miserly proportions. A dirty cement cavity, cramped with dead verdure, where sea lions had once glided for a bit before being forced to make a turn. Impossibly, despite four decades of dereliction, the stagnant concrete bowl still issued the scent of decaying marine life.

On the opposite side of the broad paved area was the domed concrete structure he had seen from below, with a painted roof designed to resemble ice and snow. It had once housed penguins. The only flightless bird remaining was the worn, sad and peeling stone creation he'd seen above the treetops. From this angle, age and rustication had made its one visible eye mad with what looked like panic.

The doors to what was called the Arctic Arena were long gone, but the stench that wafted from out of the darkness overrode Jason's curiosity to see beyond the aperture.

When he called out for Electra again, he wasn't answered by a shriek from the treeline, but his cries did incite the repetitive scrape of what sounded like the raking of dry leaves from inside the Arctic Arena. Whatever was disturbing the most recent leaf fall was not, he was sure, his date.

The area below and around him felt neither *stable* nor safe. Having now burned right through his patience and any reasonable and reliable sense of where he now was, when he tried to push on to locate his date at the very summit, he tripped over his feet twice. His breathing was ragged, his thoughts hapless. His clothes were sopping and his throat was salted with a terrible thirst.

Up. Some deep and rarely used instinct told him she would be up there, waiting at the top. He continued upwards.

He found Electra at the summit.

She sat at one of a score of metal picnic tables, arranged outside a boarded-up restaurant with a red roof. She looked preoccupied, if not bored again, like she did at work. Her lovely pink lips had been freshly glossed and were parted as she gazed at the one-storey reptile house on the far side of the outdoor dining area. She'd crossed her legs and allowed the hem of her skirt to slither back to a pair of golden stocking tops, each welt impressed with short suspender clips.

Her companions were nowhere in sight.

Jason could not readily find the will to speak, and had his thoughts unlocked from the stupefied paralysis brought on by his fatigue and fear, he could not be sure of what he might say to her about his experience below.

More than the sudden presence of Electra, it was the air temperature that brought him to a halt. A withering heat smouldered through the whitish vapours above him and sank upon the dining area. He stripped his overcoat from his shoulders and arms. Sweat clouded his shirt and jeans. The heat of his body may actually have steamed into the thick atmosphere. He couldn't be certain.

"You took your time," Electra said with a cruel smile.

"Where... the others?" Jason blinked the sweat out of his eyes and looked at the sky; there was no sun.

"You want to know why it was done?"

"Sorry?"

"I'll show you the way."

"What?"

Electra screamed out, "We're ready!"

Behind the closed metal doors of the reptile house, something began to thump and thrash itself against the walls, the ceiling and the floor. The sounds suggested an impressive weight and size. The occupant then made a circular swishing sound in what might have been sand. The metal doors shook within their frames.

Jason fell as much as turned to the bench where Electra sat, but pulled up short when the girl stood and raised the hemline of her tight skirt to her waist. What would have been a shocking though arousing exposure, in other circumstances, now struck Jason as crude and unpleasant. Electra's hairless sex was barely concealed by the transparent black underwear she wore, cut like shorts around her shapely buttocks and tummy. Her strong legs shimmered in nylon.

"We've got to be like beasts to go with the others. Quick. Do it quickly," she said, and dropped her head back as if she were already in the throes of ecstasy, or suffering a fit.

Despite his revulsion, Jason's penis thickened and unfurled like some insensible python, motivated alone by scent and instinct.

The girl was offering herself, but whether it was to him, or something else, he wasn't sure. What he took for her anticipation of an imminent appearance from within the reptile house, and of whatever it actually was that coiled, writhed, and butted against the old metal doors, made Jason whimper like a child. Electra's moans were either caused by her own fear, or arousal, or both.

Beneath the summit erupted a din of bestial shrieks, bellows and roars as if the zoological gardens were full again, and anticipating a long overdue feeding time. The treeline around the leaf-strewn picnic area began to thrash like a clash of arms in some ancient battle. Heat from an invisible sun beat Jason's uncovered head more intensely and boiled his thoughts into higher spikes of panic and terror.

"Come on. Let him into your heart. Into your heart," Electra said, as she lay back upon the picnic table and widened her thighs.

Jason fled for the mouth of the path that must lead down and away from the summit.

A much older female voice cried shrilly from behind the shuttered ice-cream counter of the derelict restaurant. "Lie down with the little black lamb!"

Jason tried to look in that direction but lost his balance and fell, cutting both knees and hands. The pain sobered him enough to get back to his feet.

The double doors of the reptile house were broken apart from within. They grated horribly across the paving. A great hot stench of rotten meat and chitin belched like poison gas across the summit.

Two painfully thin women in dusty black gowns came through the opening and staggered across the paving. As they stumbled forward, they batted the sides of their heads as if to concuss the very horrors concealed within their skulls.

Electra thrust her sex higher into the air, as if eager for penetration.

The two haggard female spectres fell to their knees and wept. Between them leapt a thick black form.

Propelled out from the reptile house and into daylight it came, like a horrid tongue. A girth as thick as a soil pipe flopped heavily against the dirty ground. The thing's head slapped the paving just short of Electra, a head covered in soiled bandages that were open and reddish at their conclusion. What Jason glimpsed of the form's black hide appeared as sandy as that of a dead leviathan found upon a beach at low tide.

Jason fled over the lip of the hill.

A great turnstile ground behind him, or somewhere within the low, hot clouds above. He bit through his tongue and kicked off both shoes.

Halfway down the hill, he climbed over the wall of a reeking enclosure once intended for brown bears, and then squashed himself deep inside the open cage at the rear of the pen. The occupant within, half-buried under the dead leaves, appeared even more frightened than he felt.

ROUNDABOUT
by Muriel Gray

Danny decided it was time to shift The Dark Thing on the Blowbarton roundabout.

"I'm going to shift The Dark Thing."

Armaan and Bill looked at each other.

"Pffft," snorted Armaan.

Bill leant back in his chair, took a slurp of tea, then wiped his mouth.

"Good luck with that, mate." And then snorted too.

"I'll take the truck."

Armaan opened the desk drawer, fumbled, then slid the van keys across the desk.

"Keep the hazards on. It don't like the hazards."

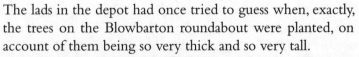

The lads in the depot had once tried to guess when, exactly, the trees on the Blowbarton roundabout were planted, on account of them being so very thick and so very tall.

"S'jungle in there," said Eddie, once, back in the day, when he'd returned, overalls ripped.

To settle the matter Danny had phoned the Traffic Department, but Traffic doesn't share information with Parks and Leisure.

"Dunno, mate," the bored guy had said. "Be on the council

website somewhere, won't it?"

Instead, being garden labourers, they worked it out. Goat willow, hazel, few tall limes and some wide-spreading sycamores. Bit of self-seeded birch and rowan and there it was. Proper bit of woodland. Thick round the edge with cotoneaster. Layers of vicious long-thorned berberis and hawthorn. Twenty years at least they calculated. Maybe twenty-five tops. That's when planning had made the new retail park build this roundabout. It was very large indeed. Five intersections all meeting. To bypass or join the motorway.

But if they couldn't say exactly when it was planted they could certainly remember when they'd stopped mowing it. It had been after The Public Art Project. Well, more specifically, after The Public Art Project had been cancelled and cleared away.

It was Bill who'd decided.

"Let's stop mowing it," he'd said.

"They'll notice," said Danny.

"Pffft," said Bill. "Not round the edges like. Course they'd notice that. Keep that trim. Just the middle. You know?"

They'd all nodded.

"Yeah. That'll work," said Danny.

And it did. Long as you kept the hazards on.

Danny didn't have a plan. He realised it soon as he bumped the truck up onto the grass. Stupid time of day to choose, frankly. The traffic coming off the motorway was already solid and the four exits were queuing back fifteen car lengths or more. But it was still light. That's what mattered. Sun still up there in the sky, somewhere beyond the grey blanket of cloud. Doing enough of its thing for this part of the north to qualify as still being in daylight.

Drivers didn't normally honk at the truck when it slowed and stopped on roundabouts. Parks and Leisure. Who honks at Parks and Leisure? The big ride-on mower in the back, few shovels, wheelbarrow, all pressing up against the wire mesh cage. What'd they expect? It's going to stop isn't it? But then there's always one. And there was. Coming fast round that blind arc and having to brake like crazy. Leant on the horn like he'd slumped over and died at the wheel. Red and shaking and stabbing a finger out the window as he accelerated past Danny's green truck, parked minding its own business half on the verge, engine idling, hazards already flicking orange. Danny just looked back. *That chump's going to have a heart attack one day*, he thought. *Keep shouting and honking like that? He'll slump over and die at the wheel. You see it all in this job.*

Just over an acre, Blowbarton. When you took in the three-metre strip of grass circling the whole thing, the bit they still mowed, maybe a bit more. Since he didn't have a plan, and it was lunchtime, Danny thought he'd have a sandwich. Agnes had made them with meat paste today. He unwrapped one and chewed at it as he looked around. This side, on the west, the foliage only let you see two exits round the edge of the curve and then down onto the north-bound carriageway of the motorway. On the north-east though, you could see the boundary of the new estate, over the bridge. Just the roofs, mind.

"Can't have that," Armaan had said when that had started getting built. They'd agreed.

"Too close."

"Still can't get at it on foot though, can ya?" said Eddie. "Not across six lanes."

"Kids, though. They can cross the motorway. Over the bridge an' that."

"Kids get everywhere," said Danny.

"Yeah?" Bill had nodded. Everyone had thought about it for a while.

"They want hanging baskets."

"Who?" snorted Bill.

"The new estate," said Armaan.

"Pffft," said Bill.

"They ain't getting 'em. Not council, is it?"

"That's what I told 'em."

"Good," said Bill.

They'd been quiet that day. Thinking. Next morning Bill got the whiteboard out of the cleaner's cupboard, knocking over some mops and spilling a box of hoover bags. He'd drawn a plan of the roads round Blowbarton and the new estate, where the old abattoir used to be. But the blue and red wipe-clean felt tips had run dry, so it didn't look quite right with just two colours instead of four.

He put it away and nobody mentioned it again. Except the cleaner. She asked who'd been in her cupboard and nobody was man enough to own up.

Danny looked at the biscuit in his hand and decided that the meat paste sandwiches had been enough. She made good sandwiches, Agnes. Nice salty white bread. Wanted him to eat fruit for a while, but he left it in the bag, so she stopped. He checked the time on his mobile phone to see if lunchtime was officially over, then put it down on the seat while he slid the plastic lunch box back under the seat. He looked into the dense undergrowth.

Without a plan this could be tricky. They all knew it needed shifting, but nobody had thought of anything clever yet. Eddie had once spent a morning collecting all the skulls and bones at the edge you could reach by just sticking your arm in, and loading them into the wheelbarrow. He'd waited to see what would happen, sitting on the lowered tailgate of the truck reading his whole newspaper, back to front at least twice, and smoking a couple of fags. But The Dark Thing didn't budge. It might have rustled a bit, he'd said. Over on the east, under the limes. Or maybe it had been the wind. Or a car transporter. They could whip up a tree something fierce as they passed, the height of those things. But if he was honest, The Dark Thing didn't seem to care. So he'd just brought back the bones and they'd all looked at them. A lot of foxes. And rabbits, obviously. But also a roe deer. Head off, ribs snapped and sucked dry of marrow. That caused some interest.

"That's come a way," said Eddie.

"Nice beast," said Bill.

"My uncle shoots 'em," said Armaan. "Got a gun licence. Cause he's got a field he lets out near Drub."

"Where's that then?" asked Bill.

"Near Cleckheaton."

"That ain't helping."

"S'nice. Got an 'orse in it."

They decided to grind down the animal remains and use them for bonemeal. They mixed it all into the planters outside the new leisure centre. Begonias were lush that year.

Danny got out of the cab, zipped up his green boiler suit and put on his yellow high-visibility waistcoat. He leant on the door and peered into the dark, thick mass of foliage under the trees. If you knew where to look you could still see the stump of The Public Art Project. They were supposed to have taken the whole metal rod out, but they'd been given the task in

December. So obviously it got a bit ropey in there, the light fading at four, a whole hour before they were due to clock off. So Eddie had taken a buzz saw to it and chopped it off at the weakest point, just below shoulder height. Just so they could get out of there quicker. While the sun was still up.

"Won't see that from the road," he'd said.

Bill had driven round twice to check.

"Can't see it from the road," he'd confirmed.

Now the ragged top of the metal post was smooth, wreathed in brambles and quite hidden by the bushes in front. But the shape was still there. If you looked hard. That was only three years ago. Nature worked fast.

Danny tried to remember the name of the artist but he couldn't quite place it. It was one name. Like famous people who didn't need two. But he remembered he was from London, because Danny had been one of the crew handling the installation of The Public Art Project, and the artist with the one name had shared a fag with him. Well to be honest the artist had been smoking a joint, while the stone-carved animal thing was being winched up off the low-loader. With its hazards on.

That had reminded Danny of once, back in the day, when the orange hazard lights on their green truck were flashing in the gloom of dusk outside the gates of the crematorium. Armaan had said, "S'like a campfire, innit?"

"Ya wha'?" said Bill.

"Campfire. Them flickering lights. Like flames. Comforting."

"Pfft," said Bill.

"Fire. Used to keep the wolves off. Cavemen an' that."

"Keeps the cops off us, don't it?" said Bill.

"Yeah," said Armaan.

Danny had asked the artist what was it like in London then, and the artist had said it was all right. But he'd not been there much because he'd been in the army, and that he'd had the carved animal thing brought back from Afghanistan or somewhere like that after he'd found it in the desert, buried in the sand. Then he'd come home and decided to be an artist instead of killing people.

He'd asked him how much flats cost in London now compared to Bradford and the artist looked bored and said he didn't know, because he lived in a commune where material things didn't matter. Danny wasn't sure what that meant but he'd nodded and they'd just smoked and watched The Public Art Project coming off the truck.

Danny couldn't really decide what it was, but then he didn't know much about art. It wasn't very big; about the size of two large watermelons. The artist had made a big long metal pole, the one that Danny and the boys had dug into the middle of the roundabout, just next to the biggest sycamore with the thick healthy bole. They'd thought of using a mini digger but Bill said no, because they'd have to take down the big trees to get it in, and you didn't take down trees in Parks and Leisure unless you had a felling order from the council.

They didn't have a felling order, so they dug it in with pickaxes and then poured cement, and none of the trees got damaged except for a few snapped branches here and there. At the top there was a big oval shape, made out of wood, like a giant egg cup, and that was where the carved stone thing was going to fit into. Like an egg into an egg cup.

It wasn't very nice. It was an odd misshapen thing and looked like a kind of damaged horse. But with overlong, sharp, bared teeth and crazy eyes in the front of its head instead of the side. One of the eyes was painted with flaky red stuff, and Danny thought the other one had been too, but the paint must have come off and it was just kind of stained maroon. It looked very old and broken. Nobody, except the artist, liked it.

"What you reckon that is when it's at home then?" Armaan had said.

"Waste of money," said Bill. "That's what it is."

"Can't even see it proper," said Eddie. "Not if you're coming off the west junction."

"Probably for the best you can't," said Armaan. "'orrible, innit?"

"Waste of money," repeated Bill.

They'd watched as the winch swung the head clumsily into the egg cup thing, while the artist shouted and waved his arms about, until it was settled and he'd stood back and admired it.

The artist with one name told them it was called *Conqueror* and that it was looking south-east, to all the bits of the world we'd conquered and spoiled.

"Why?" Bill had asked. "What's it looking for?"

That had pleased the artist a great deal and he'd crouched down for a minute, with his arms over his head in a way that nearly made them go and get help. But just in time he got up again, and held Bill's shoulder, which the lads could tell Bill didn't like one bit, and had said really slowly, like it was the last line in a film or something, "Redemption, mate. It's looking for our redemption."

Danny decided to leave the truck idling, walk round the grass perimeter, and take the barrow. The traffic was heavy and he'd better look as if he was busy in case anyone from the council was passing. He'd thrown the big net in the back, the one with the telescopic expanding handle that Eddie ordered to get dead squirrels out of trees. They'd never found any dead squirrels in trees yet. It was just something Eddie admitted he'd read on his daughter's Facebook page. But they had it now. And it might be useful.

He put the net in the barrow and set off clockwise round the grass strip.

When he came to the place where they'd found the artist's car, he stopped and set the barrow down. The years had smoothed away all the deep tyre marks, but Danny, all of them in fact, knew the exact spot where it had been towed from. The gorse was particularly thick behind, and a willow in front that somebody had been daft enough to start coppicing seasons ago, probably Eddie, was now a living basket of shiny impenetrable twigs.

Danny took out a piece of chewing gum and looked out from the roundabout in the direction the car had been facing. From this slightly raised terrain he could see over the top of the traffic roaring round in front of him in an endless stream, to the motorway heading east and the distant, bland landscape beyond. You could see a long way. If there was anything worth looking at.

The police had concluded the artist's small, cheap car had crashed, because the bumper was so deeply embedded in the high part of the soft grass verge. The passenger door was wide open and they never found the artist.

"Did a proper runner," Eddie had said.

"Pffft," said Bill. "Not surprised."

"Waste of money. Whole thing."

Danny and Armaan had been there when they towed the car off. Bill said they were going to have to get topsoil in to fix the grass, but Armaan was good at shovelling and raking, so they never did.

Danny had had a chat with the traffic cop watching the truck take the car away. He'd said the petrol tank was completely empty and the battery was dead. Danny thought about that later. A lot.

"Well that's ripe," Bill had said when he'd finished reading the local paper.

That was the time after The Public Art Project had been up for a while, and after the artist had crashed, and then done the runner and never come back. After the artist had to talk all the time on the local news, and reply to angry letters in the paper and nasty things on Facebook about why it was good when everyone else thought it was bad. Nobody liked it. Some people said it distracted drivers and it might cause a nasty accident. Other people said it was a waste of money, and it was ugly and stupid when there weren't enough nurses and the libraries were shutting down. Most people didn't know what it was supposed to be.

"Whassat then?" Armaan had asked.

"Says he was mental or something."

"Who?" said Eddie.

"The artist. The Public Art Project."

"Yeah?" said Armaan.

"PTSD," said Bill. "Pffft."

"You wha'?" said Armaan.

Nobody knew what that was, but Eddie said he might have heard it was something to do with the army.

So when the artist crashed and ran away and never came back, because, they all suspected, he was mental after everyone being so unkind about his work that he liked and nobody else did, they waited a while and then the council said they could take The Public Art Project down. On account of nobody liking it.

The egg cup thing and the carved horse head thing inside the egg cup thing were taken away by a big truck from London, and the lads were left to take down the metal post. After that the Blowbarton roundabout only got mentioned on the local news or the newspapers or Facebook because of the tailbacks on the motorway, or if one of the junctions was closed for roadworks.

Danny had thought a lot more, and for a long time after,

about why the artist's car had no petrol and a flat battery. It wasn't until long after they'd first started noticing The Dark Thing that he worked out why that might be. But by that time the police weren't interested in a minor car crash years ago on a busy roundabout without CCTV, and a mental artist who'd run away.

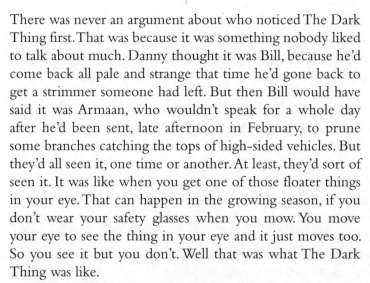

There was never an argument about who noticed The Dark Thing first. That was because it was something nobody liked to talk about much. Danny thought it was Bill, because he'd come back all pale and strange that time he'd gone back to get a strimmer someone had left. But then Bill would have said it was Armaan, who wouldn't speak for a whole day after he'd been sent, late afternoon in February, to prune some branches catching the tops of high-sided vehicles. But they'd all seen it, one time or another. At least, they'd sort of seen it. It was like when you get one of those floater things in your eye. That can happen in the growing season, if you don't wear your safety glasses when you mow. You move your eye to see the thing in your eye and it just moves too. So you see it but you don't. Well that was what The Dark Thing was like.

"Like a shark shape movin' under a boat," said Armaan, the one time he'd talked about it, not meeting their eyes.

"Seen a shark then?" said Bill with interest.

"Nah. Seen 'em on them telly wildlife programmes."

But they knew what he meant. If you tried to look straight at it, it moved with your eye and all you saw was nothing at all.

That should have been fine. Not doing any harm, was it? Just a thing that was there but you couldn't look right at. Trouble was that you knew it was looking at you. And you could feel it wasn't looking in a nice way.

"Best left," Eddie had said. When he came back one day, rattled. That's all he would say.

But now Danny was here. He hadn't left it. He'd thought about it for too long. The estate. What might happen if The Dark Thing didn't just watch any more. And so here he was. With his net. For taking dead squirrels out of trees.

Someone changing lanes honked at someone else. He jumped.

Danny entered the main thicket by way of the hazels. No thorns. Easier to push through, though still tricky. Even for a cloudy day it was darker in the undergrowth than he'd expected. The high leaf canopy shut out the sky altogether and the bushes below were tightly entwined. Even the constant roar of traffic was muffled in here, like the noise of a street from a curtained basement. As he moved slowly and carefully towards the centre of the roundabout he tutted as the net kept snagging on things.

He had a plan of sorts now. Not a very clever one. But a plan. Danny was going to sit against a tree in the middle, a place where he knew he could still see the hazards of the truck flickering through the leaves. Then he would wait, with the net, and see what happened. The big sycamore right in the centre, slightly raised, was in full leaf. He headed for that.

There was all sorts in here. People these days just rolled down their windows and chucked out any old thing.

"Pigs, ain't they?" Eddie had said once, while they cleared up the central reservation near the station.

"Pffft," Bill had replied, as he picked up half a bra with the long-handled grabber and dropped it into a plastic bin bag.

Blowbarton was as bad. Danny stepped over crushed cans and polystyrene cartons. Crisp packets and bottles. And as he moved deeper towards the middle, all the way in between the normal rubbish were bones. Lots of them. Small skulls and broken pieces. You didn't get them on the central reservations. Not that he'd seen anyway.

It gets hungry, he thought. *Just as well these roundabouts are full of things to eat.* The lads had always liked knowing that. Their secret. Your average driver speeds past and never has half a clue about the wildlife living in these wooded islands, right in the middle of an ocean of traffic, where no human ever treads. It's why the foxes brave the lethal motorways to get to them. Plenty of mice and voles and rabbits living secretly and quietly in their leafy safe haven.

He reached the tree, put down the net, cleared a spot on the ground against the trunk and sat down. It was sandy. Almost completely sand, in fact. Under the leaf mould. That was odd. If you'd taken a vote from the lads about the pH of the Blowbarton soil, most would have guessed clay.

"That border outside the library," Eddie had said once, back in the day when they were working out what to plant.

"Yeah?" said Bill.

"Too acid. Needs azaleas."

"Pfft," Bill said.

"Tellin' ya," said Eddie and then he sulked.

Bill made them plant lavender. It all died. Eddie was pleased. Since then they always dug in peat or dug in lime. But who planted in sand? Nobody planted in sand. Some chumps they must have been, those who planted up Blowbarton all those years ago. *Still*, thought Danny. *Worked. Didn't it? Look at the growth.* He'd mention sand to Bill when he got back. Maybe it would help over at those five-a-side pitches, where nothing decent would grow in the beds at the entrance.

There were a lot more bones in the sand beneath the leaves here. Tiny things. Delicate like toothpicks. Danny ran his fingers through the fine grains, sand like you'd expect on one of those Caribbean beaches. And all the little bones peppered through it like shells on a beach. Then he just sat and waited.

It wasn't a bad day. Not too cold. Not too warm. Been dry for weeks, so not damp. And no wind to speak of. He looked around. *If it wasn't for The Dark Thing*, he thought, *you could live in here*. It was quite nice. So hidden. So secret. The orange hazard lights flashed on and off far away through the tiny gaps in the undergrowth, and Danny thought he should take some pictures. To show the lads he'd been right into the centre. Show he'd meant it.

He put his hand in his jacket pocket to fetch out his mobile. It wasn't there. It was still in the truck. On the seat if he remembered. He tutted, and took out some more chewing gum instead. No matter. *It would be good to work in here again*, he thought. Once he'd shifted The Dark Thing and it was safe. His eye roamed over the bushes needing trimming, and the trees needing pollarding. And then he looked at the other things on the ground.

There was a shoe. They found shoes all the time. Usually trainers. They could never work out why. This was an unusual shoe though. More of a boot. Dirty and half buried in leaves, you could still make out it had once been bright blue and shiny. Red laces. *Like something a student would wear*, thought Danny. *Or an artist*. He took the net, pulled out the telescopic handle and gingerly poked at the crepe sole.

In the canopy a breeze stirred the leaves and Danny looked up. It wasn't a car transporter. It was here in the middle. The tree quivering above him.

It was The Dark Thing. He could feel it looking.

Danny thought about what to do next. He knew where it was, because it was all dark at the very far edge of where his left eye would reach. Maybe if he kept his eyes forward but moved his head.

He tried that. It moved at the same speed and was still as dark. Maybe even darker.

Then he thought he might try closing his eyes, moving his head to where he thought it was and then opening them really fast.

Trouble was Danny's heart was beating very fast now, because he was scared. He didn't want to close his eyes. What he wanted to do was to get up and run away. But he was here to do a job. He was here to shift The Dark Thing and that was that. So he glanced across at the comforting flicker of the hazard lights through the leaves, then swallowed hard and closed his eyes. He shifted his head a few inches to the left and then opened them again. A shape moved. Much too fast to see. But a shape.

This is a good plan, thought Danny. He shifted slightly against the tree, because he'd sunk a way into the fine sand a little and it was uncomfortable. The Dark Thing was to his right this time. His heart was still beating loud and hard in his ears, but he closed his eyes again. *I'll wait longer this time*, he thought. He turned his head and counted to five. He opened his eyes.

It was a very odd shape. Danny wondered if that was because it was closer now or because he had surprised it. But as it whipped out of his vision, like a fly-fishing line from a river, it left behind an impression this time. Big, like an animal, but in a distorted human shape. With much too big a head. Like a horse. Or a bit of a horse. Or something. It was a horrible shape.

He looked down at the net and wondered if a device for getting dead squirrels out of trees was big enough to throw over something you couldn't see and was bigger than a person and half a horse. And something too frightening to look at.

He shifted again and glanced down. His legs were covered in sand now and trying to move them was difficult. He pushed himself up with one arm, but it just made them sink in deeper. Danny was starting to panic. The Dark Thing was still watching him. He knew it was. It was very black indeed to his right now, and the shadow it made was filling his vision save for the part that could still see the orange hazard lights blinking through the trees.

The shoe that he'd been looking at when The Dark Thing came, was still lying in front of him. It bothered him. Danny pushed out the net handle again and gave it another poke. This time he jabbed it hard enough to turn it over. Sticking out the top of the boot was a bone. It looked like a leg bone.

There was one time, back in the day, when they'd found something terrible.

Armaan had shifted all the dead wood and unused sacks of manure from up against the chicken wire behind the medical centre.

"You wanna come 'ere!" he'd shouted in quite a high voice for a man. Armaan never shouted.

They'd all come. There was a leg sticking out from under a tarpaulin. It was in dirty trousers, and had a sock. But no shoe.

"'at's not looking good," said Bill.

They sent for help. Turned out it was a person. Who'd died. A methadone user who the people at the medical centre knew. The lads had to answer some questions from the police that came, but then they took the body away and nobody mentioned it again. It wasn't even in the paper. Bill had checked for a few days.

Danny looked at the bone in the boot and wondered if this would be in the paper when people knew. He thought it probably would.

He looked down and realised that he was nearly up to his waist in the sand now. He couldn't move his legs at all. It seemed like everything around him was growing very dark indeed.

Danny knew then what was going to happen. The Dark Thing was just waiting.

A plan would have been a good idea, thought Danny. After all, he knew what had happened to the artist's car. The petrol tank was dry because it had run out keeping the hazards going. And then the battery would have run out after that. Just like what was going to happen to Danny's truck. The orange light would stop. The campfire would go out.

There was no point in shouting. And no phone. So he thought for a minute. His fags and lighter were in his top pocket. Danny fumbled and found the lighter. *There's a bit of luck*, he thought. Could have been in his trousers and they were under sand now. Out of reach.

He pulled a few dry twigs towards him and made a little pile. The deadfall was dry as tinder under here.

Before he lit it, he could feel The Dark Thing quiver. That made him happy. Was it fear or fury? He hoped it was both. He hoped that even if it didn't die, because maybe it was very old and couldn't, that it would go back to wherever it came from and carry on hiding from campfires, waiting in the dark for desert people to make mistakes.

This new plan was a gamble all right. But then only metres away, hundreds and hundreds of drivers were passing by every hour. Hundreds. One would stop to help. Maybe not the people who threw bottles and cans and trainers out of their windows, or honked at folk when they pulled up onto the verge. But maybe a kind truck driver. Or a lady coming back from the shops. Maybe even a firefighter off duty. You never knew. Someone would stop. Someone would come and help. And then it would be all over.

He flicked the lighter and put the flame to the pile of kindling. It caught like a dream and he fed it with dry leaves and more twigs until it was quite the blaze, crackling and hissing. He waited until he was sure it was nice and hot and then gently nudged the fire into the deadfall, watching as it spread rapidly up into the dead grey branches of the willow. Then Danny closed his eyes.

"Wha's it say then?" said Eddie.

"Pffft," said Bill, putting the paper down. "You don' wanna know."

Armaan got up to put the kettle on.

"They never get nothin' right, them journalists," said Bill. "Money for old rope."

"Wha'?" said Eddie.

"Bein' a journalist."

"Yeah," said Armaan.

He washed the teaspoons, because it was his turn.

THE HOUSE OF THE HEAD
by Josh Malerman

In the winter of 1974, Elvie May, six years old at the time, witnessed a haunting so jarring that, well into adulthood, it never entirely faded from the frontispiece of her mind. It didn't affect her directly in that neither she nor her family was the object of the ghost story. Though the haunting *did* take place inside her house. A second house. Her dollhouse. Pink and white, sprawling and ornate, the home was much nicer than the Mays' larger home that harbored it. And, to scale, those who lived within the dollhouse (Elvie's *people*, she'd say) had much more room to move about than Elvie and her parents did in theirs. The sizes of the nuclear families were the same; three people total in each: mom, dad, child. Elvie had her parents just like Ethan had his. For this, she related greatly to the brown-haired boy who called the dollhouse home. Both families even owned a dog, and both dogs (the big one, Elvie's Jack Russell, and the little one, Ethan's Great Dane) played vital roles in the outcome of the haunting in the winter of 1974.

As with most hauntings, and every good ghost story, the events within the dollhouse began as seemingly harmless, only somewhat suspicious, occurrences throughout the home. But, also like every good ghost story, these events escalated quickly. Elvie watched the entire arc unfold from a child's chair, her chair, the red plastic seat she occupied every day after school, impatient to know the fate of Ethan, his parents, and their Great Dane. Throughout the course of the haunting, Elvie's parents recognized the worry in their daughter and made the usual attempts to make her happy. They bought her things. They took her places. They read stories, they joked, and they coddled. But the incredible events occurring in Elvie's bedroom never crossed the boundaries of the dollhouse, and Elvie never felt it necessary to tell Mom and Dad of the haunting.

Years later, as many as twenty-five, Elvie May would tighten up when her husband, Eric, asked her to tell their friends her ghost story. He'd egg her on, incapable of comprehending the impact the experience had had on Elvie's understanding of the world outside the dollhouse. *Tell them about the Smithsmiths,* Eric would say. *Tell them the story that took place inside of a house inside of a house.* Often Elvie would turn red when Eric did this. Sometimes she hated him for it. Not because Eric was so out of line for suggesting she share, but because the images, what she'd seen take place inside the House of the Head, would return again to vivid, vibrant life, causing her to stare off into space, and shake her head no.

No no no...

"Jesus, Randy," Marsha said. "It's nicer than ours."

"It is," Randy smiled, crouched beside the pink-and-white monstrosity. Eight bedrooms. Three baths. An attic. A lounge. A library. Furnished fully, of course. When you split the thing open it was like looking into a museum. "She's gonna love it."

Marsha noted the boyish sparkle in her husband's eye. There wasn't any talking Randy out of a thing when his eyes shined so. Still, she tried.

"You spoil her."

Randy looked to her, smiling.

"I do."

"Well I don't know that you should."

"And why not? She might grow up liking her parents? What an awful position to put her in."

Marsha rolled her eyes.

"Most children rebel," she said. "So while you expect, and even plan, on her adoring us, she's going to be running for the streets before we can say teenager."

For a beat, Marsha thought she had him. A brief passage of terror rose to the surface of his eyes, then sank again.

"Look at it." He pointed to the incredible dollhouse. "It's all ready to go." Then he stepped to his wife and laced his hands on her shoulders. "Marsha, I want you to remember what it was like to be a little girl."

"Randy."

"Nu-uh… hear me out. And I want you to really imagine how you would've felt if you came home from school to find… *this* all set up in your bedroom."

Marsha crouched beside it. She studied the rooms. Then she looked to the figurines Randy had picked out.

"Only three people in all that house?"

"Just like us. And we won't add any more. That way she won't ask for a brother or sister."

"It's nice," Marsha finally agreed.

"It is," Randy smiled, eyes sparkling. "It absolutely is."

Elvie named the boy right away. Ethan was the name of Ashley Ford's older brother. Such a nice guy. So, it was Ethan, Mother, Father, and Dane (the dog's name was chosen after Elvie's own dad told her what kind of dog it was.) Dane was great. Dane was big. As big as Ethan was. The dog stood higher than the dollhouse's kitchen counter and could easily fill one of the beds in the many bedrooms. He was black all over and his muscles showed in the right light and his tail was perked up like his ears, as if Dane was constantly aware of the presence of the others in the house.

And yet, despite the magnificent dog, Ethan was clearly the star of the house for Elvie.

He wore dark-blue pants and a red sweater. His brown hair wasn't all he had in common with Ashley Ford's brother; Ethan had the same kind eyes. According to where she placed him in the house, he could even look like he was smiling. Like his cheeks were actually wrinkling up into a little smile. He had a watch, something Elvie wanted for herself. And his black shoes never left any marks on the gorgeous wood floors of her pink-and-white dollhouse.

Ethan's mother probably had the neatest outfit of the three. Tight yellow pants, an orange sweater, and green socks that showed just above her shoes. Elvie's own mom called Ethan's mother's hair a "flip." A green headband kept that flip in place.

It was "a real modern look," Dad had said. And Elvie knew it to be true.

Ethan's father was equally of the era: bell-bottom jeans, a button-down white shirt (open just where his chest hair began), and round glasses. Not quite hippies, Mom told Elvie, but certainly with the times. Ethan almost looked conservative by comparison.

The family was a lot of fun.

What was not fun was picking Ethan's bedroom. There were so many of them to choose from. Because the master bedroom was for Mother and Father, Elvie had seven remaining rooms to choose from. But the longer Elvie took in deciding, the more the *other* rooms in the house seemed viable places for Ethan to sleep. On the pool table in the first lounge, for example. On the ironing board in the laundry room. And what was wrong with the green rug covering most of the floor of the library? Ultimately it didn't matter, Elvie knew. Her dad had told her, *This house is yours, Elvie. That means you do whatever you want to with it.*

For this, Elvie could let Ethan sleep on the roof. And yet, she finally decided to place Ethan's bed in the den, giving him free run of the entire first floor of the dollhouse.

It felt like the right choice. Elvie would like a room like that.

And so life in the dollhouse began this way, and coincided with Elvie's return to school. It was an abnormally cold September (years later, Elvie would begin her telling of it that way, *It was a cold September, I remember that*, when she told her then fiancé, Eric, about the House of the Head) but it wasn't until the real winter hit that things became troublesome inside. Until then, Elvie didn't always play with her dollhouse. She played with many toys and only when she tired of them would she rearrange things inside Ethan's house.

Often she'd give Mother a book and place her in an elaborately embroidered chair only inches from Father who tended to the fire. She'd put Ethan by an open refrigerator, Mother at the top of the stairs, Father at the bottom, as though looking for their son. It was great fun to use Dane as a foil. Elvie quickly learned that she could put the dog in the bathroom, close the door, and set Mother, Father, and Ethan outside it, looking to one another for what to do.

Despite the blooming, merciless cold outside her own house, Elvie found life warm within Ethan's.

She also discovered that, despite the extremely fertile ground, she didn't enjoy placing toys inside the dollhouse, toys that didn't belong. A pony in the study might be funny, but it was also somehow irreverent. There was an independence to the dollhouse from the very beginning, and Elvie respected it devoutly.

Life carried on. And Elvie watched it from the red plastic

chair in her own large bedroom.

Ethan woke up in the den, ate dinner with Mother and Father in the dining room (sometimes in one of the extra bedrooms when Elvie was feeling a little bored), played pool in the lounge, and cooked himself eggs in the kitchen. Sometimes she let him stay in bed all day.

Michigan's winter had arrived, whether or not the calendar said so. At five below zero, the district had considered canceling school; an opportunity, Elvie saw, to play with her house. But, disappointment of all disappointments, the elementary show went on, and Elvie was forced to wear the full gamut of winter clothing: two shirts (one long, one short), a sweater, gloves, hat, jacket, moonboots and scarf. She watched heavy snowfall outside her classroom window. She saw the older kids making angels in the yard at recess. And the bus ride home was a slow one.

Once home, Mom helped her out of her layers, and Elvie proceeded straight upstairs to her bedroom, where the dollhouse, split open on its hinges, still occupied the drawing table, leaving no space for anything besides.

Something in the living room of Ethan's house caught her eye.

Elvie crossed her bedroom and knelt before it. She frowned, thinking at first that it was slobber, something Jack (her Jack Russell) had done to the house. She reached for it with a mind to wipe it clean. Then she pulled her hand from the house quickly.

It was a head.

The head of another figurine, slightly bigger than Ethan's head, sat facing her on the living-room couch. She faintly recognized the features; the wide expressive eyes, the sun-bleached discoloration, the bald spots where its hair had eroded. The head once belonged to a body, Elvie knew, but she couldn't remember which.

Because the head was positioned on the edge of the couch, she could see the red plastic interior exposed at the open hole of its bodiless neck.

Elvie hadn't put the head inside the house. Yet, there it was. On the couch. Facing her.

The head.

Elvie quickly searched the rest of the house and found Mother and Father sitting on the edge of their bed together. It looked like they were discussing something serious. Elvie had seen Ethan's mother's posture before when her own mom was lost in thought. Worry. Concern. It looked like Ethan's father was trying to console her.

Downstairs, in the den, Ethan was sitting up in bed. His bed sheet was pulled up to his eyes. It looked to Elvie like he was scared.

Had Elvie placed them this way?

She gasped, quietly, when she found Dane standing in the doorway to the living room, his snout pointed directly at the bodiless head with the red neck set on the center of the couch. Elvie could almost hear the dog growling.

"Elvie!"

Elvie jumped at the sound of her mom's voice and she accidentally kicked the drawing table that held Ethan's house. The head on the couch fell to the living-room floor and rolled toward her. It came to rest on its side, facing Elvie still.

"Let's get a move on, Elvie! We're gonna miss the previews."

Previews? Distantly, Elvie knew what her mom was talking about; tonight was movie night. There was a good one playing at the Americana downtown. But Elvie couldn't take her eyes from the head that faced her.

She looked up to the master bedroom and saw that Ethan's father was now facing the bedroom door. As if he had heard something in the house.

"Elvie! Why don't you answer me?"

"Coming, Mom!"

Elvie looked to Ethan, saw he was still mostly hidden, the bed sheet still up to his nose. Dane still stood at the living-room door, but his snout now breached the threshold.

Elvie shook her head, no, because she wasn't sure what else she could do. Whatever she'd seen, the slight alterations in the figurines, Ethan's father and Dane, must have been tricks of the light. She'd learned about tricks of the light in the kindergarten play. Elvie had played a carrot and Mrs. Dunbar had given Elvie her first taste of show business.

Your costume may appear yellow now, but under the stage lights you're gonna be as orange as a balloon.

"Tricks of the light," Elvie said to herself.

"*Elvie!*"

Finally, she looked away from Ethan's house and then quickly left her bedroom and headed downstairs.

But the look in Ethan's eyes, the bed sheet to his nose, remained lodged in her mind.

Halfway down the stairs she turned and ran back up. She flew across her room and reached into Ethan's house and took the balding head from the floor.

She tossed it beyond the drawing table, beyond her dollhouse, to the shadowed corner of her bedroom, where other toys and bright clothes lay in a heap.

It made a soft plunk as it landed.

"Fine, Elvie. We're not going."

"Coming!"

She forgot all about Ethan's house at the movies. She laughed and Mom laughed and they both agreed the movie was a good one. She didn't think about the head or Ethan or the dollhouse at all. Not until they got back home. Not until Elvie raced upstairs and rushed to her red chair and saw that the head was lying on the floor in the living room still, its wide painted eyes staring into her own.

At school the next day, Elvie couldn't wait to get home. She found herself worrying about Ethan, his parents, and Dane. She hadn't removed the head before falling asleep the night before. Instead, she'd laid on her belly, feet against the headboard, and watched the dollhouse from across her bedroom. Surely Ethan or his parents would move. They'd already done so once. Or twice. Maybe Elvie would catch them.

She fell asleep this way, and when she woke, she found they *had* moved after all. In fact, they'd moved a lot.

All bundled up and hating the fact that she had to leave, Elvie took stock from her red chair.

Mother and Father were halfway down the stairs, Father first, an arm behind him, on Mother's shoulder. They were both looking to the swinging door at the foot of the stairs, the doorway to the kitchen. Ethan was on the other side of the kitchen, standing in the dining room, his ear to the second kitchen door.

The head was on the kitchen table. Tiny forks and knives were on the kitchen floor. The red at the base of its neck showed dull enough to look purple in the early morning sun through both Elvie's window and the windows of Ethan's house.

Elvie looked for Dane.

She found him outside the dollhouse, his plastic snout touching the kitchen window, looking inside at the head.

"Who let you out?" Elvie asked.

She looked back to Mother and Father on the stairs. Had they heard something? It certainly seemed like they had. Father was protecting Mother. Ethan was listening for more. And Dane wanted back in.

The eyes of the head seemed to be wider than they were last night, as though watching both doors to the kitchen at once.

Elvie reached a gloved hand into Ethan's house. Then she

paused. Last night she'd removed it. And yet, here it was.

"Do something," she said, staring at the figurines, the people of Ethan's house. She watched them for a long time. As long as she could. She tried to make sense of the silverware scattered on the kitchen floor.

Elvie's bedroom door creaked open and she screamed as Jack raced across the carpet to her.

"You *scared* me!" she said, gripping her dog by the scruff of his neck and rubbing her nose against his. Jack licked her and Elvie smiled and then Jack got bored of being in her arms and he wiggled out of them and raced out of the bedroom, as quickly as he had appeared.

Elvie looked back to the house.

The head was no longer in the kitchen. Now it was upstairs, on Mother and Father's bed.

And yet, Mother and Father were still halfway down the stairs, looking toward the kitchen door. And Ethan was still leaning against the other kitchen door. All of them still listening, waiting to hear more of whatever had worried them in the first place.

But Dane… Dane was no longer at the window. Dane was nowhere to be seen at all.

"Elvie!" Mom called from downstairs. "School!"

Elvie got up and walked around the drawing table, walked to the back of the house.

There she saw Dane seated on the drawing room table, looking up to a second story window. Elvie knew it was the master bedroom window. The room the head was in.

"Who let you out?" Elvie asked him again.

But she imagined she must know who let him out, because her own Mom and Dad let Jack out all the time for the same reason.

Dane must have been barking too much. Must have been keeping everybody awake. Elvie imagined him trying to get their attention: *look look, come come, there's something in the house with us, something that doesn't belong.*

Elvie walked back to the front of the dollhouse and felt herself grow hot in her winter clothes. What she saw scared her deeply. Mother was on her knees, picking up the forks and knives. Father was leaning over the sink, his plastic head close to the kitchen window. As if looking or listening for Dane. Ethan stood in the kitchen, too, looking up to the ceiling.

Elvie followed his sightline, through the ceiling, to the second story, to the master bedroom, to the head upon the bed.

Elvie thought about calling out to her own parents. Thought about showing them. Instead she left her bedroom and closed the door behind her. She'd have to see what happened next when she got home from school.

What happened next was bad.

Elvie had done a good job of focusing at school. She didn't think much about the dollhouse. Laughed with her friends, listened to her teacher, made a partial snowman on recess. It wasn't until the bus ride home that she really started thinking about Ethan and his family, worrying about them a great deal.

They were being haunted. That much Elvie knew. A dead doll was haunting a family of living ones. A broken figurine had come back, somehow, got into the house, and wouldn't leave.

What did it want?

Only to scare the Smithsmiths?

Elvie had come to call them the Smithsmiths that very day. She'd referred to them by name at school, talking with Jenny Penn. Unable to keep mum, she'd told Jenny that she had a great dollhouse at home. When Jenny asked what the name of the family was who lived inside, Elvie stuttered.

Lived inside.

The Smithsmiths.

The phrase chilled her. They *did* live inside the dollhouse, didn't they? And if they could live there, couldn't they die there, too?

Before arriving home, Elvie decided she had to help them. Had to help the Smithsmiths.

She begged her mom to take her to the toy store but Mom said no. So she begged Dad instead.

Modern Toys on Seaver Street was one of Elvie's favourite places to go. Mr. and Mrs. Ogman knew a lot about toys and would talk about them if you wanted them to.

"This is the boys' section," Dad said, when Elvie led him to the back of the store.

He was right, but Elvie was looking for a boy's toy.

She was looking for a policeman.

"Really?" Dad asked. "A cop?"

Elvie nodded. "I don't have any," she said.

Dad considered this.

"Interesting. I like that you're branching out. Toys shouldn't be segregated anyway, right? It's the seventies, for Christ's sake."

Home again, Mom rolled her eyes and told Dad that he was spoiling his only daughter but Dad only smiled and winked at Elvie and Elvie brought her new toy upstairs immediately.

She found Ethan and his family sitting at the kitchen table. Ethan's father had his hands together and his head down, as if he was saying grace. Elvie's family didn't say grace, but she had friends who did. It was possible Ethan's father was praying. Dane stood by the kitchen door.

Figurines that weren't meant to play together were never the same size and scale. The policeman was a little bit bigger than Ethan and his family. Elvie placed him in the kitchen with the Smithsmiths.

Then Elvie went downstairs to have dinner herself. She ate chicken and rice and when she returned, she found the family had indeed met the policeman.

So had the head.

Elvie settled into her chair.

The policeman was standing on a chair in one of the extra bedrooms. He was halfway into the attic. Ethan and his family stood around him. Father had an arm around Mother's waist. Dane was looking up at the policeman. The policeman was looking for the head, she knew. Searching the house for it.

Elvie went to the bathroom to brush her teeth. When she returned, Ethan's mother and father stood at one end of the attic. Ethan was crouched beside Dane at the other. And between them, on his knees, the policeman was halfway into a crawlspace. Elvie couldn't see his upper half.

Elvie was happy for this. Happy the policeman was doing exactly what she hoped he would.

Her own dad came into her bedroom and asked if she wanted him to read her a story. Elvie said yes. She got into bed and Dad sat beside her and read her a story about fields of many colors, a purple sky, and red trees. When he was finished he kissed her head and turned off her bedroom light. Then he left. Elvie waited a minute, got up, and quietly went to her red plastic chair. She listened for a minute, listened for her own parents. Then she turned on the lamp by the drawing table.

The policeman was lying on his belly in the foyer.

He had no head. And the tiny plastic bulb that once connected his policeman's head to his body was red. Exposed now, for all the family to see.

Elvie clasped a hand over her mouth. She wanted to scream, *needed* to scream, but didn't want Mom or Dad to hear.

Elvie shook her head no.

No, this wasn't what she hoped would happen.

Ethan stood over the dead policeman, a plastic hand over his plastic mouth. His mother stood beside him, both her hands on his shoulders, beginning to pull him away from the beheaded figurine. Father and Dane were outside the foyer, at the foot of the stairs.

Dane was looking up the stairs.

Father was looking down at Dane.

Where is it, Dane? Where?

Father had the policeman's gun.

Elvie looked for the head, too. She searched the eight bedrooms, the attic, the kitchen, the dining room, living room, library, everywhere.

Where was it, Dane? Where?

Then Elvie found it. Kind of. In the upstairs bathrooms she saw the head reflected in the bathroom mirror. But when she searched the bathroom for the head itself, she couldn't find it. Maybe it was wedged somewhere in there, somewhere she couldn't see. There couldn't be a reflection, Elvie knew, without something to reflect.

She reached for the tub and then withdrew her hand.

Elvie looked back down to the policeman. To the red plastic of his exposed neck. She brought a hand to her own throat. She felt bad. Bad for putting the policeman in the house.

The House of the Head.

She turned off the lamp and went to bed. She fell asleep thinking of other ways to help the Smithsmiths. Other things she could do.

What could she do?

How could Ethan's father shoot the head if the head wasn't in the room where it was reflected?

But Elvie knew it had to be in there. It *had* to be.

She fell asleep to these words:

It has to be… it has to be… it has to be…

They didn't have any priest or rabbi toys at the toy store. Elvie talked to Mr. and Mrs. Ogman about it.

"You *might* be able to find something like that at a church or a temple," Mr. Ogman said. Mrs. Ogman didn't think they existed. Mr. Ogman wasn't convinced. "A lot of those places use toys to explain the testaments and whatnot."

"There aren't any priests in those books," Mrs. Ogman said.

Then Mr. Ogman had an idea. "We *do* have some Native American toys, Elvie."

"What does that have to do with anything?" Mrs. Ogman chided.

Mr. Ogman kept his eye on Elvie. "They are a very spiritual people. Probably more spiritual than a priest or a rabbi could ever dream to be. You *are* looking for a spiritual toy, aren't you, Elvie?"

Elvie nodded her head yes.

"Whatever for?" Mrs. Ogman asked.

Elvie didn't tell them whatever for.

Once the Indian entered the House of the Head, Elvie felt better about things. He was about the same size as the policeman, but he looked much fiercer. Much wiser, too. Elvie thought he looked like he knew exactly what was going on and would know how to fix it. How to end it.

Ethan and his parents were sitting on the couch in the living room. The three of them side by side by side. Dane was on all fours on the floor next to the couch. All four of them faced ahead, facing Elvie's direction. So they were perfectly set-up to listen to the Indian. Elvie placed him in front of them, standing on the living-room rug.

She sat back in her chair and studied the figurines. The Indian's back was to her. His warpaint wrapped around his chest and almost met across his back. His long black hair hung past his shoulders. He had more muscles than Dane.

He gripped a hatchet in one hand, pointed with the other. Elvie felt much better about things.

She went out to dinner with her parents. A new restaurant in town. Mom talked about the housing market. Dad talked about Jack. Said Jack was getting older. Said his vision was getting worse. Mom said it was natural. Dad agreed.

When they got back home, Elvie ran upstairs, but Mom stopped her halfway.

"How about you watch a little television with us? Would you like that?"

Elvie looked upstairs, could see her bedroom door from where she stood.

"Okay," she said.

She went back down and watched a television program with her parents. It was funny. Dad and Mom laughed a lot. Elvie liked to see and hear that.

When the program was over, both Mom and Dad looked very tired. Elvie felt tired, too, but she desperately wanted to check on the Smithsmiths.

"I'll tuck myself in," she told her parents in the hallway between their bedrooms.

"Are you sure?" Mom asked.

"Yep."

"Well, well, well," Dad said. "Jack isn't the only one getting older."

They both kissed her forehead and Elvie watched them enter their bedroom, holding hands. Then she went to her own bedroom and quietly closed the door behind her.

She got into her red chair and turned on the lamp.

The Smithsmiths were all in one room. The library. Dane,

too. The library door was closed. They weren't reading books or sitting in the reading chairs. They were all standing in the center of the room, looking up to the ceiling. Dane, too. Upstairs, the Indian was in the bathroom, both hands raised. Elvie wondered if the Indian had told them to wait downstairs. He would take care of this.

Looking at the fear on Ethan's face, she hoped the Indian would take care of it.

She heard her door creak open and she turned to see Jack peering in, looking at her curiously.

"Come on, Jack," she whispered.

Jack trotted in, tail wagging.

Elvie turned back to the house and saw the Indian was now in the hall. Arms still outstretched.

Elvie looked for the head.

She searched every room. Searched the laundry tubs. Behind the shower curtains. Under the blankets on the beds, even Ethan's bed in the second lounge. She checked the closets, the cupboards, the sinks, under the tables, and behind every open door.

When she looked back upstairs the Indian was in one of the unused bedrooms. Arms toward the walls. His face was stoic, brave. Elvie nodded. Maybe he'd rid the house of the head.

Jack barked, scaring Elvie senseless. When her heart resumed its slower speed, she gripped him close and kissed his nose.

"You're not getting older, are you, Jack?"

Jack licked her face and Elvie shushed him. Jack leapt off her lap and exited her bedroom. Elvie wondered if he was going to wake Mom and Dad.

Elvie turned her attention back to the house.

The Indian was standing on the master bed. Arms to the ceiling. Hatchet raised.

Elvie looked for the head.

She searched all the same places again.

Had he done it? Had the Indian rid the house of the head?

She couldn't help but think about Mr. and Mrs. Ogman. If the Indian did it, she would have to thank them. Maybe even tell them what happened.

Elvie got up to use the bathroom. She was too afraid to look in the mirror so she didn't. She just peed, quickly, washed her hands without looking up into the glass, then returned to her bedroom.

She got back into her chair.

The Indian hung half out the master bedroom window. She could only see his legs. Was he searching the yard for the head?

Elvie got up and walked around the drawing table.

She had to adjust the lamp to see the outside of the dollhouse.

"Oh no!" she said, then brought a hand to cover her mouth.

The Indian had no hair. No head. And the plastic that once connected his head to his body was as red as the warpaint across his chest.

He was slumped, half in the house, half out. His arms hung toward the tabletop. His hands were empty, too. No hatchet. And the hand that once held the hatchet was red, as if the plastic thing had been torn from him, removing some of the paint from his palm.

Elvie searched the tabletop for the Indian's head. She didn't see it. She couldn't find it.

She rounded the drawing table quickly, adjusted the lamp again, and sat down.

The Smithsmiths were still in the library. They were holding one another now. Still looking up at the ceiling.

Behind them, on one of the bookshelves, unseen by them, was the head.

And beside it was the Indian's hatchet, too.

"Look out!" Elvie cried.

She heard movement from down the hall. She turned off the lamp and rushed across her bedroom, dove into her bed.

Her bedroom door opened and Mom's voice was loud.

"Elvie? What happened? Did you have a bad dream?"

Elvie pretended to be waking up.

"What? No. I'm okay."

"You screamed, honey."

"I did?"

"It woke us up."

"I'm sorry."

"No. Don't be sorry." Mom entered the bedroom and sat on the edge of her mattress. "I just wanna make sure you're okay. Are you okay?"

"Yes." Elvie smiled in the dark. "Just sleeping."

"Do you wanna sleep with us tonight?"

"No." Did she say it too emphatically? Would Mom know? Mom could tell these things. Better than Dad.

"Okay, honey," Mom said. "But if you need to, if you have another bad dream, just come crawl into bed with us."

"Okay."

"Promise?"

"I will."

Mom yawned and then Elvie yawned, too. A pretend one. Then Mom left her, leaving the bedroom door open a crack. Elvie listened to her footsteps in the hall. Heard her enter her own bedroom. Heard the door close. Then she heard Mom and Dad whispering.

Elvie waited.

She waited so long that she fell asleep.

When she woke up, it was still very dark in her bedroom.

She didn't know enough about time to know what time it was. She wanted a watch but Mom and Dad laughed every time she said so. She got out of bed and hurried to the drawing table. She turned on the lamp.

She started crying. Quietly.

Ethan's parents lay on the library floor, headless, both of them. Ethan's mother was reaching for the closed library door. Without her head she looked like a dress-form. Ethan's father was bent unnaturally backwards across the reading chair. As if his back were broken. His arms lay limp at his sides. The red plastic that was once hidden by their body and clothes was exposed.

"Oh no," Elvie said, crying, "oh no no no."

Ethan was half under the writing table, his head and shoulders in the shadows. Elvie reached for him, to pull him out, to check on him, then withdrew.

The head was on the table.

It was on its side. As if listening through the table, listening to Ethan beneath it. The hatchet was beside it. Its wide eyes seemed to be looking into Elvie's own.

Dane was facing the table. Dane was still alive.

Elvie's door creaked open and Jack rushed in. She turned to shoo him away but he was coming fast. He leaped onto her lap and barked and Elvie put a hand over his mouth.

"Shh," she said. "Shh shh shh!"

Jack calmed down. His tongue hung from his mouth and he was panting.

Elvie turned back to the house.

Dane was facing her. The head was no longer on the table. The head was gone.

Elvie looked over her shoulder.

Why was Dane facing her? Where was the head? Was it here? In her bedroom?

She felt cold, winter cold, and got up to search her

bedroom. She imagined a bodiless head sliding out from under her bed. Erupting from the closet. Peering in from the hall through the bedroom door.

Elvie imagined a hatchet removing her own head.

She turned back to the house.

Just Dane still. Dane still staring at her. Or staring at her bedroom beyond her.

Elvie looked to Ethan's body beneath the table. She thought of his parents. Of the policeman. Of the Indian.

Jack suddenly leapt from her lap. Panting still he ran from her bedroom into the hall. Elvie looked around her bedroom. Then back to the house.

Dane still stared.

Elvie felt hot, too hot. It felt like the heat was coming from within her. Like her skin was going to catch fire if she didn't move.

She moved.

She stood up and knocked the red plastic chair back to the floor.

Dane still stared. Ethan still lay under the library table.

Quickly, Elvie looked from room to room, searching for the head. She didn't want to look in the upstairs bathroom mirror. But when she ran from her bedroom, into the hall, when she entered her parents' bedroom and crawled into bed with them, she couldn't be sure if the head she saw in the mirror was just her memory of the time she saw it before or if it was there this last time she looked.

Years later, as many as twenty-five, Elvie didn't like to talk about her ghost story. Eric, her husband, thought it was a great one and, at parties, egged her on, asked her to tell it. Sometimes she did. Sometimes she didn't. And every time Eric brought it up, she thought of Dane. She'd never found the head in the house. Never found it in her bedroom either. Eventually she asked Mom and Dad to help her find it. After a while they asked why she wanted it so badly, but Elvie just kept saying *because*. Finally, her parents gave up and Elvie closed the dollhouse, bringing its two sides together by its hinges. She moved it all by herself into the shadowed corner of her bedroom, where the other outdated toys and clothes sat inert in a pile for so long.

She checked her bed each night before crawling in. Checked her ceiling, too. Checked between her books and in her shoes. Checked the windowsill and the curtains, too.

She never found the head. But she thought of it often. Just like she thought of Dane.

Every time Eric brought up the House of the Head, Elvie wished she still had Dane. Wished she could pull him out of her pocket or show everybody that she wore him as a necklace and could say, *Here he is… he's still staring… Can you tell me what he's staring at? What does he look like he sees?*

And she'd think of Ethan, too, and his brown hair and kind eyes. How she never verified his end. Never pulled his body from under the table in the library in the House of the Head.

SUCCULENTS
by Conrad Williams

They went on a long bike ride under a punishing midday sun. Much of it was along well-trodden pathways through scrubby brush. Large swathes of deep sand meant there was little traction; you had to get off and push. Graham was sweating hard by the time they reached Cabo Sardão. He was grateful for the rest; glad too that he'd had to bring up the rear because Felix, his six-year-old son, was struggling more than most. The rest of the group stood around watching their arrival. One of them started a slow handclap that was taken up by the others. He gritted his teeth against the urge to offer a rebuke. *Watch your temper*, he warned himself. It was something Cherry was often remarking upon.

You're getting worse as you grow older... you need to just kick back and not let things irritate you so much... there's a heart attack up ahead, you know, just waiting for you. Remember that time...

Ricardo, their guide, was talking now in his halting but charming English, about the spits of rock reaching out over the bay. Steep cliffs fell away on either side. Earlier they had watched as intrepid bathers carrying towels inched down the sheer drop, aided only by old ropes left behind by thoughtful climbers. It seemed a big risk to take, no matter that the rewards were your own private beach.

"You walk slowly and carefully if you want to see the

stork's nest," said Ricardo. "If he trips and falls he has wings. You don't, I think."

"Do you want to see the nest, Felix?" Graham asked.

"Yeah! Is it storks with the big legs? Or is that herods?"

"Herons. They both have big legs. And so does Sheila over there."

No need for that, Graham. You're on holiday. Be friendly.

He thought of Cherry back at the apartment, gorging herself on *pastéis de nata* and drinking Super Bock by the pool. She had booked them the mountain bike activity as a surprise. *Bonding time for you and the ankle-biter*, she'd called it. When he asked her why she couldn't come along too, she grew defensive. *You know I can't deal with heights. I'd hold everybody up.*

The other members of the group began moving forward along the narrowing path. Graham took Felix's hand and followed. He watched Sheila's backside as she picked her way through the thigh-high grasses. *Keep that in your sights and you can't go wrong*, he told himself, then had to stifle laughter. He was thinking of *Star Wars* for some reason, and of Luke Skywalker guiding his X-wing down to do battle against the Death Star. *That's no moon.*

"What are you laughing at, Dad?" Felix asked.

"Nothing. Just mind your step, okay? And keep hold of my hand."

Graham was envious of those who paid little heed to the precipice. Heat haze smeared the sea-chewed promontories further south. If he squinted he could just make out the car park where they had begun their tour. His boy's hand loosened in his grip; he reinforced it, and told Felix not to mess around.

Once he could see the nest—an arrestingly large aggregation of criss-crossed sticks that lipped over the edge of the cliff, as if the stork was cocking a snook at its precarious situation—Graham felt no compunction to get any closer. He didn't want a photograph; there were no chicks, the stork was not in residence… it resembled little more than an abandoned game of Jack Straws.

"Come on, Felix," he said. "Let's get back to our bikes."

He felt his relief grow with every step nearer the trail. So far, this holiday had involved too many of the things he preferred to avoid in everyday life: heights, blistering heat, exertion. He wished he was back at the hotel with Cherry. Felix loved the pool; they could bond themselves silly in there without the worry of punctures, or falling to their deaths, or storks attacking.

Or Sheila's backside.

Our cruisers can't repel firepower of that *magnitude.*

"Are you being okay?" Ricardo asked.

"Fine," Graham choked, turning around to see the rest of the group queuing up behind them as they inched back along the path. "I must have just breathed in some pollen or something. I'll be okay in a minute."

"Take a five," Ricardo said. "There's something anyway I want you to look at."

The group stared at Graham: bovine, sweaty, ill-dressed for the weather and the activity. He could already feel the rough canvas hems of his shorts abrading his skin; there'd be blisters later, or at the very least an ugly red chafing. What happens when middle-aged people get off their arses for a week. Short-sleeved shirts striped with back sweat. Red temples. A sluggishness; a lethargy. He remembered being Felix's age: football and tag in the back garden for as long as it was light enough to see. Drinks and snacks on the lam. When did you lose that playfulness, that drive? When did you go from *let's play out* to *let's lie in*?

Ricardo was on his knees in shrubbery that looked as if it had come from a science-fiction film set. The ground was carpeted with stunted plants with thick leaves and fat clustered flowers the colour of mustard.

"See this?" he said, pulling one of the flowers clear of its receptacle. An aperture in the ovule wept clear fluid over Ricardo's fingers. He licked it clear.

"Hideous," spat Sheila, her voice cracking with amused disgust.

"Not at all," Ricardo insisted. He took hold of the ovule with both hands and teased it open. There was a clearly audible suck. "This plant she is known as 'Mother's Tears'," he said. "Because, look, she is so crying all the time."

He pulled up a few more of the plump hearts and passed them around. Everyone regarded each other blankly. Graham was reminded of the kids in his class when he handed out musical instruments for the first time.

"Now, you are watching," Ricardo continued. He lifted the parted ovule and sank his mouth into it. Sheila dropped the plant she was holding and turned her back on their guide. Her face was pale and pinched.

Ricardo wiped his mouth with the back of his hand. "Like all tears of the mother, she is sweet." He looked straight at Graham. "Now you must try."

It wasn't a request. Graham had to persuade himself that he would have looked directly at whoever was standing the closest to him. He realised now that Ricardo, though young and lean, was in fact taller and broader than him. He felt a prickle of nervousness—the same loathsome fear that came calling when he had been a child—at the idiotic thought of what the Portuguese man might do if he did not partake of the plant, which now, he recognised, possessed a musky, earthy odour. An animal smell. A human smell, even.

"I don't—" he began, but Ricardo only smiled—revealing white teeth interleaved with pale grey fragments from the ovule—and pressed Graham's hand towards his mouth. He saw the others turning away, surreptitiously ditching the plants they had been given, wiping their hands on their shorts and heading back to the bikes.

He took a bite of the flesh and felt his stomach rise to meet it.

"It's good, yes?"

Graham said nothing, but swallowed the mouthful. It was sweet, but there was a disagreeable taste too, of earth, of rust. But that was nothing next to the texture, which reminded him of the slither of tripe, eaten when he was a child, with onions. Never again.

"If you are in the hot place, and no potable water, this is saving lives."

They went back to their bikes and Graham concentrated on keeping his breakfast where he'd put it. He was irked that Felix had not watched him swallow the plant. At least Ricardo seemed to hold him in higher regard. He told Graham to hold back, that the three of them would bring up the rear.

"Your wife," Ricardo said, once they'd struggled through the remaining sandpits and found a more agreeable rhythm. "She no like the bike?"

Graham balked, convinced the man had just likened his wife to a bicycle. But then he factored in Ricardo's struggle with the language, and saw how the ambiguity had snared him. "She's not much of a cyclist, no," he said.

"You like her ass? It's nice and round, no? Perhaps too much heft."

"My wife…"

But Ricardo was staring at Sheila's backside as she struggled with the incline. Graham looked around at Felix, who was concentrating on his pedalling, and watching the butterflies flirt in the hedgerows.

"It's a little inappropriate, don't you—"

"Me, I like a big ass. I like the curvy. I'm skinny as rakes but my girlfriend? She's built like the fucking tank. Your wife. She is the nice shape. Plenty to grab on to when she take you for a big ride."

Ricardo was close enough now for Graham to be able to see his teeth again. They were small and grey, packed tightly into a mouth that seemed far too capacious for them. His lips sagged, the colour of the strawberry daiquiris Cherry ordered before dinner. Juice from the plant had dried to a glaze on his chin. Shock had shrunk Graham's windpipe straw narrow; he could produce no noise from it.

"You watch your child," Ricardo said.

Graham hauled on the brakes and slid to a stop; Felix almost collided with his back wheel. He pulled up a few feet ahead, and stared back at his dad, concern pulling all of his features into the centre of his face.

Ricardo seemed genuinely nonplussed. "What is it that went wrong? Your bike, it is old and unresponsive?"

Now he read a very definite slight in their guide's words. Ricardo knew the language better than he was letting on. Graham's arms and legs were shaking with anger. He felt weak and febrile, as if he were suffering from low blood sugar.

"What do you mean, 'watch my child'?"

"It is in all the news in the Alentejo region. You have heard of *O Sedento*?"

"No." Graham shook his head. His breath was as empty as the dry, pallid drift of seedpods collected at the side of the path. "What is it?"

"Not it. A him. A person. *O Sedento*. Meaning the English, it is *the thirsty*."

"The thirsty?"

"This is the correct."

"Thirsty for what?"

Ricardo licked his lips and his tongue was like an

undercooked steak, far too big for his mouth. He winked. "*O Sedento de Sangue.* The thirsty of—"

"The bloodthirsty," Graham corrected him.

"It is like the Draculas coming out of Pennsylvania shadows, no?"

Any other time, Graham would have found Ricardo's abject malapropisms funny; endearing even. Now they gave him the creeps. He pressed on against the pedals, trying to put some distance between him and the guide. His stomach churned.

They completed their bicycle ride at a car park where a minibus was waiting to take them back to their hotel. While the others stood around admiring the view, Graham told Felix to stand with Sheila while he paid a visit to the toilet. Once there, he urinated lustily, but was appalled to see his stream of urine was the colour of rust. Hadn't he drunk a good litre of water that morning, in preparation for this arduous task? Then it must be the plant's fault. Yes, there was the same mealy smell; it had gone through him like the odour of asparagus. No more bush tucker. He was looking forward to the evening. Steak all the way. And a carafe of wine.

He left the cubicle and washed his hands; he felt his heart perform a little tumble in his chest.

Remember that time…

Stop it. The one thing he hated about Cherry was the way she was constantly harking back. She never seemed to look forward. Forget that he had lost forty pounds over the last six months. Forget that his cholesterol levels were the lowest they'd ever been, or that he treated his body to a mainly Mediterranean diet these days. No. He imagined her at the table tonight casting disgusted looks at his red meat and chips. *You'll not be needing the dessert menu after all that?*

Remember that time…

He didn't need the reminders. It hadn't even been a

proper cardiac arrest. If anything, it was a shot across the bows. He'd been at school, patrolling the playground with his usual cup of tea (milk, two sugars) when the first signs arrived. He'd been annoyed because he'd been asked by the Head to attend a meeting that evening in his stead, and there was also a problem with Felix who was either being bullied or bullying others depending on the rumours knocking around. Also, that morning he and Cherry had somehow got into an argument during sex, and she had pushed him away. There was an ache in his jaw and a pressure growing—like indigestion—around his breastbone. Later he felt breathless climbing the stairs to the gym after work. He'd decided then, feeling mild palpitations, that exercise was not something he should be doing. A visit to the doctor the following morning led to his GP calling for an ambulance.

A cardiologist conducted an ECG and gave him the all-clear, but there were lifestyle choices to make. He made them. Now his mid-morning tea was sugarless and, invariably, green. He cut down on calories and stepped up the exercise. Butter became olive oil. Battered cod became grilled salmon. He ate salad and brown rice. The pints turned into occasional glasses of red wine. The weight fled from him. But Cherry was unimpressed. Maybe it was jealousy; as they both approached middle age, it was she slowly being overcome by avoirdupois.

Remember that time…

He wondered now, as they filed back into the minibus, whether the juice of the plant had carried some kind of poison that was deleterious to the heart. Felix sat next to him, his head against his shoulder, as he thought of his parents (long dead, both heart attacks) and their love of gardening. His father had only ever referred to a plant using its Latin name, just one of the many ways he had tried to trump his only son's greater academic achievements.

Now he thought of monkshood and belladonna, of

sweetshrub and Christmas rose. Oleander and foxglove. As a child he had loved apricots and rhubarb, but his father had wagged a finger, telling him that he was a step away from a horrible death. Rhubarb leaves contained oxalates that could cause kidneys to fail; cyanide lurked within apricot stones, and would put you in a coma from which you would not revive. He often wondered if his weight gain had come from such nightmare threats: bread and cake, as far as he was aware, could be consumed without any danger of toxicity.

He was nudged awake by Ricardo. They had arrived back at the hotel. The sun was low in the sky, but its heat seemed undimmed. It struck Graham that the juice on the guide's chin was the colour of the vernix that had coated Felix's body at birth. Stiffly he climbed out of the back of the minibus, trying to combat the beats of nausea. Felix was ahead of him, already trotting down the path to the apartments. He could hear splashing and gales of infant laughter from the pool area. Beyond that was a tennis court, and the soft *thwock* of volleys. There was no sign of Cherry in their rooms, and no note to explain where she might be. Graham chased Felix into a hot shower and they dressed for dinner. He brushed his teeth but the taste of the plant remained, an oily film on the back of his incisors.

"Let's find Mummy," he said.

Cherry wasn't at the poolside, though a lounger was adorned with proof of her occupancy: a novel by her beloved Patricia Cornwell; a drained glass carrying her plum-coloured lip imprint; the silk scarf with which she tied back her hair. He found her at the bar, another strawberry daiquiri before her, laughing too loudly at the things a much younger bartender was saying.

"We made it," he said, and sat alongside her. One split second. But he noticed it: the expression falling; her flirting over.

Cherry fussed over Felix for a while, telling him what a

big boy he was for cycling so far, and for looking after Daddy. They agreed that he could have twenty minutes in the pool before dinner. Cherry took her drink to the poolside table and Graham joined her after ordering a martini for himself.

"Productive afternoon?" he asked, as he sat down.

"No need to be snippy."

"I'm not being snippy," he said. He shifted in his seat and felt the efforts of the day leap in his muscles. His thighs sang, but it was an agreeable pain, a righteous pain. Tomorrow morning might be a different matter though.

"Did you overdo it today?" Cherry asked.

"Define 'overdo'. You booked the exertion… sorry, excursion. Maybe you were hoping it would be too much for me and I wouldn't make it back. Then you could laugh at shit bartender jokes to your heart's content."

"I do worry about you, no matter what you might think."

Graham took a deep swallow of his drink. Ice cold. And what was it they used to say back during his student days, he and the others in the cocktail club? *Drier than the dust from a druid's drill-stick.* The guy might have been trying it on with his wife, but he was an excellent barman. The martini suffused him with good will, not least because it helped to mask the flavour of the plant. He gazed at his wife, at the expression on her face, that *will we, won't we* look. She seemed ready for a scrap. Was there ever a dinner eaten that benefited from a fug of bad domestic air?

"I'm sorry," he said. "It was a good day. I had fun. Felix had fun. We missed you, that's all."

"It sounds like it," she said, but it was mock admonishment, tinged with triumph at having eked out the first apology. She smiled and touched the back of his hand. "Ten minutes more, though, and I'd have been in with that bartender."

They finished their drinks and lured Felix from the pool with promises of chocolate ice cream. Dinner was good, and Cherry did not comment on the amount of wine he pointedly consumed.

Graham carried Felix—who had been nodding off into his dessert—back to their apartment. His mood was souring again; he could still taste the Mother's Tears plant, despite the slick of pepper sauce that had accompanied his steak.

Cherry was already in her sleeping attire, and it was the kind she wore to signal to him that she was not receptive to any kind of night manoeuvres. Plain Jane knickers in beige. An unflattering sleep bra underneath one of her skin-tight yoga tops that was accessible only if you had access to a variety of chisels and pliers. He left her to her nocturnal rituals of cleansers, toners and moisturisers and returned to the bar.

He was pleased to see that Cherry's barman was off duty and had been replaced by a woman. He thought of turning on the old charm, but realised he was too tired and agitated. And he just did not feel like flirting. Pain lanced his sides, like the colic he had suffered from greatly as a child. He should have just gone to bed and tried to sleep it off, but the churning of his insides had made him jittery. Some late night fresh air—and fresh it was; cliffs of cloud were rising out to sea, signalling a storm's approach—might do his efforts to relax later the world of good.

He ordered a glass of tonic water in the hope that the quinine's analgesic effects would counter his symptoms. He took the drink into a far corner of the dining room where a TV was showing grainy repeats of the evening's football match. He couldn't tell who was playing, or what the venue was, let alone what they were playing for. But it was something to focus on while his guts seethed and the wind tested the strength of the building with growing muscle.

"Tastes good."

Graham jerked in his seat; he was not alone. What he

thought was a nest of shadow turned out to be a man leaning against the wall, arms folded. He too was watching the game and Graham had sat directly in his line of sight.

"I'm sorry," Graham said, meaning it as an apology for blocking his view, but the man took it as a request to clarify his statement.

"The taste. It is good."

"I'd prefer there was some gin to go with it, but yes, it's a refreshing drink."

"Not your glass. The juice in the body. The meal of it."

Now Graham saw that the man held a newspaper in one fist. He brandished it. Graham couldn't translate the headline, but he recognised some of the words he had already heard today.

O Sedento.

"Ricardo?"

The guide offered a loose salute in return.

"You sound as if you admire him," Graham said.

"Who said it was him?"

"A woman then. Whoever it is."

"Who said woman?"

"Then what? A witch? A curse? A bad dream?" Graham wished he'd go away. He wanted to watch grainy football on a shit TV, drink his tonic water and go to bed.

"I don't know," Ricardo said. "Maybe all of those things. Maybe none. Maybe *O Sedento* is the appetite we all carry. The best of us keep it hidden, no?" He folded his newspaper and slotted it into his back pocket. He touched a finger to his forehead. "I sorry. I don't mean to annoy. Have a good night. Do not go to bed thirsty, yes?"

Any other day and Graham—who hated confrontation, hated the feeling he might have slighted someone in some vague, infuriatingly British way—would have offered some sop in reply, bought the guide a drink, invited him to stay.

But he was glad to see the back of him. The door banged shut and through the window he saw Ricardo's hair leap in the wind before the shadows consumed him.

Graham finished his drink and headed back to the apartment. Rain was in the air now, a fine mist that the wind seemingly would not allow to settle anywhere. It seethed around him. He was soaked by the time he reached the door.

He towelled himself dry and sat in the chair. Sleep came on like a rehearsal of death. He had not felt like climbing the stairs to bed; the meat from his dinner sat heavily in his stomach as if his teeth had not macerated it first. His hands gripping the arms of the chair, looking too much like the bleached white carapaces of dead crabs they'd seen in the harbour earlier that week. His sweat was dry glue on his skin. His gut rumbled; it was as if the plant had spoiled him for any other sort of nourishment.

For some reason he was thinking of the first time he had seen Cherry, on a quadrangle in the university where they had both studied. He was coming to the end of his first year of some Mickey Mouse degree that would prepare him for no job at all; she was cramming for her finals, with a placement at a City bank already secured… but that was knowledge for the future. All that he knew at that moment was the back of her neck and that she was curled on the grass and the pile of textbooks by her side. The sweep of her neck, unusually long, the way her hair was up, stray strands teased by the breeze, the dimples either side of her spine…

He stared at those dimples until he was sure she could feel the weight of his scrutiny; she sat up, her head twitching. She planted a hand in the grass and pivoted on it. Insane dream logic showed him Felix within the circle of her arms, though he was seven years away from being born.

Everything around them shivered, as if he was watching it on a TV screen with a bad reception. And then the mown grass was gone, and he was alone with his family, on the nearby beach where an ancient ship was rusting into the shingle. She dragged Felix away, the both of them casting fearful glances back over their shoulders. They disappeared inside a giant rent on the ship's port side. He followed, but every time he called their names, the juices in his throat caused him to gag.

He pressed his hands to his eyes and pushed until he saw shoals of colour sweeping across that inner dark and when he opened his eyes again he was alone in the room and it was full night, and the storm had matured, was battering the coast and their door was flapping open in the wind.

Alien flavours rose in his craw.

"Cherry?" he called out.

There was no answer. He thought she might have drunk a little too much and decided to reignite the flame he'd seen hopping between her eyes and those of the young bartender. Or maybe she'd decided to go for a midnight dip in the pool. Or maybe she'd just conked out after her long day of leisure.

He closed the door and clattered up to the bedrooms. Empty. Felix's bed was a mess of blankets, as if he'd suffered restless dreams. Or, his mind mauled itself, he'd struggled with an assailant as he was snatched from his bed.

He checked the bathroom in the insane hope that they'd decided to have a late shower together, but every room was empty. He returned to the lower level, almost tripping on the spiral staircase, and flew into the rain. He called out but his voice was spirited away by the thrashing wind. Shutters all across the complex were rattling in their frames, or, where they had not been secured properly, were crashing rhythmically like stoked metal hearts. The trees seemed aghast. The pool area was empty. All the loungers had been tied down but some of the large cushions had been blown free and floated in the water.

Steel blades flashed behind grey cloaks lifting on the horizon. He heard the police helicopter moments after it blatted overhead and watched it, momentarily distracted, amazed that the pilot had braved the violent winds tonight. A spotlight on the chopper's belly created a beam busy with rain. It picked out the fevered tops of trees, the roofs, the edges of the cliffs. Had someone been found out there? A body on the crags? His gorge rose again and he tried to let it come: he wanted his stomach to rid itself of the textures and tastes of the plant. But its coagulated syrup was not ready to leave him just yet.

He ran through the hotel grounds to the tennis courts at the rear. In one corner was a gate, which led on to a sandy path to the beach. He was there in minutes, and could see the foam-topped combers on the sea as if they were lit from within. The helicopter was hovering as best it could above the hillside that sloped down to the cliff edge. Figures were arranged upon it, like toy soldiers on a blanket. There were half a dozen black shadows and a single figure in an acid white T-shirt. Even at this distance, Graham could see that it was Ricardo: the wavy hair, the limp posture. He held something in his hands. The uncertain spotlight flashed around and over it, but would not settle. Was it... no, Christ, no. Was it Felix's jumper?

Ricardo turned to look at him. And then raised his hand as if to wave. And then he dropped, as if he had been instantly deboned. A moment later and the sound of gunfire reached him. The light shifted on the hill; he could no longer see what was happening. The police helicopter was returning along the coast. It passed directly overhead and its light picked out the rusting remains of the ship from his dream.

Was that a figure, slipping back into one of the fissures in the hull? He was torn between going to the hill to confirm what he thought he had seen, and continuing his search for his family. If it was Felix's jumper, then so what? Maybe Felix had taken it off that morning because he was too hot. Perhaps Ricardo had simply been trying to return it. His mind could not cope with the narratives he was forcing upon everything; he had to cling to the positives. The alternative was too hideous to contemplate.

Graham stumbled back along the rocky outcrop, conscious that the ground fell away from him to needles of rock some thirty feet below. The rain slashed almost horizontally across the path, stinging his face. Here was the channel leading down to the beach where the rusted ship was incrementally disintegrating into the shingle. He passed into a zone of relative calm. Now the wind was negated he could hear the rattle of rain on the decaying hull, the crisp attack of the waves upon the stones.

Lightning jagged around the inlet. The aperture in the bulkhead where the figure had sought shelter was ink black. Iron ribs edged it, splayed inward: presumably this had been where the ship was fatally breached. He approached, conscious that the flowers Ricardo had entreated him to suck were arranged around the failing metal hull as if they were somehow taking nourishment from the oil sweating from the sumps, the soot in the stack, the endless, psoriatic rust.

At the hole he paused. Another level of quiet accumulated. There was a high stench of iron and diesel and rotting marine life. He could hear his breath, ragged in his throat, echoing in the cavernous chamber, unless it was that of another he could not yet see. He bit that thought off at the root and spat it away. He called his wife's name and it fell dead at his feet, as if poisoned by this air.

He was about to move into the ship and beggar the dangers when lightning arced once more across the night. It lit up the inside of the hull for a millisecond, but that was enough for him to be able to see what looked like the limp remains of a body hanging from a metal spar thrusting down from the ceiling. He was put in mind of filled coat hooks in winter bars. Though darkness had rushed back into the space, it remained imprinted on his retina. Emptied... drained... Or maybe just a coat after all, he hoped. But no: there were crimson-tipped knuckles, where something had been chewing. He imagined the grind of tiny metacarpals in pistoning jaws. A sound like bar snacks being munched.

He staggered backwards and slipped on one of the plant leaves. He fell into a nest of swollen stems. The smell of Mother's Tears rose like a terrible seduction. His mouth flooded with juices, all red and raw. To deny them, he tore up a fistful of flowers and sank his teeth into their centres. That sweet, brackish slime burst across his tongue and he drank it down. Now his stomach railed against the stew of textures mingling in his gut and he felt his back arch violently as he regurgitated his meal. Before darkness became absolute, he was able to gaze upon his mess and discern, within the half-digested lumps and granules, the wet gleam of a wedding band upon what was left of a finger.

DOLLIES
by Kathryn Ptacek

All the dolls I owned as a child were named Elizabeth—
which is not my name, but might have been if my mother
had figured out how to shoehorn it into my already lengthy
list of names—and they all died of smallpox.

I did not "help" my dolls by using ballpoint pens or
crayons or markers to put blue dots on their faces and arms
and legs and torsos. No, those blue dots just appeared.

And why I associated blue dots with smallpox, I don't
know. I've read accounts of that disease's outbreaks, and I don't
recall anyone ever mentioning the pustules having a blueish
cast. Nevertheless, I announced to my mother one day that
Elizabeth 1, an oversize baby doll my grandmother had sent
to me and for which she made beautiful clothing by hand that
I didn't appreciate at the time, had died from smallpox.

My mother was rather dismayed by what I said—that I
would even consider one of my dolls having died and that
I would say it was from smallpox. I mean, how many five-
year-olds know smallpox is a disease, much less one that kills?
Somehow, I knew.

Elizabeth 1 was tucked away onto a shelf in the closet as I
played with other toys. I had never much cared for dolls, had
never put a doll on my birthday or Christmas list, but that
never kept my parents and grandmothers and other well-

meaning relatives from giving me dolls. I mean, I was a girl, so I was supposed to play with dolls, right? Not really.

The few friends I had seemed to have all sorts of dolls: the ones that talked, which I always found kind of creepy; the ones that were as tall as actual kids, called the "doll twin", and which also bothered me, because that wasn't really what a twin was like, or was it? Others had collections of smaller dolls from various countries where relatives had visited. Some dolls had more clothing than anyone I knew, and they had all sorts of purses and shoes and hats, which kept my friends busy for hours. I would go over and play for about half an hour—then I'd get bored and would wander from the room where all the other little girls were dressing up their dollies.

That's where I overheard for the first time my mother whispering to Petra's mother that I was such a strange child. I felt proud at that very moment; only when I saw the expression on my mom's face did I realize that what she said was not a good thing. I never told her what I'd heard her say.

It wasn't long before another doll came into my life.

Elizabeth 2 was as tall as me—and I was a child who towered over other kids of the same age—and she was refined, with a porcelain face and hands. Dressed in some vague historical outfit, all lace and delicate material and bloomer-style undies, she was beautiful—a "Madame Alexis doll" from some company that had made these dolls for many years. My mom said she'd had one when she was my age. I was dubious about the doll being in my care, but the old lady whom my parents and I were visiting insisted I take her home. I glanced across to my mother, who nodded imperceptibly, and I said solemnly, "Thank you." I clutched the doll to my chest, and I guess anyone looking at us wouldn't have been so sure who was holding who up.

We drove home through the snow, and when I got into my bedroom, I placed the doll—already christened Elizabeth

2—in a child-sized rocker that had been my mom's. It sat alongside my twin bed with its pink comforter and cat-shaped pillows. I went into the bathroom across the hall and brushed my teeth and put my flannel pajamas on, then came back to bed, and after my parents had tucked me in—no story tonight, I said—I looked at Elizabeth 2, faintly seen in the light flooding in from outside, and I wished her a good night.

It took about a week, but that's when I noticed the first blue spot on Elizabeth 2's dainty white hand. I spit on my finger and rubbed at the spot, but it remained the same: small and blue... a shade between robin's-egg blue and navy. I was unhappy about that, because I liked Elizabeth 2, although I didn't play with her. She was one of those dolls obviously meant only for display. I had a couple of tea parties with her and my black stuffed dog and my teddy bear that had once been brown and white until my mom put him in the washing machine and now was gold and a runny brown. I poured imaginary tea for my companions, and I put thin wooden blocks on the plates—pretend cookies—and we chatted. Elizabeth 2 remained patiently sitting in the little rocking chair, her wide blue eyes staring ahead, her golden ringlets bright in the sunshine that flowed into my bedroom during the afternoons.

When the spit didn't work, I got a tissue and wet it in the bathroom, and I scrubbed Elizabeth 2's hand. Nope.

The next day I found a second spot, this one on her neck. I looked at her, and she looked back. Neither one of us said anything. By the weekend, when my dad and mom and I were going out to dinner, I had found eleven blue spots on Elizabeth 2's neck and hands. I hadn't checked her body, but I knew there were more there. I turned her in the chair and then moved it back out of the sun a bit. She was in the shadows now, and you'd have to examine her closely to see the blue spots. I figured I'd better hide them from my mom.

I suspected this was an expensive doll, and I thought I would get into trouble.

We drove to the cafeteria where we always went for dinner on Saturday nights. As I pushed the peas around on my plate, I announced, "I think that Elizabeth is dying."

My dad, about to cut a chunk off his pork chop, glanced over at my mom, who put down her coffee cup with a sharp crack and said, "I thought you put Elizabeth in the closet and weren't playing with her anymore."

I nodded, my bangs flopping against my forehead. "I did. This is the other Elizabeth. Elizabeth 2."

My mom arched an eyebrow. "The Madame Alexis doll?"

"Yup."

"She's Elizabeth, also? Don't you want to name her something else, Nonny?"

"Nope. She's named Elizabeth. She told me."

My dad tried not to smile, while my mom just watched me.

"All right, honey. But I think you should name your dolly something else. Wasn't one Elizabeth enough?"

I shrugged and grabbed a piece of buttered bread and stared down at my plate.

My parents started chatting about various things—my dad's job, my mom's office, the neighborhood, wasn't that the lady from the bank over there by the piano?—and it wasn't until I was pulling on my coat and we were heading out to the car that I realized my parents hadn't asked me how I knew Elizabeth 2 was dying and what was killing her.

Elizabeth 2 succumbed not long after that, and was relegated to the death shelf in the closet. I didn't have any dolls after that for a while—just stuffed animals. They all had different names (Froggy, Spot, Kitty… I guess I wasn't very original when it came to naming) and never got smallpox, and I was glad, because I much preferred them to dolls. I made up complex stories about these toys, and they fought battles and got married and visited other worlds, and I was quite happy with my menagerie of fluffy critters.

It was about then that my mother started coming into my bedroom at night. She'd stand by my bed and not speak or move. I kept my breathing even like I was asleep, but I watched her from beneath my lashes. Mostly, she just stared at me. One time I heard her whisper something. It sounded like, "Dolly."

I never said anything to her about the night-time visits, nor did she mention them in front of my dad—or to me at all. I realized after a while that she had sneaked into my bedroom for years… but I was just too young to remember it, I guess.

On my eighth birthday, I received a lot of presents from my grandmother (my mom's mom, the one who had given me the baby doll), but no dolls, I was happy to see. However, my other grandmother had gone back to the old country on a recent trip, and she had brought me a souvenir—a doll in native costume.

"How cute!" everyone exclaimed at my party—it was just me and my parents and grandmother—and then everyone said how much the doll looked like me, with its high cheekbones and brown hair with bangs. The doll's eyes were even brown and green like mine, and I wondered, with a faint shiver, as I traced the patterns on the little white cap on her head, how long before Elizabeth 3 died from smallpox.

Another time I heard my parents talking when they thought I was downstairs. "Do you think she knows?" my mom said. They were in their bedroom getting ready for dinner.

"She can't." My dad sounded so confident.

Knows what? I wondered.

"But she has to… she has to. How?" And then my mom started crying.

"It's okay, Jen," Dad said. "Really, it is."

My mom sobbed some more, and I slunk away to my room and half closed the door. I took my stuffed animals off their shelves and started playing with them, but they were in bad moods and wanted to fight and attack each other, so I put them back until they calmed down.

I frowned. What could I know? I didn't know anything. I was just a little kid.

"I think that Elizabeth is sick," I announced at breakfast two weeks later.

My mom glanced at my dad, who sat up straighter in his chair. I heard him give a faint sigh, then he said, "We've been meaning to talk to you, Nonny."

Guilt flooded me instantly. What had I done? I hadn't meant it—whatever I had done! Really! I knew I was in trouble. That's what "talk to" meant. I had done… something… and now I was in big trouble. Only, I couldn't think of what I had done. Was it because of that something I was supposed to know—only I didn't know?

My mom made a noise. "I don't think it's time, Derek."

"She's eight, Jen. She might as well know."

I watched as her eyes filled with tears. "No," she whispered. "Not yet."

He covered her hand with his. I shifted uncomfortably. I didn't like it when my parents touched or kissed. Didn't all little kids feel that way? It was wrong… somehow.

"Please."

"Okay. Not today."

She nodded and took a sip of her coffee, and I stared at the runny eggs on my plate and tried not to think about what they were going to tell me.

I asked to be excused right after that, and they agreed, and I fled to my bedroom and my poor dead dollies.

That night my mother visited me in my bedroom again, and she leaned down close, her dress rustling. Her breath was warm on my face. "It wasn't my fault," she whispered, and she smelled of cloves and something else... something sour. I tried not to wrinkle my nose. I didn't want her to know I was awake. She stayed there for a minute or two, just staring at me, then she straightened and turned to leave.

At the door, she stopped. "I know you're awake, Nonny. You always are."

I said nothing.

She waited a bit longer, then left. I felt wetness on my cheeks, and I realized I was crying, only I didn't know why.

My dad kept wanting to tell me... whatever. And my mom kept saying, not yet. It happened when I was ten and when I was eleven... and even when I had just turned twelve, she would beg him not to tell me. He would sigh, then nod; he didn't want to upset her even more, I knew.

I was old enough then that I could have asked my parents separately. I could have not waited for them to tell me. But I got a little stubborn, I guess. If they wanted to tell me something, wanted to discuss some weighty matter for *years* now, then they could come to me; I wasn't about to break down first and ask. Nope.

And even then, my mom kept coming into my room at night, and I still said nothing.

In school, I would sometimes watch the other kids, and I wondered if their parents did that... spied on them when they were sleeping? I wanted to ask some of my classmates, but I really wasn't good friends with anyone now. I was too shy, too hesitant to ask them if I could join in, so mostly I kept to myself and watched the others as they played outside.

Once, a girl new to the school asked me if I wanted to sit with her at lunch, and I just stared at her. I wanted to, but I didn't know what to say, and after a minute, she shrugged and turned away. She didn't try to talk to me again. I felt a little sad, and I was going to talk to my mom about it, but again, I didn't know what to say.

At home that afternoon, though, I told the dead dolls about my could-have-been friend. They listened silently. Of course.

After that non-incident with the new girl, I guess I got the reputation of being a snob or someone too stuck up to talk to the "lower lifes", but I wasn't. I just didn't know what to say or how to say it. I could talk to my dead dolls, but not living kids my own age.

The kids at school were the only people I saw, outside my folks, of course. My parents weren't big into entertaining. In fact, I don't remember a single time when they ever had friends or neighbors over to the house, and no one on our street ever asked us over for summer barbecues or pool parties. Sometimes, I would stand at my bedroom window and stare across the street at all the people gathered there… the kids racing around with each other and their dogs, and the moms and dads standing with their glasses of cold beer or soda, and I'd hear laughter and shouts and some music from someone strumming a guitar. And I'd think that it looked like a lot of fun and I wished they would invite us. But they never did. And I would stay in my room and listen to the faint laughter and all I would hear in my house was the steady ticking of the clock in the living room.

For some reason, people still insisted on giving me dolls. At twelve, I thought I was too old for them, and when Grandma gave me a doll, I would thank her politely and right after that I'd tuck the doll into the closet. I knew what would happen. Elizabeth the whatever-number-we-were-up-to would develop blue spots, and she'd die, and that would be it. I always liked to make an announcement about the doll's death to my parents... I just felt it was something I had to do. I don't know why.

So many times Dad would start to say something to me, and Mom would silently plead with him, and he'd stop and just study me and shake his head. He worked longer hours now, and I didn't see him as much, and so often I was in bed by the time he got home. And that's how it continued right up to my fourteenth birthday when I got pregnant and my dad left the house one night and never came home.

My mom said the two weren't connected, but they were. They had to be. My dad couldn't take it that his little girl got knocked up by some guy at school who was halfway cute and who had talked to her a few times and then said he wanted to show her something after the last class. Yeah, he had. Him and his two buddies. They knew I hardly talked, that I wouldn't tell anyone what happened. They were right. I was still taller than most of the girls, but had developed a figure along the way. I always dressed in baggy clothing, because I didn't want anyone to see that I had developed breasts. But I guess the boys knew.

When I missed my first period, I got a little nervous. When I missed the second one and noticed I was eating more, I knew. It wasn't until my fourth month that my mom caught on. She demanded to know if I was pregnant, and I said I guess I was... a little bit. She started crying then, and screamed at me and pleaded and demanded to know what happened. But I don't think she really wanted to know; she didn't want to know that I was held down while three sweaty boys climbed on top of me, one after the other.

My dad just looked at me without a word—*what did he want to tell me all these years?* I wondered—and said he had to go to the store. He grabbed his wallet—the black leather one I had given him last Christmas—and keys, and he went out to the car and backed out of the driveway, and the last I saw of him was heading up toward the string of stores on the edge of the development.

My mom continued to scream at me, then she'd stop and sob. She kept asking what would people think? I wanted to say that they'd think I got pregnant, and that would be it. She told me I had to have an abortion, and then two minutes later she said I had to keep the baby so I would learn my lesson. She claimed she wouldn't raise the child; we would have to put the baby up for adoption. Or no, she would pretend to be pregnant, go away, and come back with me and the baby, and she and Dad would claim it was their baby, my little surprise sibling.

She cried and yelled for hours, and after a while she got quieter. My dad should have been home by then. She tried calling my dad on his cell, but we heard the ringing in the bedroom. He had left the phone there.

By midnight Dad still hadn't returned, and Mom had called the police to report a missing person, although to them Dad didn't qualify as missing quite yet, so she called all the hospitals. She called the state police. She paced up and down the hallway, going into the living room to stare out the windows, like she might catch a glimpse of him driving by or something. And she went into every room and turned all the lights on, then flipped the outside lights on. Our house probably looked like a giant birthday cake blazing with all those lights. Why did she do that? Did she think he was lost in the darkness and needed some kind of beacon to guide him home?

She reported him missing after the requisite number of hours, and the cops put out some bulletins. Someone said they thought they saw him in upstate New York or maybe it was Michigan. He didn't call. He didn't write.

Mom and I settled into an uneasy routine with her going to work and me going to school, although once the teachers and school staff noticed the swelling of my stomach, I decided to stay home. I didn't tell Mom that. I just left for school before she went to work, and I would linger around the corner until I knew she was gone, then I'd walk home and go into my room and fall back onto my bed and stare up at the ceiling. Sometimes, I would make myself a sandwich, but mostly I sat or lay on my bed and thought about... nothing.

In my sixth month, I was home doing nothing when the doorbell rang. I went to the door; it was one of the boys. He doesn't even deserve to be named; he certainly didn't call me by my name during that entire ninety-minute ordeal. I flung open the door.

"What?"

He shuffled. "Can I come in?"

"No."

I was surprised he was here. I didn't even know he had any clue as to where I lived. Maybe he asked someone. Why, though? He had never been interested enough to visit before.

"I just wanted to say—"

"Stop. It's too late. Don't say you're sorry. You're not. You're just afraid that I will tell someone what you and your friends did."

He looked down at his sneakers, then up at me. "Yeah. But I am sorry. I didn't mean—"

I slammed the door shut, then went back to my room and my dead dollies. I took them out of the closet, and I got a wet washcloth, and I took all of their clothing off, and I carefully washed their bodies. How strange to think in a few months I would be doing the same thing for the little living being growing inside me. I wanted to feel happy or sad or something. Mostly I felt nothing.

I hadn't been to a doctor yet. My mom said she couldn't take me to a baby doctor. People would know; people would start to talk. She had abandoned her idea of us going somewhere and then coming back and pretending that the baby was hers. I wondered what she thought people would do when they started hearing a baby's cry coming from our house?

I thought we might move. Recently, she had started talking about a smaller house. Dad wasn't dead, we didn't think, but he wasn't sending money either, and Mom couldn't keep up this place by herself. I didn't want to leave. What if Dad came back after we'd moved? How would he know where to find us?

When Grandma next came to visit, she squinted at me, then at my mother and said, "This one needs to go on a diet."

Mom laughed and said we both did.

Grandma had another present for me. Another doll. I thanked her. I'm not sure why she gave me one then, as I was nearly fifteen. Maybe she thought I collected them after all these years. I put the new Elizabeth on the shelf and waited.

Mom found us a new place to live shortly after that—we were moving in with her mother. Grandma had a pretty big place, and I'd still have my own bedroom, toward the back of the house, and I liked that privacy. Mom had finally broken down and told Grandma what was going on, and Grandma had said nothing but simply pressed her lips together so they were thin and bloodless. That was when she said we should move in with her.

It took us nearly a week but we got all our stuff over to Grandma's. We had to sell a bunch of the furniture, and my mom packed up all of Dad's stuff… in case he ever came by, I guess, and wanted his shoes and jeans and jackets and whatnot. Why would he want those things when he didn't want his own wife and daughter? But I said nothing to Mom.

I could tell she was still hopeful. Grandma just shook her head; she knew better.

We settled into a fairly comfortable routine. Grandma took me to the doctor, who was amazed that the baby was so healthy. He talked to me about various options, and I just said my mom and I planned on keeping the baby. He looked across at my grandmother, who shrugged. When we got home, she said I needed to keep learning, so she took out some books and we started talking about history and stuff… It was more interesting than what I'd been taught in school. She said I could make up this year in school the following year, or maybe I could get my GED in a few years. I wondered why she paid more attention to me than Mom did.

I was working on some math problems one afternoon when Grandma said, "Your mom has had it kind of rough, you know."

I put down my pencil. "No, I didn't."

"She lost a baby."

Really? She had never said anything. I had never known about another sibling. Why hadn't she told me? Was this what Dad was trying to tell me for so long?

"Twins. She was going to have twins," Grandma said, and she sighed heavily. "You were one of them."

"I was a twin?" I blinked. I couldn't even begin to comprehend that.

"She had to make a choice. Only one baby could be born. She had to choose. You were born."

I stared at my hands. I didn't know what to say. Questions tumbled in my mind… words tried to form on my tongue… but nothing came.

"Get back to your math," Grandma finally said. It sounded harsh, but it wasn't. She wasn't into kissing and hugs and all that, and for her to be gruff with me was being kind. It's those old-world people. No mushy stuff for them.

I tried to focus, but what should have taken only minutes for me to do took me an hour. Finally I finished, and said I was going to my room, and I went in and closed the door and lay on the bed.

I cried then. For myself. For my lost twin. For my mom and dad who never told me. I cried for the baby. And I cried for that boy who might have been my boyfriend or even a friend. And I wondered if he could ever find me at Grandma's house. Could Dad?

I didn't have dinner that night—I just didn't feel like eating—and I stayed in my room. Shivering, I burrowed under the covers.

Sometime later I heard the door open, and I waited. I heard my mom approach the bed. It was the first time she'd come into my room at night since we had moved out of our own house. I held my breath.

"I know she told you," Mom whispered. "We wanted to tell you. Dad wanted to tell you. But I wouldn't let him. It wasn't right, I thought. I don't know why. We should have told you years ago. We should have." She paused and waited for me to say something, but I didn't. "It was wrong. Choosing the other twin."

"You mean you should have let both of us be born?" I asked, finally finding my voice.

"No," my mother said, "I mean that I made a bad choice. I let the wrong twin live."

I stopped talking to my mother after that. I had nothing left to say to her. I talked to my grandmother, and she talked to me, but for me, my mom didn't exist. She might as well have left like Dad did.

As I got closer to term, I realized I wasn't feeling so well, or maybe it was just part of the pregnancy. I had started to read things online, but I just didn't want to know. I didn't want to hear about all the horrible things. I wondered if my grandmother would take me to the hospital to have the baby, or would we have a home delivery? She had told me that she had been born at home, but that her younger brothers had all been born in the hospital. I wasn't sure that Grandma could deliver a baby. Not my baby.

But I didn't say anything. No one talked about the pregnancy or the baby or anything like that. Mom kept going to work, and she would come home at the end of the day, and she would eat dinner, then retreat to her room off of the living room. And I would go into my bedroom at the back of the house. I don't know what Grandma did.

Both my mom and my grandmother were out of the house when I began to feel the labour pains. I was going to call 911, but I didn't, and I went into the bathroom and squatted in the tub, and I pushed like all those women you hear about, and I huffed and squeezed, and finally I felt wetness between my legs—my water broke, I guess—and then the baby was coming, just sliding right out. I caught her before she hit the bottom of the dry tub, and I studied her in the harsh bathroom light.

So little… tiny tiny fingers. Her dark hair was plastered against her fragile skull. She was breathing, but kind of faintly. Her skin looked a little blue. I put my finger in her mouth to clear it out. She coughed once, twice, then breathed more easily.

"Elizabeth," I whispered.

I got a wet washcloth and gently cleaned her up, cut the cord, and wiped up all the blood and stuff, then I wrapped her in a fresh towel. I cleaned myself up, but left the mess in the tub. Then I went into the bedroom with Elizabeth.

I sat on the bed, and I gazed down at her. She hadn't made any noise since she was born, but I could hear the faint rasp of her breathing. My mom had made a choice. I had a choice.

I laid my fingers gently across her nose and mouth. It didn't take long. She didn't really even struggle all that much, just waved a tiny fist slowly. I watched for her chest to rise and fall, and when it no longer did, I bent down and gave her a kiss on the top of her head, and then I got up and crossed to the closet and put her on the shelf beside the other Elizabeths.

Then I sat down on the bed and waited for my mother and grandmother to come home.

THE ABDUCTION DOOR
by Christopher Golden

You've probably seen the abduction door, maybe stood right beside it and never understood the kind of danger you were in. Might be you never even noticed. That's the way it works. You step onto the elevator and it's just there, no explanation, as if there's nothing at all out of the ordinary about a smaller door set into one wall of the elevator. Not at the rear of the box—like in a hospital, where most of them have sets of doors at the front and back. The abduction door always appears on one of the other walls, illogical and even absurd. The door is too small for a person to walk through, roughly three square feet, and about eighteen inches off the floor. Of course, even if one wanted to go through that door, it doesn't make sense, does it? The only thing that could possibly be on the other side is a wall or the open elevator shaft.

That's true, isn't it?

Of course it is.

When I was a boy, my father did his best to teach me to be brave, but to him "bravery" consisted mostly of ignoring fear. My mother disapproved. She taught me to trust my fears, to explore the shuddery intuitions in life. But even my mother had her limits. Even she told me that my fear of the abduction door was silly and childish.

I wonder what she would say now.

Mostly, I suspect, she'd be screaming.

I'm fairly certain that I was nine years old the first time I noticed the abduction door. That would've been 1986. My parents had taken me to New York City for the Macy's Thanksgiving Day Parade. I'm an only child, so they spoiled me rotten in those days, and I loved every minute of it. When I think back on that weekend, so many images cascade through my mind—the crowds of people lining the sidewalks in Times Square, the massive character balloons floating overhead, the marching bands and floats and Santa waving directly at me, the orange scarf my mother wore, my father's cold-reddened cheeks… so many. But the image that remains the most vivid is my second glimpse of the abduction door.

Not the first glimpse, because with the first glimpse I felt only curiosity. It was the second glimpse that etched a lifelong terror into my mind, the way some things can only manage to do when you're nine years old.

My parents always blamed the bellman, a true New Yorker named Cyril. In his red-and-black uniform, skinny, sixtyish, white-moustached Cyril seemed almost a part of the hotel itself, as if he'd stepped right out of the lobby wallpaper and would slide back into it when his shift ended for the night. We'd gone out for our Thanksgiving dinner and returned to the hotel—I don't remember the name, but it doesn't matter now, does it? The abduction door isn't there. Not in any predictable sense, anyway. The point is that we'd come back from dinner and Cyril had one of those wheeled carts filled with somebody's luggage and we were all waiting for the elevator together. I'd noticed the abduction door on our way out to dinner—not before that, though we'd been up and down the elevator half a dozen times since checking in.

Cyril looked wise to me. Old and wise, somehow more

a part of the place than the younger people behind the registration desk.

"What's the little door for?" I asked him.

"Say again, kid. What's that?"

My parents shared the smile reserved for mothers and fathers who believe fully in the precociousness of their children and assume that everyone will find their offspring charming.

"The little door in the elevator, on the side. Where does it go?"

Cyril didn't smile. It's important for you to understand that. He didn't smile, he didn't wink at my parents, he didn't crouch down with a popping of arthritic knees or smooth his moustache. His brows knitted together and he glanced at the elevator doors. Above the elevator, the numbers were counting down toward L.

"Started working in hotels in Manhattan when I was still in high school," Cyril said. "In those days they still had elevator operators in some places. This one old fella called it 'the abduction door'. Said kids got snatched right in the middle of their elevator rides… sometimes grownups, too."

I stared at him, forgetting to breathe.

"Hey," my dad said. "That's not okay, man. He's only nine. Kids his age, they believe all that stuff. Tell him it's just a story."

Cyril smiled then, but his eyes were dull and glassy, like doll's eyes—like he wanted to do anything but smile. "Course it's just a story. Sorry, little man," he said to me. "Don't mean to scare you. All these old hotels have creepy stories—ghosts and stuff—but that's all they are. Stories."

He smoothed his moustache now. Glanced away from me. I knew he was lying.

"Do they ever come back?" I asked.

"Stop," my mother said, but I wasn't sure if she was talking to me or Cyril.

"Funny you should ask," the bellman said, and now he

leaned on the baggage cart, one foot up on it like the stalwart hero in some old movie. Relaxed and confident, and so I knew the next words would be the truth. "About a month ago—no word of a lie—I'm waiting on the elevator and the doors open and this boy runs out. Little kid, couple of years younger than you. He's scared out of his wits and he grabs onto me and won't let go. Says he got away. Someone grabbed him in the elevator but he got away from 'em. Thing is, we got security cameras on every floor, right? None of the footage showed this kid getting on the elevator, not on any floor. He just appeared on the elevator while it was moving, then jumped out when it hit the lobby."

I could hear my heart drumming in my chest. My mother protested and my father got in between me and Cyril, threatening his job. I think maybe Dad even grabbed him by the red lapels of his uniform until Mom pulled him away. Cyril said he was just trying to erase what he'd told me about the abduction door, figured the story about the little boy escaping would put it right. My father muttered about him being a fucking psycho. When the elevator door dinged, all four of us flinched.

My dad pointed at Cyril. "You can take the next one."

Cyril held up his hands in surrender, but once my parents and I had gotten into the elevator and the doors were closing, I heard the skinny old bellman finish his story.

"Crazy thing was, when they tracked the kid's parents down, they found out he'd vanished from a hotel elevator in *Pittsburgh*," Cyril said. "Figure that one out."

The whole ride up to our floor, I stared at my feet. My parents fumed, determined to call the front desk and raise holy hell about Cyril's behaviour, but I barely heard a word that passed between them. Their fury washed over me, but I kept staring at my feet until the elevator reached the tenth floor and juddered and squealed to a stop. For a breathless moment, it seemed the doors would not open, that we would be trapped inside, suspended, waiting to fall.

Something creaked over my left shoulder. I peeked, and I saw it there. Just a glimpse, through the screen of my father's arm and my mother's purse and the shopping bag in Dad's hand. The abduction door.

You can imagine how fast I got the fuck off the elevator when the doors finally slid open.

A quarter century later I'm in Los Angeles with my wife and daughter. We don't live here. Nobody lives in L.A., not really. Tori and I have moved around a lot in the nine years since Gracie was born. Some of that nomadic spirit sprang from me being relocated for work, but several of those moves came because Tori couldn't stand to remain living in communities where she'd humiliated herself so badly. Alcoholism and schizophrenia make hideous bedfellows, but Tori has them both. She fights that two-front war valiantly and most days she wins, but on the other days, things get uglier than you can imagine.

Or maybe you can imagine, after all. If so, I'm sorry for you.

At nine years old, Gracie has seen and heard things no child should see or hear. Doubtless she's got a little maelstrom of love and hate churning inside her that she can't even understand, but somehow she's the sweetest, kindest, gentlest kid you'll ever meet.

Even today, when Tori had a schizophrenic break while we were shopping on Third Street Promenade in Santa Monica, and started screaming at a woman busking on a street corner, convinced that the woman was an alien insect creature—one of millions invading our world—and that her song had taken control of our minds. Tori thought she had to get us away from the music, and monitor us for behavioural changes, and kill us if we showed any sign of alien insect control. Out of mercy, you understand.

The doctors at UCLA Medical Center explained this last part. Fortunately, Tori hadn't come right out and told Gracie and me that executing us was her fallback plan. Maybe you're thinking shit like that only happens in Oscar-bait movies, and for your sake I hope you keep on believing that, I hope you never have a reason to come to terms with what can really happen during a schizophrenic break.

They put Tori on a 5150 hold at UCLA Med, which basically means they're keeping her for observation against her will, and even if I wanted to get her out of there, I couldn't. I'm told sometimes these episodes are fleeting, easily treated by adjusting medications… and other times they go on for months. Maybe forever.

By the time Gracie and I flee the hospital it's after dark. My eyes are so tired it feels like there's sand in them, and though Gracie has been a trouper, she's flagging. I can see it. The strain of having to pretend that everything's okay, having to nod earnestly and tell me Mommy's going to be all right—because that's the kind of nine-year-old she is—has exhausted her. I drive us back to the Hotel Beaumont—or just "the Beaumont" if you're a local—and let the valet make the car vanish for us. We don't talk to anyone, barely look at anyone, as we trudge through the lobby. The Beaumont has been restored so that it looks precisely the way it did in the early 1940s, in the age of the Hollywood studio system, when producers and directors met for drinks around the swimming pool in the courtyard, when aspiring starlets sunned themselves by day and sat listening to the big band in the dining room, hoping Frank Sinatra or Burt Lancaster might spot them and turn them into the next great leading lady.

Gracie and I keep our heads down. "You hungry, sweetie?"

"I'm okay, Daddy." She's too tired even to push the call button beside the art deco elevator doors, so I do it for her.

"We could order room service."

The elevator dings and we wait for two elderly women to get off. They're so old they might well have been a pair of those aspiring starlets hoping to catch Burt Lancaster's eye. Gracie and I shuffle onto the elevator as if we're even older and I smile weakly at the thought. I punch the number seven and the doors glide shut.

Head hung, I feel the elevator moving. It shifts and rattles as if it's an actual relic of those ancient days and not just made to look like one. My thoughts are with Tori, then. All I can see in my mind's eye is the fear etched on her face, the lunatic certainty that the world is secretly infiltrated by dark forces and that somehow she can save us by murdering us. I begin to well up with tears, but I can't let that happen. Not now. Gracie needs me. Sweet Gracie, who looks so much like her mother.

"What do you say, kiddo?" I ask. "Room service?"

Nothing. Then a muffled sniffling noise that I figure means my daughter—whose very existence takes my breath away—is finally crying, overwhelmed by the horror of what's become of her mother.

"Oh, hey, Gracie, it's—" I say as I turn toward her.

Just in time to see the long, spindly arms. The filthy hands. The stained fingers. Just in time to see them drag my little girl through the abduction door. It's the matter of a heartbeat as she vanishes. I scream and lunge, reaching out to catch the edge of the little door, but I'm too late and it clicks shut almost silently. It should close with an earth-shaking clang, but that click is so quiet.

I scream her name, but only twice. All my life I've been wary of the abduction door, I've kept my distance, I've been vigilant. It waited until I let down my guard and now…

I pound at the door, dig my fingers into the crease between its halves. The metal is oddly cold and it hums with a vibration completely divorced from the rattle of the elevator. Tears are streaming down my face and my jaw is clenched and I can feel myself snarling savagely and I know that is only right. I'm savage now. My Gracie, my baby girl… she's been taken and the only part of me that's left is the animal part. The most ancient part. This is what it is to be a parent, to love a child. It's ancient and bestial, and I claw at the edges of the abduction door and I crack a fingernail and blood drips but I manage to force the fingers of my left hand into the crease between the halves of the abduction door and I start prying, and hope ignites and my tears now are tears of rage and determination.

The elevator slows. Dings. I hear the real doors, the full-size doors, start to slide open and I turn, thinking, *Help me, they've got Gracie.* My fingers slide out.

A thirtyish guy with too many muscles for his silk t-shirt to contain gets on. He stares at me for half a second, maybe wondering if he should wait for the next elevator. Maybe he sees my tears and my hunched posture—maybe he sees the animal in me—but it's L.A. and surely he's seen stranger things than me.

"Help," I say, and I turn back to the abduction door.

But it's gone. With the stopping of the elevator, it has been erased.

"No," I say quietly. As quiet as the click of the horrid little door. I say it again, louder this time, and I run my fingers over the wall of the elevator, over that smoothness where Gracie has gone. I'm about to scream when I hear the clearing of muscle man's throat and I whip my head around to stare at him.

He's wary, suspicious, but not scared. One fist is clenched. His brow is knitted, and I think he wants to help but he's also ready for trouble. Maybe those muscles aren't just for show.

"You okay, brother?" he asks.

I can't speak. Can't even take my eyes from him now. We stand like that, locked in a moment of tense possibility, until the elevator dings again. The door opens and he steps off with a single backward glance and a shake of his head. I think he mutters something like "this fucking town," but I can't be sure.

Then he's gone, and I'm alone again on the elevator.

Alone. *Oh, Jesus, Gracie.* The tears come hot and fast now and I put myself into the corner of the elevator, staring at the smooth place on the wall, and I settle in for the long haul. Waiting for the abduction door to reappear. I could call the police, but what am I going to say that anyone would believe? They'd put me in the room next to Tori's at UCLA Med, two-for-one, a special on 5150s today.

So I ride the elevator and I wait. I ride all night.

I hear the woman's murmur before I feel her touch. My eyelids flutter and I see her standing before me, one hand still on her rolling carry-on. Dark and lovely, so neat in her flight attendant uniform, she gazes at me with open and genuine concern, the kind of real humanity that is so absent in our daily lives that it's shocking when you come face-to-face with it.

"You okay?"

I nod, struggling to stand upright. I'd been propped in the corner of the elevator, more or less asleep on my feet. Now I scrape the grit from my eyes and try not to release the sob rising in my chest. I nearly spill it all, nearly tell her the truth that would surely get the police involved and end up with me dragged off the elevator, but I can't get off. I can't. So I choke back the unshed tears.

"Long night," I manage, realizing how awful I must look.

How exhausted and worn, like some barroom drunk who'd stumbled into the wrong hotel.

"We've all had them," she says gently, trying to reassure me with her smile. Instead her kindness only makes me want to scream.

I want to ask the time but I've drawn enough attention to myself. I figure it's early, that she's heading off to an early flight. The elevator slides downward without stopping and dings at the lobby. She gives me one last reassuring glance and steps out, and I miss her painfully, this woman who offered me a moment of comfort. I want to scream after her. I want someone to help me, please God just help me get my baby back.

The elevator closes. Ticks quietly, awaiting its next summons. A minute or so passes and there's a hum, and it's rising again. Someone else is awake besides the flight attendant, someone else headed out into the pre-dawn hours, and I think of Tori in the hospital and I know—*I know*—I can't get Gracie back by myself.

The numbers illuminate as the elevator climbs. Trembling, I exhale and lean back against the wall, and then I see the abduction door out of the corner of my eye. My keys are out of my pocket even as I turn toward it. The elevator rises and the floors pass by and I know that when it reaches its destination the door might vanish again, so I jam my car key into the crease between doors and lever it hard, not caring about the key or the car. I get my fingers in and the metal edge scrapes the skin and blood wells up but after a second the door gives way. No snap or crack or wrenching of metal, it just gives, almost like it wants to.

The elevator starts to slow. I stare at the space yawning on the other side of the abduction door, the impossible space. Where the elevator shaft ought to be is a narrow corridor, both there and not there. It moves with the elevator, disorienting because I can feel myself in motion but the view through that little door makes it appear that I'm not moving at all. The shadows are fluid in that impossible space, shifting and yet solid at the same time, so that it looks like the unfocused mist of a dream but it feels real and *Gracie's in there*, my Gracie, and if the elevator stops…

I take a breath before I hurl myself through, fingers throbbing, scraped raw and now outstretched as I fall hard to the floor on the other side. The way my elbow cracks as it strikes the floor sends jolts of all-too-real pain up my arm, but the blur of my surroundings stays the same. Real and unreal. I hear the ding of the elevator as if it's right next to my ear, so loud, but when I look up the abduction door has closed. A little smear of my blood remains in the crease.

I should be screaming. I stand and the world tilts under me and I should be screaming because none of this is possible, not with any of the mechanics of any universe I've ever been taught to believe in. I should curl into a ball and cry in terror, but that image pricks my heart and I shake off my terror and shock, because I'm not here as the child trapped in a nightmare, I'm here as the father, and it's my job to free her.

"Gracie," I say, her name a prayer, a mantra, a battle cry.

The world is all narrow corridors and strangely angled doors. The shadowed, shifting halls are filled with the smell of roasting meat and my mouth waters. My stomach tightens. It's been a day and a half since I last ate and the mist in the claustrophobic corridors is the smoke from the ovens of this jagged maze.

I nearly trip over the first one, a man in a torn and stained pinstriped suit. He's unshaven and emaciated and I think of a thousand homeless men I've treated like ghosts in my life. I've given money to some of them, bought meals for one or two, but I'm not absolved for all of the times I've passed them by. This one flinches as I stumble and skirt around him.

"Sorry," I mutter, because I can't care about him. Gracie is here somewhere.

Just as I realize I ought to ask him about her, I see the next one. A woman huddled in an alcove in jeans and a blood-smeared sweatshirt. Beyond her, on his side, is a dirty, naked man whose filthy beard seems much too large for his withered body. A rattling wheeze comes from his chest and it's a half-second before I realize he's crying.

"Go back," says the woman in the alcove. Her eyes are full of the same gentle humanity I saw in the eyes of that flight attendant, back in the world. At least they look that way for a second before I recognize terror in her gaze. Terror and despair. Maybe that's all humanity ever was.

"Go back," she says again. "Just go."

"Whoever you're looking for," the pinstriped-suit man says from behind me, "it's not worth it. Go now. The price is too high."

I stare at the alcove woman. At the blood on her sweatshirt and the screaming sorrow in her eyes. "It's my daughter," I tell her.

She only looks at me sadly and then turns her back, shaking, hugging herself. The naked man on the floor begins to wail and she kicks him hard in the side and screams for him to be silent. Pinstriped-suit cries out that I should go back, but instead I run past them… I run past a dozen more scarecrow men and women in the coalescing shadows, the twisting narrowness of this place. I find a set of spiral stairs and I descend, forced to duck my head.

When I pause, heart pounding, I hear the whispers of children and I can barely breathe, suffocated by my own hope as I wind down the steps. The smell of roasting meat is so tantalizing that I have one hand over my tight, grumbling belly, as if my hunger is a child growing there.

At the bottom of the stairs is a smoky chamber whose

floor is a latticework of glass panes, but the first step I take, my foot catches in the glass and I tumble forward onto my hands and knees, fingers plunging into the soft, warm, malleable membrane I'd imagined to be glass. It's a honeycomb of strange windows, and I peer down through the sticky mucous and I can see that each one of those panes in the latticework of the floor is not a pane but a *pen*, and inside each of those pens is a child. And below the honeycomb of stolen children is another chamber, where horrible, spindly figures move back and forth to wide-mouthed ovens whose fire—when their doors are opened—turns the honeycombed prison a furious red. The smoke wafting from those ovens makes my mouth water like nothing I've ever smelled before and I weep at the hunger and the revulsion as I see what's being placed into those ovens. I retch but I won't take the time to be sick. Instead I crawl on hands and knees above the gelatinous honeycomb prison, using the strong latticework between the pens to keep myself from sinking entirely, and I whisper her name.

Over and over, I whisper for her. "Gracie. Gracie, please. Gracie, can you hear me?"

I don't hear her answer. Instead, I look down through the cloudy honeycomb pane by pane, pen by pen, until I see her face staring back at me. She's talking but I can't hear her voice. She's crying and her beautiful face, my little girl's beautiful face, is contorted with terror, but it's her.

I've plunged my hands down through the honeycomb pane and am dragging her out before I can even ask myself if it's possible. I know it must be, and it is, and she's stinking and covered with that sticky mucous membrane, but she's in my arms. I shush her as she cries against my chest. I shush her as she turns and vomits whatever's in her belly, and I see some of that hideous honeycomb in her puke and I nearly throw up as well.

The smell of cooking flesh chokes me but I gather her into my arms and then I'm rushing back up the spiral stairs and down that corridor. Arms reach for me, those pitiful scarecrows who told me to go back, told me to give up, and I hate them now. Despise them for even suggesting it. Still they reach for me as if to stop me and I knock a dirty, sneering man aside. Others turn their backs, sobbing as if I've committed some atrocity and they can't bear to look at me. Alcove woman sees me coming and shakes her head sadly, but it's the filthy bearded man who snaps his head up, drags himself into the narrow corridor, and screams at me.

"Stop!" he shrieks. "You don't know what you're doing!"

But I know exactly what I'm doing. Gracie's warm against me and I've never been more sure of anything in my life.

"Daddy," she says. "Daddy, I want to wake up!"

My little girl thinks she's dreaming. I won't ever tell her she's been awake all along.

The pinstriped-suit man doesn't move as I skirt around him, and a moment later I'm there. Half of me is convinced the abduction door will be gone, but it remains, its solidity sure and unsure, the walls themselves almost opalescent with their uncertainty about their own impossible nature. I cradle Gracie against me and touch the door. When it took her, it was warm and the metal seemed to hum, but now it is cold and silent.

The elevator. It's not moving. I'm certain that's it. If I just wait—

"Daddy, please," Gracie says, and she looks up at me and coughs and I wipe the last remnants of that stinking mucous from her lips and I know I am getting her out of here. I am getting her home.

I wait, one hand on the abduction door, not hopeful. *Certain*.

I hear shuffling and whispers and I glance over my shoulder

and see them, those human scarecrows. Pinstriped-suit man and filthy naked guy and alcove woman and a dozen others. Gracie catches sight of them and cries out for me again, but all I can do is hold her more tightly against me with one arm while I keep my other hand against the cold, still metal of the abduction door. I want to scream at them to stay away, those poor husks, but they're not coming any closer. They only watch us, doing nothing. Watch us with pity in their eyes.

I feel the hum against my hand as the metal of the abduction door begins to warm and I want to roar my victory at them. Fuck their pity.

With my hand against the metal I can feel the rattle and rumble of the elevator in motion. I try to jam my scraped-up fingers into the crease, to force the door from this side. I'm sure I can hear—

"Voices," Gracie says. "Do you hear—"

"I hear them." And I do, voices on the other side of the abduction door.

The hum subsides and the metal cools just a bit and I feel my hope collapsing within me, feel my certainty die. But only for a moment, because the hum returns and the metal warms and the elevator on the other side of the abduction door is moving again, but this time there are no voices.

I push and it opens so easily that I whimper with relief and tears stream down my face. Our world is there, on the other side. The elevator lights flicker a bit and I hear tinny music playing inside and I wonder if it's the same elevator or another, on the other side of the world, but I know it doesn't matter. Not a bit. The elevator is empty but moving, the numbers above the door are dinging and I don't know how long it'll stay open, so I pry Gracie away from me. She clutches at my jacket but I tear her loose and half-shove half-drop her through the open door. The sound of her thumping to the elevator floor is the greatest sound of my life and she turns, so brave now, and tells me to come on, Daddy. Come on. Hurry.

But I can't.

There's no barrier. The door remains open. Gracie's standing now, eyes wide, calling for me to come through after her but too terrified to get near the abduction door again.

I just can't. My body will not follow her. I'm wailing inside. Raging. I raise my hands but I can't make them move toward the opening again, can't make them reach through. I feel the shuffling presence of the scarecrows around me, these lost humans who told me to go back, who told me I didn't know what I was doing. They say nothing now, just watching me, part of the shadows of this nothing space.

The elevator dings as it slows to a stop, about to open.

I scream my daughter's name. Gracie cries out for me as the abduction door slams shut, and only now are my hands my own again. I pound against the door. I jam my fingers into that crease and a nail cracks down the middle and blood spills out and all I can hear is the echo of my daughter calling for me.

I put my hand against the metal. It is cool and still.

I round on the scarecrows. They've started to wander away, some muttering and shaking their heads. I grab pinstriped-suit man by the lapels and slam him against the wall with such force that his skull bounces off it, but all he can do is cry and then he's sliding down the wall and I can't hold him up. I let go of his suit and he curls into a mound of sorrow at my feet.

Alcove woman hasn't wandered away.

"Please," I whisper to her.

"You took one of theirs," she says.

"No, I... I took my daughter back."

"That's not how they'll see it. You took one of theirs and now they won't set you free until you give them thirteen in return."

I stare at her. The words echo strangely in my head, no sense to them. As impossible as this place.

"Give them?" I say at last. "How the hell am I supposed to give them thirteen children?"

Her face crumples and her lips tremble. She reaches up to wipe fresh tears from her eyes. "Don't you see? That's what the door is for."

And then I do see. Her tears are not for me.

Numb, I look up and down the shifting, narrow corridor at the withered husks of people who inhabit this place and I understand. They weep not for me, not for Gracie, not even for the children. They weep for themselves because they've all done precisely what I've just done and now they're trapped here.

Give them thirteen in return.

The filthy, ragged mothers and fathers scattered up and down this corridor are all abductors themselves, now. They're monsters, stealing other people's children until they've given back a tithe of thirteen to pay for their own.

Or they're hopeless, unable to bring themselves to do it, to steal someone else's child, and they know that as a result they are trapped in this hell forever.

I scream my daughter's name.

And I wonder what I will become.

THE SWAN DIVE
by Stephen Laws

I really don't remember my night walk across the Tyne Bridge. But I was aware that I had reached that part of the pedestrian walkway halfway across, right over the river, where the water was deepest. I'd driven across the bridge many times, of course, on the way to work; too many times to count, I guess. Just one of those things in everyday life—you do it so often on autopilot that you barely think about the journey. But I'd always been aware of that particular section of the bridge, with its central girder-strut and the crosspiece of ironwork next to the concrete barrier. I realized that a small, subconscious part of me had been thinking about this place when I was very low, when the depression had kicked in. Perhaps I'd been figuring out that this was the place I'd eventually end up, when all my options had gone.

Traffic flashed behind me, uncaring, as I walked to the rail and braced my hands. I looked through the gaps in the barrier, strained to look down at the water, but couldn't see it. Only utter black.

I'd have to climb up on to the barrier if I wanted to look down and possibly see the water. I could see the lights of the office blocks and buildings glittering on the river from the shoreline of Newcastle Quayside on my left and Gateshead on my right. But I didn't want to look at those.

I wanted to look at the water directly beneath me.

I wanted to see ripples on the water there.

I looked back at the traffic flashing behind me. A car horn blared, but it wailed and vanished in the night and was nothing to do with me.

You want someone to care? Is that it? You want a car to stop and someone to say: "Hey, you! Don't do it!"?

"No," I said aloud. My voice sounded strange. Not like me at all.

I turned back, braced my hands—and clambered up onto the parapet. I hugged it like I was sitting astride a sawhorse or something. The concrete was icy cold, even though the night was warm. Wind ruffled my hair, but there was no caress in it. I still couldn't see the water below. The darkness down there was as black as the night sky above. If I didn't look up across the shoreline, it was like being on a bridge across limbo.

I got to my hands and knees and stood.

It was easier than I expected, and the fear that I also expected just wasn't there.

I turned to look at the traffic. I had no fear that I might lose my balance and go over backwards. How strange.

The traffic still didn't care. It had places to go.

But this was where I had to be.

I turned in small, tight steps away from the traffic— one-two, one-two—expecting to lose my balance at any moment. A small part of me, deep inside, was surprised that I didn't. Now I was facing the other way, looking out across the River Tyne and with that wind on my face, coming in from the unseen North Sea miles away in the darkness. The Sage building on the right-hand Gateshead side was like a huge glass-and-metal spaceship, multiple coloured lights shimmering on the river water. But when I looked down, directly beneath me, I still couldn't see ripples or light on the water down there. Just black.

And I realised now, for the first time, why this particular place had drawn me. Since this was presumably the point of deepest water, might it not be that when I went over, maybe (just maybe) I'd possibly survive the fall? If I jumped and hit the concrete quayside (or struts on the way down) then there was no way I'd survive. But if I was guaranteed to hit the water, then perhaps I wouldn't be killed outright? Sure, the height and the impact of hitting the water from here would probably kill me (remember that joke from *Butch Cassidy and the Sundance Kid* about a ridiculous fear of drowning when the chances are that the fall would probably kill them anyway?). In which case, job done. But what if I did survive the fall? What if I didn't drown? And what if I was dragged out of the river, and was resuscitated or whatever, might not kind people then set about convincing me that life really was worth living? That there were people out there who cared and that I could set about starting again with new hope in my heart and a new life-affirming outlook?

"Yeah…" The wind took my word away because it didn't believe it.

I looked out along the river and wondered what I'd do next.

I raised my arms on either side till they were parallel and shoulder high.

Now how did I think to do that?

I wondered when the fear would come; wondered when the utter emptiness inside would be filled with it. When it came and filled that hollow in my guts and heart, would I fling myself backwards from the parapet onto the walkway, weeping and shaking? Or would it steal away this weird and newfound sense of balance and make me stumble and fall from the bridge—now twisting and screaming and clawing at the air as I tried to scramble back?

Not a jump, I thought. *No, it has to be a dive. That's it, a proper dive, like I used to do at college. A swan dive—that's it. A forward dive with my legs straight together, my back arched and my arms stretched out from the sides, then brought together over my head and down—just before I hit the water. Although I haven't done this for years, it will be the best dive I've ever performed. My swan dive will be a swan song.*

The fear hadn't come.

The fear might not come at all.

I bent my knees slightly in preparation.

I wanted to see the ripples on the water directly below. I needed to see light down there; any kind of light, however dim. But now I realised that I would only see that just before I hit the water. It was all part of the "test". I'd have to make the dive like it was a promise. My part of that promise was to make the dive—and the promise would only be fulfilled, the ripples and the light would only be revealed, when I did what had to be done.

I hadn't taken a drink that night—hadn't needed one for the first time in a long, *long* time—but it all made complete sense.

Was a small part of me still waiting for a blaring car horn, or a voice from behind calling out urgently that I should stop?

No, of course not.

Will the fear come?

No, of course not.

The wind was now rushing in my face, no longer warm but cold and fiercer than before. I suddenly realised—without being conscious of having made the decision, but with the pull of gravity changing all over my body—that I had begun the dive.

My eyes were open, and my head was tilted back—but even so I had to squint against the rush of cold air on my eyes. My body was tilting straight down, my back was arching, and I held my legs straight—now up and above me as my face swung down.

This was my last, perfect dive.

I opened my eyes.

And fear, that hateful liar, was upon me—as I knew it would be all along.

I saw, at last, the reflection of my face in the water; white as the moon and with crater blur-lines of the river surface distorting that visage—and my arms were held wide. It was a perfect reflection of my swan dive. My widespread arms, embracing the reflection, now swiftly bent forwards as if to caress my face, just before the joined palms and pointed fingers met to pierce the surface of that black water. A perfect reflection of my face swarmed up to kiss me.

But those blur-lines were quickly changing the shape of my face into something else.

Something that was not *me*.

Something that was larger and terrible and a monstrous parody of me.

In that soul-freezing moment of horror and realisation at what I had done, I could see in that split-second that I was not looking at *my* reflection at all.

Just as I had dived from the bridge and was about to shatter the surface of the river, something was quickly *rising* from below to meet me; something that was mirroring and adopting the same pose as me—and was, face-to-face, about to dive *up and out* of the river directly beneath me.

I think I screamed then. But I can't be sure.

In the next moment, there was an explosion of dark water that engulfed me, filling my mouth and lungs. Something *enfolded* me then in a terrible grip that just as suddenly expelled that gushing intake of foul liquid from my lungs in one long and barking cough. I gasped for air as my head seemed to whiplash on my neck. There was a great roaring in my ears, and a sound like massive canvas sails flapping, as my torso remained gripped in that embrace. I was now aware that, far from falling, my trajectory had instantly somehow reversed, and I was flying upwards. My scrabbling hands tried to grip something, but slid on what felt like rapidly moving wet leather as that flapping sound continued, together with a roaring like a great waterfall. My arms and legs floundered helplessly as surely as if I was on the end of a bungee rope. I was being borne upwards into a freezing night sky.

I had been snatched back up into the air by something that had erupted from the river at the very point where I had sought to enter it.

Spray flew from my eyes, and my vision was filled with a distorted, twisting kaleidoscope of neon, bridge girders and streetlights. Panting like an animal, I sucked in short gasps of freezing air that agonised my lungs. Suddenly, I was a boy again—strapped into the whirling "cup and saucer" ride on Newcastle's Town Moor when the Hoppings fair came to town; and just as suddenly, with a juddering *smack* I was back in real time again, dropped on my hands and knees onto hard concrete, retching and gasping for air, river water pooling around me.

Stark streetlight threw a pool of shadow around where I knelt, and when I weakly lifted my head I saw that— somehow—I was at the top of the side road called Bottle Bank, running parallel to the bridge on my right and winding down to the quayside while the Tyne Bridge soared on ahead across the river. I was on all fours, in the middle of the steeply winding road, when logic dictated that I should be dead and drowned.

A greater shadow than the one in which I knelt suddenly moved into my sightline. It was man-shaped but surely much too big to be a man, and with something profoundly *wrong* about it as it stepped silently up to me. Its horribly long arms were held wide in a cruciform, but those arms looked more like... no, they surely couldn't be *wings*? They weren't like the silhouette-feathered wings of a bird, or the smooth black velvet-leather of a bat's outstretched wings; but more like the dactyl-claw spread of some jet-black pterosaur, or a black angel from…

Further thought was snapped from my mind by that sound again, the canvas flapping of a sail, not unfurling this time but furling, and the shadow quickly folded in upon itself until the arms (or wings) had merged with that terrible central shadow. Now it was only the shadow of a too-big man, and when he took another step, our joint shadows became a single pool of darkness. And when I began to raise my head to look more closely, a voice said, *"I would advise you NOT to look."*

I could feel the deep bass of that voice in the concrete beneath me, and I somehow instinctively knew the dreadful truth of the warning in those words. There was something utterly hellish in the tone of that voice—unlike anything I had ever heard in my life, and impossible really to describe. But I knew that if I looked up and saw the face of whatever it was, I would go mad.

Terrified, I kept my head down.

And then the voice said: *"Follow me…"*

When the huge shadow detached itself and moved, I had no choice but to follow, rising from all fours with dirty river water dripping from my body and splashing in the puddle that I had made. And with every shambling step, I knew— just *knew*—that I had to keep my head down if I wanted to stay sane, despite the burning desire to look up and take in the details of what seemed to have been my dreadful saviour.

I said that the figure was big, somehow too big for a man; in my peripheral vision it seemed to me that it was wearing a black gown or cloak that furled and swept at the figure's base as it moved. But it was like no material I had ever seen. It reflected the bridge lights in its contours and creases, and although it had a glistening wet look, it was *not* wet. It was neither leather nor plastic, nor any kind of fabric I'd ever seen. But the way that it swirled suggested that it was moving around hidden feet and legs as I followed behind—I couldn't be sure. What I could be sure of, though, was that I was following dutifully behind this—whatever it was—just as obediently as a servant follows a master, down Bottle Bank towards the river.

Cars were flashing past on the bridge above us, and the Hilton Hotel was on our left as we moved. Surely someone somewhere could see us? What kind of dream was I having?

The Shadow kept walking, slowly and leisurely, and I matched its pace behind with no will of my own.

Suddenly, from behind, there was a shriek and squeal of tyres that made the road vibrate through the soles of my shoes. I froze, shoulders hunched, and waited for the inevitable impact as a choking cloud of burning tyre rubber enveloped me. I whirled back to see that a car had taken the Bottle Bank slip road from Gateshead at high speed, not expecting to find anything in the middle of the road. The car had pulled up only yards from where I stood, and its headlights blinded me. I heard a car door open and then slam shut with anger— but I still couldn't see the driver.

"What the *hell* is the *matter* with you?" yelled a male voice. "You might be tired of living, but *I'm* not!" The voice continued, getting louder as the driver came angrily closer. "Fucking idiot!" Out of the headlight glare now, I could see that he was a middle-aged guy in a blue boiler suit and cap. Maybe he'd finished his shift and was driving home to his wife and kids, and the last thing he wanted on the journey home was to run down some idiots on the slip road. I saw him reach the front of his car, and when we made eye contact he kept on coming. By the look of anger on his face, harsh words clearly weren't going to be enough for what had obviously been a *very* hard day at work for him.

"Bloody druggie! Is that what it is? Get stoned out of your bloody head then walk in front of my car, get yourself bloody well mangled, get my car buggered up, cost me an arm and a leg, get my licence taken off me, fuck my job up, get me in the papers..." It was all coming out non-stop.

And suddenly the man in the boiler suit froze, then stumbled several steps back and put his hand on the hood of the car. His mouth was wide open and his eyes were bulging white under the harsh streetlight. He was staring, not at me, but behind me, to where the Shadow stood, silently waiting.

"Oh my God," he said in a small, strangled voice that was filled with fear. "Oh my good God. What... the hell... is *that*?" He staggered back, groping along the hood to the driver's door and without taking his gaze from the Shadow. His terror was terrifying *me*, and I shrank in on myself as I saw my accompanying Shadow swell on the periphery of my vision. I hunched down and tried not to look as the boiler-suited man screamed like I've never heard a human being scream before. Then I heard the car door slam as he managed to get back into the vehicle.

I heard that canvas sail begin flapping again, slow but getting faster as the car engine coughed and died, coughed and died. In his panic, the boiler-suited man was stalling the engine as he tried to reverse away. Now the flapping was so quick that it sounded like the *whup-whup-whup* of a helicopter rotor blade gathering speed and power as everything around me became a chaotic maelstrom of whirling images. I squeezed my eyes shut and became a child again—crying aloud when there was an explosive crack like a gigantic bullwhip, a terrible impact of shattering glass and splintering metal exploding all around me. A deep-down part of me really—*really*—didn't want to see anything, but when accompanying heat and light blasted out of that explosion, my eyes flew open again, and I saw...

The car that had almost run me down was on its side, rolling away past me down Bottle Bank—over and over—in a shroud of billowing orange flame and black smoke. Each crashing impact crumpled and rent its bodywork, scattering debris, its doors flapping open and slamming shut on every turn. It was as if it was in the grip of a tornado that had snatched it up and flung it away.

But there was no wind.

The car flipped up from its side and spun on its rear wheels, the chassis beneath briefly exposed, and then there was a *crump* as it hit the stone buttress of the bridge on the other side of the road in a cloud of sparks and black smoke, before falling sideways again and spinning to a stop, upside down, in the middle of the road.

I could see the glass-cobwebbed side window on the driver's side.

Even from here, I could see that the driver—the man in the boiler suit—was still alive. His dazed and blood-smeared face was pressed up against that cracked glass, hammering at the crazed pane with the flats of both bloodied hands and screaming a silent scream. He had lost his cap. His hair was lank and red.

I winced and averted my head when the Shadow fell over me again. At all times, a part of me wanted to look up at the face of its owner while another part dreaded to know—and all I could do was look back and fix my gaze on the bloodied, terror-stricken driver. His fingers had found cracks in the spiderweb fractures and he was clawing a hole there, pressing his mouth to it and screaming for help. I could hear nothing over the roar, flap and billow of smoke and the purple-orange flare of petrol flame from the fractured tank on the other side of the car.

"*Elton,*" said the Shadow, and it was as if a great shadow-arm had been laid paternally over my shoulder, even though I felt no physical touch. I could feel *power* emanating from its presence; it was like standing next to some dark industrial generator, thrumming with invisible and soul-shuddering energy.

"How do you know my name?" The sound of my own voice surprised me. I thought I'd lost the ability to speak.

"I know many things," the voice continued. *"And I know you."*

"Thank you," I said—and I knew that it was a ridiculous thing to say. It felt like the voice of a frightened child in the presence of an abusive parent. And then I heard myself say: "What's your name?" The driver had clawed chunks out of the side window now, and got his face and mouth right up against the jagged aperture. When he screamed this time, I could hear it loud and clear above the other noise.

"Help me, *please*! For God's sake, help *meeeeee*!" I stared at his contorted face, and knew that the terrifying companion who towered over me in darkness was considering my question carefully before answering.

Surely to God someone in the hotel complex across the way could hear the noise and come to help—come to get me out of this terrible nightmare?

Purple-orange flame ignited inside the car behind the driver's twisted and bloodstained face. His eyes widened so much that I thought they'd pop and burst. He could feel the heat but couldn't turn to look. His mouth was moving, but no words were coming now.

"Swan," said the Shadow at last. *"You can call me Swan."* And although I knew that it wasn't his—its—name, I knew why he—it—had chosen the name.

The flame in the car suddenly flared completely orange as it swamped the driver's face and hands. His red hair crisped, frizzled and flared to nothing. His flesh melted and peeled like wax on a department store mannequin, lips curling in an involuntary sneer as they burned and crisped, revealing yellowed skull-teeth that were now much longer in his face than before—and I knew that he would have screamed again had he not swallowed that blossoming flame into his throat and lungs. The shock of it made him look like a man suffering from bad indigestion as he gulped and gasped, rather than a man burning alive—and it was the most horrifying and obscene thing I had ever seen in my life.

"Be quiet now, Elton," said Swan. *"While I feed."* The driver's eyes popped and flowed. His jaw kept working soundlessly in flame, as if repeating, *Yeah, yeah, yeah…*

The car was filled with fire, black smoke gushing from the shattered windscreen and wheel rims. There was no human movement of any kind in there now.

The Shadow—Swan—said: *"Come…"*

And I knew that he had finished feeding—and *oh God, God, God*—I was afraid, as the darkness overwhelmed me again. I felt the same constricting embrace around my ribs and torso that had saved me from the river.

Smoke, sparks, the whirling girders of the Tyne Bridge—another whirling maelstrom of wind and image and neon and the flapping sound of those great canvas sails that I knew must be wings—and we were flying again.

Into the night.

I didn't know how this could be.

It simply *was.*

This time there was no sensation of having been transported and dumped back down on the ground in a different location. As that whirling maelstrom became too much for me to bear and I could feel my gorge rising—that point where fear and nausea become the same terrible thing—I was at the point of vomiting, when suddenly I was in an unknown alley down by the quayside. Flames were reflecting on warehouse rooftops a long way away, and I could hear the lonely wail of an unseen fire engine.

I froze and looked down again.

Was I safe?

Had the thing that called itself Swan gone?

There was no traffic in this alley and I had no idea what time it was other than it was late at night. I had the strange feeling of being on a stage. Was I in the real world? Or had I been transported to some other parallel, hellish dream existence? Was I some kind of ghost, some kind of player in a staged and dreadful dream world?

I could feel the ice-cold water of the River Tyne on my body. My clothes were still soaked, and the wind was chill on my skin.

And then the voice again said: *"Come…"* I wanted to fall to my knees, weeping and pleading.

But the Shadow moved past me, down the alley towards the river—and I averted my eyes as before. Sight of the Gorgon would turn a human to stone; the sight of Swan would result in something much, much worse.

I followed again.

Head down, glancing at the swirl and movement of the cloak at Swan's base, I could hear a noise; a strange, whimpering sound like a frightened child.

Swan said, *"Be quiet."* I realised that I had been the one making the noise.

I was instantly silent.

"Tell me, Elton," Swan continued as he led and I followed. Head bowed, I was as eagerly attentive as a condemned prisoner awaiting pardon from an execution. *"What is the sweetest meat? The meat of a lamb or the meat of a wolf?"* I did not want to consider the connotations of the question, only give a response that would please.

"The meat of a lamb?"

"No, Elton. You are wrong." I whimpered, but Swan seemed not to notice.

"*The meat of the wolf is sweeter. And I will tell you why.*" We had taken a turn behind the darker buildings that screened the river from us but I could see neon lights reflecting ahead on the pavement, though I dared not look up ahead with Swan walking in front and leading the way.

"*The lamb suckles from its mother,*" continued Swan in that low and soul-shuddering bass voice. "*And the mother takes its sup from the earth and the things that grow upon the earth. And that is sweet, Elton. Yes, that can be sweet. But the—oh, the wolf. It preys upon the lamb and it hunts and kills and eats of the lamb's meat and drinks of its blood. And the lamb's terror is in its blood and in its meat. So can you not see, Elton, that the blood and the meat of the wolf—that which preys upon the lamb—is so much sweeter?*" We had reached the building that had been throwing its neon reflection into the night. There was a reflection of a red neon sign in a puddle at my feet. It was upside down, and at first it looked like an alien language. Then I made sense of it: "Juniper Diner".

"*Stop here,*" said Swan, coming to a halt.

I stopped.

His shadow obscured the neon sign in the puddle, ripples flowing across the dirty water. At first I thought that he—it—was moving forward again. I started forward, and then came to an immediate halt.

Swan hadn't moved at all.

But something was happening to his shadow.

The ripples on the puddle increased, but there was no wind. When they stopped, I saw that something had happened to my captor. Even though I could never look at him properly, I could see in my peripheral vision—and in the water's reflection—that Swan had *changed*. He had somehow shrunk and was now no longer much, much bigger than a man—now, my saviour and captor was the size of a normal man.

"*Take my hand,*" he said, and I saw a shadow arm reflected

in the puddle as it reached for me. At that moment, it was like being back on the Tyne Bridge, just at the moment when I'd found myself climbing up onto the stone escarpment and preparing to make my dive. My instinctive terror of Swan should have robbed me of all strength and will. At the very least, it seemed, I should be shrinking back from that shadow hand, falling to my knees in that neon-lit puddle with my very soul dissolving around me. But just as I'd climbed that stone barrier without will, I saw my arm rising without will towards the shadow hand, and a small whimpering thing inside that was me but also not me, accepted that when we touched, I must surely die.

But I did not die.

I was aware that my hand had been taken, was aware that it had been gripped but—how to explain—there was no physical sensation of contact at all. My hand was seized both externally and internally, but in a way that I can't describe, so that when Swan moved forward, I was tugged along behind him as surely as if I had been on a leash. And like a fearful child, so deathly afraid of Swan's wrath, I quickly made up the space between us, head down, so that I didn't have to be tugged again.

The glass door of the building banged open as we entered—and now, from my peripheral vision, I could see that we had entered a bar-diner. It was brightly lit and something inside told me that Swan could have brought great darkness inside with us, but he had chosen not to. The lights flickered, a bulb popped somewhere and someone said, "Fuck!" The tiled floor beneath me was cracked and stained; anonymous rock music was playing on a radio somewhere and I was aware of figures hunched over Formica-covered tables. Swan walked to a corner bench table and sat with his back to the room. Still holding his hand, I dutifully sat next to him. The black cloak that covered him pooled on the bench beside me so much like liquid that I expected it to run off the edge and drip on the floor.

"What's the word I'm looking for?" asked a male voice from somewhere behind.

"Faggot?" replied another.

"No, man. That's the American word for men who hold hands."

"Men? I don't think so. No—the word you're looking for is 'gay'."

"Gay? They look happy to you? Don't look happy to me. Look fucking miserable if you ask me."

"Queer. That's the word."

"Nah. Homo. That's the word."

"Hey, you two! What's the word for people like you?" When there was no answer, the first voice said: "I think the word is *deaf*!" The others in the diner laughed.

Suddenly there was a presence by my side. I turned to see a young man in a kitchen apron. His face was white and hard, as if the blood had been drained from him.

"Listen," he said in a quiet voice, his lips hardly moving. "I'll take your order if you want. But if you'll take my advice, you'll leave now. I know what those fellas are like." I wanted to speak, but couldn't. And why wasn't he reacting the way the boiler-suited guy on the Bottle Bank slip road had reacted to my companion? Had he somehow made himself *less* frightening?

"I mean it, man. You and your pal best leave now."

"I'm not calling the cops," continued the waiter. "That'd be three times this week, and I'll lose my licence. You better be getting out of here…"

"Leave them alone," said the first disembodied voice again. "What's the matter with you? Can't you see that the lovebirds want to be left alone?" I heard the sound of seats scraping back from tables. The waiter made a moaning sound—"Don't say I didn't warn you"—and vanished from sight.

I screwed my eyes shut, acutely aware of the approach of several threatening presences from behind.

"Tell you what?" said another voice. "Why don't you show us how it's done?"

"Yeah. Boy-girl action—we know how that goes."

"And girl-girl," a new voice sniggered.

"Yeah, that as well. But boy-boy, that's something else. Why don't you show us how it's done…?" I don't know how many of them there were, but I knew that they were standing right behind us now.

"I think you two have been knobbing each other so much that you really *have* gone deaf." Now there was impatient shuffling.

"You better speak. Bad manners not to speak when you're spoken to." Another snigger.

"Hey, you! Big man in homo black! You turn around when I'm speaking to…" I felt a rough hand on my shoulder, just as Swan's grip on my left hand was released. It felt more like something dissipating than being let go. I could feel Swan slowly turning to face our antagonists.

Someone drew in their breath with a loud hiss.

Someone said: "Fucking… *hell*!" And when the screaming started, I hunkered down so that my head was almost in my lap, my hands tight over my ears.

Swan was no longer sitting beside me.

Glass shattered, and the screaming went on and on.

The bench on which I sat juddered, but I hunkered down even tighter.

I felt something fly over me into the table at which I was sitting. Something crashed and the rock and roll music screeched to a halt. I swatted hard at my head when sparks landed on me from above, then quickly resumed my position, willing myself to wake up or be somewhere else; anywhere but here, anywhere but now. Someone close by me was making choking sounds and something wet and warm splashed across my hands. I kept them held tight to my ears, not wanting to hear; not wanting to be any part of the hell that was taking place in that diner.

Only one person was screaming now, but it was so high, shrill and horrifying that I couldn't tell whether it was a man or a woman. And each individual shriek was matched equally by the sound of something gradually being *torn*. Inch by inch. It was a rough and terribly *wet* sound, and also somehow obscenely *intimate*. The shrieking became an insane babbling and God, oh God, I didn't want to hear any more. I prayed for it to stop but it just went on and on.

I have no idea how long the hellish sounds continued but when they did eventually stop, I realised that I was rocking back and forth like a small child trying to console itself. I stopped rocking—and gingerly took my fingers away from my ears.

Glass crunched on the floor behind me.

I flinched, but before I could clap my hands to my ears again, Swan said: *"Open your eyes and look at the table."* All of the diner's ceiling strip lights had been shattered except one that gave enough light to show the littered and glittering crimson pool before me. I did not—dared not—look around me, but I could tell that the diner had been completely wrecked.

"Put your hands in the blood, Elton." I did as I was told, making ripples spread to either end of the Formica table; heard it dripping and splashing from the ends onto the floor.

"Make hand prints."

"Where?"

"Anywhere. Everywhere."

I was like an eager child at a finger-painting competition, splashing my hands and then patting the dry patches of table, the bench on which I was sitting, on myself.

"Enough," said Swan.

I waited for further instruction, trying not to see Swan's reflection in the smeared crimson pool on the table.

"Do you know why I asked you to do that?" I could feel the reverberation of Swan's voice in the tabletop, making ripples shimmer and spread.

"My fingerprints?" I heard myself reply.

I could *feel* Swan smile. *"And your DNA. Now—we have to personalise things."*

"Personalise?"

"Where do you live?"

"Apartment 12a, Arbon Buildings on—"

"Oh yes, West Jesmond."

"How do you know?"

"With me, Elton, a little goes a long way. By the time we're at your home, I will know a lot more." I saw the dark, indeterminate reflection of Swan's arm in the bloodied table as it stretched towards me. I flinched even from the sight of that, not wanting to see its details. But I knew that he wanted me to take his hand again. I did so. Again, I felt my hand taken but was unaware of any physical sensation.

I allowed myself to be led out of the ruined diner, my head always down and looking at the details underfoot. I tried to make sense of a curious, ragged image that I had to step over. It was only when we had walked outside again into the cold night air that I realised it had been a severed human head, its face matted with straggling hair.

"Would you like me to sing to you?" asked Swan.

"No thank you."

"Very well." Again, my world tilted and I screwed my eyes shut as I was taken into that awful embrace. It seemed to me that I was not breathing—that I had not been breathing before when Swan had enfolded me this way—as if the act of breathing was not required when it happened. Another

thought came to me. Was this what it was like when you plunged into the River Tyne, and the shock of it made you gasp water into your lungs instead of air—so that you didn't breathe, just gasped in water until you drowned? It was somehow like that, and somehow not. I'm sorry, I know that isn't clear, but Swan's embrace contained the terrible essence of what I'm trying to convey. The awful flapping began again and we were travelling once more.

I willed myself unconscious. I'd done it before, years ago, when I was writhing in pain on a hospital trolley waiting for a hospital bed to become free. I was suffering with bacterial pneumonia and every joint in my body was screaming with pain. I'd somehow *made* myself black out to escape from it. I did that again now.

I'm not sure whether what followed was a dream but it seemed like a dream. There had been none of that sickening suffocation this time, none of that feeling of being transported through the night and the terrible flapping and buffeting that accompanied it. But now I was on the shadowed internal staircase of my apartment block in West Jesmond. The communal door in the hallway was shut and I had no awareness that I had used my pass key to come through it. But I was halfway up that first flight of stairs and a small, shrinking part of me wanted to believe that I would be able to wake up completely now; perhaps begin to understand that I'd suffered some kind of mental breakdown and that if I could only get to my apartment, everything would be all right again.

When I began to turn to look up the stairs, it was as if the whole stairwell was underwater, suffused with blue undersea light; my turning was in slow motion as if I was an underwater swimmer. In that moment, I knew that any chance of awakening was hopeless and that Swan was up there—on the stairs.

Waiting for me.

I hoped that Mrs Abermont, who lived on the first floor landing, didn't "accidentally" open her front door as usual when she heard someone on the stairs so that she could engage in a brief and trivial conversation with whoever was there.

Because if she did, she would die.

"No she won't," said an unseen Swan from the darkness up ahead of me.

"Why?" My voice seemed slow and dragging.

"Because you like her."

I ascended.

Was I indeed dead and at the bottom of the River Tyne? Was this why I felt as if I was swimming up from the depths; as if the worn carpet on the stairs was swirling like mud beneath my feet as I ascended?

Mrs Abermont did not appear on the landing, thank God.

I did not look up on the second or third flight of stairs as I kept onwards and upwards. But I knew that Swan was up there, leading the way to a place that he could not possibly know existed—but somehow did.

I heard my apartment door open.

I entered that deeper underwater darkness, and made my way to the living-room sofa. Swan was ahead of me, but somehow the door closed of its own volition and locked.

I sat, head down, and listened to Swan—his presence somehow all-consuming in that living room; moving in the dark like liquid, picking up and examining ornaments and framed photographs from the shelves and tables. Dried flowers from a vase beside the television were scattered absently at my feet, and I heard the telephone jiggle in its cradle, followed by the pages in my personal telephone book riffling and turning.

"Ah," said Swan at last. *"Now I understand."*

"You do?" Again, my voice sounded like a small, frightened child wanting desperately to be understood.

"Oh yes. Come here." I stood, not looking, like the naughty boy at the back of the classroom, now called to the front for punishment. I took two steps, a third—then hesitated.

"I really don't want to look at you."

"It's best that you don't, Elton. Two more steps, if you please." I did as I was told, and now was close to the telephone table.

Suddenly, the telephone was in my hand.

"Does it have to be her?"

"Yes. Tell her to come over."

"Do I have to?"

"Yes. Tell her to come over alone."

"But she won't come over alone. She'll bring him as well."

"I know. But tell her anyway." I dialled the number.

For a moment, I couldn't get my breath.

The telephone continued to ring as I struggled to control my breathing. I could feel my heart hammering and my throat constricting.

"What?" When she answered, her voice was sharp and sleep-blurred—but heartbreaking in its familiarity. "What the hell…?"

"Susan?"

"What? Wait—bloody hell. Is that *you*, Elton?"

"Is he with you?"

"Have you any idea what *time* it is, you stupid bastard?"

"Is he *with* you?"

"You're drunk. Fucking typical. Ringing me at this time of the morning. I've told you before. If you—"

"Do you want those papers signed or not?" There was a pause at the other end. I needed it. I could hardly get my words out. Finally, I broke the silence.

"Well *do* you?" Swan whispered beside me. It was like a cold and foetid wind in the room, making the curtains swirl. Papers and magazines rose and flapped to the floor. *"I've signed them."* Even that whisper made cups and saucers shiver and rattle on the kitchen table.

"I've signed them," I said, as instructed.

"But you've got to come and get them…"

"But you've got to… got to come and get them."

"Say: 'Come alone.'"

"Come alone…"

"Well…" Susan cleared her throat on the other end of the line. "Well, all right. Good. Not before time. I'll come by later."

"You'll come now."

"You'll come now…"

"And you'll come alone."

"…and you'll come alone."

"I'm at my place."

"I'm at my place."

"But if you don't come now—come alone now—I'm going to burn those papers and you can forget all about the divorce. You and lover boy will have to wait your time out before you can do it without me."

I repeated what Swan whispered. A plate crashed and tinkled in the kitchen.

"All right, you bastard. I'm coming. But they better be signed."

"They're signed," I said, without prompting.

"Oh, and, Susan," whispered Swan. A news circular flapped in front of my face. I swiped it away.

"Oh, and, Susan…"

"You're a bitch."

"You're a *bitch*." I gave the last word added emphasis as darkness was laid on my hand and I put the phone down.

"Now she definitely won't come alone."

"I know."

"They're not signed." I kept my eyes on the telephone. "The divorce papers. They're not signed."

"I know they're not."

"Is that what you want?"

"It's what we want."

"What do I do now?"

"Go. Wash. Change."

"I don't understand."

"You're covered in blood, Elton."

"Oh."

I did as I was told, like an automaton. There was no room for thought.

"Go sit on the sofa and wait." I did as I was told.

"Switch on the television." I did so.

It was football. Newcastle United were playing an away game. Normally, I would have been at the pub, watching the game with friends. Or here at home, watching with a couple of cans.

"You're a Newcastle United fan," said Swan from somewhere in the apartment. His voice seemed constantly near, constantly reverberating in the walls, the floor and ceiling—but he could be in any part of the room. He'd made a matter-of-fact, ridiculously mundane statement, requiring no response. A mere detail, but I knew that Swan now knew all about me. I don't know how long I'd been watching the television, taking in no details of the game or the action, when Swan said: *"They don't stand a chance this year. Their defence is all wrong. Not enough aggression from the forwards."* The other side scored a goal and the crowd exploded in response.

"See?" said Swan, matter of fact.

And then the doorbell rang.

How long could it have been since I made that telephone call? There was no way of knowing, but surely it couldn't have taken what seemed to be such a short time. Time in

Swan's presence seemed to lose all meaning.

Swan was not in the living room. I had no sensation of him physically leaving, but his presence was no longer there—and I knew that I could look up safely.

The doorbell rang again and I waited for an instruction, wherever Swan might be. No such instruction came and now there was an angry knocking at the door.

"What do I do?" I asked.

There was no answer. No instruction.

Now the doorbell was ringing continuously and the angry knocking became more impatient.

"What do I *do*?"

"Elton!" Susan's muffled but furious voice came from the landing outside. "You better open this door!"

"*Please?*" I begged, now daring to look around the room. Papers lay scattered everywhere, ornaments examined and discarded. Football pundits were analysing the now-finished game on the television.

"I can *hear* you," threatened Susan. "Open the door!" I rose tentatively from the sofa and made my way to the front door as if walking on thin ice. The ringing, banging and angry words continued. When I unlatched it, the door instantly flew open against me with a crash, the edge catching me painfully on the elbows as I instinctively threw up my hands to protect my face.

And, of course, Greg the nightclub bouncer—with whom my soon to be ex-wife had taken up—was the first to come through that door. He slapped my arms down and took me with one hand by the throat, propelling me back across the room to the sofa that I had just left. With one brutal shove, I was sprawled backwards, choking for air—as Susan slammed the door shut and came in behind Greg, ready to launch herself at me.

Greg stopped her. I saw Susan's arms flailing as he prevented her from getting at me and tried to calm her down.

"Stop, stop, stop…" Greg tried to get her to look at him. And then, finally: "*Stop!*" She stopped.

Susan stepped around him, giving him the kind of glare that she usually reserved for me. She had no make-up on, hadn't had time to get ready—and I knew that in itself would have infuriated her. Her hair was not as perfectly attended as usual, and she angrily snatched back a wayward strand as she turned her familiar glare back to me.

"Okay, Elton. Where are the papers?" I sat up, looked around—and waited. But there was no sense of Swan's presence at all.

"Elton," continued Susan, her teeth gritting my name as if she were chewing ice cubes.

I looked around again.

Nothing.

"Where are they, Elton?" Each of Susan's ice-pick words contained its own promise of instant violence.

"Swan?"

"What?" said Greg.

"Swan? Where are you?"

"What the fuck?" Greg's exasperation was beginning to show. "What the fuck are you talking about swans for, Elton?" He liked to exaggerate the pronunciation of what he considered to be my very poncey name.

"You see?" said Susan, hands on hips as she turned back to Greg. "I told you—he's pissed again. Look at the state of this room." I laughed. More hysteria than humour. I just couldn't help it. They both looked genuinely shocked when I did so.

"No bottles or cans," I pointed out. "Look around. You won't find any booze or empty bottles anywhere."

"You little…" Greg loomed forward again, filling my vision entirely. He smelled sour; smelled of her. Just as effortlessly as before, he took me by the throat again, squeezing my windpipe shut. With no effort, he held me up in the air off the sofa as I beat at his arm. It felt like steel cable—perhaps made of the same stuff as the cables on the Tyne Bridge. In that moment, my reason for being on that bridge, making ready to make that swan dive, was instantly crystallised in my mind. Susan's bitter vitriol, the constant cheating—now with this swine, the latest in a long line of men who could give her "what she wanted". The constant betrayal and shame, the depression, despair and humiliation. Let that steel-cable-bridge-arm keep my windpipe closed. Let him take the life out of me, just as I'd been ready to give it up earlier that night. Susan had brought me to this point, even to the bizarre nervous breakdown that had led me somehow to believe that I had jumped from the bridge when I hadn't; that had led me to create the horrifying figure of the thing that called itself Swan—something that existed only in what was now my shattered and irreparable mind.

I went limp in his grip, the weight of my body dragging his arm down. His eyes widened, taken by surprise but now angered at what somehow seemed to be a physical challenge to his muscle-bound bodybuilder's physique. He gritted his teeth and had to bend his knees to keep me up in the air, when he could just as easily have let me drop to the sofa.

"Where are they?" demanded Susan.

I grinned at the ape that was holding me up. Now his eyes were bulging with effort and anger.

"Where *are* they?" he demanded.

I just kept on grinning.

"You scrawny little *bastard*..." Greg looked like he was being challenged in a one-armed contest to lift the world's heaviest dumb-bell on an episode of *World's Strongest Man*.

I was a dumb-bell, all right.

And I'd win this challenge when he killed me.

"Let him go!" Susan's face leered in close. "Take your

hand off his throat. How can he talk if you're choking him?" It was the excuse that Greg needed.

He pitched me back on the sofa, face now beaded with sweat.

Susan was in my face now, slapping me as I retched.

"Where are they? Where are the papers?" I was done. I just wanted this harpy out of my face, out of my apartment, out of my life. I pointed to the bureau by the telephone. Susan gave me a good one across the cheek that helped me breathe again and then tottered to the bureau. I'd forgotten that there were papers all over the floor. Had it blown off…?

But *what* had blown it off, if it hadn't been…?

Greg joined her, snatching and grabbing at papers on the bureau and the floor. I heard Susan muttering angrily as she hunted.

"Living like a pig… crap all over the place… this time of the morning…"

Then Greg said: "Here—here it is," snatching a paper up from the floor.

After a brief pause while they looked at it, I knew what was coming next.

"You bastard!" Susan turned back to snarl at me. "You *haven't* signed it!" Maybe if I smiled at her again, Greg really would kill me. It seemed like an option. I watched his face go red with anger. Could he *really* love her that much? Or was it just pure frustration with me?

Susan stormed back to me, holding the paper in front of her. Greg loomed behind her as she thrust it into my face.

"Sign it!"

"What with?" My voice sounded raw and strangled.

"Greg, find a pen."

Now she was standing with her hands on her hips, foot tapping on the floor while Greg hunted for a pen.

"Bet he can't even read or write." I don't know why I said

it. The words just came out. So when Greg lunged back and punched me on the side of the head, it wasn't unexpected. But it made everything tilt, with Susan and Greg swinging in and out of my vision.

"Try the bedroom," said Susan. "He's got some kind of desk in there."

"Nice of you to remember." The words just came out again.

Greg glared at me and stalked past.

"Does he know what a pen looks like?"

I heard Greg come to a halt and waited for him to return for another blow; saw Susan glare at him and then snap: "Just get a *pen,* Greg!" Greg made some kind of frustrated sound. Then I heard the bedroom door open.

And then I saw the expression on Susan's face change. Her look of rage blurred and shifted. Her eyes grew wider, her jaw dropped—and what was becoming a frown of puzzlement began to morph into something else.

Something was happening behind me, but I was too dazed—too displaced inside my own head—to turn and see. I could only watch in fascination as the expression on Susan's face continued to change. I realised now that I was expecting to hear Greg begin to scream; perhaps the same kind of screaming I had heard earlier that night in the diner. Because now I knew that what I had begun to think were just bizarre creations of a nervous breakdown had really happened after all. And that was why I should be hearing Greg screaming in a high falsetto quite unfitting to the masculine image he liked to project. That screaming should be accompanied by horrible ripping sounds and the hot pattering of blood on the living-room carpet. But no—all I could hear was a sound like... how do I explain... rapid breathing. Short staccato gasps that sounded almost like the sounds of lovemaking; rapid, hissing intakes of breath that could be of pain or pleasure. And all this was happening as a gigantic winged shadow began to rise up across Susan's body, the figure backlit by the light in the bedroom doorway—a shadow that swelled and broadened and rose as those huge wings flexed. Her face fell completely into that shadow now as it rose. Susan's mouth was wide open and she should have been screaming, her shadowed face contorted and her eyes glittering with terror. But no sound was coming out of that mouth at all.

God help me—as much as I had loved her enough to end my life when she left me for whatever was now left of Greg—I could feel a red-hot coal of hate deep inside me, which could not be denied at this last moment. And God help me again, I tried and failed to find some pity inside that might prevent what was to come.

"I can't," I said.

"*I know,*" said Swan in that horrible, familiar resonating voice that shook the living-room furnishings.

"I'm sorry, Susan." They were such hollow words.

I screwed my eyes shut, bent over double just as I had done in the diner, and buried my face in my hands.

And when Susan was finally able to give vent to that shrill and piercing scream, I screamed too; trying and failing to drown out the other terrible liquid and rending sounds.

I was enfolded in darkness and snatched away as my scream broke down into hoarse sobs. Cold wind was buffeting me again and that terrible *flap, flap, flap* surrounded me once more as I was propelled into the night. Somehow, I could still hear the dying echoes of Susan's screaming even though I knew that I was no longer in my apartment and that Susan had received the terminal separation from me that she had so desired. But those echoes were becoming something else as I kept curled up like a foetus in Swan's awful embrace with my eyes still firmly screwed shut.

They had, impossibly, become the strident ringing of a telephone.

And then I heard: "999. What is your emergency, please?"

"Police," said Susan's voice over the sound of rushing wind. *"I need the police."* How could that be Susan's voice when I knew that Susan no longer existed?

"Your name, and the nature of the emergency, please?"

"My name is Susan Perdue," said Swan in Susan's stolen voice. *"And I've just been assaulted by my husband, Elton Perdue."*

"Where are you now, Mrs Perdue? Can you give me…"

"You've got to stop him. He's killed my boyfriend and some people at the Juniper Diner down by Gateshead Quayside—and he's got a gun."

"He's got a *gun?*"

"He's got a gun and he's on the Tyne Bridge. I mean—he's on the Tyne Bridge right now, and he's…"

"Mrs Perdue, please calm down and tell me…"

"He's just rung me. He's on the Tyne Bridge and he's got a gun and he says he's going to start shooting at the cars going past and he's going to get his own back before he jumps…"

"He's there, on the Tyne Bridge, *now?*"

"He says he's going to get his own back, do you hear me? Get his own back and then he's going to jump off the bridge into the river and kill himself."

"Mrs Perdue! Don't…" And then the voices were cut off by the buzzing of a disconnected line—just as I fell on hard concrete, my hands and knees slapping painfully as I was dropped in a crouching position. The utter darkness that had enveloped me was swept away like a velvet, swirling cloak.

I didn't need to look up to know that I was back in the same place on the Tyne Bridge where the horror had started.

It was night, and traffic was passing unheeding as usual. Keeping my head down, I scanned my immediate surroundings to locate Swan and make sure that I didn't make the mistake of looking up directly to see him.

"So…" My throat was ragged and raw. I coughed and retched before continuing. "So you've tied it all up. Got me back to where it began." When there was no answer, I hoped that he—that it—had gone. But really, I knew I couldn't be so lucky.

"Are you there?"

"Yes," came that hideous, sonorous voice somewhere off to my right. *"I'm here."*

"Why don't you just kill me?"

"How ungrateful that would be of me, Elton. After everything you've done for me."

"You've fed well, then?"

"Oh yes. So many wolves. Such tender meat."

"And now everyone thinks that it will have been me who did the killing. The diner. The apartment."

"Of those that can be found, yes. And don't forget the man in the car down below on the bank."

"I've had a busy night."

"Indeed."

"You need me. People like me. To feed you."

"Yes, Elton. Without you and your kind, I wouldn't exist." There was a flurry of movement from Swan and I cowered, covering my face. He was lying. He did intend to kill me after all.

But no, as the wind flapped around me, I knew that Swan had jumped up onto the parapet; to the exact spot from where I had made my swan dive, and given my terrible saviour his—its—name.

"So that's it, then? This is when it ends?"

"That's up to you. You have choices, Elton. You still have choices."

"What the hell *are* you?"

"Not a wolf, not a lamb."

He was silent then, and for a moment I really thought that

I was going to get a proper answer.

But then the distant wailing of police sirens swirled in the air.

Swan laughed. Or at least made a low and shuddering sound that could have been a laugh.

"Goodbye, Elton." And then Swan was gone, over the edge of the parapet and into the night.

I lurched to my feet and ran staggering to the parapet, hoping—I think—in that moment of desperation that I might have even a momentary glance of the face of whatever it was that had caused such horrifying mayhem. Maybe the shock of seeing Swan properly would do more than send me mad. Perhaps—mercifully—it would kill me.

But as I lunged to look over the edge, all I saw was a massive shadow like a giant black seabird, suddenly folding black bat-like wings tight behind its back as it plummeted into the water. There was no explosive splash—just a thin plume of foaming black water that spurted high and dissolved into spray. For a brief moment, I saw a swift underwater flash of something like glittering scales as Swan sped deep and away into the River Tyne. When I leaned back, I could see lights and a police cordoned area below on Bottle Bank where Swan had killed the driver and destroyed his car.

The sound of police sirens was very loud now as I turned from the parapet. Bracing both hands behind me on the cold stone, I saw the flashing lights of not one but two police cars—one speeding towards me from the Newcastle side of the bridge, the other from the Gateshead side. Behind them, in both directions, I could see that the police had also cordoned off the roads and stopped the traffic.

I turned and clambered back up onto the parapet as the first of the police cars slewed up onto the pavement, mere yards from me. All doors opened simultaneously as the four officers erupted from the car. They were wearing black flak jackets, clearly armed. As the second car stopped, they spread out—and one of them had his gun aimed directly at me. Couldn't they see that I was unarmed, despite what Swan/Susan had told them? The officers in the second car appeared to be unarmed as they too began to form a half circle, hemming me in on the parapet.

"Armed police!" said the officer with the gun. "Get down from the edge!"

"No, wait!"

One of the unarmed officers was holding up his hand to the armed policeman. "Mr Perdue. Why don't you come down and we can talk?" So some of them wanted to blow me off the bridge; others wanted to be my friend.

"You still have choices," Swan had said.

I looked out across the river—to the Newcastle and the Gateshead sides. Cities full of wolves and lambs, and sometimes things that shouldn't exist but do—like Swan.

Now one man wanted to shoot me, the other wanted to save me.

Should I do something to make the first kill me, or climb down to the other and be taken away; tried and sentenced to life for the murders that had occurred that night?

Or should I just finish what I'd originally started, and take a second swan dive from the bridge? I knew for a fact that this time Swan wouldn't be there to catch me.

I looked at the gun.

I looked at the outstretched hand.

And then I looked down over the parapet to the dark water below.

Like Swan had said—I still had choices.

But which way to dive?

Which way, indeed?

CONTRIBUTORS' NOTES

Alison Littlewood's latest novel, *The Hidden People*, is about the murder of a young woman suspected of being a fairy changeling. Her other books include *A Cold Season*, a Richard and Judy Book Club selection, *Path of Needles* and *The Unquiet House*. Her short stories have been picked for several "Year's Best" anthologies and won a Shirley Jackson Award for Short Fiction. They have been collected in *Quieter Paths* and *Five Feathered Tales*. Alison lives in a house of creaking doors and crooked walls in Yorkshire, England. Visit her at www.alisonlittlewood.co.uk.

Stoker and World Fantasy Award nominee, winner of British Fantasy and International Horror Guild Awards for his short fiction, **Stephen Gallagher** is a novelist and also a creator of primetime miniseries and episodic television. In the US he was lead writer on NBC's *Crusoe* and creator of CBS Television's *Eleventh Hour*. Among fifteen novels are *Chimera*, *Oktober* and *Valley of Lights*. He's the creator of Sebastian Becker, Special Investigator to the Lord Chancellor's Visitor in Lunacy, in a series of novels that includes *The Kingdom of Bones*, *The Bedlam Detective* and *The Authentic William James*.

Angela Slatter's debut novel, *Vigil*, was released by Jo Fletcher Books in 2016, and the sequels *Corpselight* and *Restoration* will follow in 2017 and 2018 respectively. She is the author of eight short story collections, including *The Girl with No Hands and Other Tales, Sourdough and Other Stories, The Bitterwood Bible and Other Recountings, Black-Winged Angels, Winter Children and Other Chilling Tales* and *A Feast of Sorrows: Stories.* Her work has been adapted for the screen, and translated into Japanese, Russian, and Bulgarian. Angela has won a World Fantasy Award, a British Fantasy Award, one Ditmar Award, and five Aurealis Awards.

Brady Golden's short fiction has appeared in *Mythic Delirium, DarkFuse 2,* and on the podcast *Pseudopod.* He lives in Oakland, California, with his family.

Nina Allan's stories have appeared in numerous magazines and anthologies, including *Best Horror of the Year #6, The Year's Best Science Fiction #33,* and *The Mammoth Book of Ghost Stories by Women.* Her novella *Spin,* a science-fictional reimagining of the Arachne myth, won the BSFA Award in 2014, and her story-cycle *The Silver Wind* was awarded the Grand Prix de L'Imaginaire in the same year. Her debut novel *The Race* was a finalist for the 2015 BSFA Award, the Kitschies Red Tentacle, and the John W. Campbell Memorial Award. Her second novel *The Rift* was published in 2017. Nina lives and works on the Isle of Bute in western Scotland. Find her blog, The Spider's House, at www.ninaallan.co.uk

Brian Keene is the author of over fifty books, mostly in the horror, crime and dark fantasy genres. His novel, *The Rising*, is credited with inspiring pop culture's current interest in zombies. In addition to his own original work, Keene has written for media properties such as *Doctor Who, The X-Files, Hellboy, Masters of the Universe* and *Superman.* Several of Keene's novels have been developed for film. He has won numerous awards and honours, including the 2014 World Horror Grandmaster Award, 2001 Bram Stoker Award for Best Non-Fiction, 2003 Bram Stoker Award for First Novel, 2004 Shocker Award for Non-Fiction Book of the Year, and Honours from United States Army International Security Assistance Force in Afghanistan and Whiteman A.F.B. (home of the B-2 Stealth Bomber) 509th Logistics Fuels Flight.

Chaz Brenchley has been making a living as a writer since the age of eighteen. He is the author of nine thrillers, two fantasy series, two ghost stories and two collections, most recently the Lambda Award-winning *Bitter Waters*. He has also published Chinese fantasy as Daniel Fox, and urban fantasy as Ben Macallan. He lost count of his short stories long ago. His work has won the British Fantasy Award and a Lambda Award. He has recently married and moved from Newcastle to California, with two squabbling cats and a famous teddy bear.

A.K. Benedict's debut novel, *The Beauty of Murder*, was shortlisted for an eDunnit Award and is in development for an eight-part TV series. Her second novel, *Jonathan Dark or the Evidence of Ghosts*, was published in February 2016 and *The Stone House*, a tie-in novel for *Doctor Who* spin-off *Class*, was published in October 2016. Her poems and short stories have featured in journals and anthologies including *Best British Short Stories*, *Magma*, *Scaremongrel* and *Great British Horror*. Her first audio drama, *The Victorian Age*, was released as part of the *Torchwood* range at Big Finish, while her second, *Outbreak*, was a three-part *Torchwood* drama co-written with Guy Adams and Emma Reeves.

Brian Lillie is an American writer, moviemaker, and musician from Ann Arbor, Michigan. His stories have appeared or are forthcoming in *Into the Darkness: An Anthology, vol.1* (Necro Publications), Space Squid, Jersey Devil Press, Albedo One, and Cutting Block Books. A *huge* horror and weirdness fan, he runs *31 Hath October*, a Halloween countdown blog chock-full of reviews, interviews and essays. He owes a gigantic debt of gratitude to his writers' group, Altered Symmetry, and would be nowhere without their help. Seriously. Check out brian-lillie. com to find out more.

Ramsey Campbell's first book appeared in 1964, and he has written horror ever since. His most recent books are *The Booking* (a novella), *Born to the Dark* (the second volume of his Brichester Mythos trilogy), and *By the Light of my Skull* (a collection of short stories). He has received the Grand Master Award of the World Horror Convention, the Lifetime Achievement Award of the Horror Writers Association, the Living Legend Award of the International Horror Guild and the World Fantasy Lifetime Achievement Award. In 2015 he was made an Honorary Fellow of Liverpool John Moores University for outstanding services to literature.

British Fantasy Award-winning **Carole Johnstone** is a Scottish writer, currently living on the island of Cyprus. Her short fiction has been published widely, and has been reprinted in Ellen Datlow's *Best Horror of the Year* and Salt Publishing's *Best British Fantasy* series. Her debut short story collection, *The Bright Day is Done*, and her novella, *Cold Turkey*, were both shortlisted for a 2015 British Fantasy Award. More information on the author can be found at www.carolejohnstone.com.

Sarah Lotz is a novelist and screenwriter with a fondness for the macabre and fake names, whose collaborative and solo novels have been translated into over twenty-five languages. She has written urban horror novels under the name S.L. Grey with author Louis Greenberg; a YA pulp-fiction zombie series, *Deadlands*, with her daughter, Savannah, under the pseudonym Lily Herne; and quirky erotica novels with authors Helen Moffett and Paige Nick under the name Helena S. Paige. Under her own name, she is the author of *The Three*, *Day Four* and *The White Road*. She currently lives in a forest with her family and other animals.

Adam L.G. Nevill was born in Birmingham, England, in 1969 and grew up in England and New Zealand. He is the author of the horror novels *Banquet for the Damned*, *Apartment 16*, *The Ritual*, *Last Days*, *House of Small Shadows*, *No One Gets Out Alive*, *Lost Girl* and *Under a Watchful Eye*. His first short story collection, *Some Will Not Sleep: Selected Horrors*, was published on Halloween, 2016. *The Ritual*, *Last Days* and *No One Gets Out Alive* were the winners of the August Derleth Award for Best Horror Novel, and *The Ritual* and *Last Days* were also awarded Best in Category: Horror, by R.U.S.A. Many of his novels are currently in development for film and television. Adam also offers two free books to readers of horror: *Cries from the Crypt*, downloadable from his website, and *Before You Sleep*, available from major online retailers. Adam lives in Devon, England. More information about the author and his books is available at: www.adamlgnevill.com.

Muriel Gray graduated from Glasgow School of Art, and worked as an illustrator and museum exhibition designer. After presenting the iconic music programme *The Tube* a long career in broadcasting followed, including founding a television production company. An award-winning opinion writer in many publications, she is the author of three horror novels, *The Trickster*, *Furnace* and *The Ancient*, and many short stories. She was the first female rector of Edinburgh University, is chair of the board of governors of Glasgow School of Art, and a trustee on the board of the British Museum. She lives in Glasgow.

Josh Malerman is the author of *Bird Box*, *Black Mad Wheel*, *A House at the Bottom of a Lake* and *Ghastle and Yule*. He's also the singer/songwriter for the rock band The High Strung, whose song "The Luck You Got", can be heard as the theme song for the hit Showtime show *Shameless*. He lives in Ferndale, Michigan, with his soul mate Allison Laakko and their many pets.

Conrad Williams is the author of nine novels: *Head Injuries, London Revenant, The Unblemished, One, Decay Inevitable, Loss of Separation, Dust and Desire, Sonata of the Dead* and *Hell is Empty.* His short fiction is collected in *Use Once Then Destroy, Born with Teeth* and *I Will Surround You.* He has won the British Fantasy Award, the International Horror Guild Award and the Littlewood Arc prize. Recently he was a finalist for a Crime Writers' Association Dagger. He lives in Manchester with his wife and three sons, where he is at work on a haunted house novel and an interactive video game.

Kathryn Ptacek's novels, among which are *Blood Autumn, Kachina, Shadoweyes* and *Ghost Dance*, are now out as e-books from Crossroad Press and Necon ebooks. Her first collection of short stories, *Looking Backward in Darkness*, was released by Borgo Press. Her short stories can be found in *Expiration Date, Better Weird, The Year's Best Dark Fantasy and Horror 2016, Fright Mare – Women Write Horror* and *Dark Discoveries* magazine. Her poetry has been published in the *Horror Writers Assn. Poetry Showcase Volumes II* and *III.* Kathy lives in rural northwest New Jersey and shares her old Queen Anne home with lots of books, the requisite author cats, unusual teapots and the occasional visiting mouse. She can be reached at gilaqueen@att.net or through her Facebook pages.

Christopher Golden is the *New York Times* bestselling author of *Snowblind, Ararat* and *Tin Men*, among others. With Mike Mignola, he co-created two cult favourite comics series, *Baltimore* and *Joe Golem: Occult Detective*. As editor, his anthologies include *Seize the Night, The New Dead* and *Dark Cities*. Golden is a frequent speaker and instructor at libraries, schools and conferences. He has also written screenplays, video games, radio plays and an animated web series. His novels are available in languages around the world. Please visit him at www.christophergolden.com.

Stephen Laws is an award-winning horror novelist whose books, which include *Ghost Train*, *Spectre*, *The Frighteners*, *Daemonic* and *Chasm*, have been published in America, France, Germany, Spain, the Netherlands, Denmark, Italy, Australia, Poland and Japan. Peter Cushing loved his novels, but hated the bad language therein. Horror actress Ingrid Pitt organised a team search of his hotel room, concentrating on a "haunted sock drawer". Roger Corman bought him a pizza. He made Christopher Lee cry in public. He won second prize in a 1963 "Name the Sugar Puff Bear" competition. His son has a famous godfather in the genre. He plays piano, and one of his compositions was performed with full orchestra on a pre-Civil War Yugoslav television "variety" programme. This is all true.

DARK CITIES
ALL NEW MASTERPIECES OF URBAN TERROR
Edited by CHRISTOPHER GOLDEN

In shadowy back alleys, crumbling brownstones, and gleaming skyscrapers, cities harbor unique forms of terror. Here lie malicious ghosts, cursed buildings, malignant deities, and personal demons of every kind.

Twenty of today's most talented writers bend their skills toward the darkness, creating brand-new tales guaranteed to keep you awake at night—especially if you live in the dark cities.

Far worse than mythical creatures such as vampires and werewolves, these are horrors that lurk in the places you go every day—where you would never expect to find them. But they are there, and now that you know, you'll never again walk the streets alone.

Nathan Ballingrud • Amber Benson
Kealan Patrick Burke • Ramsey Campbell • M.R. Carey
Nick Cutter • Tananrive Due • Christopher Golden
Simon R. Green • Sherrilyn Kenyong
Kasey Landsdale & Joe R. Lansdale • Tim Lebbon
Jonathan Maberry • Helen Marshall • Seanan McGuire
Cherie Priest • Scott Sigler • Scott Smith • Paul Tremblay

TITANBOOKS.COM

DEAD LETTERS
AN ANTHOLOGY OF THE UNDELIVERED, THE MISSING, THE RETURNED...
Edited by CONRAD WILLIAMS

The Dead Letters Office: the final repository of the undelivered. Love missives unread, gifts unreceived, lost in postal limbo. *Dead Letters: An Anthology* features new stories from the masters of horror, fantasy and speculative fiction, each inspired by an inhabitant of the Dead Letters Office, including tales from Joanne Harris, China Miéville & Maria Dahvana Headley, Adam L.G. Nevill and Michael Marshall Smith.

Joanne Harris • Maria Dahvana Headley
China Miéville • Michael Marshall Smith • Lisa Tuttle
Ramsey Campbell • Pat Cadigan • Steven Hall
Alison Moore • Adam L.G. Nevill • Nina Allan
Christopher Fowler • Muriel Gray • Andrew Lane
Angela Slatter • Claire Dean • Nicholas Royle
Kirsten Kaschock

"Those who enjoy dark fiction and horror should pick up this collection" NY Journal of Books

"The all-star writers who contributed to this volume did indeed deliver" Pop Mythology

"Sometimes haunting, sometimes terrifying, this is a strong collection of tales" SciFi Bulletin

TITANBOOKS.COM

For more fantastic fiction, author events, exclusive
excerpts, competitions, limited editions and more

VISIT OUR WEBSITE
titanbooks.com

LIKE US ON FACEBOOK
facebook.com/titanbooks

FOLLOW US ON TWITTER
@TitanBooks

EMAIL US
readerfeedback@titanemail.com